Crossing to Safety

Crossing to Safety

Wallace Stegner

WINGS BOOKS
New York

This 1997 edition is published by Wings Books®, a division of Random House
Value Publishing, Inc., by arrangement with Random House Inc., New York.

Wings Books® and design are registered trademarks
of Random House Value Publishing, Inc.

Printed in the United States of America

Library of Congress Cataloging-in-Publication Data

Stegner, Wallace Earle, 1909-1993
    Crossing to safety : a novel / by Wallace Stegner.
        p.   cm.
    ISBN 0-517-18776-0
        1.   Family--United States--Fiction.   I. Title.
    PS3537.T316C76   1997
    813' .52--dc21   97-
16919   CIP

Random House
New York • Toronto • London • Sydney • Auckland
http://www.randomhouse.com/

Crossing to Safety
ISBN: 0-517-18776-0

*For M.P.S., in gratitude for more than
a half century of love and friendship,
and to the friends we were both blessed by.*

I could give all to Time except—except
What I myself have held. But why declare
The things forbidden that while the Customs slept
I have crossed to Safety with? For I am There
And what I would not part with I have kept.

ROBERT FROST

Crossing to Safety

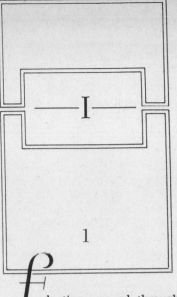

I

1

*F*loating upward through a confusion of dreams and memory, curving like a trout through the rings of previous risings, I surface. My eyes open. I am awake.

Cataract sufferers must see like this when the bandages are removed after the operation: every detail as sharp as if seen for the first time, yet familiar too, known from before the time of blindness, the remembered and the seen coalescing as in a stereoscope.

It is obviously very early. The light is no more than dusk that leaks past the edges of the blinds. But I see, or remember, or both, the uncurtained windows, the bare rafters, the board walls with nothing on them except a calendar that I think was here the last time we were, eight years ago.

What used to be aggressively spartan is shabby now. Nothing has been refreshed or added since Charity and Sid turned the compound over to the children. I should feel as if I were waking up in some Ma-and-Pa motel in hard-times country, but I don't. I have spent too many good days and nights in this cottage to be depressed by it.

There is even, as my eyes make better use of the dusk and I lift my head off the pillow to look around, something marvelously reassuring about the room, a warmth even in the gloom. Associations, probably, but also color. The unfinished pine of the walls and ceilings has mellowed, over the years, to a rich honey color, as if stained by the warmth of the people who built it into a shelter for their friends. I take it as an omen; and though I remind myself why we are here, I can't shake the sense of loved familiarity into which I just awoke.

The air is as familiar as the room. Standard summer-cottage taint of mice, plus a faint, not-unpleasant remembrance of skunks under the house, but around and through those a keenness as of seven thousand feet. Illusion, of course. What smells like altitude is latitude. Canada is only a dozen miles north, and the ice sheet that left its tracks all over this region has not gone for good, but only withdrawn. Something in the air, even in August, says it will be back.

In fact, if you could forget mortality, and that used to be easier here than in most places, you could really believe that time is circular, and not linear and progressive as our culture is bent on proving. Seen in geological perspective, we are fossils in the making, to be buried and eventually exposed again for the puzzlement of creatures of later eras. Seen in either geological or biological terms, we don't warrant attention as individuals. One of us doesn't differ that much from another, each generation repeats its parents, the works we build to outlast us are not much more enduring than anthills, and much less so than coral reefs. Here everything returns upon itself, repeats and renews itself, and present can hardly be told from past.

Sally is still sleeping. I slide out of bed and go barefooted across the cold wooden floor. The calendar, as I pass it, insists that it is not the one I remember. It says, accurately, that it is 1972, and that the month is August.

The door creaks as I ease it open. Keen air, gray light, gray lake below, gray sky through the hemlocks whose tops reach well above the porch. More than once, in summers past, Sid and I cut down some of those weedlike trees to let more light into the guest cottage. All we did was destroy some individuals, we never discouraged the species. The hemlocks like this steep shore. Like other species, they hang on to their territory.

I come back in and get my clothes off a chair, the same clothes I wore from New Mexico, and dress. Sally sleeps on, used up by the long flight and the five-hour drive up from Boston. Too hard a day for her, but she wouldn't hear of breaking the trip. Having been summoned, she would come.

For a minute I stand listening to her breathing, wondering if I dare go out and leave her. But she is deeply asleep, and should stay that way for a while. No one is going to be coming around at this hour. This early piece of the morning is mine. Tiptoeing, I go out onto the porch and stand exposed to what, for all my senses can tell me, might as well be 1938 as 1972.

No one is up in the Lang compound. No lights through the trees, no smell of kindling smoke on the air. I go out the spongy woods path past the woodshed and into the road, and there I meet the sky, faintly brightening in the east, and the morning star as steady as a lamp. Down under the hemlocks I thought it overcast, but out here I see the bowl of the sky pale and spotless.

My feet take me up the road to the gate, and through it. Just inside the gate the road forks. I ignore the Ridge House road and choose instead the narrow dirt road that climbs around the hill to the right. John Wightman, whose cottage sits at the end of it, died fifteen years ago. He will not be up to protest my walking in his ruts. It is a road I have walked hundreds of times, a lovely lost tunnel through the trees, busy this morning with birds and little shy rustling things, my favorite road anywhere.

Dew has soaked everything. I could wash my hands in the ferns, and when I pick a leaf off a maple branch I get a shower on my head and shoulders. Through the hardwoods along the foot of the hill, through the belt of cedars where the ground is swampy with springs, through the spruce and balsam of the steep pitch, I go alertly, feasting my eyes. I see coon tracks, an adult and two young, in the mud, and maturing grasses bent like croquet wickets with wet, and spotted orange Amanitas, at this season flattened or even concave and holding water, and miniature forests of club moss and ground pine and ground cedar. There are brown caves of shelter, mouse and hare country, under the wide skirts of spruce.

My feet are wet. Off in the woods I hear a Peabody bird tentatively try out a song he seems to have half forgotten. I look to the left, up the slope of the hill, to see if I can catch a glimpse of Ridge House, but see only trees.

Then I come out on the shoulder of the hill, and there is the whole sky, immense and full of light that has drowned the stars. Its edges are piled with hills. Over Stannard Mountain the air is hot gold, and as I watch, the sun surges up over the crest and stares me down.

We didn't come back to Battell Pond this time for pleasure. We came out of affection and family solidarity, as adopted members of the clan, and because we were asked for and expected. But I can't feel somber now, any more than I could when I awoke in the shabby old guest cottage. Quite the reverse. I wonder if I have ever felt more alive, more competent in my mind and more at ease with myself and my world, than I feel for a few minutes on the shoulder of that known hill while I watch the sun climb powerfully and confidently and see below me the unchanged village, the lake like a pool of mercury, the varying greens of hayfields and meadows and sugarbush and black spruce woods, all of it lifting and warming as the stretched shadows shorten.

There it was, there it is, the place where during the best time of our lives friendship had its home and happiness its headquarters.

When I come in I find Sally sitting up, the blind closest to the bed—the one she can reach—raised to let a streak of sun into the room. She is drinking a cup of coffee from the thermos and eating a banana from the fruit basket that Hallie left when she put us to bed last night.

"Not breakfast," Hallie said. "Just *hazari*. We'll come and get you for brunch, but we won't come too early. You'll be tired and off your clock. So sleep in, and we'll come and get you about ten. After brunch we'll go up and see Mom, and later in the afternoon she's planned a picnic on Folsom Hill."

"A picnic?" Sally said. "Is she well enough to go on a picnic? If she's doing it for us, she shouldn't."

"That's the way she's arranged it," Hallie said. "She said you'd be tired, and to let you rest, and if she says you'll be tired, you might as well be tired. If she plans a picnic, you'd better want a picnic. No, she'll be all right. She saves her strength for the things that matter to her. She wants it like old times."

I let up the other two blinds and lighten the dim room. "Where'd you go?" Sally asks.

"Up the old Wightman road."

I pour myself coffee and sit down in the wicker chair that I remember as part of the furniture of the Ark. From the bed Sally watches me. "How was it?"

"Beautiful. Quiet. Good earthy smells. It hasn't changed."

"I wish I could have been along."

"I'll take you up later in the car."

"No, we'll be going up to the picnic, that's enough." She sips her coffee, watching me over the rim of the cup. "Isn't it typical? At death's door, and she wants it like old times, and orders everybody to *make* it that way. And worries about us being tired. Ah, she's going to leave a hole! There's *been* a hole, ever since we. . . . Did you feel any absences?"

"No absences. Presences."

"I'm glad. I can't imagine this place without them in it. Both of them."

Long-continued disability makes some people saintly, some self-pitying, some bitter. It has only clarified Sally and made her more herself. Even when she was young and well she could appear so calm and withdrawn from human heat and hurt that she fooled people. Sid Lang, who is by no means unperceptive, and who was surely a little in love with her at one time, used to call her Proserpine, and tease her with lines from Swinburne:

> Pale, beyond porch and portal
> Crowned with calm leaves, she stands
> Who gathers all things mortal
> With cold immortal hands.

Her cold immortal hands got to be a joke among us. But long before then, back during the years when her mother was having to stash her like a parcel in any convenient place, that was when she learned quiet, the way fawns are supposed to lie unmoving, camouflaged and scentless, where their mothers leave them. Some hand, very early, brushed her forehead serene as stone; she seems as tranquil within as without. But I have known her a long time. The refining of her face by age and illness that has given a fragile elegance to her temples and cheekbones has concentrated her in her eyes.

Now her eyes give the lie to her passive, acceptant face. They are smoky and troubled. She fixes them on her hands, which she folds, unfolds, refolds, and speaks to. "I dreamed about her. I woke up dreaming about her."

"That's natural enough."

"We were having some kind of fight. She wanted me to do something, and I was resisting her, and she was furious. So was I. Isn't that a miserable way to . . ." She pauses, and then, as if I have contradicted her, bursts out, "They're the only family we ever had. Our lives would have been totally different and a lot harder without them. We'd never have known this place, or the people who have meant the most to us. Your career would have been different—you might have been stuck in some cow college. Except for Charity, I wouldn't be alive. I wouldn't have wanted to be."

"I know."

I am sitting with my back to the window. On the bed table is a tumbler of water that I set there for Sally last night. The sun, coming in flat, knocks a prismatic oval out of the tumbler and lays it on the ceiling. I reach out my foot and kick the table. The rainbow image quivers. I lift a hand and block the beam of sun from the glass. The rainbow goes out.

Sally has been watching me, frowning. "What are you telling me? It's all over? Accept? I get tired of accepting. I'm tired of hearing that the Lord shapes the back to the burden. Who said that?"

"I don't know. I didn't."

"Maybe it's true, but I don't need any more shaping. I wake up here where everything reminds me of them, and I'm dreaming we're quarreling, and I think how I let myself judge her, and how long it's been, and I just want to weep and mourn."

Rebuking herself, she makes a disgusted face. We look at each other uncomfortably. I say, because she seems to need some expression of distress from me, "I'll tell you one place I felt absences. Last night. I knew Charity wouldn't be out with a flashlight cheering our arrival, but I expected Sid. I suppose he's needed up there. But I felt how serious it is, my heart went down, when only Hallie and Moe appeared as a proxy welcoming committee. This morning I forgot again, it felt as it used to."

"I wish she didn't have this idea we'll be too tired to come up this morning. Isn't it like her? I guess noon will have to do. Will you get me up? I need to go."

I get her into her braces and lift her under the arms and set her on her feet and hand her her canes. With her forearms thrust into them she lurches off to the bathroom. I follow, and when she stands in front of the toilet and stoops to unlock her knees, I ease her down on the seat and leave her. After a while she knocks on the wall and I go in and lift her up. She locks her iron knees again and stands to wash at the washbowl, stained by minerals in the spring water. After a few minutes she comes out, her hair combed and the sleep washed from her face. By the bed she stoops once more to unlock her knees, and sits down suddenly on the rumpled covers. I lift her legs and straighten her out and put the pillows behind her.

"How do you feel? Okay?"

"Maybe Charity is right. I do feel tired."

"Why don't you sleep some more? Want the braces off?"

"Leave them on. It's less nuisance for you if I have to call you."

"It's no nuisance to me."

"Oh," she says, "it has to be. It has to be!" Her eyes close. Then she is smiling again. "How about peeling us an orange?"

I peel us an orange and pour the last coffee from the thermos. Braced against the headboard with her legs making a thin straight line under the blankets, she shapes her face into one of its game, sassy looks, as if to say, What fun!

"I like this *hazari* idea," she says. "Don't you? It's like Italy, when we woke up early and you made tea. Or the Taj Mahal Hotel in Bombay. Remember *hazari* there? Only there too it was fruit and tea, not fruit and coffee. All we need is a big ceiling fan, the kind Lang broke by throwing a pillow at it."

I look around at the bare walls, bare studs, bare rafters, and naked green blinds. Every element of the compound, even the Big House, is much the same. Charity imposed austerity evenhandedly on herself, her family, and her guests. "Well," I have to say, "not *quite* the Taj Mahal."

"Better."

"If you say so."

She drops to her lap the half-clenched hand with the half orange in it—the hand that will never quite unclench because while she was in the iron lung all of us, even Charity who thought of everything, were so concerned that she go on breathing that we forgot to work on her hand. It stayed clenched there for too long. Now for a moment her controlled serenity, her acceptance and resignation, her stout and stoical front, dissolve away again. The woman who looks out at me is emotional and overtired.

"Ah, Larry," she says accusingly, "it does make you sad. It makes you as sad as it does me."

"Only when I laugh," I say, for emotional or not, she puts up with long faces no more than Charity does. She lets herself be rebuked, lets me tuck her in, lets me kiss her, smiles. I draw the blinds. "Hallie and Moe won't be here for two or three hours. Sleep. It's only five in the morning, Santa Fe time. I'll wake you when they come."

"What are you going to do?"

"Nothing. I'll be out on the porch, looking and smelling and recherching *temps perdu*."

Which is what I do for a good long time. It is no effort. Everything compels it. From the high porch, the woods pitching down to the lake are more than a known and loved place. They are a habitat we were once fully adapted to, a sort of Peaceable Kingdom where species such as ours might evolve unchallenged and find their step on the staircase of being. Sitting with it all under my eye, I am struck once more, as I was up on the Wightman road, by its changelessness. The light is nostalgic about mornings past and optimistic about mornings to come.

I sit uninterrupted by much beyond birdsong and the occasional knocking and door-slamming of waking noises from the compound cottages hidden in the trees off to the left. Only once is there anything like an intrusion—a motorboat sound that develops and grows until a white boat with a water skier dangling behind it bursts around the point and swerves into the cove, leading a broadening wake across which the skier cuts figures. They embroider a big loop around the cove and roar out again, the noise dropping abruptly as they round the point.

Early in the morning for such capers. And, I have to admit, a sign of change. In the old days forty academics, angry as disturbed dwarfs, would already have been swarming out of their think houses to demand that the nuisance be abated.

But apart from that one invasion, peace, the kind of quiet I used to know on this porch. I remember the first time we came here, and what we were then, and that brings to mind my age, four years past sixty. Though I have been busy, perhaps overbusy, all my life, it seems to me now that I have accomplished little that matters, that the books have never come up to what was in my head, and that the rewards—the comfortable income, the public notice, the literary prizes, and the honorary degrees—have been tinsel, not what a grown man should be content with.

What ever happened to the passion we all had to improve ourselves, live up to our potential, leave a mark on the world? Our hottest arguments were always about how we could *contribute.* We did not care about the rewards. We were young and earnest. We never kidded ourselves that we had the political gifts to reorder society or insure social justice. Beyond a basic minimum, money was not a goal we respected. Some of us suspected that money wasn't even very good for people—hence Charity's leaning toward austerity and the simple life. But we all hoped, in whatever way our capacities permitted, to define and illustrate the worthy life. With me it was always to be done in words; Sid too, though with less confidence. With Sally it was sympathy, human understanding, a tenderness toward human cussedness or frailty. And with Charity it was organization, order, action, assistance to the uncertain, and direction to the wavering.

Leave a mark on the world. Instead, the world has left marks on us. We got older. Life chastened us so that now we lie waiting to die, or walk on canes, or sit on porches where once the young juices flowed strongly, and feel old and inept and confused. In certain moods I might bleat that we were all trapped, though of course we are no more trapped than most people. And all of us, I suppose, could at least be grateful that our lives have not turned out harmful or destructive. We might even look enviable to the less lucky. I give headroom to a sort of chastened indulgence, for foolish and green and optimistic as I myself was, and lamely as I have limped the last miles of this marathon, I can't charge myself with real ill will. Nor Sally, nor Sid, nor Charity—any of the foursome. We made plenty of mistakes, but we never tripped anybody to gain an advantage, or took illegal shortcuts when no judge was around. We have all jogged and panted it out the whole way.

I didn't know myself well, and still don't. But I did know, and know now, the few people I loved and trusted. My feeling for them is one part of me I have never quarreled with, even though my relations with them have more than once been abrasive.

In high school, in Albuquerque, New Mexico, a bunch of us spent a whole year reading Cicero—*De Senectute,* on old age; *De Amicitia,* on friendship. *De Senectute,* with all its resigned wisdom, I will probably never be capable of living up to or imitating. But *De Amicitia* I could make a stab at, and could have any time in the last thirty-four years.

ain was falling when we reached the Mississippi. Going through Dubuque we bumped along brick streets between shabby, high-porched, steep-gabled houses with brick church spires poking up from among them, and down a long cathedral-aisle of elms toward the river. To my western eyes it was another country, as alien as North Europe.

The bridge approach lifted us up parallel to the dam. We could see the broad slaty pool above it, mottled with green islands, and the bluffs of the far shore green and shining in the rain. "Welcome to Wisconsin," I said.

Sally stirred and gave me a minimal, enduring smile. We had been on the road for three days, at nearly six hundred miles a day, over all kinds of roads including miles of construction in Nebraska, and she was three months pregnant. She probably felt about as cheerful as the afternoon looked, but she tried. She stared downriver to where Iowa and Illinois were linked by a double hyphen of bridges, and ahead to where the road curved out of the river trough toward the rolling Wisconsin farmland. "Ha!" she said. "The *vita nuova*. About time."

"Another couple of hours."

"I'm ready."

"I'll bet you are."

We coiled along the bluff and up onto the top. The rain fell steadily on the narrow, right-angled road, on white farmhouses and red barns whose roofs announced Dr. Pierce's Golden Medical Discovery, on browning September cornfields, and pigs knee-deep in muddy pens. It fell steadily as we passed through Platteville, Mineral Point, Dodgeville, and was still falling when somewhere beyond Dodgeville the wiper blade disintegrated and bare metal began to scrape in a crazy arc across the windshield. Rather than delay us by stopping to get it fixed, I drove from Mount Horeb to Madison with my head out the window, my hair soaked, and water running down inside my shirt collar.

The traffic led us directly into State Street. However Sally felt, I was interested. This that we were entering was our first chance at a life. I knew that the university was at one end of State Street and the State Capitol at the other, and I couldn't resist driving the length of it once, and partway back, just to get the feel. Then I saw a hotel entrance and a parking place simultaneously, and ducked in. As I was opening the door to start sprinting for the sheltered entrance, Sally said, "Not if it's too much!"

Hair soaking, shoulders wet, I made it to the hotel desk. The clerk put both hands flat on the walnut and looked inquiring.

"How much is a double room?"

"With bath or without?"

Momentary hesitation. "With."

"Two seventy-five."

I had been afraid of that. "How much without?"

"Two and a quarter."

"I'd better check with my wife. Be right back."

I went out under the canopy. The rain, falling straight down, bounced in the wet street. In the fifty feet to the car I got soaked again. Crowding into the dense, damp interior, I had to take my glasses off to see Sally. "Two seventy-five with bath, two and a quarter without."

"Oh, that's too much!"

We had a hundred and twenty dollars in traveler's checks to last us till my first payday on October first.

"I thought maybe. . . . It's been a hard trip for you. Don't you think maybe a hot bath, and clean clothes, and a good dinner? Just to start off on the right foot?"

"Starting off on the right foot won't help if we haven't got anything in our pockets. Let's look for a bed-and-breakfast place."

Eventually we found one, a low-browed bungalow whose lawn bore a sign, "Overnite Guests." The housewife was large and German, with a goiter; the room was clean. A dollar fifty, breakfast included. We huddled such luggage as we needed through the kitchen, took serial baths (plenty of hot water), and went to bed supperless because Sally said she was tired, not hungry—and besides, we had eaten a late picnic lunch the other side of Waterloo.

In the morning, still in the rain, we went looking for permanent housing. The fall term would not begin for two weeks. We hoped we were ahead of the rush.

We were not. We saw a house for a hundred a month and an apartment for ninety, but nothing close to affordable until we were shown a small, badly furnished basement apartment on Morrison Street. It was sixty dollars a month, twice what we had hoped to get by for, but its back lawn dropped off a low wall into Lake Monona, and we liked the look of sailboats slanting past. Discouraged, afraid we might hunt for the next two weeks and find nothing better, we took it.

Recklessness. Paying the first month's rent cut our savings in half and sent us into serious computations. Take $720 a year out for rent and we would have left, out of my $2,000 salary, exactly $1,280 for food, drink, clothing, entertainment, books, transportation, doctor bills, and incidentals. Even with milk at five cents a quart and eggs at twelve cents a dozen and hamburger at thirty cents a pound, there would be little enough for drink or entertainment. Scratch those. Doctor bills, though inevitable, were unpredictable. The going rate in Berkeley for delivering a baby was fifty dollars, prenatal care thrown in, but there was no telling what the price was here, and no estimating the cost of postnatal care and the services of a pediatrician. We had to save everything we could against the worst possibilities. As for incidentals, they were going to be very incidental indeed. Scratch those too.

In a way, it is beautiful to be young and hard up. With the right wife, and I had her, deprivation becomes a game. In the next two weeks we spent a few dollars on white paint and dotted swiss, and were settled. The storeroom next to the furnace, warm and dry, would be my study until Junior arrived. I set up a card table for a desk and made a bookcase out of some boards and bricks. In my experience, the world's happiest man is a young professor building bookcases, and the world's most contented couple is composed of that young professor and his wife, in love, employed, at the bottom of a depression from which it is impossible to fall further, and entering on their first year as full adults, not preparing any longer but finally into their lives.

We were poor, hopeful, happy. Nobody much was yet around. In the first week, before I had to report to the university, I wrote a short story—or rather, it wrote itself, it took off like a bird let out of a cage. Afternoons, we felt our way into that odd community, half academic, half political, that was Madison in 1937. We parked the Ford and walked. From our apartment it was a mile and a half around the

Capitol and up State Street and up Bascom Hill to my office in Bascom Hall. Once school opened, I walked it, to and from, each day.

Sally, who would have liked working and who watched our budget with a miser's eye, put a card on the departmental bulletin board advertising that she typed theses and term papers quick and neat, but neither term papers nor theses were in season then, and she got no takers. As soon as I started teaching, she had some long hours alone.

That deep in the Depression, universities had given up promoting and all but given up hiring. My own job was a fluke. At Berkeley the year before, I had read papers for a visiting professor who happened to like me, and who telephoned when Wisconsin developed a last-minute opening. I was a single cork to plug a single hole for a single season. My colleagues, instructors of one or two years' standing, were locked in and hanging on. They made a tight in-group, and their conversation tended to include me only cautiously and with suspicion. They all seemed to have come from Harvard, Yale, or Princeton. The Harvards and Princetons wore bow ties, and the Yalies went around in gray flannels too high in the crotch and too short in the leg. All three kinds wore tweed jackets that looked as if apples had been carried in the lining.

I didn't even have an office mate to talk to. My supposed office partner was William Ellery Leonard, the department's literary lion, famous for an eccentric theory of Anglo-Saxon prosody, for his romantic and tragic private life as told in his long poem *Two Lives,* for his recent tempestuous marriage to and betrayal by a young woman known around the campus as Goldilocks, and for his former habit of swimming on his back far out into Lake Mendota, wearing a boar helmet and chanting *Beowulf.*

I was looking forward to William Ellery with considerable interest, but almost at once I discovered that his aggravated agoraphobia kept him from venturing more than a block from his house. I had been stuck in with him because his office, though inalienable, was spare space. She'll have to sleep with Grandpa when she comes. In the year we roomed together he never once came to the office, but his pictures, books, papers, and memorabilia stared and leaned and toppled, ready to fall on me where I had scratched out working space in a corner. Coming there at night, I felt his presence like a poltergeist, and never stayed long.

That was the way our new life started: two weeks of isolated settling-in followed by a week of registration, transfers, room changes, and the first meetings of classes—the beginnings of a recognizable routine. Then at the end of the first week of classes there was a reception at the chairman's house. I washed the Ford and we dressed up and went, unconfident and watchful. There were forty or fifty people whose names we never properly heard, or confused with others, or promptly forgot. Some of the younger faculty, including a couple I had found pretty condescending, hung so hungrily around the sherry that out of pure pride I refused to be like them. Sally, even stranger in that company than I was, stuck with me.

We spent most of the two hours with older professors and their wives, and probably got an instant reputation among our peers for sucking up. Naturally we were both at our most charming. I even think Sally had a good time. She is gregarious, people interest her just by being people, and she is much better on names and faces than I am. And she hadn't been to any kind of party, even a departmental tea, for a long time.

I suppose we were both a little depressed at leaving those colleagues, strangers though they were, unknowns with the most profound portent for our future, and going home to our cellar, where we ate the stuff that was good for the budget but not especially for the soul. After dinner we sat on the wall above Lake Monona and watched the sunset, and then we went back in and I prepared for my classes and Sally read Jules Romains. We were tender with one another in bed: babes in the woods, lost in a strange indifferent country, a little dispirited, a little scared.

3

One day the next week I came home about four. I came down the steps hoohooing, feeling that Sally needed a show of cheerfulness and a promise of news from the outside. Coming from bright afternoon into our cave, I stopped in the doorway, struck blind. "God, darling," I said, "why do you sit in the dark? This place is like the back entrance to a black cow."

Somebody laughed—a woman, not Sally. I found the light switch and revealed the two of them, Sally on the couch and the other in our not-too-easy chair, with a tea tray on the homemade coffee table (more boards and bricks) between them. They sat smiling at me. Sally has a smile I would accept as my last view of earth, but it has a certain distance about it, it is under control, you can see her head going on working behind it. This other one, a tall young woman in a blue dress, had quite another kind. In the dim apartment she blazed. Her hair was drawn back in a bun, as if to clear her face for expression, and everything in the face smiled—lips, teeth, cheeks, eyes. I mean to say she had a most vivid and, I saw at once, a really beautiful face.

Astonishment. I stood blinking in the doorway. "Excuse me," I said. "I didn't know we had company."

"Ah, don't call me *company*!" the visitor said. "I didn't come *over* to be *company*."

"You remember Charity Lang, Larry," Sally said. "We met at the Rousselots' tea."

"Of course," I said, and went in and shook her hand. "I couldn't see when I came in. How are you?"

But I didn't remember her at all. Even in the crowd at that stiff reception, how could I have missed her? She ought to have showed up like a burning lighthouse.

Her talk was as animated as her face. Every fourth word was underlined—she had the habit of feminine emphasis with a vengeance. (Later, when we diverged into different associations and we got letters from her, we discovered that her writing was the same way. You couldn't read it except in her tone of voice.)

"Sid says you two have got to know each other at *school*," she was saying. "And he brought home *Story Magazine* with your *story* in it. We read it aloud in bed. It's *splendid!*"

My God. An audience. Just what I've been looking for. Pay attention to this delightful young woman, she is obviously somebody special. Her husband too, evidently. Sid Lang. Do I know him? With difficulty, while murmuring false modesty to his enthusiastic wife, I track him down in my mind: spectacled, sober-suited, fair-haired, soft-high-voiced, friendly, forgettable, undistinguished by song, plumage, or nesting habits from a dozen others. At least not one of the snooty ones, and obviously a man to cultivate. I excuse him for not having put himself more forcefully forward. Perhaps, perceiving me to be a writer of power and promise, he was diffident.

Is that the basis of friendship? Is it as reactive as that? Do we respond only to people who seem to find us interesting? Was our friendship for the Langs born out of simple gratitude to this woman who had the kindness to call on a strange young wife stuck in a basement without occupation or friends? Was I that avid for praise, to feel so warm toward them both because they professed to like my story? Do we all buzz or ring or light up when people press our vanity buttons, and only then? Can I think of anyone in my whole life whom I have liked without his first showing signs of liking me? Or did I (I hope I did) like Charity Lang on sight because she was what she was, open, friendly, frank, a little ribald as it turned out, energetic, interested, as full of vitality as her smile was full of light?

Between the taking of a cinnamon toast and tea she let drop bits of information that my mind scurried to gather up and plaster against the wall for future use, like a Bengali woman gathering wet cow dung for fuel. She came from Cambridge. Her father was a professor of religious history at Harvard. She had gone to Smith. She and her husband had met while he was a graduate student at Harvard and she, after graduation, was marking time working as a docent in the Fogg Museum.

She could not have disclosed these facts to a more susceptible ear than mine. Despite my disillusion with some of my bow-tied colleagues, I was ready in 1937 to believe that the Harvard man was the pinnacle of a certain kind of human development, emancipated by the largeness of his tradition and by the selective processes that had placed him in it from the crudeness of lesser places. He had looked on Kittredge bare, he had been where John Livingston Lowes loved and sung, he had read in the enchanted stacks of Widener and walked in thoughtful conversation along the Charles. Certain eastern women's colleges, in their separate but not quite equal way, produced female variants of the same superior breed.

Charity was clearly one of these. Born to Harvard, she had gone to Smith and returned to marry Harvard. She had grown up in contact with the beauty and the chivalry of Cambridge. She, and presumably her husband as well, represented the cultivation, good manners, consideration for others, cleanliness of body and brightness of mind and dedication to high thinking that were the goals of outsiders like me, dazzled western barbarians aspiring to Rome. Mixed with my liking was, I am sure, an almost equal deference, a respect too sincere to be tainted with envy.

And here was this Harvard/Smith woman obviously enjoying cinnamon toast and Lipton's Orange Pekoe in our basement, and she and her Harvard husband professed to admire a story by Larry Morgan, lately from Berkeley, California, and before that from Albuquerque, New Mexico.

Further information: The Langs had two sons, the younger, Nick, a baby barely a year old; the older, aged three, named George Barnwell after Charity's father and known as Barney. Charity grumbled cheerfully about him. She thought he must have been prenatally influenced. He had been conceived on an expedition into the Sahara, and he had the exact character, including the stubbornness, the evil eye, and the distressing voice, of a baggage camel.

Wait a minute, we said. The *Sahara*? You're kidding.

But she wasn't. When they decided to get married, Sid dropped out of graduate school for a semester. They had been married in Paris, at the house of her uncle. . . .

Ah, said Sally, it must be nice to have relatives who live in Paris!

"Well, they *don't* any more," Charity said. "Roosevelt replaced him—*fired* him, I guess you'd have to say."

Roosevelt did? Fired him from what? What did he do?

I thought Charity blushed, and in the circumstances I thought blushing was another evidence of the civilized sensibility and modesty of her kind. It had just struck her how something that she took for granted would sound to our ears. "He didn't do anything. Nothing to get him fired. It was just that the *government* had changed. He was Ambassador to France."

Oh.

"And then we took this long wedding trip," Charity said. "Down through France and Spain to Italy, Greece, the Middle East, Jerusalem, Egypt. We were quite mad, we wanted to see *everything.* I'd gone to school in France and Switzerland, but Sid had never been abroad, not once. We wound up in North Africa, Algeria, where we rented camels and went off into the desert for three weeks."

She said it breathlessly, slurring the gorgeous details, obviously wanting to get out of the appearance of place-dropping she had got herself into. But good Lord, ambassador uncles and three-month wedding trips and expeditions into the Sahara, those meant not only family distinction, but amounts of money unlikely in our times and inconceivable from our sparse cellar.

"What makes you think the camels marked Barney?" I asked, just to keep the revelations flowing. "Has he got a hump, or a cleft palate, or what?"

"Oh no, *nothing* like that," Charity said, almost crowed, delighted and hyperbolic. "He's quite beautiful, really. But he's got their grumpy *disposition.* Their grumpy disposition and their inch-long eyelashes." Her laugh was as clear and uninhibited as everything else about her. "Did you notice how I was avoiding Dr. Rousselot the other day? You know how he looks, with those sad, long cheeks?" She pulled her face down with her fingertips. "I didn't dare glance at him, even, because I'm pregnant again, and I had this *horrible* feeling that if I let my eyes even touch him, this new one would look like *him.*"

"Pregnant?" Sally said. "You too? When? When is it due?"

"Not till March. And are *you*? When's yours?"

"The same time!"

That ended the revelations about the rich, cultivated, and romantic background of Charity Lang. She and Sally fell on each other. You never saw two more delighted people. If they had been twins separated in infancy, and now revealed to one another by some birthmark or other perepetia, they couldn't have been more exhilarated. "It'll be a *race*!" Charity said. "Let's keep *notes,* and compare. Who's your obstetrician?"

"I haven't got one yet. Is yours a good one?"

A big ringing laugh, as if parturition, which sometimes brought the clammy sweat of apprehension to Sally and me, were the most fun since Run Sheep Run. "I guess so," Charity said. "I really don't know him very well. He's only interested in my *uterus.*"

Sally looked a little daunted. "Well," she said, "I hope he'll like mine."

I made to rise. "Excuse me," I said. "I believe the only wholesome thing is to blush a deep crimson and leave the room."

Hoo hoo, ha ha. We filled the basement with our laughter and our discovered common concern. Charity wrote the name of her doctor in a large scrawl on a three-by-five card (she kept a pack of them in her purse). Then she snapped the purse shut and held it on her lap as if about to spring up and go. But she wasn't going, not yet. In a lamenting voice, she cried, "Look what I've done! I came over to get to know *you,* and all we've done is talk about Sid and *me.* I want to know all about you. You're both from California. Tell me about it. What did you *do* there? How did you meet?"

Sally and I looked at each other and laughed. "Not on a camel expedition."

"Ah, but in the West you've got things every bit as good. Those big open spaces, and all that freedom and opportunity and sense of *youth,* and the *freshness* of everything. I wish I'd grown up there instead of in stuffy Cambridge."

"With permission," I said, "you're out of your mind. The Berkeley English Department is Harvard and water."

"It would have been fine if we'd had any money," Sally said. "Neither of us did. Do."

"Were you both students? How *did* you meet?"

"In the library," Sally said. "I had a part-time job charging out books in graduate student carrels. I noticed him because he was always there, and every day there'd be about twenty new books to be charged, and twenty old ones to be returned to the stacks. I thought anybody that industrious was bound to get somewhere, so I married him."

Charity was very interested, like someone peeking through a microscope at a bunch of paramecia. Fascinating, all those cilia and pulsating vacuoles. Her smile was irresistible; you *had* to smile back. She said to me, "I gather you had nothing to do with it."

"A willing victim," I said. "I kept seeing this gorgeous girl with big Greek eyes padding around with her charge slips and keeping me honest with the desk. When she tore up an overdue notice, I knew she was the one."

"You're right about the eyes," Charity said, and turned her attention on Sally. "They're the first thing I noticed about you at the Rousselots'. *Are* you Greek?"

"My mother was."

"Tell me about her. Tell me about *both* your families."

I could see Sally becoming diffident. "We haven't any. They're all dead."

"*All?* Both sides?"

Defensive on the couch, Sally shrugged a quick little shrug and threw her hands up and let them fall in her lap. "Everybody close. My mother was a singer. She died when I was twelve. I was brought up by my American aunt and uncle. He's dead now, and she's in a home."

"Oh, my goodness," Charity said, and stared from Sally to me and back. "So you had no help from *anyone*. You had to do it all alone. How did you manage?"

If Sally was getting diffident, I was getting edgy. Interest is one thing, prying is another. I have never welcomed dissections of my insides. I waved an airy hand. "There are all sorts of ways. You give placement exams. You read papers for professors. You help some Dr. Plush on a six-thousand-dollar salary make his textbooks. You teach sections of Dumbbell English. You work in the library for two bits an hour."

"But when did you study?"

Sally blurted out a laugh. "All the time!"

"Did you do that too, work your way and finish your degree?"

"No," I said. "Like a dumb Greek peasant she hitched herself to the plow. She gave up her degree to support us. As soon as this baby is born and weaned you'll see me herding her down State Street headed for the Graduate Studies office."

"Oh, it wasn't that much of a do," Sally said. "I wasn't close to finishing. Anyway, I was in Classics, and who studies Classics anymore? I couldn't have got a job if I'd finished my degree. Larry was obviously the one."

Charity had a fine narrow head that nodded and turned on her neck like a flower on its stalk. I had seen that comparison in poetry; I had never seen a person who suggested it, and I found it fascinating. Her smile came and went. I could see her mind pouncing on things and letting them go.

"The short and simple annals of the poor," I said fatuously.

"Well," she said, "*I* think it's admirable. It's not as if you'd been run through the assembly line, like some of us, having fenders and *headlights* bolted on. You've done it yourselves."

Sally said, with a quick, shy, proud glance at me, "I'm glad you think he's admirable, because I do too. He used to amaze me, how he'd be there in that carrel day after day and night after night. I never came that he wasn't there. At first I thought he was some kind of grind. Then I found out. . . ."

"Sally, for hell's sake," I said.

But she had to get in her brag, confession, whatever it was. She needed something on our side to match that Paris wedding and those camel rides.

"See, both his parents were killed," she said. She flushed, but she was going to tell this new friend all, like some teenager at a slumber party. "When you were what?" she said, with a look that barely reached me before it fell. "Twenty? Twenty-one? Anyway, when he was a senior at New Mexico."

When Charity wasn't taken over by her smile, her face was still intensely alive. Without her usual gush, without any theatrical emphasis, she said, "What did you do?"

"What would I do? I took the roast out and turned off the oven. I buried them. I sold the house and furniture and everything but the car and moved into a dorm. I went back between semesters and made up the examinations I'd missed. When I graduated, I went straight off to Berkeley to graduate school, because school looked like the safest place to be."

"Was there money in the estate to help you through?"

"Estate? Well, I guess that's what it was. I got about five thousand out of it. I put it in the bank and the bank failed."

"What rotten luck," Charity said. "Were they traveling somewhere? Was it an automobile accident?"

I suppose there was a certain bravado involved, or I would have turned her questions off. But I decided that if Charity Lang wanted to know all about us, let her hear it. Let her find out how different other lives were from hers. I said, "We had a boarder in Albuquerque, a world-war buddy of my father's. He came and went, around for a few weeks and then gone for months. He had an old Standard biplane tied together with piano wire that he used to fly upside down around county fair racetracks, and take up wing walkers and parachutists. A barnstormer. He used to let me wear his British officer's boots to school, and when things were slow he'd take my girl and me up. Nobody beat my time in high school. So this pal of mine ended by orphaning me. He took my folks for a joyride on their wedding anniversary and ran them into the side of the Sandias. I was home studying and minding the anniversary roast."

In the subdued light Charity sat still, her hands on the purse in her lap. Her head tilted, she made a half smile as if about to say something placatory or humorous. But all she said, and still without the inordinate emphasis of her customary conversation, was "That's terrible. Both of them. Were you very fond of them? What did your father do?"

"He ran an auto repair shop," I said.

So much for family backgrounds. So much for animated afternoon conversations, too. I seemed to have squelched her curiosity. Within a couple of minutes she was turning her watch to the light and crying that she must go, Barney would have absolutely *devoured* the nanny, or smothered Nicky. But first, could we come to dinner Friday evening? They wanted to know us *well,* as soon as possible. They didn't want to be deprived of us a *minute* longer than they had to. Wasn't it *luck* that What's-His-Name Jesperson went to Washington to work for Harold Ickes, and that we had been picked to take his place? He was such a fud. Could we make it Friday? It would be just two or three couples, young faculty we probably knew already, and her mother, who was visiting from Cambridge. *Please* be able to come.

It crossed my mind, and if it crossed mine it had already passed through Sally's, that we had a humiliatingly blank calendar. One quick look established the fact that we had no more pride than we had engagements. Friday, then.

We walked Charity up the three steps from the basement, and around the house to where her car was parked in the street. It was not a fancy car—a Chevy station wagon about the age and condition of our Ford—and it could have stood a wash. The back seat had some rolled-up clothes in it, obviously headed for the cleaners.

"I feel we're going to be such friends!" Charity said, and hugged Sally and gave my hand a hard squeeze and climbed into the driver's seat and irradiated us with that smile. *"Start keeping notes!"* she said to Sally. Ox-eyed Sally, she of the Demeter brow, she had no residue of impatience at having been pried at, as I did. She hadn't been bothered by Charity's curiosity. She had invited it. She had poured us out like a libation on the altar of that goddess.

We stood waving as Charity drove away toward the Capitol dome that showed above the trees. All right. I admitted it: a charming woman, a woman we couldn't help liking on sight. She raised the pulse and the spirits, she made Madison a different town, she brought life and anticipation and excitement into a year we had been prepared to endure stoically. Our last impression of her as she turned the corner was that smile, flung backward like a handful of flowers.

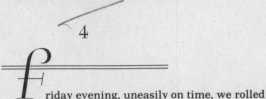

4

*F*riday evening, uneasily on time, we rolled along Van Hise Street under big elms. The western sky was red, and there was light enough to read the numbers painted on the curb. A car length past, we stopped and looked the house over.

To my rank-conscious eyes it looked like a house with tenure—big front lawn with maples, unraked leaves thick on the grass and in the gutter, windows that stretched like a nighttime train. Above the door an entrance light showed two brick steps, a flagstone walk, and the heavy leaves of a lilac hedge along the driveway.

"It's a Charity sort of house," Sally decided. "Sort of ample and careless. No side."

"Lots of front."

"Not the kind that puts you off. No iron stags. No "Keep off the Grass" signs."

"Did you expect them?"

"I didn't know what to expect." She shrank her shoulders together in the gold-embroidered Chinese dragon robe that was almost the only relic left from her mother's operatic career, and laughed a little. "I liked her so much I can't help wondering what *he'll* be like."

"I told you. A friendly house detective."

"I can't imagine her married to a house detective. What'll I talk to him about? What's he interested in?"

"Spenser's *Faerie Queene*?" I suggested. "The *Marginalia* of Gabriel Harvey?"

She was not amused. In fact, she was definitely nervous. Peering like a burglar at the lighted house, she said, "Her mother, too. Did you know her mother was one of the founders of Shady Hill School?"

"What's Shady Hill School?"

"Oh, you know!"

"No."

"Everybody knows Shady Hill School."

"Not me."

"Well, you should." I waited, but she didn't enlighten me. After a minute she said, "Charity was telling me about her. She sounds formidable. She'll probably expect me to converse in French."

"Converse in Greek. Put her down. Who does she think she is?"

She said restlessly, "I wish I'd asked what people would be wearing. What if everybody's in a long dress, and I come out from under this robe in my two-year-old short thing? The robe's too fancy and the dress isn't fancy enough."

"Look," I said, "it isn't her uncle the ambassador's. If we aren't presentable they can send us home."

But when I started to open the door she yelped, "No! We don't want to be the first. We don't want to be sitting here when the others come, either. Drive around the block."

So I drove around the block, slowly, and when we got back, two cars were unloading. Their occupants gathered under the arc light, where bullbats were booming after insects and a chilly Octoberish smell of cured leaves rose from the ground, the indescribable smell of fall and football weather and the new term that is the same almost everywhere in America.

I knew the three men: Dave Stone, from Texas via Harvard, who looked like Ronald Colman and spoke softly and had already impressed me as one of the younger faculty I could be friendly with; and Ed Abbot, another friendly one, on leave from the University of Georgia while he finished his degree; and Marvin Ehrlich, one of the high-crotch, short-leg, baggy-tweed contingent. He had let me know a day or two earlier, while loading his pipe and scattering tobacco crumbs all over my desk, that he had studied with Chauncey B. Tinker (Tink) at Yale, and then had gone on to Princeton to read Greek with Paul Elmer More. He had also quizzed me on how I happened to have my job—whom I knew on the senior faculty, who had recruited me— how much he had to watch out for me, in other words, in the competition for promotion. I had reacted to him as if he were ragweed, and was not especially happy to see him now.

I knew none of the wives, though Sally did, and they said they had met us at the Rousselots'. Lib Stone was a thin Texas belle full of laughter, Alice Abbot a freckled girl from Tennessee, with white eyelashes. Wanda Ehrlich was notable mainly for her shape, which bulged her clothes until her eyes popped.

The Stones and Abbots shook hands with great friendliness. Ehrlich was putting away his goddamned pipe, and acknowledged us with a lift of the head. His wife (I reconstruct this after many years, and without charity, small c) gave us a smile that I thought curiously flat in so plump a face. It struck me then, and strikes me again now, how instantly mutual dislike can make itself evident. Or was I only reacting to their indifference? They did not appear to value me, and so the hell with them.

At least Sally could be reassured. No long dresses, and no wrap a tenth as gorgeous as her dragon robe.

Ed Abbot was antic, and full of party spirit. Going up the walk, he scared the bullbats with a rebel yell and spooked a cat out of the shadows. In two bounds it disappeared under the lilacs, while he helped it on its way with a screech. *"Yander goes a critter!"* Out of Wanda Ehrlich came a laugh like a hiccup, inadvertent and incredulous. "Ed, you cracker," said his wife, "you'll rouse the neighborhood."

Laughing, smiling, or being superior, each according to his kind, we clustered under the light. Since I was closest to it, I pushed the bell button.

There is nothing like a doorbell to precipitate the potential into the kinetic. When you stand outside a door and push the button, something has to happen. Someone must respond; whatever is inside must be revealed. Questions will be answered, uncertainties or mysteries dispelled. A situation will be started on its way through unknown complications to an unpredictable conclusion. The answer to your summons may be a rush of tearful welcome, a suspicious eye at the crack of the door, a shot through the hardwood, anything. Any pushing of any doorbell button is as rich in dramatic possibility as that scene in Chekhov when, just as the Zemstvo doctor's only child dies of diphtheria and the doctor's wife drops to her knees beside the bed and the doctor, smelling of carbolic, takes an uncertain step backward, the bell sounds sharply in the hall.

I suppose this bell sounded in the hall. But no dazed and haggard doctor answered the door. This door was yanked open, exposing the brilliantly lighted interior, and in the doorway stood—who? Theseus and Ariadne? Troilus and Criseyde? Ruslan and Liudmila?

Oh, my goodness. House detective, did I say? Did I mention Spenser's *Faerie Queene*?

Side by side, dressed for the party, shouting welcome, blinding the dim porch with their smiles, these two were the total antithesis of academic mousiness, economic depression, and the meager living that had been our tenement for most of our conscious lives. To our dazed eyes, they were as splendid a pair as lamplight ever shone upon.

Charity I was prepared for, more or less—the fine narrow head, the drawn-back hair, the vivid face, the greetings that managed to be excitedly personal even while she was dividing them among eight of us. She was dressed in a white ruffled blouse and a long skirt made, apparently, of a Paisley bedspread or tablecloth with a hole cut in the center. Her pregnancy didn't show yet. By February, she would look like a Mississippi River tug pushing a three-by-five tow, but right then, in her doorway, crying greeting, she looked simply tall, beautiful, exotic, and exuberant.

But Sidney Lang, he overwhelmed the sight. He wore an embroidered shirt that I thought might be Greek or Albanian or Jugoslav, but that might have come from Mexico, Guatemala, North Africa, or some tribal culture in the Caucasus. And dress was the least part of his transformation. Something had enlarged and altered him. If this had happened in recent years, I would be compelled toward images of Clark What's-His-Name throwing off his glasses and business suit and emerging in his cape as Superman.

This English instructor in his Balkan or whatever it was shirt, standing by his beautiful wife and crushing the hands of his guests, was by Michelangelo out of Carrara, a giant evoked from the rock. At the university, in his gray suit, he had seemed of no more than medium height, perhaps because he stooped so attentively to hear the slightest word from the person he was talking to, perhaps because his neat, fair hair made him look somehow ineffectual. Walking with me to a class the day before, he had all but skipped to keep in step, inclining his head to hear the wisdom that dropped from my lips, and I had felt at once flattered and superior. Now, ordering me into his house, roaring his pleasure at our presence, demanding coats for stowing in the closet, he was a djinn. He walked among the treetops and was taller than the trees.

Our hands, offered two at a time because that was how they were demanded, passed from Charity's to Sid's. "Oh, Sally Morgan, how absolutely *lovely* you are!" cried Charity as she passed Sally on. "You belong on a Ming scroll!" And to Wanda Ehrlich, coming next, "Wanda! How *nice* to see you! Come in, come *in*!"

I saw Wanda register the difference between Sally's welcome and her own. I saw Sid seize Sally's hands with such a passion of greeting that she bounced from the impact. His forearms were massive and dense with blond hair. Golden hair sprouted from the throat of his embroidered shirt. His eyes, with the steel-rimmed spectacles off, were strikingly blue, and the teeth in his square face were as white as Charity's. He was not only the most robust English teacher I ever saw, but the most charming. With his power turned full on, he could win anybody. In all moods his face fell into pleasant lines, and he had a kind of enthusiastic antique gallantry that blew Sally away. He held her hands high and had her pirouette under them—in effect, they boxed the gnat. "Absolutely lovely is right," he said. "Oh, beautiful, beautiful! Charity told me, but she didn't do you justice."

She began to undo the loops of her robe, but he stopped her. "Don't. Keep it on. I want to show you off to Aunt Emily."

He left the rest of us to fend for ourselves, he put an arm around her shoulders and propelled her toward the living room. Being hauled like a captive into a cave, Sally threw me a look: amazement, amusement, a Bronx cheer for my powers of description.

Trailing after them into the living room, we were presented to Aunt Emily, Charity's mother. Even Charity called her Aunt Emily. She was a lady with gimlety brown eyes and the grim smile of a headmistress who has seen all sorts of naughtiness and still loves children, or swears she does.

"Ah," she said when it came my turn. "You're the man with the literary gifts. And such a beautiful wife. Charity and Sid have told me how much you've added to the English Department."

"Added?" I said. "We've barely arrived."

"Obviously you've made an impression. I hope we can talk, though the way this costume party is starting out, I may not see you again."

I liked her. (She flattered me.) "I'm at your command," I said. "All it will take is a seductive signal with your fan."

"I'll have to get a fan and lie in wait. They tell me you're a writer of great promise."

Who could resist? There lay the evening before us, more full of promise than even myself. The mere prospect of a square meal could cheer me in those days, and here there was much more—light, glitter, chatter, smiles, dressed-up people, friends, audience. A girl who came across the thick carpets bearing canapés turned out to be a freshman from one of my classes. I liked her seeing me in those surroundings. Books everywhere. Paintings on the walls that were not Van Gogh or Gauguin prints but original oils by Grant Wood and John Steuart

Curry. I read them as evidence of how enthusiastically these New England Langs had adapted to midwestern life, giving up (I supposed) Winslow Homer for the Hayloft School.

And more. Remember, this was 1937, only four years out of Prohibition and deep in that Depression that is like the Age of Fable to today's young. Only last month our grandson in La Jolla, twiddling the dials of his five-hundred-dollar stereo in search of the Eagles or James Taylor, interrupted some reminiscence of mine by saying, "Yeah, Grandpa, tell about the time you and Grandma saved up for a week for a couple of nickel ice-cream cones." His 1972 irony is close to our 1937 reality, but to him it will never be anything but a wisecrack. Nickel ice-cream cones make him snort. Any respectable ice-cream cone costs sixty or eighty cents, and a three-decker a dollar and a quarter. And saving up, what is that?

What was true of ice cream was triply true of liquor. Whatever else it did, Prohibition really did inhibit our drinking. In Albuquerque before 1933, our student parties had involved homemade wine or home brew explosive with yeast, sometimes with a stick of grain alcohol or ether in it if we happened to have a medical student among us. Faculty, if they had any hoarded or bootlegged supplies, did not share them with students. In Berkeley, after repeal, faculty receptions did blossom out with jugs of sherry that had been manufactured in haste and aged on a truck coming up from Cucamonga. Student parties graduated to grappa—raw California brandy—or punch. Punch we created in a bowl in the spirit of research, making it up out of fruit juices, soda, and whatever intoxicants we happened to have—gin, rum, grain alcohol, grappa, or all four. These we stirred together and colored pink with the synthetic grenadine syrup called Yum.

Yum.

Now here at the end of the room beyond Aunt Emily was a table burdened with Haig and Haig, Sunnybrook Farm, Duff Gordon, Cinzano sweet and dry, Dubonnet *rouge et blonde,* Dutch gin, Bacardi. Some Madison liquor store (I had not yet been in one) had been plundered to lay that table, though it turned out that the Langs themselves drank only a little Dubonnet, and Aunt Emily drank nothing at all.

Ed Abbot, coming up beside me to inspect those riches, was so shaken that his knees visibly wilted. He clutched his brow, and clutching it, bent to read labels. His lips moved. "Oh my," he said. "Oh my." And then, more strongly, "When does the sacrifice begin? Do you-all need a victim? *Please!"*

Sid stepped behind the table and called for orders. The gentlemen deferred to the ladies. Of the ladies, one spoke. "I'll have a Manhattan," said Wanda Ehrlich, without please.

Those were the days of the silver cocktail shaker. Robert Montgomery's way with it in the movies had instructed us all. Sid seized his, uncapped it, filled it with ice. His hand moved over the crowded bottles and selected a sweet Cinzano, hovered again and descended on a Haig and Haig Pinch. But Ed and I cried out with one voice, and his hand stopped.

"What's the matter? Whiskey and sweet vermouth? And bitters? God, *I* don't know, I was gently reared. I yield to my betters. Here, one of you make it."

So Ed Abbot became bartender, beating me out by four one-hundredths of a second, and the rest of us came to the party.

I have heard of people's lives being changed by a dramatic or traumatic event—a death, a divorce, a winning lottery ticket, a failed exam. I never heard of anybody's life but ours being changed by a dinner party.

We straggled into Madison, western orphans, and the Langs adopted us into their numerous, rich, powerful, reassuring tribe. We wandered into their orderly Newtonian universe, a couple of asteroids, and they captured us with their gravitational pull and made moons of us and fixed us in orbit around themselves.

What the disorderly crave above everything is order, what the dislocated aspire to is location. Reading my way out of disaster in the Berkeley library, I had run into Henry Adams. "Chaos," he told me, "is the law of nature; order is the dream of man." No one had ever put my life to me with such precision, and when I read the passage to Sally, she heard it the same way I did. Because of her mother's uncertain profession, early divorce, and early death, she had first been dragged around and farmed out, and later deposited in the care of overburdened relatives. I had lost my security, she had never had any. Both of us were peculiarly susceptible to friendship. When the Langs opened their house and their hearts to us, we crept gratefully in.

Crept? Rushed. Coming from meagerness and low expectations, we felt their friendship as freezing travelers feel a dry room and a fire. *Crowded* in, rubbing our hands with satisfaction, and were never the same thereafter. Thought better of ourselves, thought better of the world.

In its details, that dinner party was not greatly different from hundreds we have enjoyed since. We drank, largely and with a recklessness born of inexperience. We ate, and well, but who remembers what? Chicken Kiev, saltimbocca, escallope de veau, whatever it was, it was the expression of a civilized cuisine, as far above our usual fare as manna is above a baked potato. A pretty table was part of it, too—flowers, wine in fragile glasses, silver whose weight was a satisfaction in the hand. But the heart of it was the two people who had prepared the occasion, apparently just to show their enthusiasm for Sally and me.

They put Sally on Sid's right, distinguished above other women and exposed to his full gallant attention. Over other conversation I heard him telling her a romantic story about their honeymoon, about a time in Delphi when a man they had met on the boat to Itea fell over the cliff and they were three days finding his body. Sally was a little high. A smile hung on her lips and her eyes were on his face, ready for cues that would move her to amazement, concern, or laughter. As for me, I was king of the castle between Charity and her mother. They quizzed me on a hundred California subjects from Yosemite to Dust Bowl refugees, and not only they but others near us, Alice and Lib especially, attended my answers as if I had been speaking from the sacred cave. How lovely it is to be chosen, how flattering to have such bright eyes on you as you divide the light from the darkness.

After dinner, coffee and brandy in the living room. While my awed freshman student was serving coffee and Sid went around with his tray of snifters and his bottle of VSOP, Charity put a record on the phonograph. *"Now!"* she cried, and flopped onto a couch. "Now we'll all sit for a few minutes and just digest and *listen!*"

But Marvin Ehrlich had carried from the table an argument about the Spanish Civil War he had been having with Ed, a continental neutral. And I had found a place on a sofa beside Charity's mother, and thought it my duty as a gentleman to make small talk.

As I was settling back after putting Aunt Emily's cup on the coffee table for her, I heard Marvin say, ". . . rather go fascist? You've got to go one way or the other. Want to join up with Franco and Mussolini and Hitler? What's the matter with being on the side of the masses?"

"Masses?" Ed said. "What masses? Americans don't know anything about any masses. Masses are a European notion, they're a cheese that won't travel."

"No? What about the middle-class masses?"

Hoots from Ed.

To Aunt Emily, as the strains of clarinet and strings swept the room, I made what I hoped was drawing-room conversation. "What is it about Mozart that makes him sound so happy? Is it just the tempo, or is there something else? How do you make pure sound sound happy?"

"Shhhhhhh!" Charity said, to both Marvin Ehrlich and me, and as we subsided into digestion and attentiveness she salved our severally bruised feelings with the most forgiving of smiles.

I don't know how English Departments are now, for I escaped them years ago. But I know how they used to look. They used to look first class. They used to look like high serene lamaseries where the elect lived in both comfort and grace. Up there, scholars as learned and harmless as Chaucer's Clerk of Oxenford moved among books and ideas, eating and drinking well, sleeping soft, having three-month summer vacations during which they had only to cultivate their inclinations and their "fields." Freed by tenure, by an assured salary, by modest wants, by an inherited competence, or by all four, they were untouched by the scrabbling and scuffling that went on outside the walls, or down in the warrens where we aspirants worked and hoped.

We knew that vision was only partly true. Some of our superiors were indeed men of brains and learning and disinterested goodwill, but some were stuffed shirts, and some incompetents, and some timid souls escaping from the fray, and some climbers, and some as bitter and jealous as some of us were at being inadequately appreciated. But still there they were, up in the sunshine above the smoke, a patch-elbowed, tweedy elite that we might improve when we joined it but that we never questioned. Especially during the Depression, when every frog of us was lustful for a lily pad.

Early in our stay in Madison Professor Rousselot, who was much admired by his junior faculty for his elegant stone house, his snow-white handkerchiefs, his way of taking razor-thin slices off a baked ham or turkey, his mots and aphorisms, his quotations for every occasion, and his summers in the reading room of the British Museum, gave me a hint of how things were. We were talking about one of my fellow instructors who had a sick wife. "Poor Mr. Hagler," Professor Rousselot said. "He has only his salary."

Ah, yes, Professor Rousselot. Many of us understand. Poor Mr. Morgan, he too has only his salary, and comes from the boondocks besides. There are several like poor Mr. Hagler and poor Mr. Morgan. Poor Mr. Ehrlich, for example. He has only his salary, and he comes from Brooklyn, and hates it. He tries hard—harder by far than poor Mr. Morgan, who is a little arrogant in his barbarism. Poor Mr. Ehrlich has labored to benefit from what he was taught by Tink and Paul Elmer More. He smokes the right mixture in his Dunhill pipe, he works on his profile, he wears the right flannels and tweeds, he can recommend the right nutty sherries. But he gives himself away, like the Russian agent who ate jam with a spoon.

Neither of us may in fact make the club, but poor Mr. Ehrlich is in even worse shape than poor Mr. Morgan, for Mr. Morgan, besides being a little arrogant, is uncomplicatedly upward-mobile, whereas Mr. Ehrlich is bent on tearing down the demo-plutocracy whose airs he affects. He snows you with his Yale-Princeton superiorities at the very moment when he is trying to sign you up in the Young Communist League. He seems to Mr. Morgan to be hung up halfway between the British Museum and Red Square, paralyzed by choice.

I spend a minute on Marvin Ehrlich not because he matters to me, or ever did, but because that evening, by his failure to make it into the junior version of what we all coveted, he emphasized my own euphoric sense of being welcomed and accepted. Maybe we were all anti-Semitic in some sneaky residual way, but I don't think so. I think we simply felt that the Ehrlichs didn't permit themselves to be part of the company.

Marvin never did get over his flushing resentment at being shushed by Charity. And when, after the music, she stood in the middle of the room and blew a police whistle and ordered us to get ready for square dancing, the Ehrlichs didn't know how and refused to learn. Dave Stone coaxed them with some real hoedown music on the piano, and Charity told them how easy it was, Sid would call only the very simplest things. The rest of us formed a square and waited. No go. Since Dave was needed at the piano, we were one short. After a while we replaced the rug and accepted the songbooks that Sid passed out.

Brand new, my mind said to me. Ten of them. I peeked at the price on the dust jacket of mine. $7.50. Seventy-five dollars for songbooks, just for one evening.

The Ehrlichs didn't sing, either. They sat with the open book between them and moved their lips and made no sound. Maybe they were tone deaf, maybe they had grown up to other kinds of songs. But their eyes burned with resentment and reproach.

Certainly what we sang could not have evoked their scorn. None of your "Home on the Range" stuff, nor bawdy ballads, nor tunes remembered from Boy Scout campfires. No no. We sang things that Tink himself might have applauded: "Eine feste Burg," "Jesu Joy of Man's Desiring," "Down by the Salley Gardens." Martin Luther, Johann Sebastian Bach, William Butler Yeats. That was a civilized bunch of people. All of them, barring the Ehrlichs, could carry a tune. And behold, Sid turned out to be a glee club tenor, Sally Morgan was a real contralto, a rich inherited voice, Larry Morgan could at least sing barbershop, and Dave Stone was a genius on the piano. We rolled our eyes and held long reverberating chords.

"Why, how well you did that!" cried Aunt Emily, and clapped her hands. "You're practically professional!" We were all applauding ourselves. On the piano bench Dave nodded gravely and beat his hands together. We were full of self-congratulation and the discovery of a shared pleasure. And there sat the impossible Ehrlichs, smiling and smiling, with their useless book open and their mouths shut, hating what they envied.

After a while Charity saw their discomfort, and sent a look across the room to Sid, who stood up and wondered if anyone was getting dry. Several of us answered his call, and as we stood with glasses in our hands, prepared for more choral song or whatever Charity's agenda had in mind, Sid picked up a volume of Housman's poems from a table, opened it, and said in his light, pleasant, hurried voice, "Listen. I'd like your opinion on something. Listen."

"Shhhhh!" Charity said. "Sid has a question for you poetry critics."

We hushed. Sid stood by the piano, cleared his throat, waited for full quiet, and read, taking it seriously. I didn't know it then, but this was one of his roles—starting an intellectual hare.

Easter Hymn

If, in that Syrian garden, ages slain
You sleep, and know not you are dead in vain,
Nor even in dreams behold how dark and bright
Ascends in smoke and fire by day and night
The hate you died to quench and could but fan,
Sleep well and see no morning, son of man.

> But if, the grave rent and the stone rolled by
> At the right hand of majesty on high
> You sit, and sitting so remember yet
> Your tears, your agony and bloody sweat,
> Your cross and passion and the life you gave,
> Bow hither out of heaven and see and save.

We stood or sat, waiting. "What's the question?" Dave Stone asked.

"Does it satisfy you? Is it good Housman?"

"Satisfy how? It's good Housman, sure. It's a good poem. It should be read aloud every morning in Madrid and Barcelona."

"Larry, does it satisfy you?"

"Sure. I believe in all that unquenched hate. I guess I didn't know Housman was tempted by Christianity, though."

"Exactly!" Sid cried. "Exactly! Doesn't that strike an odd note, for him—that plea for salvation? That's not the old stoic. That's not the fellow who said 'Play the man, stand up and end you/ When your sickness is your soul.' It makes me wonder if he really wrote this. He didn't publish it, it's one his brother found among his papers. You know what I think? I think Lawrence Housman got the stanzas mixed. I think he printed the stanzas in the wrong order. Wouldn't it be more Housman if they were reversed? If it ended 'Sleep well and see no morning, son of man?' "

As a diversion, it was successful. We were all pretty high, we were all the kind of people for whom reading poetry aloud—lily parties, we used to call them—is neither odd nor sissy. A brisk argument ensued. We went to other volumes of Housman for corroborations, and volumes of Housman led us to other poets. Before long we were ransacking the packed bookshelves so we could read some favorite. That was how, within a few minutes, Sally and I, but mainly Sally, managed to give the Ehrlichs the coup de grâce.

Looking through the shelves to nail down some point or other, I found an *Odyssey* in Greek. I was astonished. Why should Sid, who I was sure didn't know Greek, own Homer in the original? An affectation, like Ehrlich's pipe? A feel for completeness, a need to have the total poetry of the world at his fingertips? A sense of what the well-bred house should contain? Had Charity's father, a classical scholar, given it to them in an absentminded moment, forgetting it was Greek to them? Anyway, I was surprised. I had thought we might be the only household in Madison that gave shelf room to Homer and Anacreon and Thucydides. And we had them not because of anything I could do with them but because of Sally.

I plucked the book from the shelf and turned around and said, "Sally! Read us some Homer. Bend our minds with some hexameters."

General consternation. "Do you read *Greek*?" Charity said. "Oh, please, yes! *Quiet,* everybody. Shhhh! Sally's going to read Homer."

Sally protested, but let herself be coerced. Half drunk and proud, I watched her stand up by the piano and get herself together. Her eyes went over us, she sobered the smile on her mouth. She has great dignity and presence when she is cornered, and when she reads that antique poetry she can bring tears to your eyes. It is much better than if you could understand it. She chants out of a remote time with the clang of bronze in it.

We hushed. She read.

She not only brought tears to some people's eyes, she brought down the house. Cheers, applause, excitement. Isn't she great? God, I wish I could do that. But no sooner had the clapping died out into a babble of talk than the Ehrlichs rose to leave. "Oh, no!" Sid and Charity said. "The evening is young. Stay awhile." But I noted a point at which they tacitly agreed not to press the Ehrlichs further. The Ehrlichs shook hands with Aunt Emily, still beaming on the sofa, and as they came past me, Wanda bent her overupholstered body close and said something tense and furious.

I was caught unready. "What?" I said. "I'm sorry, I didn't hear."

"My husband can read Greek too!" Wanda said, quite loudly, and went on out to where Sid was holding her coat and Charity was opening the door. Host and hostess, with their shining smiles, they cried the Ehrlichs out. "Goodnight, goodnight. Thank you for coming. Goodnight." Returning to the living room, they made a wry, disconcerted face at the rest of us.

Altogether, a lovely scene. I felt guilty and triumphant. There we were, still in the warmth and light and grace of that room, while those who didn't belong, those who hated and envied, those who were offensive to Athena, went out into the chilly darkness. I knew how they felt, and I hated it for their sakes. But I also knew how *I* felt. I felt wonderful.

The party broke up a little while afterward, and guess which couple was the last to go. Neither Sally nor I had ever known people like the Langs, neither of us had ever spent so exhilarating an evening. And just as we were getting ready to go, the Langs found themselves unwilling to part with us. Aunt Emily had gone up to bed, the door had closed on the Abbots and Stones. Standing with Sally's dragon robe in his hands, Sid said suddenly, "Don't go yet. How about a walk? Wait, it's got chilly, this won't keep you warm. Charity, where are the burnooses?"

She knew, and brought them—long white cowled woollen robes that covered us from skull to heels. We got into them, all four of us, and went out into a night of frost. If anyone had looked out his window he might have thought he was seeing the ghosts of Fra Lippo Lippi and his pals weaving back to the monastery after a night on the town.

I remember how quiet it was, how empty the streets at that hour, how our feet were loud on pavement and then hushed in grass and then crackly in leaves. There was a glint of settling frost in the air. Our voices and breaths went up and got mixed with the shadows of trees and the bloom of arc lights and the glitter of stars.

It was like nothing I had known either in Albuquerque or Berkeley. It looked different, sounded different, smelled different, felt different. And those two people were the newest and best part of it. It is there in my head now, as bright and dark as Housman's vision of human hate, but with the opposite meaning. We talked and talked. We told each other what we liked and what we had done and what we wanted to do. If we quit talking for a minute, in flowed that frosty, comforting midwestern night.

"Don't you think of this place as an *opportunity*?" Charity asked us. "Don't you feel the way we do, how young and promising it is, and how much there is to be done, and given, and taught, and learned? Sid and I feel so lucky. Back in Cambridge some people felt sorry for us, going away out to Wisconsin, as if it were Siberia. They just don't *know*. They don't know how warm and friendly and open and eager it is. And bright, too.

"Maybe the students aren't as well trained as Harvard students, but a lot of them are just as bright. If there are Winesburgs in the Middle West it's because people don't give them a *chance* to *become* anything. They expect too much too soon. They won't stick it out and give what they ought to give. Instead, they run away to Chicago or New York or Paris. Or else they stay home and just grumble and knock and talk about spiritual *poverty*.

"I don't know about you, but Sid and I think a little city like this, with a good university in it, is the real flowering of the American dream. Don't you feel it? It might have felt like this in Florence in the early fifteenth century, just before the big explosion of art and science and discovery. We want to settle in, and make ourselves as useful as we can, and help it grow, and grow ourselves. We're determined to give it our absolute best. Before we're all done with it, let's make Madison a place of *pilgrimage*!"

She went on like that for blocks, while Sid murmured, and agreed, and prompted, and listened. She said a lot of things we might have thought or hoped but would have been embarrassed to express. Never in our lives had we felt so close to two people. Charity and Sally had their competitive pregnancies, we were all at the beginning of something, the future unrolled ahead of us like a white road under the moon. When we got back to their big lighted house, it seemed like our house too. In one evening we had been made at home in it.

All of us felt it. We must have. For in front of their gate, before we drove away still wearing their burnooses, we fell into a four-ply, laughing hug, we were so glad to know one another and so glad that all the trillion chances in the universe had brought us to the same town and the same university at the same time.

5

*M*adison. It comes back as broken scenes.

We sit in ragged lawn chairs on the ragged lawn. I am grading papers through a hangover headache, Sally is still trying to get through Jules Romains' *Men of Good Will*. Saturday, not quite noon, the morning after we came home from the Langs' dinner party wearing their romantic burnooses and too stimulated to sleep. We talked, we made love, we talked some more, finally we wore out. Now it is the next day.

It is a fair blue day, Lake Monona is tepeed with white sails, there is a bright chop on the water that my aching eyes avoid, focusing out of duty on the pages of a freshman theme describing Observatory Hill. Something strikes my eye, I laugh out loud, Sally looks up from her book.

"Listen to this. 'The top of the hill is round and smooth, worn down by centuries of eroticism.' Is she pulling my leg, or is this one for Dave Stone's boner collection?"

"I suppose she means 'erosion.' "

"I suppose she does. But yearning speaks between the lines. It's like that headline, 'Pen Is Mightier than Sword, Says Wilson,' that left out the slug between 'Pen' and 'Is'. Inadvertence is the truest humor."

"Is it, now."

The wind moves the silver maple over our heads, and some leaves rustle down. Offshore a boat comes about with wooden knockings, watery slappings, a pop of canvas. And now, from the corner of the house, voices. There are Sid and Charity, dressed for outdoors, full of urgency. Can we come on a picnic? Since we have no telephone yet, they took a chance and just made a lunch and *came*. Last night was their wedding anniversary. They were going to pour champagne for a finale, but then the Ehrlich business sort of damped the party and they didn't. But they want a celebration, and they want us along. They know a hill out in the country where you can see a long way, where last spring they found pasqueflowers, and where now there might be hickory nuts. No need to bring anything—it's all packed.

Vigorous, vital, temperate, and hence not hung over, they flush us out of our culvert of duty. We bundle our books and papers inside the basement door, we manage to contribute some apples to the picnic supplies, and we pour around the house to their car.

Out in front, the mailman is just arriving. He hands me a letter and I see the return on the envelope. My eyes jump to meet Sally's. A hope as startling as a stray bullet ricochets off up Morrison Street. When I stick my finger under the flap, Sally frowns slightly: Not now, don't open your mail in public. Sid is holding open the station wagon door.

But I can't wait. I never could. I have been opening my mail in public all my life. I can no more refrain than Noah could have refrained from taking the sprig of green from the dove's beak. Already moving to get in the car, I rip open the envelope and snatch a look. I let out a yell.

Sally knows instantly, but Sid and Charity stare. "What is it? Is it good news of some kind?"

I pass Sid the letter. *Atlantic* wants my story, the one I wrote in the week before the beginning of classes. They will pay me two hundred dollars.

The Langs join us in a war dance around the station wagon, and all the way out into the country their excited faces turn from the front seat to shine on us. They ask a hundred questions, they burst with pleasure, they warm us with their total, generous happiness in our good luck. Everybody's tap is wide open.

Once we have parked and started down a country road between stripped cornfields, with crows cawing over, Sally and Charity go on ahead. Sid carries a big Adirondack pack basket that he will not let me spell him with. The girls, after their first briskness, dawdle, stopping often to examine roadside weeds, and we consciously slow our pace so as not to catch up.

I can hear Charity's high animated voice doing most of the talking. She is endlessly volatile and enthusiastic and provocative. I gather that she is back on baby-making, telling Sally not to be afraid, to *give* herself to it and get the most out of it. Herself, she intends this time to be conscious the whole time. She will not take any ether unless it gets unbearable, which she does not expect it to do, being the third time. She has worked out a system: She will take a little flag into the delivery room, and when she can't bear any more, if it comes to that, she will raise the flag as a signal to the anesthetist. She wishes she could rig a mirror so that she could *see* the birth.

I am guessing, but not wildly. Their talk often goes like that. As for me, I walk in the mellow sun with that letter in my shirt pocket as warm as if it had life. Two hundred dollars are a tenth of a year's pay. I wrote that story in a week. If I could go on doing even a quarter that well and that fast, I might double Wisconsin's salary. I tell myself I will do just that. I decide that for Christmas I will get Sally a portable phonograph and some records, to cheer up her basement during the winter months and give us something to listen to together, the way the Langs do.

Beside me, Sid walks under his pack basket as if it weighed no more than his shirt. He is earnest, I have discovered. His grappling, wrestler's mind is not quick, but it will not let go of an idea until he has pinned it or it has patted the mat. The *Atlantic*'s letter has turned him to the subject of writers and writing.

He believes that all serious writers have a vocation, a sort of mystical call. What they exploit is not intelligence or training, but a glorious gift that is also an obligation. He believes I have it. He wonders that I have never written poetry—he thinks I am a poet manqué, and he surprises me by quoting lines from the one story of mine that he has read (the only one I have ever published), to illustrate what he calls the particularity and brightness of my images, my sense of place, my verbal felicity.

"You know how to do it," he says almost plaintively. "You could study for years and not *learn* how to do what you do. Right from the first paragraph of your first story, you know how. Now you've done it again. In a week. My God, it takes me a week to get my pencils sharpened and my rump comfortable in the chair. I envy you. You're an instrument that blows no blue notes. You're on your way."

Pleasant things to hear, though hearing them from him embarrasses me. I soak up the praise but feel obliged to disparage the gift. I believe that most people have some degree of talent for something—forms, colors, words, sounds. Talent lies around in us like kindling waiting for a match, but some people, just as gifted as others, are less lucky. Fate never drops a match on them. The times are wrong, or their health is poor, or their energy low, or their obligations too many. Something.

Talent, I tell him, believing what I say, is at least half luck. It isn't as if our baby lips were touched with a live coal, and thereafter we lisp in numbers or talk in tongues. We are lucky in our parents, teachers, experience, circumstances, friends, times, physical and mental endowment, or we are not. Born to the English language and American opportunity (I say this in 1937, after seven years of depression, but I say it seriously) we are among the incredibly lucky ones. What if we had been born Bushmen in the Kalahari? What if our parents had been undernourished villagers in Uttar Pradesh, and we faced the problem of commanding the attention of the world on a diet of five hundred calories a day, and in Urdu? What good is an ace if the other cards in your hand are dogs from every town?

Sid has picked up a stick from under a tree, and he swings it on thistles and milkweed stalks along the road, causing explosions of fluff and seeds. In a tone so surly that it surprises me, he says, "What if you're born in Pittsburgh and your father thinks literature is a frill, for women and sissies?"

We walk on in silence. "Is this you?" I ask finally.

Between beheadings of roadside weeds he looks at me sidelong. "My most vivid memory of my father is the total incomprehension— the contempt—in his face when I told him I wanted to major in English literature at Yale. That and the red hairs that sprouted on the backs of his hands. His hands always made me think of some clean, well-manicured strangler. I was afraid of him from the time I learned to walk. That hand with its pink fur was the symbol of power, callousness, philistinism, Presbyterian bigotry, business ruthlessness, everything I didn't want to be ruled by. Is that what you'd call bad luck, or should I have been stimulated to surmount it?"

Caught off guard, and more than a little incredulous, I say cautiously, "But you did surmount it. You did go ahead and study literature. You're teaching it."

"Not with his blessing. I was in economics till he died, then I switched. And sure I'm teaching, but that wasn't exactly the idea."

He has taken off his glasses and tucked them into his shirt pocket and buttoned them down. At once he looks less scholarly, more robust, and more cheerful. Many times, later, I saw that change. Glasses, and winter pallor, and his teaching uniform, could make him look like Milquetoast. Outdoors, and with a summer tan, he was somebody else.

Out of the corner of his eye he is studying me. "Your father was a mechanic, Charity says."

"Yes."

"Did he have any opinions about poetry? Did he think it's a frill?"

"I doubt that he ever thought much about it."

"So he left you alone to develop your gift."

"He was a hard-working, home-brew-making, ballgame-going, lawn-mowing, decent, unintellectual man. We got along very well, generally. I think he was proud of me. He used to tell me, 'Do what you like to do. It'll probably turn out to be what you do best.' "

"Ha!" Sid says. "He was a wise man. That's all it would take." He swipes at some goldenrod and kicks the litter off the road. "It would have made a lot of difference to me if my father had said anything like that to me. If he'd been proud instead of baffled when I published a couple of poems."

"You write poetry?"

"I used to. I tried to, never very successfully, never with much encouragement. I was the only son, I was supposed to step into banker's shoes after a good long humbling training of twenty years or so. I don't suppose he had any objection to poetry as a hobby. But to study it seriously, make it a career, that simply undid him. So I went into economics. A month after I went back to New Haven for my junior year, he dropped dead. At midterm I switched to literature, and I've felt guilty ever since. End of stupid story."

We walk. Crows flap over. The woods on the hill ahead glow yellow and bronze. "Why is it the end of it?" I ask. "Why feel guilty?"

He ponders that, shrugging the pack basket higher on his shoulders. "I suppose you're right," he says. "Maybe it didn't have to be the end of it. And I did go back to writing poems. I never quit, in fact. I published a few, mostly in little magazines but some in other places— *The Nation, Saturday Review.* But every time I wrote one I could feel his eyes on me. Every time I published one I'd read it with his eyes, and gag. Then I went to Harvard to graduate school, and you know how that is. You spend so much time filling the cistern that you don't have any time or strength to do any pumping. Then teaching—other things. I've just sort of let it lapse."

"Recite one."

But he won't. I understand that his father is still looking over his shoulder telling him they're amateur and unworthy of a grown man's time. He would be overcome with embarrassment to expose them to a real writer, one with the *Atlantic*'s letter in his pocket. Though I can't see that poems in *The Nation* and *The Saturday Review of Literature* are necessarily lesser things than a story in *Atlantic,* and would have been very high on myself if I had made those magazines as an undergraduate, I don't grant him his premise that there is a deficiency in him, kindling or match or both.

Full of abounding conviction that what we elect is not beyond us, I urge him to start writing again, turn it out, not let anyone discourage him. Graduate school, after all, is over; his life is what he wants to make it; he has passed all the examinations required of him. I have the insufferable confidence of a small success.

But he won't talk about his poems. He turns the conversation to that banal subject, fascinating to non-writers, of why writers write. Ego enhancement, sure. What else? Psychological imbalance? Neurosis? Trauma? And if trauma, how far can trauma go before it stops being stimulating and becomes destructive? Academic pressures to publish, do those mean anything? Not much, we agree. How about the reforming impulse, a passion for social justice?

Are writers reporters, prophets, crazies, entertainers, preachers, judges, what? Who appoints them as mouthpieces? If they appoint themselves, as they clearly do, how valid is the commission? If Time alone makes masterpieces, as Anatole France thought, then great writing is just trial and error tested by time, and if it's that, then above all it has to be free, it has to flow from the gift, not from outside pressures. The gift is its own justification, and there is no way of telling for sure, short of the appeal to posterity, whether it's really worth something or whether it's only the ephemeral expression of a fad or tendency, the articulation of a stereotype.

But the fact is, you *can* tell, don't I think? He quotes me, seriously, the old bromide about a pretty good poem being like a pretty good egg, and asks me if anyone could feel good about laying pretty good eggs.

I can't help suggesting that he has overlooked an important inducement, and that outside pressures do count. The libraries are full of authentic masterpieces that were written for money. Grub Street turns out good things almost as often as Parnassus. For if a writer is hard up enough, if he's far down enough (down where I have been and am rising from, I am really saying), he can't afford self-doubt and he can't let other people's opinions, even a father's, keep him from writing.

"Or a wife's?"

Again I am astonished. "Don't tell me Charity is against poetry."

Swinging his stick, he walks with his head down, brooding at the road. "She wants me to get promoted."

"Poems will help with that. This is an English Department, after all."

Sid holds his nose delicately with thumb and finger as if shutting out a bad smell. "Charity's got a very practical head, a hell of a lot more practical than mine. Last year she made a study of all the ranking professors and associate professors—what they'd done to get promoted to tenure. The results were what you'd expect. A scholarly book is best—write *The Road to Xanadu* and you're in. Next best is articles, but it takes a lot of them. She cites me DeSerres, who takes a single idea like perfectibility and lays out a whole string of thinkers and writers on that bed, one after the other. Jefferson on Perfectibility. Freneau on Perfectibility. Emerson on Perfectibility. Whitman on Perfectibility. You can practically do it out of the indexes to the collected works."

"Don't tell me Charity likes that bullshit better than poetry."

"No. She just thinks I have to write it for a while. It's like politics, she says. First you get elected, doing whatever you have to do; then you can vote your principles. Academics have it better than politicians because if you're a congressman, say, you have to get reelected every two years, but if you're a teacher all you need to do is get promoted to associate professor and you're as safe as a justice of the Supreme Court. They may never promote you from associate to full professor, but they can't fire you."

"Why is it so important to be safe?"

He must hear something scornful in my voice, because he looks at me sharply, starts to reply, changes his mind, and says something obviously different from what he has intended. "Charity's family are all professors. She likes being part of a university. She wants us to get promoted, and stay."

"Yeah," I say. "All right, I can see that. But if I were in your shoes I might feel like utilizing the independence I've already got, rather than breaking my neck to get promoted into a kind I might not like so well."

"But you aren't in my shoes," Sid says. It sounds like a mild rebuke, and I shut my mouth. But after a few seconds he adds, squinting my way, "Ask Charity about the fate of poets in this English Department. They've got just one, William Ellery, and he's a pariah."

"He's got tenure."

"Not because he's a poet. Because he's an Anglo-Saxon scholar."

"I hate to think you'll have to write articles about Floyd Dell on Perfectibility for six or seven years before you can write poetry again."

"That's about it."

"Well, good luck," I tell him. "Count on my reading you when tenure has brought you independence."

Laughing, he shakes his head. Ahead of us Charity and Sally have climbed through a fence and started up a hill crowned with yellow trees. We follow, saving our wind for the climb.

When we arrive, our wives are clearing a space of limbs and nut hulls. We spread a blanket. Charity opens the basket and lays out fried chicken wrapped in wax paper, a wooden bowl of ready-mixed salad, French rolls already buttered, a jar of artichoke hearts, celery sticks, fruit, cookies, napkins, paper plates. And our Jonathan apples, to make us feel we have contributed. Sid and I lie on the ground and crack hickory nuts between rocks. The view is spreading, bronzed, conventionalized like a Grant Wood landscape. The air smells of cured grass, cured leaves, distance, the other sides of hills.

Charity looks up, as brilliant as a flash from a heliograph. "We're ready. *Sid?*"

He rises promptly. His arm goes into the hamper and brings out a sodden sack. Inside is a wet towel with ice chips in it, and inside the ice chips is a magnum of champagne. (I have never seen one, but I am literary, I recognize it.) Abruptly he is manic, reviving the shouting conviviality of the night before. His excess leaves me faintly uncomfortable. "Celebration!" he cries. "The day of Jubilo!"

He untwists the wire, the cork explodes up into the hickory leaves, he shakes the bubbles off his hand. "I know it's show-off to blow the cork. Experts do it with a discreet sigh of gas. Well, better over-stimulated champagne than no champagne."

We hold up our Dixie cups and he fills them. With the enormous bottle in one fist, he raises his cup with the other. "What an occasion! How marvelous to be in on it! We salute you at the beginning of a great career."

"Wait," I protest, and Sally says, "No, no, no! It's *your* day, it's your fourth anniversary. Here's health and happiness forever and ever."

Stalemate. We stand with our uplifted cups throwing bubbles above their rims, and our smiles are uncertain but our intentions honorable and unselfish. After a moment Charity saves us. "It's *all* our day, yours and ours too. Here's to all of us."

Sitting on our blanket among twigs and yellow leaves and dusty blue asters, we sip what is probably the first champagne that either Sally or I ever drank, and are promptly refilled, and refilled again. In the circumstances, it doesn't take much to exhilarate me. So I am caught in the wrong mood when Sid, looking down as if with distaste into his cup, repeats the toast with variations. "To all of us. May we all survive the departmental axe."

"What are you talking about?" I say, somewhat raucously. "I'm cannon fodder, I'm a nine-month wonder. But if anybody's in, you are."

"Don't kid yourself. Rousselot was inquiring delicately just the other day what I'm working on. By the time they vote in April or May you'll have a bibliography as long as your arm, and I'll have my little undergraduate poems."

Our faces, I am sure, reflect our degrees of understanding of what is going on. Sally knows nothing about any poems, and is only curious and interested. I know about them but don't believe they are as amateur as he suggests, or that Charity is really opposed to his writing them. Charity doesn't know what Sid may have said to me but knows he must have said something. Her eyes flick from his face to mine and back to his.

Sitting cross-legged with the salad bowl in her lap, she makes a sudden, impatient face and bends far over the bowl and straightens up again. "Oh, *bosh,* Sid! Have some *confidence* in yourself! You're a splendid teacher, everybody says so. Go on being that. If they demand publications, *write* some. Just take it for granted you're going to be promoted, and they won't have the nerve not to."

At me she smiles with all her vividness and urgency, a smile meant to tell me that my luck with the *Atlantic* has hit him, and she knows it, and knows I know it, and wants me to know that it is nothing serious. It's not *your* fault, she seems to say. If he sounds discouraged it's only because your letter started him thinking about *us*.

Troubled that what started as a celebration has begun to sound tense, I hold out my Dixie cup for more champagne. "Let us be unignorable," I propose.

"Exactly!" says Charity. "You have to take your life by the throat and *shake* it." She shakes a double handful of air, strangling it, and

we all laugh. We sidle away from Sid's anxiety and whatever it is between him and Charity. We fill our plates with chicken and salad and rolls, we eat with our eyes contentedly grazing on the countryside, in shade as temperate as the air of Eden, colored gold by hickory leaves. And then, as Charity rises to her knees to help us to more, she freezes, tilts her head listening, and makes a shushing motion with her free hand. "Oh, listen. Listen!"

A sound like a big crowd a good way off, excited and shouting, getting closer. We stand up and scan the empty sky. Suddenly there they are, a wavering V headed directly over our hilltop, quite low, beating southward down the central flyway and talking as they pass. We stay quiet, suspending our human conversation until their garrulity fades and their wavering lines are invisible in the sky.

They have passed over us like an eraser over a blackboard, wiping away whatever was there before they came.

"Oh, don't you *love* them!" Charity says. "Sometimes when we stayed late in Vermont, or went up late for the color, we'd see and hear them like that, coming over Folsom Hill. Someday you've got to visit us there. We've got all *kinds* of room. How about next summer?"

"Next summer," I tell her, "if they'll let me, I'll be teaching summer school, and maybe cleaning out steam tables at the hospital in the evenings, and driving a cab nights. Come spring we will have a little hostage to fortune."

"Summer after next, then."

"Summer after next I may be wearing out shovels for the WPA."

"Pooh," she says. "Sid's right, by then you'll be famous. *Please* plan on coming. You can write all day except for mealtimes and picnic times and swim times and walk times."

Sally's big eyes, liquid, shiny with champagne and feeling, touch mine, and she shakes her head as if in disbelief. The hickories move in the light wind, and a nut thumps down. "Don't extend any invitations you don't want accepted," Sally says. "It's dangerous to wave raw meat around tigers."

"We never invite if we don't mean it," Sid says. He looks into his Dixie cup and looks back up as if surprised at what he found there. The future, maybe. "God, how marvelous that would be! That's a standing invitation. Anytime you can, for as long as you can."

In that fine place, in the ripened Indian summer weather, those two once again choose us. In circumstances where smaller spirits might let envy corrode liking, they declare their generous pleasure in our company and our good luck. What we felt last night when we fell into a laughing bearhug and fused our frosty breaths outside their door, we feel again on this placid hill. We have been invited into their lives, from which we will never be evicted, or evict ourselves.

But I have become aware of unexpected tensions in their relationship, and to my own surprise have begun to feel a little protective of a man whom only last evening I thought the luckiest and most enviable man alive.

Another afternoon. We are skating on Lake Monona, just off our snow-mounded wall. Silvery air, slatey sky, spidery clinging flakes of snow, red runny noses, a cold wind, laughter. January, probably; I have the feeling that Christmas has passed. The girls are both noticeably pregnant. Sally is being extremely cautious, for ice skating was not her most natural sport in Berkeley, and she is afraid of falling and doing harm to the child she carries.

Charity is so unapprehensive as to seem reckless. "If you're going to fall, you'll fall on your *bum*," she says. "There's nothing *there* to get hurt but you."

Only a week or so ago, out on a country hill beyond Middleton, I watched her and the blue-blooded wife of a visiting Irish professor coasting on Flexible Fliers. The Irish lady bellyflopped like a ten-year-old. Charity at least had the sense to sit on the sled and steer with her feet, but she didn't have the sense not to race. They came together down the hill, screeching. As they passed under a big oak they hit soft snow. Their runners dropped in, the sleds stopped, the ladies went skidding, the Irish woman on her stomach, Charity ponderously on her bum. "Jesus Crust," the Irish lady said, or I think she said. Wiping snow off their faces, shaking it out of their mittens, beating it out of their clothes, laughing their heads off, they went plowing back up, dragging their sleds, for another run.

Now here we are, still advocates of the strenuous life and healthful exercise in the open air, out on Lake Monona on skates. This time cautious Sally has been persuaded to join in, though God knows why this seems safer than coasting. Here, iceboats sneak up silently behind you and pass with one up-reared runner skimming your head. There is even a little airplane that lands and takes off on the ice. You skate, believe me, with one eye over your shoulder, especially if you are on blades for the first time in your life, and most especially if you are pregnant, almost ready to pop your cocoon.

Charity's eyes are snapping and her nose is red. She wipes it with the back of her red mitten. "It's not so different from roller skating, only *teeterier*. Don't lean back, lean forward. Just push off and let yourself *swoop*." She swoops, heavy and graceful. Out farther, Sid is sprinting, cutting corners, braking with a shower of shaved ice when an iceboat cuts across his bows.

Meantime, I am limping around on the insides of my ankles. When I try to help Sally get started, I slide out from under myself and pull her down in a soft huddle on top of me. Obviously she needs better instruction than mine. Sid, observing, glides in, lifts her up with encouraging words, takes her left hand in his right, lays his left arm around her shoulders, fits her right arm around his waist. Tentative and floundering, she is skated away with, begins to feel the rhythm, begins to make cautious strokes. There they go in increasingly confident arcs, out away from the rougher inshore ice and onto the open lake. Watching and applauding, I pay insufficient attention to my own peril, and *bomp*, I go out from under myself again and bruise my tailbone on the ice.

I remember the gray, snow-spitting afternoon, the bite of cold wind on chin and cheeks and brows, the cold of feet cramped into too-small borrowed skate shoes, the throttled-down whistle and mutter of the plane landing behind me, the vision of a racing iceboat shearing away with one runner off the ice and the operator spread-eagled on the deck, and the sight of Sally and Sid leaning and stroking, and Charity gliding by, portly and exhilarated, encouraging me while I flounder flabby-ankled, and fall down, and get up, and fall down again.

But I remember even better the hour afterward in our basement, hot buttered rum and Sally's cinnamon rolls still warm from the oven. Red faces, tingling skin, exuberant vitality, laughter, and for Sally and me the uncustomary pleasure of giving instead of taking.

There sit our two podded wives close together on the couch, whispering and intimate, two months away, rosy with the heat of indoors. Coming from the kitchen bringing the rum bottle and the teakettle for a fresh round of drinks, I see them there, and think how in those two women four hearts are beating, and it awes me.

ecollection, I have found, is usually about half invention, and right now I realize that there is much about Sid and Charity Lang that I either invented or got secondhand. I didn't know them in college, or when they met and married, and so I have neither memory nor documentation to draw on when I start to imagine what they were like when they first came together. I have only this Vermont lake and its associations, and the stories that they themselves, or Comfort, or Aunt Emily, told us.

First Sid had them feeling sorry for him and rather wishing he would go away. Then he won them over. That in itself is surprising, for neither Charity nor her mother was ever comfortable with a man she couldn't predict and manage. Maybe the circumstances disarmed them. On the other hand, from the very beginning they may have managed him more than they seemed to. When a male ballet dancer lifts and carries his partner around the stage in a *pas de deux,* he looks as strong as Atlas, but any ballerina will tell you there is a good deal in knowing how to be lifted.

"Who *is* this boy?" I can imagine her mother asking. "Do we know him? Do we know his family?"

Suppose they are sitting on Aunt Emily's porch, looking down across waist-high ferns and raspberry bushes to the lake. It is a day of traveling clouds. The porch is a sheltered pocket, though the wind is strong enough to scrape limbs across the roof. Emily Ellis is knitting. Her needles dart and withdraw, her finger with its loop of yarn makes swift circles, she pauses to pull stitches along one needle and tug another yard of yarn loose from the ball. Her eyes are brown and sharp, her face wears an expression at once interested, amused, and self-contained.

Charity, sprawling in the porch swing, her hair in pigtails, waves an opened letter as if waving away smoke. "*I've* only known him a few months. He's a graduate student at Harvard. You wouldn't know the family—they live in Pittsburgh."

Her mother's hands pause. Her lips tighten. She says tartly, "It's not out of the question that people worth knowing should live in Pittsburgh. Did you invite him?"

"*No!* I came up here to get away from him."

"What's the matter with him? He sounds pushy."

"Pushy is what he absolutely *isn't*. He's a pushover. He's in *love*, Mother. He's suffering. He hasn't seen me for a week."

"Oh, dear me," her mother says. She counts stitches, moving her lips. "How about you? I suppose you're suffering too."

"Then you suppose all wrong. All I'm suffering from are his impetuous *advances*." She laughs and hoists one foot up on the back of the swing. Her mother looks at the exposed leg until Charity takes it down again.

"You don't want him to come up, then."

"How can we stop him? He says he'll be *passing through,* and would like to drop in. Passing through, my eye. He's not headed anywhere but right here. Why couldn't he say so?"

"Perhaps he feels he has to have an escape, in case you don't make him welcome. Would he be sensitive that way?"

"He would if *you* didn't welcome him. He's *painfully* polite to his elders, and he has such a wild idea of the intellectual distinction of this family that he practically genuflects when he speaks Daddy's name."

"It's not unbecoming in him to respect scholarship. How long would he expect to stay?"

"Who knows? Until we drive him away? He's set himself the goal of reading all of Restoration drama this summer, but he might think he can do that as well up here as in Cambridge."

Her mother's hands are moving again, swift and automatic. "Well, if you don't want him, we can give him tea and send him on his way."

Charity's expression incorporates a slight frown. "I don't know. Wouldn't that seem a little . . . ? We could put him in the dorm."

"Comfort is sleeping there."

"She could go over to Uncle Dwight's."

"But must not be sent over," her mother says. "Arrange it as you like, if Comfort is agreeable. On the other hand, if you don't want him around, he should be discouraged at once. Firmly."

Charity stands up, tall and square-shouldered. Seen only from the neck down, she could be thought a bit gangly. With her head on, she is something else. Her neck is long, her head small, molded by the tight braids. Her eyes are hazel, her teeth white and even. Her mother correctly thinks her a striking young woman, and her mind ventures off into speculations. "All right," Charity says indifferently. "If he's a pest we'll just shoo him off."

"Nevertheless," says her mother, "let me give you a word of advice. It is neither decorous nor kind to mislead a boy in the condition you say he is in. Unless you're serious, or think you might be, don't encourage him. As the saying goes, I don't want his blood on the rug. Remember that."

So Sidney Lang, at the end of his first year as a graduate student in English literature, makes his entry into the world of Battell Pond. He arrives, at a guess, about midafternoon, having started from Cambridge at first daylight and driven hard in the rain only to realize, an hour short of his destination, that he will arrive at lunch time. He pulls off the road and sits for two hours, missing his own lunch and watching the peaks of the White Mountains to the south and east appear and disappear in the alternations of sun and rain. Accustomed to making every hour count, he reads a hundred pages of *Middlemarch* while he waits.

When he is sure that his arrival will interrupt neither lunch nor possible after-lunch naps, he drives on. He comes to the village—white frame houses on a single street with a single cross street, nothing very picturesque—and following Charity's instructions, goes on one mile to some mailboxes mounted on a wagon wheel. A dirt road leads him left between a farmhouse and a pair of lakeside cottages. At once he is engulfed in dense, dripping woods. The track is rutted and chuck-holed, full of puddles, humped with roots. Even dimmer tracks lead off to glimpses of cottages and lake. Both sides. He seems to be on a narrow peninsula. Keeping right, he arrives in a clearing before a weathered shingled cottage. The car parked on the grass he recognizes as Charity's. Both front windows are open. He leaps out, rolls her windows shut, and crowds back into his own car to ponder strategy.

His view is cut off by the cottage. Off in the woods on the right, a weathered gable shows through the trees: the dorm, though he doesn't know then what it is. On the left, a path curves behind a clump of young conifers and into thick woods. That leads, though again he doesn't know, to George Barnwell Ellis's think house, a shack heated by a sheet-iron stove, where a single hanging light bulb shines down on a desk loaded with books in three dead languages and learned journals in four living ones. Here Professor Ellis has been engaged for ten summers on a book about the twelfth-century heretical sect called the Bogomils. He will still be working on it when he dies, fifteen years from now. He has already distinguished himself with his book on the Albigenses.

Sidney Lang looks at the door that is the only break in the wall of shingles facing him. Hoping that Charity might have been watching for him, he waits for it to open. But the longer he waits, the more he is convinced that that door has not been opened in years. It looks rusted shut and mossed over. A plank walk leads around the cottage on the right-hand side. To welcome him from there, Charity would have to come out in the rain.

For a few minutes more he waits, imagining her under a big umbrella, dazzling the downpour with her smile. She does not appear. No one appears. He hears only the steady patter and rustle and drip of rain in the wet woods, and the gush of water from the downspout at the corner. The woods around him are an intense, wet green. Even the air is green.

Eventually, reluctantly, he reaches his slicker from the back seat, shawls it over head and shoulders, opens the door, sets his L.L. Bean moccasins down on the drenched grass, and is committed. Hunching, he hurries around the house on the slippery walk. From around the corner he hears the steady sound of a woman's voice.

Emily Ellis's porch is less porch than command post. It is fifteen feet deep and runs across the entire front of the cottage, railed and low-eaved and sheltered even in the worst weather. I never saw it empty of people, never saw it without a partly solved jigsaw puzzle spread out on a card table and the swing full of dominoes, rummy, and Chinese checkers, rarely saw it without someone playing bridge, either Aunt Emily teaching some children or Aunt Emily and George Barnwell engaged in their intent, competitive afternoon rubbers with Uncle Dwight and Aunt Heather.

The bridge table is at the far end, out of the traffic, which is incessant. Though the Ellis daughters are grown, Charity out of Smith, Comfort halfway through, there are innumerable cousins, nieces, nephews, grandnieces, grandnephews, neighbor children, and the children of visitors and guests. Just inside the door is a circulating library of wholesome books, among which I have noted *The Wind in the Willows, The Boy Scout Handbook,* the entire *Pooh* canon, *Black Beauty, Little Women, The Yearling.* There are also piles of the *National Geographic.*

Aunt Emily believes in the freedom of summer. She doesn't much care what the children do so long as they do *something,* and know what they are doing. It is idleness and randomness of mind that she cannot abide. When the children go on a hike, she packs bird and flower guides into their knapsacks, and quizzes them on their return to see if they have learned anything. When she accompanies them on an overnight camping trip, sleeping in her own worn pup tent, they can count on instructive fireside talks on the stars. And on rainy days such as this she sits like a confident spider in the midst of her web until boredom drives all the children on the Point to her porch, where she reads to them or teaches them French.

What she is doing now is reading *Hiawatha.* She is fond of Longfellow, whose house is a landmark on Brattle Street hardly a block from her own, and she perceives the rightness of *Hiawatha* in this setting of northern woods. She reads loudly, to be heard above the rush and patter of rain.

> By the shores of Gitche Gumee,
> By the shining Big-Sea-Water,
> Stood the wigwam of Nokomis,
> Daughter of the Moon, Nokomis.
> Dark behind it rose the forest,
> Rose the black and gloomy pine-trees,
> Rose the firs with cones upon them;
> Bright before it beat the water,
> Beat the clear and sunny water,
> Beat the shining Big-Sea-Water.

All the little Indians in a half circle around Aunt Emily are getting an imprinting that will last for life. The sound of her voice reading will condition how they look upon themselves and the world. It will become part of the loved ambience of Battell Pond, a glint in the chromatic wonder of childhood. These small sensibilities will never lose the images of dark woods and bright lake. Nature to them will always be beneficent and female.

When he heard the owls at midnight,
Hooting, laughing in the forest,
"What is that?" he cried in terror.
"What is that?" he said. "Nokomis?"
And the good Nokomis answered:
"That is but the owl and owlet,
Talking in their native language,
Talking, scolding at each other."

Some of those children, years later, may awaken in the night from a dream of that strong voice chanting Iroquois myths in Finnish trochees, and their souls will yearn within them for the certainty and assurance and naturalness and authority of the time Aunt Emily dominated.

In primitive cultures, Aunt Emily will tell anyone with whom she discusses the rearing of children, the young learn by imitating their parents. Girls learn household tasks and the feminine role, including motherhood, by playing house and looking after their younger brothers and sisters. Boys follow their fathers to field and forge, and ape their ways with tools and weapons. Both boys and girls may be instructed in the proprieties of symbolic occasions by medicine men, shamans, and specially delegated elders, just as in our society they are sent to school and set to read books. But in our society (she means Cambridge), men (she means men of education and culture) no longer work with tools or use weapons. Girls can still imitate their mothers, but a man-child finds little in his father's activities that he can make games of. Women must therefore provide models for both girls and boys, and steer them into paths they might not find for themselves, and above all encourage them in the strenuous use of their minds. Precisely what Nokomis did for her orphaned grandson Hiawatha.

About the abdication of male authority she is, of course, right. A quarter of the male population of New England escaped during the California Gold Rush. Another quarter vanished into the Civil War, and either died or kept on going. Those without the vigor to be Argonauts or warriors stayed to see their work taken over by the Irish, Portuguese, Italians, and French Canadians. They lost some of their political power but kept most of the status. The best of them (she means men like George Barnwell Ellis) continue in the tradition of Emerson and the enlightened divines. They teach at Harvard or the lesser academies, they are scholars and moralists, they love Nature. Also, though Aunt Emily can't be expected to think of this, they prepared the way for the New Humanists whose thinking dominated many college campuses in the 1930s. I studied under a couple of them, and was advised for the good of my soul to read others.

They were people such as Irving Babbitt of Harvard, from whom Sid Lang tried to learn the decorum, the *nil admirari*, and the dry reasonableness he was never quite able to attain to, and Paul Elmer More of Princeton, under whom Marvin Ehrlich devoutly read Greek. Ernest Hemingway once guessed that all New Humanists were the product of decorous intercourse. There was one at Wisconsin who directed Ed Abbot's dissertation on romantic excess in *Comus*. Ed, who had more in common with Comus than with either Milton or his dissertation director, summarized his own position in a quatrain:

> So nail the punch and spike the beer,
> The fucking Comus Club is here.
> We'll kill the man who would insist
> That Comus was a Humanist.

But back to Aunt Emily. New England women, left behind, had few men to pick from except the Irish, Portuguese, Italians, and French Canadians, all of them religiously, economically, and socially unacceptable. Some women turned mannish and assumed roles that their men had once performed. Some espoused causes, affiliated themselves with Abolition or Susan B. Anthony or the antivivesectionists, marched in parades, got themselves arrested, wrote strong letters to the press, addressed meetings, and generally became characters without ever forgetting they were ladies. Even those who found mates among the reduced numbers of New England men found themselves doing things unfamiliar to their grandmothers. These matured as matriarchs, the others as old maids. The clear lesson of New England's history is that when there are not enough suitable men around to run the world, women are perfectly capable of doing so.

It is a fact that no child ever followed George Barnwell Ellis to his work, or aped his way with any tool. His routines are simply not imitable. He appears mistily and cheerfully at breakfast, and shortly disappears—in winter to his office or to the Divinity School, where a child would have a difficult time finding anything at all to do, and in summer up the path to his think house, which by his assumption and Aunt Emily's interdict is off limits to the young.

In winter he reappears for dinner, but in summer, a less rigorous time, he has another pattern. At precisely twelve he comes with his stiff-legged walk, his thin hair on end, around the corner of the porch. He plucks yesterday's damp swimming suit off the rail and goes in to change. He and Aunt Emily walk together down to the dock, and there, while Aunt Emily launches into the cold water like a sea lion, displacing a big bow wave, and swims across the cove and back, a good half mile, George Barnwell paddles and putters in the warmer shallows, mostly on his back to avoid flooding his sinuses. When Emily surges up, blowing and exclaiming and shaking her fingers, they come together back to the porch, where the hired girl will have timed lunch for their arrival.

After lunch, Aunt Emily reads or knits on the porch, while George Barnwell disappears into his bedroom for a nap. At two-thirty he emerges, looking aimless but actually as relentless as a guided missile, and goes back up the path to his rendezvous with the Bogomils. At five he returns to the porch, where Aunt Emily, George's brother Dwight, and Dwight's wife Heather will be waiting at the bridge table. What Miles Standish used to get out of encounters with hostile sachems, George Barnwell gets out of a tight rubber of bridge. After dinner he will read a detective novel until ten, and go to bed.

No medicine man he, as *Time* might once have said. He is mild, agreeable, wryly humorous, abstracted, distinguished and therefore to be respected, helpless and therefore to be looked after. Aunt Emily's attitude toward him is not greatly different from her attitude toward any child. On command, like a well-bred spaniel, he will sit, stay, or speak. He will even sing, as lustily as the children though never on key, when Aunt Emily dragoons the extended family into an evening of music and leads them through "Frère Jacques," "Who Will Carry Me over the River?", "Ach, wie schön ist mir am Abend," "Claire de Lune," "Au Près de ma Blonde," and "Why Doesn't My Goose Sing As Well As Thy Goose?"

Most of the time George Barnwell never notices the children, for most of his time he spends in twelfth-century Bulgaria. It is accepted that whatever the children learn, they learn from Aunt Emily. And any child who undergoes Aunt Emily's instruction is a post under a pile driver. When Aunt Emily reads, you listen.

Eventually some not-quite-harness-broke child looks up and sees Sid Lang, his glasses streaming and his slicker draped over his head, standing at the corner. She nudges her neighbor, she puts her hand over her mouth. Thus early does Aunt Emily's influence persuade the young that adult males are an intrusion or an irrelevancy. As awareness of him becomes general, heads turn, eyes roll, giggles are smothered. Aunt Emily goes on obliviously chanting, Sid stands dripping at the corner. Then somebody's giggle breaks into the open, and Aunt Emily looks up. Her eyes follow the children's eyes. She of course knows who this has to be, but she says nothing. She waits, radiating control.

Sid starts to speak, finds a frog in his throat, clears it, and says in a strained tenor, "I'm sorry. I didn't mean to interrupt. Is this . . . ? I was looking for Charity Ellis."

"Come in under cover," Aunt Emily says, "and sit down. We'll be through in a few minutes."

He comes in under cover, sinks into a warped wicker chair, slides his wet oilskin off his head. He is goggled and giggled at until Aunt Emily, lifting her book, says a single word: "Now!" He feels undoubtedly that he has made the worst possible entrance, and will not be forgiven. Aunt Emily reads again.

> "And the birds sang round him, o'er him,
> 'Do not shoot us, Hiawatha!'
> Sang the robin, the Opechee,
> Sang the bluebird, the Owaissa,
> 'Do not shoot us, Hiawatha!' "

For five or six minutes Sid is chained to the wicker chair while Hiawatha in his magic mittens visits his father Mudjekeewis at the doorways of the West-Wind. The rain falls swishing, a curtain between porch and lake. Distracted by his presence, the girl children whisper behind their hands. Aunt Emily reads on. But during the brief pause while she ordered Sid Lang under cover she has got an impression of this young man whom Charity is so suspiciously indifferent to.

Fairly standard graduate student. Poor, of course, as they all are these days. Poorer than most, to judge by the frayed cuffs of his khaki pants and the blotch on the front of his work shirt as if it had been washed with chocolate in the pocket and the stain then ironed in. Fine fair hair. Skin less tanned than it ought to be this far into the summer. Nearsighted, from the way he squinted when he removed his glasses to dry them. Eyes a striking forget-me-not blue. Pleasant square face, a little gaunt. Quick, eager smile.

Aunt Emily believes she knows how he feels, stuck there in a chair like a visitor to a kindergarten. Looking up briefly, she meets his eyes, his eager smile. Painfully polite to his elders, Charity says. Nothing wrong with that. But he follows the reading so attentively that she is impatient. Surely a student at his stage should have progressed beyond *Hiawatha*.

Then sneakers thud on the walk, and Charity bursts around the corner with a newspaper over her head. Sidney Lang forgets *Hiawatha* and leaps to his feet. Aunt Emily closes her book and dismisses the Indians with a wave. They scatter to Chinese checkers, rummy, and ginger-ale-and-grape-juice. For the grown-ups there are introductions.

Though she observes that he can hardly look away from Charity, speckled with rain, laughing, her color high, Aunt Emily concedes that Sid Lang does have a respectful manner. He is almost too deferential, and she can see how he might sometimes fret Charity, who is direct and opinionated and enjoys argument. At the same time, she remembers that Charity, given the chance to scotch this visit, did not do so. She looks anything but bored or fretted now.

"Mr. Lang will want to bring in his things," Aunt Emily says. "Have you got his quarters ready?"

"That's what I've just been doing."

"Oh, no no no no no!" Sid cries. "I can't stay. I only came by to say hello. I've got to go on."

Charity looks at him out of clear skeptical eyes. "To where?"

"Montreal. I'm on my way to see a friend in the McGill Medical School."

"Can't he wait?"

"I don't think so. He . . . we arranged that I'd meet him for dinner tonight."

"It's four hours to Montreal," Aunt Emily says, "and it's pouring. You can't possibly make it. At least you must stay tonight and see if Battell Pond won't show off a little better tomorrow."

"Oh, that's not it. It's beautiful, rain and all. What a beautiful pocket of quiet. But I don't want to barge in and put you all to trouble."

"I've already made your bed," Charity says. "If you don't lie in it I'll be *furious*. So will Mother."

"And it's dangerous to infuriate me," her mother says. "Charity will show you where to put your bag."

Now Sid is embarrassed. "The fact is, I don't have a bag. I didn't even bring a clean shirt. I just took off."

"To drive," Charity says, "to Montreal. To dinner. You do need a keeper. You must have brought *something*. Books? I never saw you without a green bag of books." To her mother she says, "He reads *everywhere*—in the subway, between the acts at plays, at intermissions in Symphony Hall, on picnics, on *dates.*"

This speech conveys considerable information to Aunt Emily. She watches Sid's eyes close in mock agony, while a really very engaging smile takes over from the sheepishness on his face. "Well, there's so much to read, and I'm so far behind. Everybody's read ten times more than I have."

"What did you bring?" Charity asks. "Restoration dramas?"

"I'm taking a rest from those. I've just got some hole-fillers. *Middlemarch, The Idiot,* things like that, novels I should have read but haven't."

"Then let's put them in the dorm before they mildew," Charity says, "and then take a walk in the rain. I want to show you Folsom Hill and I won't *tolerate* your bringing a book along."

"Dress for it," says Aunt Emily. "I see you have proper rain gear, Mr. Lang. Charity, take an umbrella. There's no need to risk grippe."

"An umbrella? In the woods? The woodpeckers would die laughing."

About to say something tart and sensible, Aunt Emily closes her mouth on it. "As you wish." To Sid she says, "We have few rules here, but for the girl's sake we do like people to be on time for meals. Dinner will be at seven."

"One thing I'm very prompt about is meals," Sid says. (Good, thinks Aunt Emily, not such a stick as he seemed at first.)

Charity goes inside and comes out in a raincoat. "No hat?" her mother asks.

Sid says, "I've got a sou'wester in the car."

"Then what will you wear?"

He surprises her. He runs his hand back to front across his head, ruffling the short fair hair, and says in a Yiddish accent, "Vot's to get vet? Vot's to get hurt? Anyway . . ." He lifts a finger, and intones:

"I want to drown in good salt water,
I want my body to bump the pier."

"Bless me," Aunt Emily says, "what an extraordinary sentiment. Who wrote it?"

"Samuel Hoffenstein," Sid says. "In the manner of the early Millay."

He grabs Charity's arm, and they are gone.

Up to here, I have no trouble imagining. I know how Battell Pond first struck Sid because I remember how it first struck me, and I have many times heard Aunt Emily tell the tale of his first visit, giving it a quality at once humorous and romantic: a fairy story involving a sequestered princess, a prince in pauper's clothing, a remote place accessible only by back roads approximately as difficult as a sword-edge bridge.

This summer colony is so discreet and understated that from either road or lake it hardly shows. Of its two thousand or so summer residents you rarely see more than a couple of young people in a canoe, a woman at a mailbox, or a gray scholar disappearing toward his think house. Exceptions: summer auctions, and the village store at the hour when the *New York Times* is delivered. Then you will see scores, maybe hundreds.

Battell Pond is out of a Hudson River School painting, uniting the philosophical-contemplative with the pastoral-picturesque. It is not a resort. It is the total opposite of a resort, for the academics who dominate it in summer and pay most of the taxes have quietly scotched all movements for an airport, a movie house, a second gas station, even motorboats on the lake. What Sid Lang saw first in the summer of 1933 was not visibly much different from what George Barnwell Ellis and Bliss Perry began after a buggy tour before the turn of the century. Candles and oil lamps have reluctantly given way to electric lights. Some cottages now have telephones. The rotting planks of porches and docks have been replaced every six or eight years. Not much else has changed.

My problem is not in imagining Battell Pond, but in guessing what Sid and Charity may have said and done that afternoon and on the days thereafter that he stayed, postponing without letter, telephone call, or explanation his dinner date in Montreal. The love scenes of my friends have never been my long suit or my particular interest, and anyway I don't know that at that point she was sure she wanted him, though I am pretty sure she did. Moreover, a Vermont downpour is no setting for amorous scenes. So I will simply take them on the walk they would probably have taken.

They go back through the wet woods to the main road, turn left on that for a hundred yards, and wedge through a gate with a faded sign: *Defense de Bumper,* some professor's joke. A dirt road, the road I walked this morning, burrows along the hillside under overhanging trees—sugar maple and red maple, hemlock, white birch and yellow birch and gray birch, beech, black spruce and red spruce, balsam fir, wild cherry, white ash, basswood, ironwood, tamarack, elm, poplar, here and there a young white pine. Being her mother's daughter, survivor of many a hike with bird, flower, fern, and tree books, Charity knows them all. Sid, whose family has summered in the Carolina mountains among other forests, and a few times on the Cape where eels and alewives are more significant than trees, knows few of them, but welcomes instruction.

The road climbs curving out of wet ground thick with cedars, and up onto a plateau meadow where Jersey cows, beautiful as deer, watch them with Juno eyes. Along the trail the ferns are dense, drooping with wet, twenty kinds of them. Again he does not know them (in my experience, ferns are an exclusively feminine expertise), and she tells him: hay-scented fern, wood fern, sensitive fern, cinnamon fern, ostrich fern, interrupted fern, Christmas fern, bracken, maidenhair—names that are as pleasant to his ear as the woods smells are to his nose. In the intervals between clumps of spruce, the moss spreads a green carpet, inches thick, feather-soft, with the candles of ground pine and the domes of spotted orange mushrooms rising out of it.

Sid treads on it in his wet moccasins. He jumps up and down as if on a trampoline. He stoops to press it with his flat hand. "God," he says, "I want to roll in it. Any minute now a leprechaun will pop out from under one of those toadstools."

"Those are not toadstools," Charity tells him. "Those are mushrooms. Deadly Amanita mushrooms. *Ne mangez pas.*"

"You know everything that grows here. That's wonderful."

"Not so wonderful. I grew up here."

"I grew up in Sewickley, Pennsylvania, too, but I couldn't tell you the name of one thing that grows there. One, maybe. Lilacs."

"You didn't grow up with my mother."

There they are, smiling at each other in the dwindling rain. He loves the even whiteness of her smile, as who doesn't; though as for smiling they are about equal, they both have what he disparagingly calls a rush of teeth to the mouth. The rain drips off the brim of the yellow sou'wester, and he thinks it the most fantastically attractive head covering he ever saw. I suppose he has an impulse to bed her right there in the pneumatic moss, reproducing a scene between Lady Chatterley and her gamekeeper that he has reread several times in a borrowed, bootlegged copy. Her eyes are laughing and alive. I suppose he reaches for her. I suppose she fends him off. That is what girls did in 1933. They walk again.

A partridge comes out of a tree above them with a startling rush of wings. They see a snowshoe rabbit (not a rabbit, she tells him, it's a varying hare, they only *call* them rabbits). By now they are walking between half-obliterated stone walls and ancient, broken maples, along what was once a road. The sloping meadows on both sides are on their way back to woods. She tells him about the farms that used to be up here, and shows him foundations overgrown with roses gone wild, and heliotrope, and browning lilacs, and Virginia creeper rank as weeds.

At some unnoticed moment the rain has stopped. Off to the west, high and far off, blue shows, and when they climb the last pitch onto a summit marked by the stone hearths of picnic fires, there are the mountains to westward. Those too she names as they reveal themselves: Camel's Hump, Mansfield, Belvidere, Jay. A thin sun gilds them. He spreads his slicker dry-side-up on the grass, and they sit.

The view from Folsom Hill is not grand in the way of western landscapes. What gives it its charm is the alternation of wild and cultivated, rough woods ending with scribed edges against smooth hayfields—this and the accent dots of white houses, red barns, and clustered cattle tiny as aphids on a leaf. Directly below them, across the shaggy top of a lesser hill, is the lake, heartshaped, with the village at its southern end. Hardly a cottage (the local word is "camp") shows around the lake, hardly a dock or boathouse. Green woods and greener meadows meet blue water, and it all looks nearly as wild as it must have looked to General Hazen's men, cutting a road to Canada through these woods during the Revolution.

Sid breathes it in, sucks it in through his pores. If there was ever a romantic who should not have studied with Irving Babbitt, he is the one. He is more Hudson River School than Asher Durand, more transcendentalist than Emerson, more kin to fox and woodchuck than Thoreau.

"You never told me," he says. "It must be the most beautiful place on earth."

"Not that beautiful, but beautiful enough. I love it up here. I'm glad it's quit raining. Maybe tomorrow we can paddle around the lake."

"Should I stay tomorrow?"

"Will your McGill friend worry?"

This is pure malice. He cuts the McGill friend off with a chop of the hand. "Do you want me to stay?"

Expressive shrug. Enigmatic smile.

"Are you annoyed that I followed you up here?"

"No."

"Why did you run away from Cambridge?"

"I didn't run away. I came up here for my vacation."

"And didn't even tell me where you were going. Of course you ran away. I had to find out from the Fogg where you'd gone."

"I decided on the spur of the moment."

"Because of me."

"Not *everything* has reference to you!"

"But this did."

Shrug.

"Charity," he says in desperation, "do you want me to go? I'll go right now if you say so. I do have a friend at McGill. He isn't expecting me, that was all blather, but he exists. I'll get out of your way in five minutes if that's what you want. How do I know you're not playing games? I love you, does that mean anything? I'll hang around forever if there's a chance, but I don't want to be a pitiable nuisance. I want you to marry me. I'll do whatever it takes, if it takes years. But I won't have you stringing me along because you feel sorry for me."

"Of *course* you're not a nuisance," she says. "Of *course* I want you to stay. *Mother* wants you to stay. I'm glad you came, I truly am. I hoped you would. But marry you! How could we get married when you're still two or three years from your degree? Everybody's starving in breadlines, and there we'd be without a job or prospects, and *years* from getting any. Your mother might support you as long as you're in school, but she won't if you're crazy enough to get married."

"There are ways."

"What would you do, rob banks?"

"If that's what it took. The question is not how we'd manage, it's do you want to."

She looks at him with clear eyes from under the brim of the sou' wester. He grabs for her hand and she pulls it away. Gritting his teeth, he sits looking off down the hill. Distant, half smiling, she says nothing, but when she changes her position, bracing herself and leaning backward, he discovers that one of her hands is again within reach. This time he covers it with his own and will not let it go. Leaning close, he all but roars in frustration and desire, "Charity . . . !"

With her other hand she sweeps the long wet grass and sprinkles him with cold drops. "Dampen that ardor."

"You bloody witch. Tell me one thing."

"Of course."

"If you wanted me to follow you up here, why didn't you invite me?"

"I couldn't be sure it would match Mother's plans."

"You could have telephoned and found out."

"No, I couldn't. We don't have a telephone up here."

"You could have written."

"The mail takes *days.*"

"So you just left without a word to me."

Her laughter bursts out. "You found me."

Pulling at her hand, he tips her toward him. "Charity . . . !"

But she looks at the watch on her wrist, exposed by his pulling, and yanks her hand free and jumps to her feet. "Good Lord, dinner's in twenty-five minutes. We can't be late, not your first day. That'd be *fatal.*"

"Fatal to what?"

But she is already running. He sweeps up the slicker and comes after her like a big yellow bat, swooping down the wet hill between the broken stone walls and the old maples. They run all the way home. One minute before the hired girl Dorothy brings on the soup tureen, thirty seconds before George Barnwell Ellis drops his head to say grace, they pant up to the table and scramble into the two empty chairs. Charity has thrown a sweater over her shoulders to dignify her dress for dinner, he has comb marks in his wet hair.

Aunt Emily gives them a sharp, searching look. Comfort, at nineteen a younger, softer, prettier, less striking version of Charity, has already dropped her chin for the prayer, but lets her eyes wander to Sid, on her left, and then to Charity, across the table. George Barnwell, seeing all chairs filled, does not pause for introductions. He folds his hands and looks benevolently at his plate. "Heavenly Father, we thank Thee for all Thy loving care. Bless us this day, and sanctify this food to our use. Amen."

Amen.

I can't imagine Sid Lang venturing into the Ellis household without preparing himself. He probably looked up George Barnwell in *Who's Who,* the *Directory of American Scholars,* and the card catalogue of Widener. He might have thumbed through the vast volume on the Albigenses, the seventh person in history to do so. He might even have checked the book out and brought it along in his green bag along with *Middlemarch* and *The Idiot.* For he felt the obligation to read everything, and both his passion for Charity and his respect for learning would have made him look upon George Barnwell Ellis as a gold thread in the tapestry of human thought.

Alone with Professor Ellis he would quickly have established a relationship, as he did with all professors whom he respected. He would have primed the pump, asked questions, listened with attention. But the other presences at the table were distracting, and since introductions had been suspended in favor of grace, and George Barnwell clearly didn't have the slightest idea who the young man at his table was, Sid found himself exposed to Aunt Emily. She would not have held still for intellectual conversation anyway. She had lived too long with her husband to let him wander into shop talk. "Hush, G.B.," she had been known to say in company. "Nobody wants to hear about your Bogomils." Now, while Sid ate like a threshing hand (she did not know he had missed lunch), she set her eyes on him as she might have set a carving fork in a roast. That he ate so heartily prejudiced her in his favor. It had always exasperated her that George Barnwell ate so pickingly.

"You come from Pittsburgh, Charity tells me."

"Sewickley. It's a suburb."

"That must be pleasanter. From all one hears, Pittsburgh is a rather dirty industrial city."

"It's smoky, yes. We're across the river, on the bluffs."

"Has your family lived there long?"

"My grandfather came there from Scotland."

"Like Andrew Carnegie."

Laughter. "Well, not *quite* like Andrew Carnegie."

"What does your father do?"

A little glinting look through shining glasses. "My father's dead."

"I'm sorry. What *did* he do?"

"He was in business. Various businesses."

From his slight hesitation she judged that he was evading her question. Ashamed of his father? Lost everything in the crash, perhaps? Jumped out a window? The boy was practically in rags. Could he be really poor, the son of a steel worker or something like that? A thoroughgoing egalitarian, Aunt Emily would not have minded. But his laconics made her more curious.

"Where did you go to school before Harvard?"

He had a pleasant, musical voice. "Yale," he said. "Before that, Deerfield."

That accounted for his good manners. Pittsburgh could hardly have taught them to him. So respectable an educational background, moreover, argued parents who knew what was best for their son, and were able to afford it.

"Is your mother living? Do you have brothers and sisters?"

"My mother still lives in Sewickley. One of my sisters lives in Akron, the other in Chicago."

It sounded rather drearily midwestern. Possibly the boy was trying to outgrow his origins, perhaps with the disadvantage of a family financial collapse. If he was making his own way through graduate school, as so many had to do these days, he was to be respected.

George Barnwell had become aware that the young man he was entertaining was a Harvard student, and asked courteously after his studies. When he learned that Sid had taken courses with both Irving Babbitt and John Livingston Lowes, he chuckled out a story about a colleague who, seeing those two crossing the Yard together, remarked, "There go a scholar and a gentleman."

Sid Lang astonished Aunt Emily by leaning back in his chair and guffawing like a tavern drunk. His neck was as wide as his head. He was an odd one, so soft-voiced and polite, and so violently amusable. George Barnwell, surprised at the success of his joke, beamed. Charity looked opaque—annoyed with her father for retailing stale Cambridge witticisms, or embarrassed by her young man's outburst? Comfort was watching Sid noncommittally. Aunt Emily saw him become aware of the attention being paid him, and feel his way toward safer ground. He advanced the theory that the surest way to *be* a gentleman was to be a scholar. And what a place for the studious life Battell Pond was! What quiet and beauty, what time for thinking.

"Yes," Comfort said. "Up to now."

"Why? What's the matter with it now? The rain? I think the rain's wonderful, it puts such a living shine on everything."

"Oh, not the rain! Good heavens, if we couldn't stand a little rain we ought to move to Arizona. No, they're all set to spoil Battell Pond. You know the shore across the cove?"

"I don't think . . . I just got here this afternoon."

"It's all just wild woods. And some criminal bunch, some syndicate, wants to buy it and put in a cabin camp for transients, and a dock, and a gas station, and store—what's the matter with McChesney's—and maybe even a movie house and dance hall."

Aunt Emily said, "Comfort shouldn't let it upset her so, but it *is* too bad."

"Too bad?" Comfort said. "It's horrible. Imagine a lot of tourists, and motorboats, and all-night dances, and broken beer bottles, and all the rest of it. The cove is where all the little kids catch perch. That's where the bullfrogs congregate. That's where it's fun to drift along in a canoe and watch minks and weasels on shore."

"It'll *ruin* the view from our porch, Mother," Charity said.

Sid was attending carefully. "Is it inevitable? Couldn't you fight it in town meeting?"

"Town meeting's not till March," Comfort said. "They rig it that way so the summer people aren't here to vote. Anyway, some people around here obviously want a resort. They think it'll bring on prosperity. They're all such money-grubbers! So's Herbert Hill. He doesn't have to take their dirty money."

"He's a poor farmer," her mother said. "We can't expect him to turn down a good offer simply because it will inconvenience us."

"Us and everybody else on the lake."

"How much money?" Sid asked.

"I don't know. Eight thousand, is it? For just those twenty acres of shore. Whole farms, with buildings and stock and machinery, are going for less."

"Couldn't people get together and raise the money? Wouldn't this Herbert Hill rather sell to his neighbors than to a syndicate?"

"Perhaps he would, but where do his neighbors find eight thousand dollars these days? Most summer people don't make half that much in a year. The Battell Pond Association got him to hold off for thirty days, but I haven't seen the money forthcoming."

"I swear if they build that over there I'll burn it down," Comfort said.

"Of course you'll do nothing of the kind," her mother said.

"She might," Charity said, "and I just might help her."

"The minute they build it," Comfort said.

Dorothy took away the plates and brought a bowl of strawberries and a pitcher of cream. The table had gone cranky. Again Aunt Emily saw Sid, sensitive as an uneasy hostess, adjust to the changed tone and try to divert the conversation. He turned to Comfort, pushing his glasses up on his nose, and asked her how her name happened to be Comfort. He would have thought that since the first daughter was Charity, the next should have been Faith or Hope.

He asked it teasingly, and his eyes included Aunt Emily in the question, asking her to take this as a conversational gambit only, as essentially well meaning as the wagging of a dog's tail.

Unfortunate. Comfort apparently thought he was condescending to her as the kid sister. She had not been happy to vacate the dorm, which she and her friends used as a clubhouse, and move for an unknown term over to Uncle Dwight's. She also hated jokes about her name, which she said made her sound like a featherbed. Now she gave Sid a smoky glance and replied that after Charity was born her parents had given up both Faith and Hope.

"Why, you ungrateful *wretch*!" Charity cried. "After I joined your arson conspiracy."

"Naming you Comfort may have been our highest expression of hope," Aunt Emily said, and pushed back her chair, ending the conversation and the dinner.

Dorothy cleared away. George Barnwell rose, shook Sid's hand and said he hoped they would see more of him, and excused himself to his bedroom and his detective novel. Charity, from across the table, threw Sid a look full of amusement, commiseration, and malice. Comfort disappeared in a cloud of sparks. Aunt Emily, her knitting already in her hand, looked out into the porch.

"Why, there's going to be a sunset. Battell Pond is going to show you its better side after all, Mr. Lang."

"Sid," Sid said. "Please. Being called Mr. Lang makes me nervous."

"Come on, Mr. Lang, sir," Charity said. "You can take me for a canoe ride along Comfort's enchanted shore. Unless you'd rather read."

Aunt Emily later, making a story of it, suggested that Sid had come out of the West like Young Lochinvar and taken them by storm. It wasn't a bad story, or entirely untrue, but during those first days she didn't think of him as Lochinvar. She thought of him as a pleasant young man who simply wouldn't do, and she brooded a good deal about how to tell him and Charity so. Interference, she understood, would cause unhappiness, perhaps serious unhappiness. But better a little now than more later.

It took her no more than that first afternoon to discount Charity's assumed indifference. She was as gone on him as he was on her, and the next days proved it. They could spend all day on a hike or picnic or canoe expedition and still be full of each other at dinner, almost the only time the family saw them. They could be out till all hours—twice Aunt Emily turned her flashlight on the clock when she heard Charity sneaking in, and once the clock said nearly two and the other time nearly three—and still look at one another over the breakfast table as if dazed by the wonder of what they saw.

Aunt Emily had no idea what they did when they were together; she had to rely on Charity's good sense. Seeing them swimming off the dock, or canoeing around the cove, she could feel a pang like regret. Charity was what she was, a most striking, vivid, headstrong, exasperating, often infuriating young woman. Sid Lang, helping her into the canoe and shoving away from the dock, was a demigod. His back was now red with sunburn and his nose was peeling, but his neck was strong and his back broad. When he dipped the paddle, the canoe shot forward as if motorized.

Pumping him, she had brought up mainly acceptable opinions. It was true that Sid admired Franklin D. Roosevelt, whom the family was divided about because he had already indicated he would replace Aunt Emily's brother as ambassador to France. But Sid also loved books, had earnest, high-minded ideas and a passion for poetry, felt that each individual should try to leave the world a little better than he found it. On the other hand, he was vague about the future and not at all sure that it involved teaching. He seemed to be in graduate school mainly because he couldn't think of anything better to do. For a penniless student who ought to be burning with ambition, that seemed odd, even ominous.

Once, half humorously, he told Aunt Emily that what he would really like to do was retire to the woods, such woods as these, where there would be books, music, beauty, and peace, and just walk and read and think and write poems, like a Chinese philosopher of the Taoist persuasion.

They had some dinner-table arguments on that topic. Those were not the most logical years to be advocating philosophical retirement, even for poets. Poetic speech in those days was supposed to be public speech, and bring thousands to the barricades. Literature was for mobilizing the masses (the middle-class masses), Doing Good, and Righting Wrongs. So when Sid, in defense of his vague disinclination to become engaged in social betterment, enlisted poetic support, saying:

> "I will arise and go now, and go to Innisfree,
> And a small cabin build there, of clay and wattles made,
> Nine beanrows will I have there, a hive for the honey bee
> And live alone in the bee-loud glade"

he started Charity to bouncing in her chair.

"Oh, *pooh,* Sid! That's a splendid poem, but it's not a plan for a *life.* It's defeatist, it's total retreat. Poetry ought to be a by-product of living, and you can't have a by-product unless you've had a product *first.* It's *immoral* not to get in and work and get your hands dirty."

"You can get your hands dirty in nine beanrows."

"Yes, but what are you doing? Feeding your own selfish face. Indulging your own lazy inclinations."

"Charity, really," her mother said.

Sid was not offended. "A poem isn't selfish. It speaks to people."

"*If* it's good enough. Has any poem ever moved you to action?"

"I just quoted you one."

"That's not action, that's *inaction!* Really, Sid, the world needs people who will do things, not run from them."

"I don't admit that poetry is running from anything, but what would you suggest instead?"

"Teaching."

"Teaching what?"

"What you're studying. What you know."

"Poetry."

"Oh, you . . . ! You twist things. Look, there are so many empty minds in the world that teaching them *anything* is worthy activity. A teacher enlarges people in all sorts of ways besides just his subject matter."

"And a poem doesn't?"

They were getting heated. No, Aunt Emily decided, only Charity was. Though Sid defended his position, he listened to her as if her warmth fascinated him. Her cheeks were rosy with vehemence. She sat back in her chair, momentarily at a loss, as if his question were unfair, and thought a moment, and burst out again.

"You want to make me sound like a philistine. All I'm saying is that poetry isn't *direct* enough most of the time. It doesn't concern itself with the vital *issues.* It may be nice to know how a poet feels when he looks out his window into a fresh snowfall, but it doesn't help anyone feed his *family.*"

"Charity," Comfort said, "you argue like a corkscrew."

But Sid would not accept the chance to laugh the argument away. "Let me get you straight. You think poetry isn't communication on any significant level, but you think teaching is, even if the teacher is teaching poetry. It's okay secondhand, but not firsthand."

"I told you," Comfort said. "A corkscrew."

"You keep out of this," Charity said. Her cheeks were pink. She looked aggrieved and misunderstood. "All I'm saying," she said to Sid alone, "is that poetry-making isn't the basis for a full life unless you're an absolutely *great* poet, and forgive me, I don't think you are, not yet anyway, and won't be until you find something to do in your life so that the poetry *reflects* something. It can't just reflect *leisure.* In this world you can't have leisure unless you cheat. Poems ought to reflect the *work* the poet does, and his relationships with other people, and family, and institutions, and organizations. You can't make a life out of nine beanrows. You wouldn't have anything to write poems about but beans."

Laughter. "Well," Sid says, "I have to take a job, is that it?"

"I don't know what you're studying for, if not some sort of job."

"What if I said I'm studying because I think a poet ought to have his head filled with ideas?"

"Then I'd say the ideas you get out of books are secondhand ideas, and the ones you need for writing poems are firsthand ones. Your training leads straight toward the teaching profession, doesn't it?"

"Usually."

"Why not in your case?"

"I'm not sure I've got what it takes to be a good teacher."

"Are you sure you've got what it takes to be a good poet?"

"No."

"Well."

"That's what I'm trying to find out."

A lull. Charity, fixing her eyes on him hard, smiling and frustrated, said, "Well, you'll have to grant me one point."

"What's that?"

"Teaching at least pays a salary."

"I know," he said. "Poverty and poetry are twin-born brats."

"See?" she cried in triumph. "You just proved my point. You taught us all something. If you hadn't been studying to be a teacher you wouldn't know that line, or who said it. Who did?"

"Samuel Butler, I think. And if he hadn't written it, no teacher would be able to teach it."

"This is getting excruciating," Comfort said.

Aunt Emily was making up her mind that the subject must be changed, and was opening her mouth to do so when Charity fired one Parthian shot. "You think you want to withdraw and write poetry because you're afraid you can't *contribute* any other way. But you can! Why should you undervalue yourself? You've got all the makings. You can do anything you want if you want to enough."

Comfort looked at the ceiling. "Lives of great men all remind us we can make our lives sublime."

Sid ignored her, looking at Charity. "You believe that?"

"What I said, or what my impertinent sister just said?"

"What you said."

"You bet I do. So should you. Anything you want to do you *can* do."

"And if I want nine beanrows and a hive for the honeybee?"

Shrugging, dismissing the very idea, she said, "You don't need a higher degree for that. Any monk or bum can do that." Leaning forward, frowning urgently and then breaking into a smile, she said, "Just go at it the way you're going at you-know-what."

"I've got special reasons there. And it was your idea."

"What difference does that make? The will to do it is what matters. There's always some special reason."

He was attending, half smiling, totally absorbed in her voice, as if it came out of a burning bush. Aunt Emily perceived that he was easily led, that he wanted the kind of direction and reassurance that Charity was prepared to give him. He paid too much attention to other people's opinions, including, unfortunately, hers. Now he shrugged, nodded, accepted. Aunt Emily could not help asking, "What is this you-know-what?"

Instantly Charity's face changed from argumentative to gleeful. She laughed out loud. "You'll find out. Oh, are you going to get a surprise! There's going to be an *announcement*. Maybe tomorrow."

Everybody looked her way, awaiting further enlightenment, but she had said all she was going to. It sounded ominous. In fact, it persuaded Aunt Emily that by letting things drift for only five days she had already waited too long. She subsided into watchfulness. But when Dorothy was clearing the table and George Barnwell had rolled his napkin into its ring and Charity had stood up, already in flight, her mother said, "Are you going out again this evening? I had some things I wanted to talk over with you."

"Can they wait till tomorrow? We have to go down to the village and make some telephone calls."

"Telephone calls? To whom?"

"That's part of the surprise. Won't tomorrow do?"

"I suppose it might if I were sure I'd see you tomorrow."

"You can be sure. At breakfast."

"All right."

She watched Charity go around the table, drop a kiss on her father's feathery head, and take Sid's arm. "Come on, Mr. Lang, sir. We'll be late." There they went, she in her dirndl and sweater, he in his wrinkled khakis.

Somewhat grimly, Aunt Emily took herself out onto the porch. She sat a long time in the dusk, knitting by ear, thinking and planning, annoyed by Charity's lack of common sense. Such an airy dismissing of warnings—for she knew precisely what her mother wanted to talk to her about. Such total lack of realism, with her infatuated faith that people could do anything they wanted to if they only wanted it enough. With Sid, at least, Charity's theory was sound. She could do anything she wanted with *him*. He had no better sense than she had.

Well, tomorrow's encounter. She would begin by pointing out that her sister Margaret, with Molly and three children, was coming on Sunday, and would require the dormitory. Sid's visit must therefore be terminated. That would bring on the promised announcement, which she would have to oppose. Then the fat would be in the fire—hurt, tears, protestations, anger, the whole rest of the summer with a sullen Charity moping around the place, unhappy and rebellious and embittered. Perhaps there would be the necessity of resisting her return to Cambridge, where she would be out of control. There would be the unpleasant duty of watching the mail—not to intercept it, she would not stoop to that, but to make sure that the break was clean.

If she could not persuade them, then she would have to extract a promise that they would wait until Sid finished his degree, assuming he went for a degree, and found a job. No more than Charity did she take seriously those nine beanrows. So, the degree—two more years, perhaps three, longer in any case than their infatuation was likely to last. If they surprised her by holding out, why then God bless them, they would have proved something. She found herself wishing, against her sense of the realities, that they would do just that.

None of her planned program came to pass.

They arrived at the breakfast table late, after George Barnwell had already gone to his think house. Aunt Emily appraised their bottled excitement and waited. She had to wait only the thirty seconds it took for Sid to shove Charity's chair under her and go around to his own. He was barely seated when Charity said, "Mother, we promised you a surprise. This is it. We want to get married."

Aunt Emily set down her coffee cup. "That's not entirely a surprise."

"Do you approve?"

Aunt Emily looked from her daughter to her daughter's young man. He had taken off his glasses and was polishing them. Perhaps he felt that he looked more approvable with his blue eyes exposed. But it wasn't that, it wasn't that he lacked anything personally. He was a thoroughly pleasant young fellow. She caught his eye and smiled, meaning to be kind, thinking, What a pity, what a pity.

"No," she said. "I'm afraid I don't."

She expected them, Charity at least, to break out in arguments and expostulations. But Charity only took a sip of her orange juice, sat back in her chair, and said with a smile that her mother thought offensively confident, "Why not?"

"I'm surprised that you have to ask."

"Is there something wrong with Sid?"

"No," Aunt Emily said, and could not forbear laying her hand on Sid's for a moment. "I'm very fond of Sid, as you must know. But marriage—children, you just don't know what you're doing."

Holding her mother's eye, Charity finished her orange juice. When she put down the glass, the little smile was still on her face. "If you're so fond of him, why do you object? He's healthy, he's intelligent, he's got all his *limbs,* he doesn't stammer, he's not disfigured in any way. What's the matter with him?"

"Nothing's the matter with him," Aunt Emily said. "Nothing in the world. What's the matter has nothing to do with him personally. It only has to do with the times, or the timing. Even if he were sure he wants to be a teacher, he has years of study ahead before he can qualify for a job, and perhaps several more before he can support a wife. If you tell me you'll work to support *him,* then I have to think that the wildest folly. I've seen too many student marriages like that. The wife goes to work and stops growing while the husband grows beyond her. I don't want that to happen to you, and neither does Sid, I'm sure. Your father's salary won't stretch to help support the two of you. You want something that simply isn't possible. I wish it weren't so."

"Is it only economics, then?"

"Only economics," Aunt Emily said. "There's your inexperience speaking."

Charity laughed so freely that her mother was irritated. "Ah," Charity said, "there's something you don't know. If economics weren't a problem, you'd approve, is that it?"

"You'll have to explain."

"*Would* you?"

Now Aunt Emily was truly irritated, trying to be kind and being pushed by this insolent girl into something like a quarrel. "How can you even suggest that economics isn't a problem?" she said. "Forgive me, Sid, but it seems I have to point out some facts. How can there be no economic problem when Sid doesn't even have a spare shirt? All the time he's been here I've been wondering how I could steal the one he's wearing so Dorothy could wash it. No, you're being absurd."

Sid surprised her with one of his bellows of laughter. They were both laughing. "His *disguise* is too good," Charity said. "He had me fooled, too, till lately. What would you say if we told you Sid's father was for quite a while, and in several business ventures, a partner of Andrew Mellon? Would your objections disappear then?"

For the space of several calming breaths Aunt Emily sat still. Then she said to Sid, "Is this true?"

"I'm afraid it is."

"You're *afraid* it is! What is this? Why the disguise? Why does the son of a partner of Andrew Mellon come visiting with chocolate stains on his only shirt?"

"Because he wants to be *himself,* not somebody's relative," Charity answered for him. "His father was a fierce banker and businessman, and wanted Sid to step into his shoes, but Sid liked books and poetry, which his father thought frivolous. (And so do you, thought Aunt Emily, but did not say it.) They didn't agree on anything, practically. So even when his father created this trust for him . . ."

"He was sure I'd never be able to support myself," Sid said. "I took it as a gesture of contempt, sort of."

". . . he wouldn't use the money. His mother sent him a check to buy a new car last Christmas and he sent it back. He tries to look like the poorest student in Cambridge, but actually he's as rich as *Croesus.* He leaves all that money accumulating in the trust and lives on a hundred a month." Crackling with vitality, vivid as a revelation, she threw an enchanting smile at Sid, sitting diffident and charmed, and added, "I'm going to help him break *that* habit."

Aunt Emily had gradually assembled herself. She said drily, "We don't see many rich people these days, and since I objected on economic grounds, I must ask you a question. *How* are you rich? Real estate frozen by bank failures? Stocks fallen through the floor? Factories in receivership? Charity mentions a trust. How is that managed?"

"Very conservatively," Sid said. "My father set up funds for my sisters, too, a good while before he died, and he added to all three of them in his will. The Mellon Bank manages them. My sisters draw on theirs, but I never have. It got hit pretty hard by the crash, but it's recovered some. I think there are three or four million in it. I can call the trust officer and get an accounting, if you'd like."

Caught between a laugh and a cough, Aunt Emily put her fist to her mouth for a moment. "No. As an approximation, I think three or four million will do."

Charity jumped to her feet and flew around the table and wrapped her arms around her mother's head. "You think it's all right! I knew you would!"

Disentangling her hair, Aunt Emily said to Sid, "If you didn't want to use your father's money before, why do you change your mind now?"

"Because he's got *motivation!*" Charity said.

"No, let him tell me. Perhaps you've persuaded him that his scruples aren't sound. Perhaps later he'll wish he'd preserved his independence."

"But his scruples were . . ."

"Please," Aunt Emily said. "Sid?"

He was looking at her steadily, wearing a diffident smile. "You think I tempted her with my glittering gold?"

"I don't think it hurt your chances."

Now his smile grew broad. "But she said yes before she knew."

"When she thought you didn't have a spare shirt to your name?"

He nodded.

"And you're sure you won't regret taking this inheritance? You won't feel you've betrayed your principles? Because I don't mind telling you, if you really do despise wealth, and if your differences with your father went very deep, then I think your scruples were honorable, not foolish."

"I suppose it was whimsical," Sid said. "He wasn't a monster, or a crook, or anything. He made his money honestly, or as honestly as any banker. It was just that he thought more of it than I felt he should, especially since he was such a stiff Presbyterian. I wasn't ashamed of it. I just didn't want to get trapped in it, and I didn't want to take it from him as a contemptuous handout to an incompetent. But he's gone, and the money sits there. I suppose I could give it to my mother or my sisters, but they don't need it. I'd rather spend it on Charity."

"And you're both absolutely sure."

They were.

"You thought I'd resist you," Aunt Emily said. "If I did, it was only because I thought I must, for your own sakes. Well, bless me, this is all very astonishing."

"Shall we go up and tell Daddy?"

Aunt Emily thought only a second. "No. He wouldn't like being interrupted. We'll tell him at lunch."

"There's something else," Charity said, her eyes on Sid. "Do you want to tell her, or shall I?"

"You."

"You and Comfort won't have to worry about the development across the cove," Charity said, and went back around the table into Sid's arm. "Sid's bought the land, the whole *shebang*, from Herbert Hill. We called his trust officer last night, that's why we had to go into the village. Sid gave Herbert two thousand more than the syndicate had offered, and it's *all settled*. Isn't it something?"

"There's no other name for it. Don't tell me any more, I couldn't take it in." With the two of them before her, she standing, he sitting with his arm around her as if in an old-fashioned wedding photograph, she felt at once dazed and fond. So much good fortune, for such really deserving children. "I suppose you'll be taking an apartment in Cambridge," she said, with her eyes as usual down the road.

"That's something else we want to talk to you about, Mother. Do you know when Uncle Richard plans to leave Paris?"

"Richard? Why? Last time he wrote, he expected not to be replaced until late summer or fall. He certainly isn't going to leave until that man puts him out."

"Would he let us be married at his house, do you think?"

"Why, I suppose. But don't you think Cambridge. . . ."

"I'd like a *Paris* wedding. I won't really believe I'm Cinderella otherwise. You and Daddy and Comfort could get a trip out of it."

"Of course we'll try to do it the way you want, if we can. But it would be very expensive to take everyone abroad."

Charity dropped her arm from around Sid's shoulders and fished a worn brown wallet out of his hip pocket and shook it in the air. "Please," Sid said. "It would give me the greatest pleasure."

"My goodness," Aunt Emily said. "Well, I'll write Richard and see."

"*Cable* him!"

"Is there that much of a hurry?"

"Yes. Because after we're married we want to take a trip, a real Grand Tour. Sid's going to drop out of school for the first semester—I'm willing to make *that* much of a concession to the beanrows and honeybees. And we've got to find an architect right away before we leave so we can settle on plans for a house, and a guest house, and a think house. By next summer we want a regular compound over there across the cove so we can wave dishtowels at each other from porch to porch."

"Bless me," said Aunt Emily, for about the fourth time that morning. "You don't waste any time."

"Would *you*?" Charity said.

7

And so, by circuitous and unpredictable routes, we converge toward midcontinent and meet in Madison, and are at once drawn together, braided and plaited into a friendship. It is a relationship that has no formal shape, there are no rules or obligations or bonds as in marriage or the family, it is held together by neither law nor property nor blood, there is no glue in it but mutual liking. It is therefore rare. To Sally and me, focused on each other and on the problems of getting on in a rough world, it happened unexpectedly; and in all our lives it has happened so thoroughly only once.

I remember little about Madison as a city, have no map of its streets in my mind, am rarely brought up short by remembered smells or colors from that time. I don't even recall what courses I taught. I really never did live there, I only worked there. I landed working and never let up.

What I was paid to do I did conscientiously with forty percent of my mind and time. A Depression schedule, surely—four large classes, whatever they were, three days a week. Before and between and after my classes, I wrote, for despite my limited one-year appointment I hoped for continuance, and I did not intend to perish for lack of publications. I wrote an unbelievable amount, not only what I wanted to write but anything any editor asked for—stories, articles, book reviews, a novel, parts of a textbook. Logorrhea. A scholarly colleague, one of those who spent two months on a two-paragraph communication to *Notes and Queries* and had been working for six years on a book that nobody would ever publish, was heard to refer to me as the Man of Letters, spelled h-a-c-k. His sneer so little affected me that I can't even remember his name.

Nowadays, people might wonder how my marriage lasted. It lasted fine. It throve, partly because I was as industrious as an anteater in a termite mound and wouldn't have noticed anything short of a walkout, but more because Sally was completely supportive and never thought of herself as a neglected wife—"thesis widows," we used to call them in graduate school. She was probably lonely for the first two or three weeks. Once we met the Langs she never had time to be, whether I was available or not. It was a toss-up who was neglecting whom.

Early in our time in Madison I stuck a chart on the concrete wall of my furnace room. It reminded me every morning that there are one hundred sixty-eight hours in a week. Seventy of those I dedicated to sleep, breakfasts, and dinners (chances for socializing with Sally in all of those areas). Lunches I made no allowance for because I brown-bagged it at noon in my office, and read papers while I ate. To my job—classes, preparation, office hours, conferences, paper-reading—I conceded fifty hours, though when students didn't show up for appointments I could use the time for reading papers and so gain a few minutes elsewhere. With one hundred and twenty hours set aside, I had forty-eight for my own. Obviously I couldn't write forty-eight hours a week, but I did my best, and when holidays at Thanksgiving and Christmas gave me a break, I exceeded my quota.

Hard to recapture. I was your basic overachiever, a workaholic, a pathological beaver of a boy who chewed continually because his teeth kept growing. Nobody could have sustained my schedule for long without a breakdown, and I learned my limitations eventually. Yet when I hear the contemporary disparagement of ambition and the work ethic, I bristle. I can't help it.

I overdid, I punished us both. But I was anxious about the coming baby and uncertain about my job. I had learned something about deprivation, and I wanted to guarantee the future as much as effort could guarantee it. And I had been given, first by *Story* and then by the *Atlantic,* intimations that I had a gift.

Thinking about it now, I am struck by how modest my aims were. I didn't expect to hit any jackpots. I had no definite goal. I merely wanted to do well what my inclinations and training led me to do, and I suppose I assumed that somehow, far off, some good might flow from it. I had no idea what. I respected literature and its vague addiction to truth at least as much as tycoons are supposed to respect money and power, but I never had time to sit down and consider *why* I respected it.

Ambition is a path, not a destination, and it is essentially the same path for everybody. No matter what the goal is, the path leads through

Pilgrim's Progress regions of motivation, hard work, persistence, stubbornness, and resilience under disappointment. Unconsidered, merely indulged, ambition becomes a vice; it can turn a man into a machine that knows nothing but how to run. Considered, it can be something else—pathway to the stars, maybe.

I suspect that what makes hedonists so angry when they think about overachievers is that the overachievers, without drugs or orgies, have more fun.

Right after breakfast I went to the furnace room and wrote till ten minutes to eleven. Then Sally drove me to the foot of Bascom Hill. I climbed the hill, arriving in class just as the bell rang, and taught from eleven to four. Then I walked home, graded papers till dinner, and after dinner prepared for the next day's classes or went to the furnace room and wrote some more.

Sally had a part in everything I wrote, most of which I read to her after bedtime or during breakfast. She was critic, editor, gadfly, memory bank, research assistant, typist. She decided when things were good enough to be sent out, when they needed doing over, when they wouldn't do at all. And when I was shut in the furnace room or off at school, she had her own occupations, almost always with Charity.

They were together all the time. Charity, expending herself in twenty directions, pulled Sally along with her. Though she had no musical ability herself, sang sharp, and always pitched a song so high you had to be a castrato to sing it, Charity was intensely fond of music. She was backing a young pianist friend for a Carnegie Hall concert, and she and Sally went often to hear this young woman play. They both sang in the university chorus, with weekly practices and occasional performances. They went to many concerts, with or without Sid or me. Most of those were free, but when they were not, there always seemed to be an extra ticket in Charity's purse, a ticket she said had been bought for someone who in the end couldn't use it.

They attended movies, plays, lectures, art classes, photography shows, teas. They took walks. From January on, there were baby showers and other shared preparations. And after March, which I remember well, Sally had some recovering to do and the baby to look after, a diaper case if there ever was one, and us without a washing machine. Fortunately Charity had one, and a hired girl as well. The waste of our offspring got washed away, like sin, over on Van Hise Street.

Once or twice when the weather let up they took a stepladder out to the two acres that the Langs had bought in the suburb called Frost-wood, and climbed on its slippery steps to test the view or the solar exposure. For Charity had made up her mind when Sid took the Wisconsin job that they were not going to be like other instructors, kept for three years and then turned out to start all over again in some other, probably lesser, place. Sid was going to be so superior, and together they were going to make themselves so indispensable to the university and the community, that there could be no question of their being let go. She had spent the first year finding land she liked. They would spend this one planning the house they would build on it. No cautionary words had any effect on her. If you wanted something, you planned for it, worked for it, and made it happen.

"It's making a schizophrenic of me," Sid said to me on one of the midnight walks he was fond of. "I want her to have this palace, if that's what will please her, but I keep thinking of all the eyebrows that will go up among the senior members of the department—takes a lot for granted, doesn't he?—and the envy and jealousy a lot of my colleagues will feel. And maybe there are guys from the gashouse district who will see this schoolteach building a castle in the middle of a depression, and Jesus, look, he's got three hundred windas to bust. But Charity has the answer to at least one of those problems. She's going to make the house a weekend rest home for broken-down instructors. Even you may apply. Our friends are going to keep the guest rooms occupied, and we're going to lay down a law for ourselves: We never accept invitations on weekends. It's all going to be country walks, rough tweeds, a brace of setters, and on Sunday evenings square dances and Varsovianas and korobotchkas and a convivial punch bowl."

That was on a night when he was feeling good after a day that had gone well. Other times, he was less relaxed. "It'll look arrogant," I heard him tell Charity once. "It'll look as if we thought we could buy our way to promotion, or as if we thought ourselves so grand we could assume it. There's absolutely no guarantee we'll be here longer than this year and next. Do you want to build it just to move out of? At least let's not pour any concrete till the department has voted."

"Pooh," Charity said. "I'd like to *see* them uproot us. Just have some confidence."

"Caution would be more appropriate."

"No, sir," she said. "You don't budge me."

She already had an architect drawing plans, and she was not restraining his imagination. She and Sally went over sketches and scale drawings by the hour, and scratched them up with criticisms and questions and second thoughts, and sent them back to be done over. And over.

Sometimes Sally and I discussed the Langs in bed, bed being the only place where we found much time to discuss anything. Our basement, warm from the furnace just beyond the partition, and lightless as the womb, was a good place to rest the eyes and mind and hear the things that Sally saved up to tell me.

"She wants a lot of children," she reported. "A real lot—six or seven, the last four preferably girls."

"Well, she's going about it the right way," I said. "She'll have them by the time she's thirty. What'll she do then?"

"I don't know. Be fulfilled, I guess. That's what she thinks children do for a woman."

"How about Sid? Are six or seven children going to fulfill him too?"

I could feel her thinking about that in the dark. Finally she said, "I think she thinks fatherhood doesn't mean that much to a man. She thinks a man should be fulfilled by his work."

"Yeah. What if the department doesn't choose to fulfill him?"

"You and he are always talking that way. Charity just won't accept the possibility."

"I know she won't, and it's not very bright of her. She's reckless. I doubt that Sid is going to be fulfilled if he finds himself with a half dozen children and a big house and no job."

"At least they've got money."

"That does help," I said. "It even helps her hire a nanny to look after the children she's already got, so she can be out promoting culture and singing in the chorus and cleaning up Wisconsin politics and being kind to the wives and children of starving instructors. That's a pretty dispersed lady."

"But she's so organized!" Sally said. "She can make time for all sorts of things, and for all that hectic social life, and still be with the children in the morning, and again before dinner, and again at bedtime. She gets them up and she tucks them in, and she sings to them, and reads to them, and plays with them. She's a wonderful mother."

"I didn't say she wasn't. I was just wondering if Sid is as enthusiastic about this program as she is. I even wonder sometimes if she's as enthusiastic as she thinks she is."

More pondering. "Maybe she's a little inconsistent," Sally said. "She wants all those children, but one of her reasons is so she won't have too much time to give to one or two. She thinks children in a big family have the benefit of a certain amount of neglect. Her mother dominated her, she says. They clashed a lot, I guess. Well, you can imagine, those two. So Charity wants six or seven so she won't make the same mistake her mother made. She thinks neglect is good, so long as it isn't really neglect, so long as the mother is thinking and planning and guiding and keeping an eye on things."

"You can count on Charity to be doing that."

"Yes." More thinking silence. Then, "Sometimes I wonder, though. She's great, she's thoughtful, and loving, she's kept a book on both of the children since the day they were born—you know, first smile, first tooth, first word, first sign of individuality as they develop. Pictures at every stage. She's teaching Barney to count and tell time and read already, they set aside a half hour every afternoon. She's simply incredible, the way she can organize a day. But one thing, I don't think I ever saw her pick up one of those cute kids and give him a big squeeze, just because he's himself, and hers, and she loves him. When we get ours, don't let me have an agenda every time I'm with him."

"I'll try to remember, if my own agenda lets me."

Laughter, then quiet. Finally Sally says, "We shouldn't talk about her this way. Just think what it would be like without them."

"I have," I said. "It'd be Worksburg for me and Dullsville for you. I hope all her plans work out. I hope she has seven children, all with an IQ of 160 or above. I hope the last four are girls. I hope they grow up in that big house in Madison and have every summer in Vermont among the cousins, and love their mother and respect their father and do well in school and grow up to be ambassadors to France."

"Amen," Sally said. "I'll tell her you wished that, shall I?"

"Pray do," I said.

No, Sally was not lonely. Nor were we ever, to my recollection, diverted more than briefly from one another. We loved our life; we never looked up from it except when rallies for the Spanish Loyalists ruffled the waters of the university and upset the state house, or when Governor Phil La Follette made some alarmingly fascist-sounding proposal, or when Hitler's frothing voice over our radio reminded us that we were on a bumpy gangplank leading from world depression to possible world war.

We weren't indifferent. We lived in our times, which were hard times. We had our interests, which were mainly literary and intellectual and only occasionally, inescapably, political. But what memory brings back from there is not politics, or the meagerness of living on a hundred and fifty dollars a month, or even the writing I was doing, but the details of friendship—parties, picnics, walks, midnight conversations, glimpses from the occasional unencumbered hours. *Amicitia* lasts better than *res publica,* and at least as well as *ars poetica.* Or so it seems now. What really illuminates those months is the faces of our friends.

About November first I began a novel. Once I had begun it, I couldn't have stopped it if I had wanted to. I wrote on it every morning, I wrote on it evenings, Saturdays, Sundays. I finished a draft in six weeks, and revised the whole thing in a marathon burst during the Christmas holidays. Two days after New Year's I sent it off to a publisher.

Older and wiser, I would have put two years into a book that I wrote in two months. Some of my haste was a stupid pleasure in breaking records and making every minute count. I knew a miser's joy in the way the manuscript from week to week gained thickness and heft. The routines of work were the sacred routines of my life, not to be broken. I think I am correct in remembering that the morning I took the manuscript to the post office I came home, and instead of savoring the accomplishment, salvaged the hour before class to start a book review.

By mid-January Dave Stone, Sid, and I were at work on one of those anthology textbooks that young instructors hope will look impressive on a *vita.* Stone, Lang, and Morgan, *Writing from Conviction.* But I didn't steal from my writing hours to work on it. I stole from evenings, from Sally, from class preparation, and from sleep.

If I had kept a journal, I could go back through it and check up on what memory reports plausibly but not necessarily truly. But keeping a journal then would have been like making notes while going over Niagara Falls in a barrel. Eventless as our life was, it swept us along. Were we any less a Now Generation than the one that presently claims the title? I wonder. And it may be just as well that I have no diary to remember by. Henry James says somewhere that if you have to make notes on how a thing has struck you, it probably hasn't struck you.

8

*H*ere is one thing that eventually struck me: March 19, 1938, a Saturday.

Morrison Street, afternoon. We have visited Charity in the hospital and I am walking Sally around the block, slowly because she is heavy and near her time, cautiously because there are still icy patches on the sidewalk. The air is clammy, cold in the nostrils, but it can't be really cold, for when the sun breaks through the clouds, the roofs steam. Trickles of thaw creep from under slumped drifts along curbs and driveways. Here and there are patches of unappetizing black lawn.

We have been speaking of the groundhog. Figuring on my fingers, I have discovered that it is already more than six weeks since he ducked back into his hole on a bright February second.

"Is it six weeks more of winter, or two months, if he sees his shadow?" I want to know. "Six weeks, isn't it? Spring should already have started."

"I don't know," Sally says. "But I *wish*! I wish it would come. I wish this baby would come."

"You want to lay that burden down."

"I sure do. Did you notice how *slim* Charity was in that hospital bed? A broomstick. I bent over to kiss her and could hardly reach her for *this* in the way. She's going home on Tuesday and here I am, still as big as a beer wagon. I wonder if it isn't hatred that finally tells us to give birth. When we hate it so much we can't stand carrying it any more, we get rid of it."

"Concentrate on hate, then." I help her across an icy spot crusted with cinders. "You lost the baby derby, but you're a cinch for second. Fix your mind on that. Silver medal."

Big and mournful, her eyes turn on me. Her face is broader, she looks frumpy in her cloth coat that will button only partway down. I know and love this woman well, but she is not the girl I married. I wonder if, on the morning after she has finally had this incubus, I will walk into her room and find the old girl intact and beautiful, as Sid found Charity. He has not relished her pregnancy. Several times lately he has walked clear over from Van Hise Street and got me to chug around the block with him near midnight. God pity Charity when she is well. He has a lot of energy to work off.

Well, God pity Sally too.

"Silver medal," she says. "If there'd been twenty contestants I'd have been sure to finish last. Once, for a paper for Mr. Gayley, I wrote something on the first Isthmian Games. According to Pausanias there was a Roman running in them. Plautus. Flatfoot. That's who I feel like."

"I thought Plautus was a dramatist."

"There's more than one Flatfoot in the world." She slaps her galosh down in a wet spot, splashes us both, and laughs. "But doesn't Charity look fine? She says she was conscious nearly the whole time. Oh, I want it to happen!"

"If you produce something like David Hamilton Lang, will it be worth the effort?"

"Oh, yes! Don't you think he's beautiful? He looks like Sid."

"I thought he looked like an irritated lingcod."

"Oh, faw on you. He's darling, with his silky hair and his little perfect hands. It's the perfection that's so wonderful."

"I suppose anything looks perfect if you've had to carry it for nine months. But that kid won't look like much of anything till he's been out here a while where it counts. I don't expect ours to look like me till he's thirty."

"I hope he never looks like you, if that's the way you feel."

"I hope he looks like you. I hope he isn't a he. Anyway, the first item on the agenda is getting him born. Concentrate on hate." I grab her arm and hustle her into briskness, calling a cadence: *"Hate-*two-three-four, *hate-*two-three-four!"

In ten steps she is breathless, and slows us down. She says, "You'll lose your writing room when he comes. What'll you do?"

"Use the office?"

"People will always be interrupting you."

"I'll lock the door."

"But if you're up there all the time I won't have the comfort of hearing you hammering away like a mad woodpecker."

"Maybe we can move the typewriter into the living room. Babies sleep all the time, don't they? Maybe we can condition him to drop off the minute he hears me roll a sheet of paper into the machine."

She stops. "I've had enough. Let's go back." Going the other way, she says, "What *will* you do?"

"Pitch a tent, or build a lean-to, or change shifts. Something. Don't worry."

"It's going to be a lot different."

"I'll say. Better. We'll make it."

We walk between steaming roofs, along the drying sidewalk. On the left, between houses, we can see the lake, still icebound, but with slush on top of the ice. Papers and bottles float in it, and after sunset will freeze in. There are neither skaters nor iceboats, only warning signs sticking up here and there. In a week or two, if the groundhog knows what he's doing, the dirty snow and litter and all the paralysis of cold will be swallowed by bright water, and crocuses will be popping up in flowerbeds under south-facing walls, and lawns will show faint green under the winter soot. I have never seen spring in a really cold country, but I have read books, I know what to expect. I put my arm around Sally's thick waist.

Passing the landlord's door with its two mailboxes, I check. A letter. I read the return address. I freeze as an antelope might freeze at the hot scent of lion.

Mailbox scenes are the dramatic moments of our totally undramatic life. In any cast of characters playing *Morgan Agonistes,* the messenger is not a bit player but a principal, and he wears the uniform of the U.S. Postal Service. There we stand in that ambiguous afternoon that can't make up its mind whether to be latest winter or earliest spring, at a time in our lives when the smallest pebble on the track could derail us. I avoid Sally's eyes as I rip open the envelope, and then I read, but not aloud, for fear it's bad.

Tableau. "What is it?" Sally asks. "Who's it from?"

I pass her the letter. It says that Harcourt Brace and Company have found my novel provocative and touching. They think my characters are cut from the real, unassuming stuff of everyday life. They like my combination of irony and pathos, they like my feeling for the tears of things. They want to publish my book in the fall, and can offer me an advance of five hundred dollars against royalties.

Again I am struck by the meager scale of these successes, and by my own response to them. The letter from the *Atlantic* was printed on me in Nubian type, like a headline from the old *Vanity Fair* of the twenties, but this more significant letter leaves only a blur. Already blasé? Hardly. More likely stunned. The first was only a short story, and could have been a lucky accident. This was a novel, an extended effort, and corroboration. The sun ought to break through the clouds and flood Morrison Street with glory, there should be thunder on the right, we ought to throw our stocking caps in the air and caper and cheer. Instead, we look at each other almost furtively, not to say or do the wrong thing, and go around the house and down the steps into our basement, and there, just inside the door, fall into a long, silent hug.

Sally knows I wrote the last chapters of this book in tears, typing as fast as I could and unable to type as fast as the words wanted to come. She knows I wept some more, revising it. It had been corked up a good while—the story of my decent, undistinguished, affectionate, abruptly dead father and mother, and the glamorous friend who periodically brought excitement, adventure, and romance into our house in Albuquerque; who kept them up late with stories of far places, who used them, and sponged on them, and borrowed money from them that they knew he would never pay back, and who finally, in one of his large gestures of half-drunken good will, took them up for an anniversary joyride in a plane that should have been in the shop. The ending was appropriate for him but not for them. It was not the right reward for generosity and devotion.

Yet now, having held in grief and resentment, and evaded thinking too much about the episode that changed my life with the finality of an axe, here I am exalted by having made use of it, by having spilled my guts in public. We are strange creatures, and writers are stranger creatures than most.

Shouldn't we call Sid, so he can let Charity know? Sally asks, and I say hell yes, call the Stones too, and the Abbots, call everybody who was ever pleasant to us, and tell them the Morgans are holding open house and require their presence. I will go and buy the makings.

In my half-hour trip downtown I buy more bottles (including, God help me, an echo of my Yum days, a bottle of sloe gin) than I have bought in my entire life up to that time, and as I write a check for them I have a warm, confirmed sense of bank account, a flush of security even in a spendthrift moment. We have been living on my salary and putting away whatever I make from writing. Now, in a little while, will come a check that will dwarf those pittances. I feel better than secure; I feel rich and gloriously confident.

The only party food I know—rye bread, mouse cheese, potato

chips, and salted peanuts—I buy in quantity, and add a can of coffee in case we are short at home. Driving back, I note that the days have got longer. At four-thirty there is still plenty of daylight left. Clearing clouds are blowing southward over Lake Mendota.

As I start down our steps I can hear them inside. They must have dropped everything and come running like a volunteer fire brigade. I push open the door and they burst into applause. Dave Stone, who has recently taken up the recorder and carries one with him wherever he goes, tootles me a theme from Handel: "See, the conquering hero comes!" Cheers. Hands relieve me of my bags.

True to the potluck morality of our time and status, they have brought contributions, whatever their iceboxes contained, whatever they could grab up or had begun to prepare for their own dinners. There is a plate of cookies on the sink drainboard, and somebody's idea of a salad (something embalmed in Jell-O), and one magnificent item, a whole ham, fragrant, untouched by the knife, courtesy Alice Abbot's father's Tennessee smokehouse.

People keep arriving. My hand is sore from being shaken, my ears are blunted by the noise we make. Through the smoke and shouting and laughter our Christmas phonograph repeats over and over its one accomplishment, Bach's Aria for the G String, played by Pablo Casals with a piano accompaniment so insistent and percussive it sounds like a funeral march.

Alice Abbot and Lib Stone have persuaded Sally to put on the embroidered dragon robe. It is a tight fit across the middle, but it makes her regal. She queens it from the couch, tremulous, moist-eyed, so radiant she seems to give off light. I notice her only intermittently, for the party is a real fog-of-battle scene, as confused as Tolstoy's Sebastopol or Stendahl's Waterloo. First I see her serene on the sofa, then erect in a straight chair, then standing. I understand, without being able to do anything about it, or in truth being very alert to the fact that I should, that her inward tenant is kicking her around. Our eyes meet now and then. We shake our heads happily.

About six, Sid arrives, manic and roaring, bearing bottles of champagne in each hand like Indian clubs. He has a three-by-five card stuck in his breast pocket, which he gestures for me to take. It is from Charity.

YOU WRETCHED SCENE STEALER!
DON'T YOU KNOW THIS IS BABY DERBY WEEK?

NOW SALLY WILL HAVE TO HAVE *TWINS* TO GET EVEN!
BUT HOW WONDERFUL IT IS!
I *WISH* I COULD HELP YOU CELEBRATE!
MUCH LOVE, AND CONGRATULATIONS *GALORE!*

I manage to reach it to Sally through the crowd, and we have a brief, mute conversation with the eyebrows. Sid and I push into the kitchenette to open the champagne. Alice Abbot, starting to work on the ham, moves over for us and we stand side by side at the sink, pushing at the corks with our thumbs. With a sidelong, down-mouth smile, Sid says to me, "Well, I foretold this. How does it feel?"

"How does it feel to be the father of three?"

"Any fool can do that."

Whup! His cork hits the ceiling. *Whup!* Mine follows. Cheers. People drain their glasses, and hold their empties toward us, and we pour. Then Sid is lifting his glass and calling for quiet. Finally he gets it. Sally, I see, is back on the couch. I move to get to her with the champagne bottle, but she raises her glass to show me that someone has already provided.

"To the talent in our midst," Sid says. "To the marriage of match and kindling, the divine oxidation."

They drink to me while I smirk and squirm. Then Ed Abbot, glowing like a parlor heater, climbs on a chair, and with his glass against the ceiling says, "There's another kind of creation going on around here. Charity's already shown how it's done, and another demonstration may happen before our startled eyes. Here's to Sally, may her creation be as successful as Charity's and as easy as my old Georgia mammy used to say it was: 'Jus' like shellin' peas, Boss.' "

This one I can drink to. I pledge Sally with special emphasis, because Ed's is a toast I should have made myself.

I have no idea how many people come and go, though once, when I step outside for a breath of the chilly, damp evening, I see evidence in the snowdrift on the back lawn that someone has mixed too many kinds of happiness. The landlord comes down to ask if we can take it a little easy on the noise, and we have him in for a drink. About seven, Alice and Lib serve up the baked ham and rye and salad on paper plates (we have only six of the other kind). We put out the fire we have so enthusiastically built, we drown it in strong coffee, and then we start it again.

About eight, Sid goes back to see Charity in the hospital, bearing messages and vowing to return. About nine the landlord comes to the door again, apologetically. A neighbor has telephoned. For a few minutes we tune it down. Somebody asks me to read a piece of the novel, but I look at the disheveled basement and postpone the pleasure. The fact is, I have almost no voice.

Then, as we are all slumping out of exhilaration into fatigue and suppressed yawns, Lib and Alice corner me in the kitchen. They call my attention to Sally, once again in the hard chair, trying to sit up straight and pay attention, trying to smile. "She's had all she can take," Lib says. "She ought to be in bed. Shall we . . . ? Or do you . . . ?"

I down my coffee, assemble my scattered senses, and resume my responsibilities. "I'll put her down."

I go to her and lift her up. Her eyes are on me in questioning or pleading. I lead her to the bedroom door, and there turn her and aim her back at the remnants of the party. "Bedtime. Say goodnight to the nice people."

They crowd to kiss her. They really do love her, and I love them drunkenly in consequence. Affectionate, exhausted, and eager to be gone, she smiles back at them as I shut the bedroom door.

In the bedroom I help her off with the heavy metallic robe. Clumsily I rid her of her stockings and underclothes (whatever they were then, my mind refuses to replay the image), and drop her nightgown over her head and pull it down over her swollen body. With a sigh she lies back on the bed. "Ah, that's nice. Thank you, sweet. I didn't have sense enough to know how tired I was."

I kiss her belly, solid as wood under the nightgown. "Neither did I. Lib and Alice had to tell me. I spent the whole goddamned party making the most of my sudden rise to fame."

"But that's what the party was *about.*" She puts her arms up and I bend down and am pulled tightly against her. I feel the bulge of the intruder between us, I feel that her cheek is wet. "I love you," she says, squeezing me hard. "Oh, I knew you could! I'm so happy for you!"

"For us."

"For us, yes."

"Are you all right now?"

"Fine. A little tired, a little tiddly. Don't make people go home. Tell them I'm sorry I wasn't quite up to the occasion. I won't mind if they make noise."

"It's gone on long enough. I'll close it out as fast as I can."

"But aren't they wonderful!" she says. "You'd think it was *their* good luck. Hasn't it been a day? I can hardly believe it. Spring really did come."

Her voice is blurred and drowsy. I kiss her and taste bourbon. "Go to sleep," I tell her. "The next act is yours. You don't want to miss your cue."

The only people left in the other room are the Abbots and the Stones. Lib and Alice have dumped ashtrays and paper plates and disposed of bottles. They are washing glasses, with Ed wiping, while Dave on the couch accompanies them on his recorder. After all the choral uproar, renderings of "I Am Jesus' Little Lamb," and "The Boll Weevil Song," and "She'll Be Comin' Round the Mountain," the breathy wooden sound is sweet and tremulous, the meditation of a solitary flute. The room, still thick with smoke, swirls in the draft from the open door. Night air bites like menthol in my congested nostrils.

The recorder stops. They all turn to look at me. "Is she all right?"

"She's okay. I put her to bed."

"It was too much for her. We should have realized."

"*I* should have realized. But no, she loved it. She says for you not to rush off, she likes the sounds friends make."

"She's a sweetie," Alice says, "and it's been a great party, and we're ever so proud of you and know you will *go far.* But now we gotta go. We've been here so long I don't remember our address."

"Somewhere on Lake Street," Ed says. "Don't worry, I can find it. Compass in the car."

They sort out coats from the rack behind the door. As they are hunching into them, Sid returns. At first he is inclined to go straight away again, since the party is over, but I persuade him to come inside while the others leave. They go through their congratulations again. Sally is right, you'd think it was their good luck, not ours.

And now I am confronted by the two women who really produced and directed this revel, one strawberry blond with white eyelashes, the other thin and black-eyed and olive-skinned, both delightful, charming, sisters I wish I had. They stand on tiptoe, one after the other, and kiss me solemnly on the lips, immediately bursting into laughter. One tastes of Scotch, the other of sloe gin. I am flooded with a Turkish feeling of being surrounded by desirable, affectionate women.

"Don't forget the remains of your ham," I say to White Eyelashes. "It's a shame what we did to it. But it was beautiful, it was loaves and fishes."

"It's for you," she says. "While Sally's in the hospital you can nibble on it and dream of me."

More kisses. *Smooooch, mm.* Out they go into the cold, laughing, growing instantly aware of the noise they make, and shushing each other, silently stealing away. Lovely people, the best. As they go around the corner I hear a last word from Dave's recorder— Papageno's little fluty trill: Tweedle-eedle-*eet!* Tweedle-eedle-*eet!* Silence settles like dust after them, and I shut the door.

"Well," Sid says, "how *does* it feel?"

"Sid, how the hell do I know? Nobody but the publisher has even seen the book. If there are ever any reviewers, they'll probably tear it apart. First novels get filed in wastebaskets, readers never hear of them, they never earn their advances. Or so I'm told. Ask me next October, I'll have a humble answer ready."

"We had a word for that in Sewickley, Pennsylvania. Bushwah. You've broken through, your book's going to be published. Isn't that a powerful piece of evidence?"

"I've been celebrating, you notice. But I doubt it's going to change my life."

"Brother, it would change mine!"

I flop on the couch beside him and put my feet on a chair. I am dog-tired, sleepy, beginning to ache dully in the front of my skull, but curious too. "Would it? Would it make that much difference? You don't have to teach, you could quit any time you wanted. I couldn't, even with a break like this. I need that paycheck."

He gives this his considered attention. As always, he allows a notion contrary or oblique to his own to make its case. Then he shakes his head.

"It isn't as easy to quit as you think. You forget Charity's timetable. The kids are on time, I'll say that for her. She's living up to her part of the compact. But I promised her I'd stay with teaching, and give it my whole attention, without cheating, till we either get promoted or bounced. So far as she's concerned, that means till we get promoted, she won't admit the other possibility. She says our commitment to teaching is like a marriage vow. Once you've made a decision like that you should never look back. Well, I agree—sort of. Teaching's okay. I like a lot of things about it—the people you work with, the contact with books and ideas, the institutional reinforcement, the sense of doing something visibly useful. My real problem is the old publish or perish business."

"I still think you could write a few poems in your spare time without violating your parole."

He pulls down his mouth. "I promised her I'd play by the rules. Poetry's time will come, she says. She's very happy about the textbook, incidentally. Something positive for the dossier." He breathes out through his nose, audibly. "Damn the dossier. You hear what the dean said about Jesus Christ? 'Sure He's a good teacher, but what's He published?' "

We have a laugh in the bleary basement. "Well," I have to say, "I'm not a devoted teacher, and what I publish doesn't cut any ice with the department, and nobody is going to mistake me for Jesus Christ."

"You're a liar on all counts," Sid says, yawning. "They can't overlook you. And I can tell you, if I'd done what you've just done, I'd be changed. I'd be a lot surer I could justify my life."

His wool shirt is open at the neck, his wrestler's throat is exposed. He laughs and throws his hands in the air and stands up. "I should be going. Charity is betting me I can't finish an article before she comes home from the hospital. Of course I can't. The more I work at it, the less there is to say. Who the hell cares about the revelations of Tennyson's personal life in *Locksley Hall*? How about a turn around the block?"

Sid and I have a lot in common. He works as hard as I do, and that is a powerful compulsion on my respect. He reads every student theme with the care of a copy editor, he writes comments that are longer than the theme. His house is always open to students, half his women students are in love with him, his office hours stretch on past five o'clock, he prepares for his lectures as if each one were an oral exam. Yet my good luck makes me uneasy around him. Every piece of fortune that enhances me seems to diminish him, though he never fails to warm me with his admiration. He makes me feel bigger and better than I am, and somehow, in the process, manages to lessen himself.

Because I can't say any of this, I kid him. "Still walking off your biological urges. I wonder if we'll ever see you, once Charity's well."

His glance is hard and sharp, offended, as if he heard some hidden slur. Then he shrugs and laughs. "Look who's talking. I saw you bussing Lib and Alice there. Being a gentleman you could go no further, but if Sally doesn't get that baby born, Ed and Dave had better look out. How about it, is she asleep? Can you slip out long enough to stretch a leg?"

"Let me check."

I crack the bedroom door and look in, expecting darkness and even breathing. Instead I encounter light, and Sally, bulky in her night-gown, standing by the bed pulling on the sheet. She turns her head and I see that she is crying.

I slide in and shut the door. "What's the matter?"

She won't meet my eyes. "Oh, Larry, I'm such . . . I'm ashamed. I guess it was the excitement. I wasn't tight, I didn't do more than sip my drinks. But I . . . I've *wet the bed!*"

Filled with a terrible premonition, I snatch from her hand the corner of the sheet she has been pulling on, and yank it halfway off, certain it will be red with her blood. It isn't, but it is wet, and so is the pad. I pull them both off and throw them in the corner, I send her to the bathroom and hunt for a dry nightgown, which I finally find in her bag, ready packed for the hospital. I pass it through the bathroom door to her and then I go back into the living room, brushing aside Sid's questions, and get on the telephone to the doctor.

9

*A*n hour after the water sac broke, Sally's pains began. I monitored them, watch and notebook in hand, while Sid sat in the other room and read a book and hoped to be helpful. At two he drove us to the hospital. A little after three, persuaded that he could do nothing for either Sally or me, he went home. Next morning before eight he was back with a premature pot of flowers for Sally, and some rolls and a thermos of coffee for me, in case, as it happened, I was too preoccupied to get out for breakfast. All that day, Sunday, he and Charity kept track of Sally's lack of progress from Charity's room down the hall, and they were both there, Charity having talked the nurses into letting her out in a wheelchair, on Monday morning when the obstetrician decided—I had been telling him for twelve hours— that Sally couldn't take any more.

He appeared in the waiting room with his bloody rubber gloves held up at shoulder height—*her* blood, red as paint—and said, "I'm going to have to go get that babe."

At once he turned and started back in. "Go *with* him!" Charity cried. "Make them let you. *Doctor!* Doctor Cameron!"

She got him to pause, she got him to agree. She was not a woman you could argue with. They led me in and a nurse got me into a gown and mask and I watched from the side of the room, watched as much as I could stand to. Times like that are a kind of paralyzed frenzy. I was imbecilic with shock, fatigue, and fear, and close to passing out. But I was furious when the doctor looked up across the sheet humped by Sally's knees, and the eyes above the mask fixed on me. He paused. Everything paused.

"Is he all right? Get him out of here."

I understood him. He didn't want any husbands fainting on the delivery room floor while he tried to make up for having been too casual about that broken water sac. But I hated him for what he was doing and what he hadn't done, and I snarled back, "Tend to her, not me!"

The eyes stayed on me for a moment; then he went back to work. That was when the anesthetist, bending over Sally's head and watching her dials, said urgently, "She's going, Doctor!"

I had no feelings that I remember. I watched from my torpor, shocked numb, incapable of response, while they hustled and bent, clustered and dispersed and clustered again tensely. Sally told me later that she heard, away down under the ether and exhaustion and pain, and thought in surprise, "She means me!", and after a moment, "I *can't.*"

In the flurry of hypos, plasma, oxygen, whatever they did to keep her alive, the doctor quit trying to rotate the baby into position, and literally tore it from her body.

When I came out, blind and nauseated, Sid and Charity were still there. I saw them with stupid surprise. Charity swung her wheelchair around. "How is she? Is it over?"

I couldn't answer her. I found a chair and fell into it. My head reeled, the room rolled over, the membranes of my mouth were rank with ether smell. I put my head down between my knees and shut my eyes. After quite a while I felt a hand on my shoulder, and Sid's voice said, "Here, take a sip."

But even the motion of lifting my head to sip from the paper cup set the room to spinning again. My mouth was flooded with brine. I put my head down again and hung on.

"Find a nurse," I heard Charity say far off. "Get some *smelling* salts!"

Heels on rubber tile, a vast expanse of time, a sense of white, enclosing, emetic space. Then the hand on my back again, the voice. "Try this." A whiff of ammonia flamed up my nostrils. I coughed, choked, cleared. Another whiff. I waited, and after a while cautiously lifted my face from between my knees. The spinning room slowed, steadied, wobbled, slowed, fell still. Another flame of ammonia. I got my head above my belt buckle.

"Christ," I said, ashamed. "What an exhibition."

"Keep your *head* down," Charity said. "Why wouldn't you feel faint? You've been up for two days and nights."

Things were steadier. I waited some more. Sid offered me the ammonia again but I pushed his hand away. "Hahhhhh!" I said, shuddering, and sat up straighter. They swam into focus, anxious-faced, she in her wheelchair, he in his house-detective teaching suit. The waiting room's sterile lights had been overtaken by morning.

"Better?" Charity asked.

I nodded.

"What happened? Is it over? Is she all right?"

"The baby's born," I said. "I think it's a girl. I don't care what it is, so long as she's rid of it."

"But how is *she*?"

I sat up a little further. Charity's face was putty-colored without any makeup. Her hair was in pigtails. "What about this doctor?" I said. "Did he do all right by you, with his unassisted-childbirth line? I was after him all night to do a caesarean, to save her from any more of it, but he wouldn't. He kept trying to massage the goddamned baby around so it would appear politely. Even with the water sac broken, and a breech delivery, he wanted nature to take its course."

"I didn't have any such trouble," Charity said. "I had it easy. But oh, I'm *sick* I recommended him to Sally. He should have. . . ."

The delivery room doors opened and a nurse came out, bearing a squalling bundle in a pink blanket. "Congratulations, Papa," she said. "You can see your daughter in the nursery in a few minutes." She wore a professional smile. Her mask hung on its strings underneath her chin.

I sat where I was, but Charity half rose out of her wheelchair, then wheeled it after the departing nurse. "Oh, let *me!* Let me look at her!" The nurse stopped and bent and folded the blanket away from the baby's bawling face. Charity and Sid took a long, charmed look. I heard, "Oh, she's lovely! She's *all right!* Oh, what a dolly! It's all right, Dolly, it's all over. Now the whole *world's* ahead of you."

I said, "How's my wife? What are they doing in there?"

"She's fine," the nurse said. "They're doing some little—repairs, is all."

She carried her bundle away. Charity sat clapping her hands slowly and emphatically, beaming at me. Sid said, "Morgan, you and Sally do things dramatically, I must say. Now you're coming home with me and going to bed."

"I'd better stick around till she's out of the woods."

"She'll just want to rest," Charity said. "You'd better too."

"You've got a house full—your mother, and the nurse she brought, and the nanny, and the hired girl, and tomorrow you and the baby will be home. You don't need guests."

"There's a whole bloody household over there waiting for some-body to look after," Sid said. "You're their first chance."

"I wish to hell they'd bring her out," I said, and then, remember-ing, "Oh, Christ, what time is it? I've got classes at eleven and one."

"Which I am taking," Sid said.

"You've got plenty to do without . . ." But I let my protest die. I couldn't have dealt with those classes in any case, and he would be seriously upset if I didn't let him. "I'm not sure you're qualified."

"You're afraid of being shown up, you mean."

The delivery room doors opened again and two women in surgical gowns came pushing a gurney. I jumped up and walked beside it, looking down into Sally's face. She was fish-belly white, remote, un-reachable, out cold. One of the women, whom I recognized as the anesthetist, nodded and smiled at me. The gurney stopped. "She's had a transfusion," she said. "She'll be all right."

"Where are you taking her now?"

"Recovery room."

"Can I go along?"

She looked at me kindly, I thought, her mask dangling and her cap pulled up on the top of her head and her imperturbability rumpled, I supposed, by the close call. "Look, she won't need you. She'll be an hour or two coming out of it, and then she'll sleep. Why don't you go home to bed and come back after four this afternoon? We'll have her all pretty for you."

"Now you're talking," Sid said.

"Is she really all right?"

"She's fine now. Good strong pulse, blood pressure okay. You go along, we'll take care of her."

"What about the baby?"

"Didn't you see her?"

"I guess I didn't look."

Her eyes had golden flecks in the iris, and when she laughed a gold tooth showed back in her mouth. She struck me as a cheerful, humane woman, too good to be assisting that butcher of a doctor. "The baby," she said, "has a broken arm and a sore mouth. She came the hard way. But babies are like starfish, you can almost chop off a leg and they'll grow a new one. Two months from now you'll never know she had a bad time."

A broken arm and a sore mouth. My grievance grew bitterer. "Where's Dr. Cameron?"

"Washing up."

"Come on," Sid said, "you're in no shape to talk to him. Let's go."

"Come back after four," the anesthetist said.

They wheeled Sally away, corpselike. From her wheelchair Charity said, "Look on the bright side, Larry. It's over, and they're both safe. I feel *ghastly* about recommending that man, and I'll never use him again if I have *twelve* children. I'd rather have a baby in a chamber pot. But at least it's over. You and Sid go on, and you have an enormous breakfast and roll into bed. When you come back you'll probably find Sally and me comparing children."

Her color had come up. She looked radiant, undamaged. If they had let her, she could have gone home the day after having her baby. I felt envious for Sally, ghastly and etherized and patched together with twine. Good fortune was like money; those who had, got. As for me, I knew that I looked and felt and probably smelled like a cigar butt in a spittoon. Suddenly I could hardly keep my eyes open. I was really grateful to be going home with Sid, not having to drive, not even having to look.

"Did anybody ever tell you two how great you are?"

"Oh, pooh," Charity said. "What are you going to name the baby? Have you got any he-or-she names picked out?"

"You mean in all that talking she never told you?"

"No."

"There was only one name we could agree on. It was the same whether he or she. Her name's Lang."

"What?" Sid said, four times too loud for a hospital waiting room. "You mean it? Oh, say, that does us honor."

Charity was quizzing me with a speculative smile. "Really?"

"Really. Don't you kind of like the sound of it? Lang Morgan? It sounded very distinguished to us."

But Charity thought about it, pouted, and burst into a laugh. "Damn!" she said. "You've gone and spoiled everything. Why didn't Sally *think*? We had a plot to marry her to David if she turned out female. What kind of name is that going to leave her? *Lang Lang.* She'll sound like a *streetcar.*"

10

One more fragment, a crucial afternoon.

It is May, only a few weeks before the end of school. Noon. I am in my office eating a bag lunch and grading papers, with the door closed. Most of my colleagues eat together, but I have rarely felt that I can afford the time. Today I am less inclined than ever to join the cabal. The department has delayed and delayed its decisions on promotion, and everybody is on edge. Rumors expand to fill every pause in the talk, rivalries and jealousies surface, we watch each other for clues to conspiracy or secret knowledge. I have told myself that I am not part of that expectation, hope, and dread. I have done my job. If they like me and feel like reappointing me, fine. If they don't, I will manage. Meantime I have themes to read.

Bushwah, as they would have said in Sewickley, Pennsylvania, when Sid was growing up there. I would sell my fair white body in the public square to stay on.

William Ellery Leonard's fierce narrow face glares down at me from a half dozen frames on the walls. I have a certain fellow feeling for William Ellery, though I have never met him. A poet and iconoclast, he told the department where it could go. So can I, if I have to. Like him, I am a cuckoo in this robin's nest.

Bells ring. Ten minutes until one o'clock classes. But I have given my one o'clock the day off, to let the desperate spend an extra hour on their term papers, and I ignore the bells. I pick up another theme, read the first paragraph, correct a couple of misspelled words, scrawl *coh*, for coherence, in the margin. There is a tapping on the door. Damn.

"Come in."

The door opens and Sid puts his head in. "Busy?"

"Not to any real purpose."

He comes in and closes the door. His face wears a scowl. He looks forward-leaning, hollow-chested, and anxious. "Have you heard?"

"Heard what?"

"You haven't, then. They finally met. Adjourned a half hour ago. Mike Frawley brought us word."

There is such distress in his face that I say, "Don't tell me they didn't up you."

Embarrassed, he grimaces. "They didn't up me, no. But they didn't down me either. Renewed instructorship, three more years after next year."

When I stand up, I have to grab the pile of papers that starts cascading off the desk. I say cautiously, meaning to be supportive but not quite knowing what the vote means, "Isn't that all right? At least they didn't cut you off short."

He continues to look guilty and confused. "They're out of their minds. I can't imagine what motivates them, or what evidence they judge by, or what kind of department they want."

Now I begin to comprehend. "You mean they x-ed *me* out."

There is a hollow in my insides that later, when I have had time to think, I will probably fall into and drown. Without any reason to hope, I have been hoping. I manage a what-the-hell gesture, I flutter my fingers at the future that I am already dreading to take home to Sally. She has been happier this year than any year of her life.

"The least they could have done was give you the rest of a three-year appointment and put you on the ladder. That's what we all got, first round. Now some of us get an extension. But you've done more in a year than any of us will do in four or five, and they throw you out."

"No Ivy degree," I say. "No defined field. No articles in *PMLA*. No studies of romantic excess in *Comus*."

"That crap!" Sid says. "That miserable, prechewed, vomited-up, reeaten carrion! It's made a cynic out of Ed. Damn them, they enforce mediocrity. The rest of us have to play the game, but you shouldn't even be allowed to." Furiously upset, he walks around knocking his knuckles against bookcases and walls. He stops. "What they did do, in their great charity and wisdom, they gave you the two summer classes. Booby prize. You can do their slave labor through the summer until they give you the gate."

Hard times are instructive and humbling. I can't forget that I have a birth-damaged daughter, just coming around, and a still-recovering wife, and that medical expenses and the girl we have hired to help

Sally have eaten up most of our savings. I hear the word about the summer classes gratefully. Something, at least.

Sid wanders to the window, whose sill is piled with papers God knows how old, scholarly offprints God knows how unimportant, and books God knows how long overdue at the library. His lips flatten against his teeth. He almost spits.

"How many stories have you written this year? Three? And sold them all. And the novel, which will make you famous—they'll be teaching it in this lamentable institution before many years. And at least two articles. And some book reviews. And the textbook. All of it while you were teaching a full load. So they pound your fingers off the gunwale. You know why? You threaten the weak sisters. They don't want distinction around, it would show them up. Energy and talent like yours are bombs under their beds. Half of that executive committee went to college here, and to graduate school here, before they started to teach, and they've never taught anywhere but here. They're ingrown, inbred, lazy, and scared. They don't dare let people like you into the department."

He knows, and so do I, that he is talking out of loyalty and distress, not out of conviction. There is as much competence in that department as in any he or I know. What he means, and I understand, is that times are tough, and that this time I am the victim. Nevertheless, it is comforting to hear that I am wronged.

"Remember that speech," I tell him. "I may want to hear it again. I may want to quote from it. How did Dave make out?"

"Same as me—extension. They're cagy. If they keep anybody seven years they're up against the rule of the American Association of University Professors that says anybody kept for seven years has tenure even if he doesn't have rank. So they'll cut everybody off at six."

"No, no. You guys will inherit this place. And Ed's got his job waiting at Georgia. What about Ehrlich?"

"Out. Next year is terminal."

"Out! Like me. Oh, he'll be fit to be tied. All that Greek he read. All those asses he kissed. How about Hagler?"

"Out. Terminal. What they'll do now is recruit three new, cheap, eager instructors to replace the three of you. Three years from now they'll fire those and start all over."

"You and Dave are the only ones continued. That's a compliment."

"Is it?"

I understand him. If we were all in the same boat, he could be cheerful about it. But he has been preferred over most of his friends, including some that he generously thinks are his betters, and he can conceive no reason for that favoritism except that he is rich, or perhaps that his wife is socially hyperactive. That can't make him very happy.

Restlessly he turns and pushes at the casement, which gives with a creaking noise and a lifting of dust. Into the room flows the mild, soft, perfumed air of spring. He stands inhaling it. Fresh air is medicine to him, spring is an eagerness, his automatic response to stress is to walk or run or skate or ski or otherwise work it off.

"This all gives me the most profound bellyache," he says. "What are you doing after your one o'clock?"

"I'm not holding it. I'll be reading papers."

"Can you smell what it's like outside?"

"A matter of indifference to me."

"You're a bloody liar. You yearn out the window as much as I do, only you've got more willpower. How about going for a sail?"

"Where would we get a boat?"

"The Union rents them."

"Sid, I'd love to, but if I don't read these papers this afternoon I'll have to read them tonight and tomorrow, and that will take me off a story I'm trying to write. I need that story. I need it now more than ever."

Twisting the cord of the blind, he watches me, and I read him. He is at once disappointed to have got only a continuance, and miserable to have been continued while I have been rejected. It shocks his whole system of values to think that he should have been preferred over someone he likes and admires. He takes prosperity harder than anyone I ever knew.

"How did the vote go?" I ask. "Did Mike say? Did anyone vote to promote you, or keep me? Anybody we should be grateful to?"

"Oh, sure. Mike didn't say, but you know a lot of them would have voted for you. It's a conspiracy of the timid mossbacks."

"Which we would all love to be."

"Speak for yourself." He walks in a circle, jingling the change in his pocket, and returns to look out the window. "How about it? Just a couple of hours? Why don't I call Charity and ask her to pick Sally up and meet us at the dock? Can your girl look after the baby for two hours?"

"She can do everything but nurse it."

"Come on then."

I hesitate only a moment, and then I fall. Why not? What good does it do to work every minute? "Maybe we'll all drown," I suggest. "Then they'll be sorry. Who'll they get to teach their summer classes then?"

Galvanized, emancipated, already in better spirits, we go down the stairs and along the main corridor of Bascom Hall. Most of the time I have known it, it has smelled of steam heat, sodden floors, hot radiator paint, and wet wool, and icy drafts have swept it every time a student shuddered in its doors. Now the doors stand open, and a sweet, beguiling wind blows the length of the hall. Outside, men students in shirtsleeves and girls in summer dresses sprawl on the steep lawn. From where we emerge, sidewalks bulge outward and downward like lines of longitude seen from the North Pole. A professor-hen is clucking a ring of chicks around him under a tree.

Authentic spring, time of hope. I shut away the bitterness of rejection, I sweep into the back closet of my mind the uncertainties and anxieties that are going to be with us now until I can find something else, in this wasteland of the Depression, that will support us. I sweep them all into the closet along with my anger and wounded vanity and punctured self-esteem and the grim arithmetic I will soon be working on. I say to myself, self-consciously and pompously, as I once said more harshly in Albuquerque, in circumstances a lot bleaker than these, the words of the Anglo-Saxon stoic: "That have I borne, this can I bear also."

Almost cheerfully, our coats slung on hooked fingers over our shoulders, we walk down Bascom Hill toward the Union. Halfway down, I ask, "Does Charity know?"

"Not yet."

"Nor Sally either. Do we tell them?"

"Let's have our boat ride first. Why spoil it?"

"Hearing that you've made it shouldn't spoil anything for Charity."

"Made what? Charity doesn't accept anything but success. She hates stalemates. Also, hearing that they've let you go will spoil everything for her. It spoils everything for me. This place will be a desert without you two."

I am not used to such naked expressions of regard. Like his admiration, his affection half embarrasses me. I don't know what to say. I say nothing.

.   .   .

The day is breezy, cloudy in the west but clear overhead. Our boat is heavy and broad in the beam, a scow. I sit forward by the mast, Sid at the tiller, the girls on the thwart amidships. The wind tangles Sid's fair hair as he sculls us out from the dock. I do what he tells me with the jib. Later I do what he tells me with the mainsail. We lean into a long northeast tack up-lake. Settling down on a life preserver with my back against the mast, I am face to face with our two beaming women.

"*Some*body had a good idea," Charity says. "Isn't it wonderful to be *out,* and unpregnant, and free!"

Actually I am pretty pregnant with the news Sid brought me, but glad we have not spread it. The girls look very happy. With their heads bound up in *babushkas* they might be out of the peasant chorus of a Russian opera. Any minute now we will sing and dance to the balalaika. Charity is tall and striking; Sally smaller, darker, quieter. One dazzles, the other warms. In a couple of hours I will need sympathy, but for now I like being washed by the wind.

"What are the towers?" Sally asks, and nods ahead. Craning, I look. Beyond the far shore, rising out of green countryside, a cluster of tall buildings.

"Camelot?" I guess.

Sid says, crosswind, "The mental hospital."

"The one where William Ellery took his demented wife?"

"That's it."

We discuss my office mate and his really tragic life, his talent, his absurdities, vanities, and pretensions. He must have been something, in his prime. I wonder aloud how it would be to be sailing along like this and have him overtake you, swimming on his back in his boar helmet, with his eagle beak in the air and his voice filling the wind with Anglo-Saxon brag. Sid, completely in character, wonders if this stormy-bright lake might sometime in future acquire, because of William Ellery, a poetic and legendary aura such as Wordsworth and Coleridge gave to the Lake Country and Hardy gave to Dorset. We agree that until it has had a poet, a place is not a place.

"I'll bet you'll be the one to glorify Mendota," Charity says. "When are you going to write something about all of us here? Don't we tempt you as a subject?"

"Give me time."

Which, of course, they are not going to give me. Too bad, Lake Mendota, you'll never know what you missed.

Buffeted by a stiffening and changeable wind, we are led to another association suggested by this lake. A couple of years ago I.A. Richards, then a visiting professor, went sailing with a companion from the Wisconsin faculty, just as we are doing now, and at about this season. They capsized, and the lifesaving unit on the Union dock was slow to spot them. When they reached the capsized boat, Richards was still clinging to it, and as if to preserve the meaning of meaning they rescued him. But the Wisconsin professor had let go and drowned.

We drag our hands over the edge of our sluggish tub and agree that the water is very cold—the ice has been out only a few weeks. How long would a person survive if he went overboard? Ten minutes? A half hour? An hour?

We have been tacking back and forth, ducking under the swinging boom. Sid is very busy, for the boat handles badly and the wind seems to come from every direction. The sun has gone under, too, and the warmth has left the afternoon. The sky to the west is full of bruise-colored clouds, and the hospital towers on the north shore are lost in gray shrags of rain. In the hostile airs we come almost to a standstill. The canvas flaps. Sid grates out, "Oh, God, don't *luff*!" The boom comes over, we veer sluggishly onto another tack.

Sally's eyes find mine. Though the wind has stirred spots of color in her cheeks, she is still wan, for the birth business left her anemic, and she exists on liver and spinach and such things. Now she is clearly uneasy. Her face brings me back from exhilaration with the lurid light and the sense of exposure and risk. I try to incorporate into a look several confident reassurances: Our boat is a scow, unsinkable; Sid is an experienced sailor; shipwreck is something that happens only to the I. A. Richardses of the world. I know she is hoping I will suggest turning back, but I can't do that. It is Sid's expedition. He is the one to say when we should head for shore.

Then in her clear voice, clear as a pitch pipe (in a crisis, or when calling for attention, she pitches her voice as high as she does when starting a song), Charity says, "Sid? *Sid?* It's getting too rough. Turn back."

He squints at the clouds. "It's just a squall. It'll blow over."

"No. Go back. Right away."

She couldn't be more peremptory. Only I, who am facing the stern, see the resistance, the active rebellion, in his face. But he obediently prepares to come about. "Heads down! Here we go." We duck under the slow club of the boom, I feel the wind on the other side of my face as sharp as Charity's voice, and the movement of the boat as reluctant as Sid's obedience.

Off to the left and ahead, as we flounder quartering into the wind, I can see the green shore, the university buildings around and on Bascom Hill, Observatory Hill with its skeleton ski jump. I can't see the dock, which is low and obscured by spray and the heaving lake. I wonder if the lifesaving outfit on the dock can see *us*.

The boat won't sail so close to the wind, and Sid has to let it fall away a little. The wind whips and shoves, the sails lean, the boat moves like a dog hanging back on its leash. Waves smack us, the gunwales tip, we nervously high-side. The girls have buttoned their coats under their chins. There is water under the duckboards.

As suddenly as if someone has opened a valve, the rain comes. One minute I am squinting up at the thunderous blue clouds overtopping us, and the next we are being pounded by heavy rain that turns almost at once to hail. We cover our heads with our arms. In a couple of minutes it has passed; I can see it chopping the water astern and to starboard. Then I look down, feeling myself even wetter on the feet than on the rest of me, and find that the water under the duckboards has risen so that the boards are afloat. So much, in that short shower? I find a coffee can and begin to bail.

I am facing Sally and Charity, looking into their faces. They crowd together on the wet thwart, huddling into their coats. Sally gives me a wan, stoical glance. Charity cries out in cheerful outrage, "Oh, *damn* the weather! This started out to be *fun*!"

A gust explodes against us, the gunwale dips deeply, spray flies. I can't see that I have gained on the water in the bottom, and my feet are soaked. I shout at Sid, "What do you think? Shall I lower the sail?"

Sitting with their feet pulled up, looking straight ahead as if the wobbling of their eyeballs might tip us beyond recovery, the girls interpret my shout in different ways. Sally obviously thinks it a confession of crisis, and it alarms her. Charity takes it as a challenge to her leadership. "No! We're safer if we keep our *way*."

I continue to look at Sid. For all I know, Charity's judgment may come not out of sailing experience but out of a reading of Captain Marryat. But Sid is no help. He has been overruled before he can open his mouth. He lifts a shoulder, that is all. My icy hand goes back to pouring coffee cans of water over the side. The wind keeps blowing bucketfuls back aboard.

Despite everything I can do, the water gains on me. I turn to look around, hoping to find the shore and dock nearer, and my eye is struck by how low we are in the water. We are not riding the waves down and then rising buoyantly again. We are simply boring into them, heavier and lower, heading down. The line of the gunwale is aimed at the bottom a quarter of a mile ahead.

I grab up the two life preservers I have been sitting on, and throw one to Sally, one to Charity. I have time to loosen the sheet from the turnbuckle and let the mainsail pour around me, wet, cold, and enveloping. Another life preserver is there in the water that now reaches to my calves, and I throw it over Sally's head to Sid. Glaring around, I spot the last one and grab it. Sid is standing in the stern, his hand on the tiller, his eyes on the diving bow. The girls too have stood up, ready to jump. I scream at Sally, "No, the high side! The high side!" But she has no time. We heel over, the bow stays under, the mast hits the waves, and we are in the ice water.

This is not an adventure story, and being after the fact it doesn't generate suspense. Obviously we all survived. There were no heroics. Everybody behaved well.

When I came up gasping and bulging-eyed from the shock of immersion I saw Sally in her cumbersome coat trying to get the section of duckboards she was clinging to free of the sail and the fouled lines. I started to work around the mast to get to her, but Sid reached her first. Then I arrived, and the three of us paddled the duckboards around onto the windward side of the hull where Charity was hanging fast. We tied ourselves to the hulk and waited for rescue.

It seemed a fatally long time, though I suppose it wasn't more than ten or twelve minutes, until the Chriscraft roared up, jockeyed around, threw us a line, and hauled us up over the side one by one, the girls first, like gaffed fish. As they got us onto the deck, chattering, blue, and numb, they told us with demoralizing casualness, "Go below. Don't get the bunks wet."

Down in the tiny cabin we huddled together, soaked, freezing, our jaws locked so that we could hardly speak. Charity said incredulously, "Don't get the . . . *bunks* wet? What kind of . . . rescue . . . is this? Where are the little . . . barrels of . . . brandy? To hell with keeping their . . . bunks . . . dry!"

She fell onto the starboard bunk and pulled a blanket over herself, motioning Sally down beside her. We all accepted that invitation, bundling like antique New Englanders in a cold snap, while the Chriscraft bounced and roared toward safety.

It slowed, swerved, bumped against the dock. Under the eyes of twenty or thirty of the curious we staggered ashore, shoeless, squishing water. Eying us with a professional lack of expression, the rescuers relented, and let us each wear a blanket home. "What about the boat?" Sid kept asking. "I rented it. Shall I . . . ?"

"We'll take care of it. Come down tomorrow."

We hurried to the Langs' car, too cold to worry about boats or blankets, too cold almost to move. Actually we were probably in more danger than we realized. Doctors these days take hypothermia seriously, and if anybody ever had the right to be hypothermic, we did. We crowded into the station wagon, Sid drove us to our house. "Get warm," they chattered at us, and drove away. We made it around to our basement door.

Our girl Ellen, with Lang on her shoulder bawling her head off, met us. "Oh, my land, did you wreck?"

"Draw us a tub of hot water, Ellen, please. Hurry!"

Ellen started to hand Lang to her mother, but Sally was too shattered, wet, and cold. "Not now, not yet. Just get the tub filled."

While Ellen drew the tub, we sat on the bed and peeled off our soggy, reluctant clothes. A dry bathrobe should have been a sybaritic pleasure; I never even felt mine. We shuddered and shook. In the bathroom Lang's bawling drowned the sound of running water.

"Is it ready, Ellen? If it isn't, just let it run. We'll finish up."

Ellen came out of the bathroom with Lang purple-faced and unappeasable on her shoulder. We crowded past them into the steam and shut the door, threw aside our robes. "Be careful," I said. "You won't feel it. You could scald yourself."

Cautiously we felt our way into the tub and settled down facing one another, sinking in to our chins. The heat, at first not felt, moved into our hands and feet as a slow, hard ache. Our skins turned lobster red, our shuddering began to smooth out, it began to be luxurious. We smiled at each other, shaking our heads.

"That was close."

"I thought we were gone."

"Feel all right now?"

"I don't ever want to move."

"Just lie and soak."

We lay and soaked, but not for long. Out in the bedroom Lang was having an uninterrupted tantrum. Pretty soon Ellen's hesitant knuckles tapped on the door. "Mrs. Morgan?"

"What is it? Is she hungry?"

"It's nearly an hour past her feeding time. I can't get her quiet."

"Well, bring her in. No, good heavens, don't do any such thing! Wait a minute."

"I'll get her," I said.

I climbed out and hunched into my robe without toweling and opened the door a crack. Out there Ellen was rocking and patting and comforting, obviously very interested in what was going on inside. She was a broad, good-natured girl, no more than eighteen, and coming from Wausau she probably thought Madison wicked and exciting, one of the cities of the plain.

I took the baby from her. "Can you scrape us up something to eat, Ellen? We're still frozen solid. Anything, whatever there is. Warm. Just give us a few more minutes to thaw out."

Lang liked my shoulder no better than she had liked Ellen's. Burly, fat-faced, obviously overnourished at Sally's expense, she did not get my sympathy. What did she have to howl about? But I stripped off her diaper—dry, for a wonder—and shed my bathrobe again. Pink, sighing, liquefied with pleasure, I handed her to Sally, stepped into the tub, and settled down with my back against the taps.

Three in a tub. I watched my naked daughter laid against the breast of my naked wife. She found a dark nipple, her squalling died in a gurgle, her mouth worked, her eyes closed. Naked in Eden, the ultimate atomic family, pink and wet and warm, we lay entangled in the tub, and rescue was so recent, safety so sweet, that I didn't have the heart to tell Sally what had happened to us.

I watched Lang's fat fingers work in the softness of Sally's breast, and her mouth work with her feeding. Sally looked up and caught me watching. We smiled, foolishly and gratefully. I moved my foot between Sally's legs and fitted it like a bicycle seat into her crotch.

We had come out of the tub finally, Ellen had taken Lang to the furnace room and put her down, Sally and I were sitting in our eight-by-ten kitchen eating some sort of goulash and drinking hot tea with jam in it, Russian style. There was a knock on the door. Sally jumped up and started for the bedroom, but she had no chance. The door opened and in came Sid and Charity.

They stopped in the doorway, surveying our bathrobes, the remains of supper, the general dishevelment of that crowded little hole.

"Oh, thank *goodness*!" Charity cried. "You're all *right*! We'd never have forgiven ourselves if you weren't. Did you ever have such a time getting *warm*?"

"We stepped into a boiling tub and it froze over," I said. "What are you doing running around? You ought to be in bed with hot-water bottles. That's where we were going."

I was thinking, and I am sure Sally was too, what it must have taken, in the way of friendly concern, to get them into their clothes and out to their car and across town to us. Not very confidently, I wondered if we would have been capable of it. In fact, we hadn't been. It hadn't occurred to us to worry about them as they had about us.

"We were fine as soon as we warmed up," Charity said. "But wasn't it *paralyzing* in that water? All I could think of was I.A. Richards and how awful it would be if one of us couldn't hang on. And when Sid told me what the *department* has done. . . ."

She stopped. Sally was staring at her. "Oh!" Charity said, and hit her head with the heel of her hand as Sid had done that afternoon in my office. A family gesture. "*Idiot!* How stupid of me. You didn't know. Larry hasn't told you."

"She has to know," I said—and to Sally, shocked and woebegone, "we're out. But we did get summer school, so we're okay for a while. And Sid got reappointed, Sid and Dave both, so there is a God. If I hadn't been seduced into getting warm I'd have laid in champagne in the best Lang manner. How about a cup of tea? Sit down. Here, let me clear some space."

I babbled, throwing papers and my briefcase off the couch, but when I turned around they were still standing there, Sally looking ready to cry, and Charity and Sid distressed with sympathy.

"Oh, damn," Sally said. "I hoped. . . ."

I put my arm around her. Eventually we all sat down.

"What'll you do?" Charity asked.

"I don't know. Write a lot of application letters. Hope for some last-minute opening. They made it tough by delaying so long. Everybody who is going to hire has hired."

"But you've done so much! You're getting such a *dossier*. How could they not understand how good you are?"

I managed not to be too sympathetic with myself, for fear I would let out a bleat of pure self-pity. I agreed with her, I had been unfairly treated. But I suppose I had some dim awareness, too, that in her guidance of Sid, she had been right. Poetry would not get him anywhere in that department. If he wanted to stay, he should do what the system called for. If I had done that, I might well have got at least another couple of years.

"Hell," I said, "something will turn up. The novel will sell a million copies. Our textbook will get adopted in Texas and we'll have to ship it down there by the freight-car load. Sally and I will go down to the Virgin Islands and live on coconuts and bananas and write expensive and live cheap and need no clothes but a dark tan."

"You mustn't do anything like that," Charity said. "I'm sure this will only be temporary. You're too good to be unemployed for long, and we love you too much to let you go and live on some beach where we'll never see you. *Sid?* Isn't it time we made our proposal?"

He sat in our one chair, facing the three of us on the couch. He put his elbows on his knees and knotted his hands and leaned forward. His earnest glasses glinted as he checked Charity's face for some corroboration or encouragement. "I'll jump in if they make the slightest objection," she said.

"See," Sid said, "you'd be doing us a great favor. We were talking about it while we ate, and it came to both of us at once. First, have you signed a lease for this apartment?"

"Just till June first. But we can have it longer."

"You don't want it. Because we'll be in Vermont all summer and our house will just be sitting there. We'd like you to use it."

Sally and I looked at each other, each asking, neither answering.

"There's just no *point* in your paying rent for a place when ours sits empty," Charity said. "Last summer the Haglers used it. It's best if there's someone there. You can mow the lawn if it will make you feel better. But don't clean out the fireplace! George Hagler was such a model tenant that he wanted to leave the house *spotless,* and he cleaned out the ashes Sid had been half a year collecting. But you don't *have* to do anything. Just live there and keep prowlers at bay."

"What about your new house? Will you be going ahead with that?"

"I don't know," Sid started to say, but he was overridden by Charity. "Of *course* we're going ahead. They can't scare us off with a *postponement.* But the new house isn't the question. The old one is. Will you look after it for us?"

"Charity," I said. "Sid . . ." and ended up, "Sally?"

"You could write six stories and another novel," Charity said. "When one room gets dirty, move into another. After eight weeks you'll still have one clean one left."

Looking around our basement, I had to laugh. "Sally is a better housekeeper and I am less messy than appears," I said. "You catch us in disarray. We just emerged from Lake Mendota, clothed in white samite, mystic, wonderful, and we dripped a little on the floor."

As a tension-and-gratitude-breaker it was ineffectual. Nobody paid any attention. "Are you just being lovely and kind," Sally said, "or do you really need somebody in your house?"

"That answers us," Sid said. "We are not being lovely and kind. We are doing ourselves a great favor. We do want somebody in the house. You. So notify your landlord. Now there's a part two to this proposition. We asked you before if you wouldn't spend a summer with us at Battell Pond. The way things have worked out, we can't have Larry, but what's wrong with Sally and Lang driving to Vermont with us?"

"You've approached it wrong end *to,*" Charity said. "Don't ask what's wrong with it. *Nothing's* wrong with it. It's the solution. There can't be a single sensible objection. We'll have our regular girl there to look after the babies, and she's wonderful, she can handle four as easily as three. Sally can loaf and get strong again. We can all swim, and walk, and go *ferning,* and have picnics on Folsom Hill, and read poetry on the porch, and listen to music, and square dance, and just talk around the fire. It isn't luxurious at all, we don't do anything that isn't simple and wholesome and plain. Larry will have to stay here and suffer, but when he's through he can join us. *Wherever* you go next year, you can get there from Vermont as easily as from Madison. Just say you will, and make us happy. Then we won't feel so bad about taking you out sailing and nearly drowning you."

How do you deal with people like that? I said, "You're outdoing even yourselves. What do you think, Sally?"

"I don't think I should leave you alone. You'd work too hard."

"He'll do that wherever he is," Sid said.

"Think what a summer of loafing will do for Sally's health," Charity said.

They pressed upon us, at a time when we would normally have wanted to be alone with our forebodings. They wanted to express their affection and solidarity, they wanted to ease the blow the department had dealt us, they wanted to make restitution for being rich and lucky.

Sally's hair had gone curly from the steam of our bath, but the anemic pallor had reasserted itself through the temporary pink. She put her hands over her face and took them away again, ashamed.

"Would you like to?" I said.

"Could you get along?"

"If I couldn't make it in the Palazzo Lang I ought to be institutionalized."

"It might be easier for you to write without the baby around. Do you think? How long would it be? Two months?"

"There you are," I said to Sid and Charity. "She'd like to. I think it would be wonderful for her, the best thing that could happen. I can content myself with merely ducal status at the palazzo. We accept with pleasure. But neither of us will ever figure out a way to repay that sort of kindness."

"Wonderful!" Charity's eyes were so wide open that white showed all around the iris—one of the comic faces she affected when she was especially pleased. She hugged Sally, then she leaned the other way and hugged me. But the kiss that I aimed at her cheek barely grazed her. She was not much of a kisser. She had a way of turning at the last minute and presenting a moving target.

"As for repaying," she said to me in rebuke, "friends don't *have* to repay anything. Friendship is the most selfish thing there is. Here are Sid and I just licking our *chops.* We got everything out of you that we wanted."

So they did. They also got, though that they would never have permitted to figure in our relations, our lifelong gratitude. There is a revisionist theory, one of those depth-psychology distortions or half-truths that crop up like toadstools whenever the emotions get infected by the mind, that says we hate worst those who have done the most for us. According to this belittling and demeaning theory, gratitude is a festering sore. Maybe it is, if it's insisted on. But instead of insisting on gratitude, the Langs insisted that their generosity was selfish, so how could we dislike them for it?

We liked those two from the minute of our first acquaintance. After that shipwreck afternoon we loved them both, sometimes in spite of themselves and ourselves. At the time I could not have told them that. I am not sure that either Sally or I was ever able to tell them, though it had to be apparent without telling.

Just in case, I tell them now.

11

On a morning in early June I saw them all into the Lang station wagon—three adults, two infants in baskets in the back seat, two rampant toddlers imprisoned in canvas nests in the middle seat. Commiserating with Sid, condemned to drive that nursery for two and a half days, I helped Charity establish herself in front and got Sally into the back between the two baskets. In the interest of sanity she and Charity would change places every hour or two.

Only as she settled back out of reach did I realize that I was being separated from my girl for the first time in our knowing of one another. She sat there blinking and smiling. Euridice. God damn.

I leaned far in to kiss her, kissed Lang in her basket, gave a finger to the pudgy fist of David Hamilton Lang, and stepped back. The car started and pulled away with hands flapping out the windows and voices calling back things I heard only as noise. There I was, alone on Van Hise Street. Promptly, dog to vomit, I went into Sid's study and started a novel.

It was five days before I had a letter. After that they came regularly, four or five a week, and they were so full of happiness that I stopped feeling sorry for Sally and began feeling sorry for myself, left in darkest Madison while she frolicked in Arcadia.

Arcadia took shape as a place of great tranquility and order. Every morning, Sally said, Charity lay in bed for a half hour with pad and pencil, and when she got up, the day was organized. Constructive daydreaming, she called it. I suppose a nursing baby and two other children can keep any woman on a schedule, but Charity would have produced a schedule stricter than the Book of Hours without any children at all.

Besides her family obligations, which extended from her immediate family through two dozen aunts, uncles, cousins, and in-laws, she was the queen of volunteers and the princess of projects. She had a hand in church suppers, auctions, village fairs, Sunday evening concerts on the lake. She planned children's birthday parties and family picnics. She went fifteen rounds a week, by mail and telephone, with her Madison architect. She knew nearly everybody around the lake, and entertained both those she knew and those she didn't.

Much of this Sally got pulled into simply by being there, but Charity was perceptive, and honored Sally's need of rest—in fact, ordered it—and made opportunities for withdrawal from the strain of being a stranger and a guest. What her household offered in the way of warmth and ease and acceptance left Sally almost tearful. She wrote me like this:

> You like ruts, because ruts are a sign work is being done. You'd love this rut. Up at seven—we could sleep later but nobody wants to. After breakfast, Charity gets busy with the house or errands (she should wear a big ring of keys on her belt), and sends Sid out to his study. She is absolutely determined that he's going to write something this summer that will make Wisconsin promote him next year and make them wish they'd promoted him this. She bosses him like mad. He grumbles, but he goes. Then the nurse girl Vicky takes all four children up to the play room, and I come out here and sit on the porch and write to you.
>
> It may rain later but right now it's clear and still. The lake down below is a perfect mirror, with an upside-down reflection of the opposite shore and the Ellis dock and boathouse. I just saw George Barnwell Ellis's white head going up the path to his think house, and I can almost hear Aunt Emily saying, "There! *He's* out of the road. Now for the day's business." She and Charity are two of a kind. Not like me. If I had you here, and sent you out to your think house, and you went when I sent you, I'd want to tag right along.
>
> Before lunch we all take a swim, and after lunch we nap or read, and after three, on good days, we play tennis or walk. If it's raining we read or listen to records. Dinners are fun, almost always somebody interesting, and never a night without somebody. Last night it was Uncle Richard, the ex-ambassador, who is now president of Phoenix Books in Boston. And Charity's sister Comfort and her husband, Lyle Lister. Comfort is terribly pretty, and Lyle is one of the most fascinating men you ever met. You and he should hit it off. He comes from Arizona, and is a biologist, and works all over the world. He and Comfort were married right after he got his Ph.D. at Yale, and they went straight to Alaska, clear up to Point Hope, and lived among the Eskimos, in an igloo practically. If you can believe Aunt Emily, they ate nothing but seal

blubber for two years, and I know, from Comfort herself, that they had no bathroom, nothing but a chamber pot, and it was so cold sometimes they had to thaw the pot on the stove before they could dump it. She makes even that sound like an adventure.

Now he's given up arctic flora and is working on plants that have adapted themselves not to cold, but to drought. He's just back from several months in Libya, and he had all sorts of stories about caves with people and animals painted all over the walls, and a flint desert where the wind had teed up stones like golf balls, and when you looked, you could see that every stone was a tool left from a neolithic civilization that died thousands of years ago. I swear his clothes smelled of camel-dung fires. Comfort's eyes never leave his face. She's so happy to have him here that she makes me jealous.

He stole the show, but Uncle Richard is definitely Somebody, too—dignified and impressive, with a twinkle, and kind of tweedy. Naturally I told him about your novel, and he wants to meet you. Unfortunately he isn't perfectly trained in Charity's rules of order, and neither is Lyle. When we went into the living room after dinner, and Charity announced music, and Sid set the needle down on "The Trout," Uncle Richard and Lyle were still talking away, planning a book on those old Saharan civilizations and the drouth-adapted plants that they and their animals lived on. So there was the music beginning, and there we all were with our hands in our laps and our eyes downcast and respectful, and there were those two still talking. "Uncle Richard!" Charity said to them. "Lyle! *Really!*" They shushed, but neither of them much liked it. It reminded me so much of the night she shushed you and Marvin Ehrlich. I think she'd shush Franklin Delano Roosevelt if he didn't keep still for the music.

I could imagine them there in their rustic outpost of culture like colonials being British in a far land. I was homesick for those people before I ever met most of them. Some things that astonished Sally—hard beds, hard chairs, unfinished walls, Ivory soap, no liquor harder than sherry—could not dispel the impression I got of a simplicity expensively purchased and self-consciously cherished, a naturalness as artificial as the Petite Trianon, and a social life that was lively, hectic, and incessant.

While I crossed off the days on the calendar, I lived on the daily report from Arcadia. For a while, Sid's mother was visiting, and shared the guest house with Sally—the gentlest woman alive, Sally said, a *mouse,* not at all what she'd imagined a very rich woman would be like. She could see where some of Sid's qualities came from.

Mrs. Lang went away, but the dinners and picnics went on. As for me, I rose at six and got in three hours on the typewriter before my first class. I tried writing in the late afternoon, too, but even stripped to the waist I sweltered in the midwestern heat, and my arm stuck to the varnished desk and my sweaty hands smudged the paper. One more day, another, one more, yet another, a week. And nearly every day a letter to tell me how much I was missing. On the days when none arrived, I died. When two arrived in the same mail I fled out under a tree to read them at leisure with my bare feet in the grass.

Once in a while a detail left me brooding. Word of a midnight swim, for instance, a chilly impulse of Sid's. God help me, I went around for several days wondering if they had worn suits. I resented and feared their skinny-dipping while I had to grind away in the heat teaching high school teachers the elements of English literature from Beowulf to Thomas Hardy. What if, luring my wife out of my protective reach on the pretext of helping us out economically and putting her back into health, this friend of mine worked on her liking and trust? I was enough of a writer even then to imagine the whole business—courtesies, the meeting of eyes, little touchings, moments on dock or porch when no one else was there. Oh, man.

I worried about the future, too. A dozen letters had produced only one nibble. It came from a Lutheran college in Illinois, and I might have pursued even that possibility if they had not wanted me, before any further discussion, to declare my belief in the Apostles' Creed, the Augsburg Confession, and the principles of higher Christian education.

No jobs. By mid-August we would be on the street. Dreary time, best forgotten. Hot, lonely, laborious summer. No friends in town except the Abbots, and Ed swallowed by his thesis. We had a few beers together at the Union, where back in May we and the Langs had come ashore dripping seaweed, and I went once to their house to dinner. Alice was appealing. That night I kissed her beside the car and found her alarmingly responsive. Thesis widow. But she was not Sally—in fact, that little episode so inflamed me with the plausibility of my imaginings about Sally and Sid that I practically fled the premises. Besides, I liked Ed. I wished his ribald view of the academic scene could give me a clue on how to survive without it.

Even the interminable will end if it is only eight weeks long. Late one August morning—grades in, farewells said (not many), excess

Morgan household effects stored in the Langs' basement, a sack of sandwiches and a thermos of coffee in the seat beside me, I started east, or rather, northeast. I had figured out that by driving up through the Saulte instead of crossing Lake Michigan on the ferry I would save at least ten dollars.

It was like bringing the good news from Ghent to Aix. Daylight galloped, the Ford galloped, we galloped all three. Beaver Dam, Waupun, Fond du Lac, Oshkosh, fell behind. The sun wallowed down into long beds of cloud that went pink, then red, then purple. In the twilight I passed through Appleton, in the dark through Green Bay. There was a sense of dark enclosing forest opening up into lost farms and little lonely towns. A sense of dark enclosing history also—Indians in bark canoes, pork-eaters, blackrobes, fur traders, French explorers greedy for empire. Exhilarated, going the wrong way on a one-way historical street, I rattled back toward the beginnings of the Republic, toward the ancestral East that had never figured in my life, and hadn't figured in my family's for three generations. And what was more important, toward reunion with Sally and the baby. Lang would probably not know me. Sally, I hoped, would.

Menominee, when I went through about eleven, was barely alive. Escanaba, after midnight, was as dead under its hissing arc lights as something on a slab. At three-thirty in the morning an American customs man waved me through the gate at the Saulte, and a Canadian on the other side reluctantly left his lighted room and his coffee—I could see it steaming on his desk—to ask me if I had any firearms or pets, and turn away almost before I could answer him.

Half a league, half a league, half a league onward. Daylight came sickly on Sudbury's blasted heath. My nerve ends were like ingrown hairs, my head the size of a pumpkin, my fingers balloons full of water. At Sturgeon Falls I stopped at an all-night diner for a doughnut and a fresh thermos of coffee, but it was no go. I almost fell asleep starting the car, and I barely made it to a place where I could pull off, lock the doors, and lie down in the seat.

Confused hours later I awoke. Somebody tapping on the window—a provincial policeman in a Baden-Powell hat. I sat up, cleared my bleary eyes and my mossy mouth, persuaded the policeman that I was neither dead, drunk, in trouble, nor an outlaw, worked my face into flexibility, had a capful of coffee, and drove on.

It is a long way down the Ottawa. I finished my novel during that stretch, revised it between Ottawa and the St. Lawrence, and threw it away going up the Richelieu. The flat Quebec country disappointed me, and so did the shapeless Quebec houses covered with Johns-Manville shingles in colors that would have been unsalable anywhere else. Drive all this way for *this*? The day was going, too. I would never arrive in time for after-dinner music, much less dinner, much less sherry. It was already dinner time, and I was still a hundred and fifty miles away.

I ate my last sandwich, drank my last coffee, contemplated starting another novel and couldn't get interested. Instead, I recited all the poems I knew, from "Lycidas" to "The Shooting of Dan McGrew," doing my best to recall them without error from beginning to end. By the time I ran dry I was at Rouse's Point, at the upper end of Lake Champlain. The last miles to the customs station I was counting backward from one hundred by sevens, trying to persuade myself that my brains still worked.

At Rouse's Point they ransacked the car—trunk, back seat, front seat, under the seats. Either they were waiting for someone, or I looked like jail bait. They quizzed me about my identity and the reasons for my quick errand into Canada. They scrutinized such documents as I could produce. Finally, after killing nearly thirty minutes that I valued at a hundred dollars a minute, they let me go on.

Furious, I careened on down through St. Albans. It was already dusk, but I could see that the country had changed. The minute I left Quebec, the flats had given way to hills, lakes, mountains, heavy woods. The Johns-Manville houses had been replaced by clapboarded farmhouses leading through staggered sheds to big barns. In town I saw white gables, green shutters, porticoed doors with fanlights.

All right. My attention picked up. I was cheered. But sleep had me like a crocodile's jaws. Twice, after turning off on a lesser road marked "Morrisville," I awoke with the Ford slewing in the loose gravel of the shoulder. The second time, alarmed, I pulled off and ran up and down in the near-dark for several minutes. But when I got in and drove again I was still sand-blind with sleep. My eyes had sash weights on the lids, the road forked where there were no forks and curved where there were no curves. Headlights glaring in my face shocked me into alertness, but within seconds I was back fighting to stay awake. I pinched myself on the inside of the upper arm, where there seemed to be particularly sensitive nerves. I ground my eyes hard shut and stretched them wide. At once I saw something coming at me, a truck without lights. Slam of brakes, swerve, skid, shuddering stop: all alone on a dark road, nothing visible but roadside woods, black firs and spruces, ghostly birch trees.

Ashamed and scared, but not scared enough to admit I wasn't fit to drive, I went on. I got lost, unable to follow the inadequate signs and unable to read the map by the dim cowl light. At a crossroad, out in front of the headlights, I determined where I was. Glory be, only seven miles to Battell Pond.

In the village, at nearly eleven o'clock, I couldn't tell which of two streets to follow, and had to knock on the door of the only lighted house. A man in his undershirt told me to go straight on one mile. I went on, I found the Ellis mailbox among others on a wagon wheel, I went on another two hundred yards to other mailboxes on a plank. I found an opening in the trees, I turned left. There were three cars in the clearing, one of them the Lang station wagon. I pulled up and let the Ford die and turned off the lights.

Now where? I was in black woods, the sky shut off, the darkness so total I couldn't see my hands. There was a soft sound of wind up above, in the tops of the trees. Turning on the lights again, I discovered railed steps, paved with slates, leading down. Once I turned off the lights I had to grope to where my retinal memory told me the steps were, and then feel my way down them to level ground. A building loomed up on the left, blacker than the blackness around. With one hand on the wall I followed it to a corner, where a weak bloom of light fell from a window across a porch. Inside I could see a big high-ceilinged room, a single lighted floor lamp, shapes of furniture, no people. Listening, I thought I heard voices from around the next corner.

I felt my way up two steps onto the wooden planking of the porch, and past the window to another corner, and from there, my eyes adjusted by now, I saw the three heads in three chairs under the diffused light from inside.

Feet hit wood, somebody stood up. "Who's there?" Sid's voice said. "Larry, is it you, finally? Hello?"

I felt like laughing crazily. I could have rolled on the porch in my frenzy of pleasure. In my best Latin, for my classicist wife, I said the password we had used in Berkeley when she lived in a garage apartment on Arch Street and I used to come around late, unable to study any longer and needing grace.

"Cave," I croaked. *"Cave adsum."* And then for the Langs, who might not understand Latin, "Beware, I am here."

. . .

Insert a blurred, out-of-focus interval. I suppose we talked a while. I imagine that Sally and I sat close together and held hands. I am sure Sid and Charity must have urged hospitality on me—sherry? a sandwich? a piece of cake? a cup of Ovaltine?—and I am sure I was too groggy and happy to think I needed any of those. I had performed my total obligation and achieved my full desire just by getting there. But within minutes I would have begun to fade, and their consideration would have taken over.

"You must be absolutely dead," Charity would have said. "Off to bed, now. We can talk all day tomorrow. We can talk for three weeks."

She would have pressed into our hands two of the flashlights she kept by the front door for use by guests who never remembered that this was *country,* without streetlights. We would have gone stumbling, with our arms around one another, trying to walk double in a single-file path, through fifty yards of black woods to the guest house. We would have gone to bed at once and wrapped each other tightly, intending more than I, at least, could perform. And I would have gone to sleep before I could perform it.

Mumblings. Whispers. Someone was standing by the bed and looking down at me with concern. Whoever it was took my condition more seriously than I did, and I wanted to say something humorous and reassuring, but my tongue was sluggish, and couldn't find the words.

I opened my eyes and looked toward light and saw Sally, in her robe, standing in the open door talking in low tones to someone—the nurse girl, I decided. Sally was furred with morning. The light penetrated her thin robe and showed her legs. She passed Lang in her basket out the door, the whisper of her voice stopped, the girl's footsteps went along the porch and down three hard steps into soundless earth. Then Sally turned and found me watching.

"Ah! You're awake!"

"I hope so. What time is it?"

"Only eight-thirty. I thought you'd sleep longer. Don't you want to?"

"No. Come here."

She came, smiling, soft-slipper-footed on the bare wooden floor.

"Climb in."

A moment's hesitation, a glance at the windows, and then she opened and shed her robe. I watched the nightgown lift over her head to reveal her; young, soft, brown, restored from what childbearing had done to her. In a moment I had her locked against me, my face between her breasts, and I was saying into the warmth of her skin, "You're real. Oh, goddamn, you're real! Let's not do that ever again. Two months are too long. Two *days* are too long!"

Thus to awaken in Paradise. We hadn't earned it, we didn't deserve it, we didn't belong there, it wouldn't last. But how wonderful to have even a taste. I felt like the grubby child in Katherine Mansfield's story when she got a glimpse of the rich girl's dollhouse before being hustled away. *I seen the little lamp.*

All days should begin as that one did. All life should be like the three weeks that followed.

12

$\mathcal{S}$ally is right about my liking ruts. In graduate school, with more to be done than there were hours to do it in, with obligations and deadlines to meet, with classes to take or teach, papers to write or read, exams to prepare and proctor, meetings to attend, books to locate, charge out, and read—with all that haunted routine of preparation and testing, I used to dream, perhaps beguiled by the examples of Sir Walter Raleigh and Jawaharlal Nehru, of the pleasures of solitary confinement. It seemed to me that nothing could do so much for a man as a good long jail sentence.

To have all of one's physical needs taken care of by specially appointed assistants; to be marched to and from meals with neither choice nor cooking, payment nor dishwashing, on one's mind; to be sent at stipulated times to the yard for exercise; to have whole mornings, afternoons, evenings, of freedom from interruption, with only the passing and repassing of a guard's steps in the corridor to assure and emphasize it; to hear the clang of opening and closing doors down the cellblock and know that one needn't be concerned, one still had months to serve—who could not write the history of the world under such circumstances? Who could not, in a well-insulated but austerely padded cell, think all the high thoughts, read all the great books, perhaps even write one or two?

If I had known it, I *was* in jail then, my own jail, and only when Sally joined me and made my confinement unsolitary did I become aware of how completely I had shut myself in. Little by little she coaxed me out, but I came cautiously, not to expose my flanks, and my vision of the ideal isolation never changed.

Now this Vermont lake. Thanks to Charity, its routines were as fixed as those of Alcatraz, but it was a long way from being a maximum-security prison. It organized time, including free time. Like her mother, Charity could not bear randomness or lack of purpose. If your purpose was work, then arrange to do it. If it was play, set aside the time. Don't, as I heard her tell Barney once during his moody adolescence, don't just sit and *gawp*.

I found the days as Sally had described them. We did our hours of constructive work, all of us, from eight to eleven-thirty: Sid in his study, Sally and Charity with their babies and house plans and shopping and village volunteerism, I in the moving shade of the treetops on the guest-house porch, the cook in her kitchen, the nurse girl in the nursery, and God, presumably, in His Heaven.

At eleven-thirty, when the locomotive bell on the porch of the Big House clanged, we gathered for swimming, sunning, and conversation on the dock or the elephant rocks. Suddenly (Charity's planning again) we were not individuals or couples, but families, or one big family—naked babies being dipped, shrieking; Barney stretching out in knee-deep water and crying at us to watch him swim, with one foot on the bottom; Nicky sitting in the shallows and splashing; Sally, Charity, and the nurse girl wading around, helping. Sid and I spent several of those swimming periods clearing the bottom of stones and building a breakwater of them to catch sand and create more beach for the children. That was only his noon-hour project. He had dozens of others for other hours when he was released from scholarship.

After lunch we retired from one another, the children were put down, we either napped or read. I had never taken an afternoon nap in my life, but I took a few there, inadvertently falling asleep over a book. About three the place came alive again, I heard chopping or pounding or sawing and went out to find Sid repairing the dock or clearing paths or replacing a rotted porch rail or working on the woodpile.

At five-thirty another swim, at six-thirty sherry on the porch, at seven dinner, usually with one or another of the Distinctions who walked the roads of that village as unassuming as sparrows.

No bread-and-butter family atmosphere here. The children were all fed in the kitchen and were spirited upstairs before we came in from the porch. No greasy goodnight kisses, no clinging and whining to stay up. The bell rang and they were gone. I suppose Charity checked on them before she went to bed, but they were never allowed to interrupt dinner, which was social and intellectual and adults-only.

The talk was always intense, full of argument and laughter. Charity's heightened voice was always egging it on. Sid, presiding in his faded work clothes (he spent as much at Sears, Roebuck trying to look like a farmer as some people spend at Brooks Brothers) would start some intellectual hare and chase it through one or two fields and then subside when Charity cried, "Wait. Wait! Let's hear what *Larry* thinks." Or Lyle. Or Uncle Richard. Or Daddy. Or some rosy-cheeked Nobel laureate in medicine or chemistry. Or the headmaster of some academy that I had always associated with the fortunate salt of the earth.

It seemed we all outranked our host. Though he loved discussion and in other circumstances would pursue an argument for hours, at table he had the modest function of the rabbit who sets a fast pace for the first quarter or half so that others may run their four-minute miles. We ran a lot of them, we ran them every evening.

A happy, orderly, lively corner of Eden, as hushed as a hospital at quiet times, jumping with activity as soon as the social bell sounded. The evening usually ended, after the guests had gone, with a walk up and down the road, or a midnight canoe ride on the black lake under a big starry dome of sky, or a late swim as invigorating as shock treatment.

In those late hours when we were most a foursome, it was Charity who was quiet and Sid who expanded. He loved to exercise his muscles, he loved the night sky and the intimacy of night stillness. We sang a good deal, walking or canoeing, because singing was what we had most to say. Charity did not pitch those songs as she did in company. She let Sally do it, deferring to Sally's musical taste and knowledge. It evened things, somehow, that Charity had no gift that way. It let Sally give something in exchange for all we took.

When we had walked a couple of miles, or found the dock and hauled the canoe out and turned it over, we said goodnight and separated, probing the woods with our flashlights in different directions to our separate cottages. Two Adams and two Eves, an improvement on God's plan, and one I recommend to Him next time He makes a world.

He would also do well to surround His doubled first family with a web of relatives. Neither Sally nor I had any experience with families. Neither of us had grandparents, parents, sisters, or brothers. If we had cousins, they were strangers, mine scattered through the West and Midwest, hers in Greece.

Here, relatives swarmed like termites. The first time we went along on a Folsom Hill picnic, I thought Charity must have invited half the village. But no, they were all Langs and Ellises, mostly Ellises. They perched on logs and stones, sprawled on blankets, hid and raced with the kids playing Prisoner's Base or Kick the Can. What confidence they had! How fully they belonged! Roles developed without prompting. Charity, Comfort, and Sally (by now an honorary Ellis) presided over the picnic hampers; Sid over the barbecue; Lyle and I over the firewood; Aunt Emily, Aunt Heather, and the hired girls over the smaller children; Uncle Dwight over the sherry; and George Barnwell over the children's game, blinking nearsightedly in the wrong directions, cheerfully faking an incompetence double his natural gift, while grandchildren and second cousins twice-removed stole home on him, and the hilltop wind blew his wispy white hair on end.

Indispensable to those picnics was the Marmon, vintage 1931, once Sid's father's car, that Charity had rescued from sale and put to humble family use when Sid's mother bought something less grand. It was a touring car, with a top that now was permanently furled, and it had plate-glass wind wings, a plate-glass partition to separate the driver from the quality, seats that would hold ten or twelve in a pinch, and running boards that would take six more. Its snout was long and sleek, and it had extended bumpers that would accommodate still more, and an engine that from the look of the hood must have been twelve in line. That was a triumphal chariot. When fully loaded you couldn't see it for bodies, and once at the picnic site it proved itself bottomless, disgorging hampers, boxes, bags, blankets, grills, and a dozen flashlights.

When the games were over, there was eating—steaks, naturally. When the eating was over, there was singing around the fire. Light hung a long time in the sky, but the dusk edged upward and eventually crowded us all into a ring. The marshmallows ran out, the smaller children huddled in blankets or snuggled in against their parents' knees, the fire shone red in a ring of eyes. Everybody sang, whether he could sing or not—Charity saw to that. But there were solos too. "Sid, do 'Barbara Allen.' " "No, you know, the one about 'Go, little boat, like a bird on the wing, over the sea to Skye.' " "No, 'Lord Randall.' "

He had a fine, true, plaintive voice, exactly right for sad ballads, and he knew a lot of them. Their lugubrious tragedies ticked themselves out, a notch at a time, like the wooden wheels of a Seth Thomas clock. Between songs figures rose and threw wood on the fire and blotted part of the ring with their shadows, and set off showers of sparks. Sally was made to sing—she was an instant success. Even I had to sing, something hoarse and western to impress these New Englanders with the roughness of a man with the bark on: "Blood on the

Saddle," maybe, or "Strawberry Roan," or "I Shall Be an Old Bum, Loved but Unrespected."

That tribe whose size and energy amazed us, amazed us equally with their courtesy. Happily, eagerly, they expanded their circle and let us in. Professors, diplomats, editors, bureaucrats, brokers, missionaries, biologists, students, they had been most places in the world and loved no place as they loved Battell Pond. Their loyalties were neither national nor regional nor political nor religious, but tribal.

Over all that tribe, Aunt Emily was matriarch. Daughters and sons never left, sons-in-law and daughters-in-law were absorbed and naturalized and weaned away from whatever loyalties they had once had. Children were incorporated as they arrived, widows held full membership for life. Sally and I too, as if we had married into the clan.

We put Wisconsin and its failure behind us, we forgot to worry about the future. When they asked us what we did, we said that I was working on my next book. My next book. What an ego-inflating phrase. It made the future sound not uncertain and scary, but possible, and even, after a slight necessary delay, assured.

I have difficulty in recognizing those hopeful innocents as ourselves. What justification did Sally have for her faith in me? What justification did I have for faith in myself? Why did all those Ellises and Langs, down to the remotest cousin, take us at our declared value—or more accurately, at the value that Sid and Charity declared for us?

I suppose I know. To them we were no very special phenomenon—a young couple on their way up, just starting out. That family expected young people to be reasonably attractive socially, and gifted in some way. They had bred so many kinds of competence and so many examples of distinction that mediocrity would have surprised them more than accomplishment did. And they rather liked the fact that like Lyle Lister we came from nowhere. We corroborated some transcendental faith of theirs that the oversoul roof leaked on all alike.

Perhaps also, in some small way, I was Cinderella to them, as I was to myself. No matter how cold the ashes or grubby the household chores, I lived by the faith that when the time came, the glass slipper would fit my little foot, and that when I needed her the Fairy Godmother would pull up in her pumpkin coach.

She didn't even need to pull up. She lived there. In the line of succession to be chief matriarch, already accustomed to manage everybody's affairs whether asked or not, Charity dealt with our future both imaginatively and practically, along with all the other items on her daily agenda, while sitting in bed with her notebook doing her constructive daydreaming.

Her method exploited what Sally and I, in our nonentity and unawareness, had until then known nothing about: connections. Specifically, Uncle Richard, when he came up from Boston for the weekend and was ordered over to dinner along with Aunt Emily and George Barnwell.

He had been primed to ask about my book, and courteously did so. He wondered if I had a copy of the manuscript that he could read. I said I would be honored, but Harcourt Brace was publishing it, and I didn't suppose he'd want to spend his time for nothing. His eyebrows went up. Nothing? He *liked* reading good books, he had so many opportunities to read bad ones, and Charity had assured him that mine was a good one. Did I have a copy? I did. I also had the galleys, which had come the day before. Fine. Could he borrow them for a day before I sent them back?

Very flattering. He had Airedale eyebrows and a long, disciplined face like a horse on parade, and when he looked straight at you, which was most of the time, he turned out to have Aunt Emily's gimlety brown eyes. He said he understood that I was into a second novel. How did that go? I told him: slow and hard. Good, he said. Hard writing makes easy reading.

The cook came to the windows that looked onto the porch and said to Charity that dinner was ready. Charity rose and shooed us all in. "There's a spinach soufflé and it *won't wait.*"

Even the seating at table was conspiratorial, as Sally pointed out to me later—she next to Uncle Richard, to soften him up, and I across from him, on Charity's right, in the best position for talking to him. As I might have expected if I had been as sharp as writers are supposed to be, Sid started an intellectual hare calculated to get Uncle Richard running. He challenged Uncle Richard to justify a big best seller, a drugstore-lending-library romance, that he had just published.

"Didn't you betray us?" Sid said. "Just for a handful of silver, didn't you let down all those readers who expect Phoenix Books to publish only books of quality? Because of my faith in you, I bought the thing. It's a cream puff."

Uncle Richard dropped his long head and looked at Sid through the tops of his bifocals. "You too?"

"There must have been better things to choose. There are hundreds of good books written every year that never get published at all."

"Show me where they are and I'll make your fortune," Uncle Richard said.

"There have to be books better than this one. Couldn't you have left this one to some shoddy popular publisher? Seeing it on your list is like finding a *True Confessions* story in the *Atlantic*."

Uncle Richard, knife and fork in hand English-fashion, considered. He suggested that publishing was not a charitable enterprise. He named six titles on his fall list that he would be unable to publish if he weren't able to count on the sales of this one that Sid thought shouldn't have been published at all.

Being an academic table, we began deploring the level of popular taste. Only junk seemed to sell. Wasn't there any market for good, serious, intelligent, well-written books? There must be. Couldn't you count on a good book's finding an audience—small, maybe, but enough to carry it?

"Sometimes," Uncle Richard said.

"How many copies would a book like that be likely to sell?"

Uncle Richard made a balancing, delicate, *cosí-cosí* gesture with his hand.

"How many would it have to sell before its publisher broke even?"

"Depends on size and price. An ordinary novel, around thirty-five hundred."

"And you say it would have trouble doing even *that* well?"

"One out of two dozen will do that well."

Groans, the company's outward, mine inward. So much for the furtive Morgan dream that his little unheralded novel would impress tens of thousands with its irony and pity and feel for the tears of things, and deliver the Morgans by pumpkin coach to their new home on Easy Street.

Everybody at the table except perhaps George Barnwell and I understood what was going on, and nobody except the two of us was likely to have been surprised when Charity, as we rose to take coffee before the fire, proposed a *treat*. Instead of music, would Larry read a chapter of his novel? Oh, please!

Far from unwilling, I took a flashlight and went over to the guest house for the galleys. When I returned, Sid had set a lamp behind a big chair, and they were all sitting around in the glow of the fireplace, the fire shining through the amber eyes of the owl-shaped andirons, ready to listen to some *real* literature, the kind that ought to make Book of the Month and the best seller lists but would probably never lead to anything more significant than the Nobel Prize.

Afterward, when everybody had exercised his option to be enthusiastic, I found myself, just as Charity had planned it, talking solo to Uncle Richard.

Not for the last time in his life, he was extraordinarily kind. He told me that Sid and Charity were not mistaken, I had something special, I had a future if I would work for it. He wanted to know if I had given up teaching, and when I told him I was looking for a position but had had no luck yet, he advised me bluntly to stop looking. Teaching, carried on too long, could turn a good writer into a twenty-five-watt Henry James.

He thought I should settle in somewhere and finish the second novel, which he would like a chance at if Harcourt Brace didn't have me tied up with an option, or if they should turn it down. Some publishers published books, he tried to publish authors. I might find it advantageous to be with a house that was willing to carry me for two or three books. Flash-in-the-pan writers sometimes made it big with their first one, but often faded. Real writers were more likely to make it with their fourth or fifth or even sixth. Did I have any way of supporting myself? No, not unless writing would do it. I had had some luck with magazines, but not enough to live on.

Had I considered working in a publishing house? (I sure had—why else was I perched next to him like a house finch at a bird feeder?) Publishing had its disadvantages for a writer, as teaching did, and I was overqualified—you didn't need a Ph.D. to be a publisher, or to tell a good book from a bad one; in fact, many Ph.D.'s couldn't—but he thought I had the kind of instinctive perception, and liking for books, that I would need. And the pay was better in publishing, and there was no tenure to squabble and scrabble for. He himself had no openings at the moment, but things could pick up, and there was always some movement of people. I should let him know where I would be. If by chance I came through Boston, I should call him, and he would introduce me to people who might be of service to me. Or he would give me letters if I went to New York.

Which is to say, he took me under his wing, he treated me as he would have treated an ambitious and reasonably promising member of the Ellis clan. Having absolutely no other alternatives, except the vague one of going to New York, huddling in a cold-water Village walkup, and living on love and beans while I wrote my way to fortune, Sally and I decided that night that Boston, not New York, was our choice and that Uncle Richard was our hope. Only when Sally explained the evening to me did I begin to realize what Charity had done for us. Until then, I thought things had just happened.

We added up the money I had made from stories and reviews in the past year. We estimated what it would take to get by in Boston, or more likely Cambridge, where there must be cheap student housing and where the presence of Aunt Emily would be a comfort. We speculated on how realistic it was to hope to live by writing, without a backlog paycheck. We hoped Uncle Richard might occasionally give us manuscripts to read, as he had hinted he might, and that by that door I might ease into some editorial slot. We figured out what a $2.50 novel would earn, at ten percent royalty, if it sold thirty-five hundred copies, and found that if mine did that well we would have an extra three hundred and seventy-five dollars beyond the advance. We hoped the textbook, which was also in press, might get some adoptions and make us a little, though first it would have to earn back about a thousand dollars in reprint permission fees advanced by the publisher.

Somehow we would make it. As soon as the Langs started back to Wisconsin, and Battell Pond folded up for the winter, we would point the Ford toward Boston, carrying our by-now-exuberantly-healthy daughter, my portable typewriter and Sally's portable phonograph, and our bank book showing four hundred and ninety dollars savings at four percent.

Meantime there were these friends, this open-armed family, this summer weather, these peaceful mornings on the guest-house porch where, with my typewriter on a card table, and the thrushes and whitethroats singing up the last act of the summer's intense family life, I could sit among the treetops and look down through the hemlocks to the glitter of the lake and feel my mind as sharp as a knife, capable of anything, including greatness.

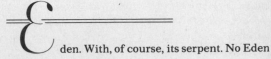

13

den. With, of course, its serpent. No Eden valid without serpent.

It was not a big serpent, nor very alarming. But once we noticed it, we realized that it had been there all along, that what we had thought only the wind in the grass, or the scraping of a dry leaf, was this thing sliding discreetly out of sight. Even when we recognized it for what it was, it did not seem dangerous. It just made us look before we sat down.

Human lives seldom conform to the conventions of fiction. Chekhov says that it is in the beginnings and endings of stories that we are most tempted to lie. I know what he means, and I agree. But we are sometimes tempted to lie elsewhere, too. I could probably be tempted to lie just here. This is a crucial place for the dropping of hints and the planting of clues, the crucial moment for hiding behind the piano or in the bookcase the revelations that later, to the reader's gratified satisfaction, I will triumphantly discover. If I am after drama.

Drama demands the reversal of expectation, but in such a way that the first surprise is followed by an immediate recognition of inevitability. And inevitability takes careful pin-setting. Since this story is about a friendship, drama expects friendship to be overturned. Something, the novelist in me whispers, is going to break up our cozy foursome. Given the usual direction of contemporary fiction and the usual contemporary notions of human character and conduct, what more plausible than that Sid Lang, a rampant male married to a somewhat unmalleable wife, should be tempted by Sally's softer nature. I have already dropped a hint of that by recalling my uneasiness about their skinny-dipping.

The possibilities are diverse, for friendship is an ambiguous relationship. I might be attracted to Charity. She is an impressive woman—though I can't quite imagine myself smitten by her, or her by me. There are other possibilities, too: Sid with me, Charity with Sally. We could get very Bloomsbury in our foursome. Anything to get this equilibrium of two-and-two overturned.

Well, too bad for drama. Nothing of the sort is going to happen. Something less orthodoxly dramatic is. Nevertheless there is this snake, no bigger than a twig or a flame of movement in the grass. It is not an intruder in Eden, it was born here. It is one of Hawthorne's bosom serpents, rarely noticed because in the bosom it inhabits it can so easily camouflage itself among a crowd of the warmest and most generous sentiments.

From the first days of our friendship with the Langs we had been aware of it, but pretended it wasn't there. Comfort, one night in a canoe, told us about an episode in Greece, when her junior year abroad had intersected briefly with their honeymoon; but instead of being alarmed or dismayed, we had chosen to be amused at something so outrageously characteristic. But on the walking trip that we took as the grand finale to that summer, a trip that both Charity and Sid—especially Sid—had been planning for weeks, we had a revelation or two that we couldn't ignore or simply be amused by.

The morning after I arrived, I found Sid's shop already piled with the gear he was assembling and mending and adapting. We would take a packhorse to carry most of it. We would be out a week. We would walk a hundred-mile circuit by the remotest back roads Sid could find on the map. We would sleep beside mountain brooks, or on the shores of little, still lakes buried in the woods, and if the weather was bad, in the lofts of friendly barns. It would be a last burst of freedom before we had to divide and go our separate ways, Sid and Charity back into the teaching suit and the departmental politics and the house-building in Madison, we to Boston or wherever the path of least resistance led.

We did walk some overgrown back roads, leading a horse named Wizard. There were days of rain, days of sun, nights of stars and storms. We met gnarled old couples on back farms, men with weathered faces and veiny rough hands, women with washed-out blue eyes and a passion for talk. We ran into French Canadians fresh down from Quebec who stopped their plows—one of them was plowing with oxen—and drowned us in a rush of *joual* that none of us could understand, not even Charity, who had spent three years in French and Swiss schools.

We ate our lunches in the yards of abandoned schoolhouses, and among the rank roses and heliotrope and goldenglow of abandoned cemeteries, and under the dooryard maples of windowless farmhouses. Sleeping in meadows, we were awakened by the snuffling of grazing cows. Sleeping in a hayloft, we were bombed by swallows disturbed by our flashlights.

Everything was as green as a salad, but with hints of fall—occasional maples burning, ferns blackened by a hard frost. We were reddened by sun and stung by yellowjackets, we ate dehydrated soup and peanut-butter sandwiches and raisins and chocolate, and once, after we passed through a village, a tough steak, and once, after we passed a farm, some tough and memorable chickens.

That trip was indeed what Sid planned it to be, the crown and climax of summer. We came to the sixth day of it rejuvenated, swearing that next year we would walk the international border from Beecher Falls to Lake Memphremagog, or do a backpack trip, without benefit of Wizard, on the Long Trail from Middlebury Gap to Jay Peak.

I remember, it seems, every detail of it until the end, when it falls apart in the memory as it fell apart in fact. The end I will have to get to, but everything that led up to it tempts me more.

It didn't begin promisingly. It began, actually, with a clash of temperament and will, a flare-up over trivialities, like a wink through the shutters showing fire inside the house.

Morning light, without gleam or glare. The rented horse stands patiently in his aristocratic bones, a superannuated Irish hunter seventeen hands high, fallen from the days when he used to jump hedges and ditches with a pink coat aboard him. The bare wooden sawbuck of the packsaddle demeans his bony elegance and emphasizes his patience.

On the ground, spread out on a tarp, is what we intend to put on him—sleeping bags, pup tents, canvas bucket, axe, coils of rope, a half sack of oats, and two big pack hampers crammed with food, utensils, sweaters, slickers, and extra socks. Sid tightens and tests the cinch. Vicky, with the two infants in their shared buggy, and Barney and Nicky held back by the hand from tearing onto the tarp and disturbing its careful order, stands back with Charity and Sally. The babies are only recently weaned, and their mothers are nervous about leaving them. Aunt Emily circles, getting us into a snapshot.

Sid grabs a hamper, I grab the other, and we heave them up and hang them over the forks of the saddle. But Charity, who has been giving Vicky last-minute instructions written out on two sheets of paper, looks up just then and cries out, "Wait. *Wait!* We have to check the list."

With his hand on Wizard's neck, Sid says in his light, musical voice, "Larry and I checked it when we packed, last night."

"Ah, but Pritchard says *always* doublecheck."

Incredulous, he stares. "You mean take everything out and repack it?"

"I don't know how else we can be sure."

"Then why did we pack it all last night?"

"I'm sure I don't know. You should have known we'd have to check."

He starts to answer, but says nothing. But old Larry, frisky and full of morning, and believing that she can't be serious, puts in his nickel's worth. "Sitting Bull no check-um on Little Big Horn. Have-um good chiefs, trust-um catch Custer."

Charity has a way of smiling more strenuously when challenged. Her color comes up, she is good-naturedly scornful. "Look who's talking! The man who only last night, with approval, was quoting Artemus Ward: 'Trust everybody, but *cut the cards.*' Well, I took you seriously. Let's *cut* the cards. Anybody can make a mistake. What if we got out fifteen miles from anywhere and found out you'd forgotten the matches?"

"Rub-um sticks together."

She is impatiently patient with my nonsense. Sid says, "We haven't forgotten the matches. There's a whole waterproof jar of them in there."

Smiling, she looks at him. "Just the same."

Incredibly, it has become a confrontation. You can feel the stubbornness in the air. It will show up in the snapshot that Aunt Emily is taking from the corner of the garage. The peripheral image I have of her over there, bending over her box Brownie unwittingly recording tension, brings to my mind another scene, also involving a camera— the scene Comfort was telling us about the other night, reporting with amusement and sisterly malice a morning in the little inn called La Belle Helene, near Agamemnon's tomb in Mycenae.

The sisters sit at the breakfast table ready for a day in Agamemnon's city and beehive tomb. Charity has on the chair beside her the product of her constructive daydreaming: camera, binoculars, guidebook, notebook, *Greek for Travelers,* a knitted woolen Cretan bag containing Kleenex, aspirin, antacid tablets, sunglasses (the November light across the Argive plain is diamond-bright), flashlight (the tomb may be dark). The honeymoon journey is two months old. Comfort joined it two days ago, in Náuplion. The three of them are the only guests at La Belle Helene. The table is littered with the crumbs of their breakfast rolls, their coffee cups contain the sludge of their coffee. In the doorway the proprietress lurks, listening with Greek xenophilia to their conversation.

Eventually Charity looks at her watch. "What on earth can be *keeping* him? We don't want to lose the whole morning."

"Didn't you say his hay fever is bothering him?"

"He likes to make the most of that. Maybe I'd better . . ."

At that moment he appears. He has his handkerchief in his hand, and he sneezes three times crossing the dining room. His eyes are red, and he sniffles. Charity bursts out laughing.

He looks annoyed. "What's so fuddy?"

"You are. You look so *lugubrious.*"

"I *feel* lugubrious."

"Well, you can't," Charity says. "You'll just have to brace up, because we've got to see *everything* here today if we're going to Pylos tomorrow."

He continues to sniffle and wipe his eyes. The proprietress comes and pours coffee and goes away again, heavy in black dress and slippers. Comfort says sympathetically, "You sound terribly stuffed. What could be blooming, this time of year?"

He shrugs. "I do' doe. Idsect spray, baybe. Roach powder? The place is crawlig with roaches."

"You'll just have to get on top of it," Charity says. "Have some coffee. Eat something, you'll feel better. Oh, come *on!* Don't be such a baby! Here, I'll take your picture and you can carry it around to remind you how not to look on your honeymoon."

She picks up the camera and points it at him. He frowns, shaking his head, and turns his face into his handkerchief to sneeze again. When his face comes up, the camera is still aimed at him. "Don't!" he says sharply.

And there it is. Confrontation. Challenge and response. "Why, of course I will if I want to," she says.

His voice rises. "I'm asking you, don't snap that thing."

She puts her eye to the finder, aims, and clicks the shutter. Furiously he stands up. For a moment he seems to grope for words. Then he goes out, back toward the room.

Comfort says nothing. Charity, though she smiles, is a little tight around the mouth, and her cheekbones are pink. "He'll be back," she says. "Anyway, I didn't take it. There's no film in the camera. But I couldn't let him get away with that, telling me what I can and can't do. Could I?"

The moral, Comfort says, is not to accept an invitation to any honeymoon except your own. But the instant, fighting assertion of will that Charity has demonstrated is something Comfort knows from way back. It is what she grew up with as Charity's younger sister. It is what caused so many clashes between Charity and Aunt Emily. It is what shows now while Wizard waits patiently to be loaded.

For a second or two Sid stands looking at the ground, his eyes veiled. Then he unhooks the hamper from his side of the saddle. I do the same. We spill the painstakingly packed contents onto the tarp. Expressionless, Sid turns his hamper upside down to show that it is empty—a little angry showmanship there. Charity gets out her stenographic notebook and a pencil. Sally discreetly gives her attention to the babies side by side in their buggy.

For the next half hour I hand things to Sid one at a time and he repacks them while Charity checks them off. Aunt Emily says her good-byes and leaves—time to get George Barnwell fed and off to his think house. Finally the tarp is clear except for tents, sleeping bags, axe, oats, and ropes. Consulting her pad, Charity asks, "Where's the tea?"

An extraordinary expression passes over Sid's face—defeat? outrage? resignation? the *wish* for resignation?—and he says, "In here. You just checked it off."

"No, I didn't." Then, when he starts to speak, "I'm sorry, Sid, I *didn't.*"

"I called it out."

"You can't have."

I expect him to call on me to back him, and there is nothing I would so happily avoid. But he says nothing. Stalemate. At last he says, almost surlily, "What if it isn't there? Let's get started. Do we need tea? We've got coffee."

"Tea is lighter to carry," Charity says, as if reciting a lesson. "You can take enough tea for *months* and only add ounces to your load.

Pritchard says the Hudson Bay York boats *never* carried coffee, only tea. They stopped to boil the pot every noon. Tea kept them going."

This extraordinary speech we all greet with silence. The silence lengthens while Sid stares at her. Finally he says, "Are we going in a York boat? Are we going for months? Will it help the weight problem to carry tea if we're taking coffee too? Anyway the tea's in there, I know it is."

"Then why don't I have it checked off?"

The answer to that is unthinkable. Standing on the sidelines, I have the impression that somebody should laugh. Me? No. Charity has to know how preposterous she is being, but having said what she has said and taken the stand she has taken, she is planted, she will not budge. Somebody else can budge, and if Sid does, we'll be unpacking and repacking those hampers all over again.

Then Sally saves the day, saying quietly, "I'll just go get some." She starts toward the Big House. In the gray morning we stand around pretending nothing is the matter, there is only this trifling delay.

Very soon Sally is back with a box of tea bags. I cram it inside the top edge of my hamper, and we hook the hampers back over the saddle. Then the pup tents, sleeping bags, ground cloths, oats, axe, bucket. Then the covering tarp. Looking impenetrable, Sid throws a tense diamond hitch over the load. He has been practicing in his study when Charity thought she had him pinned down to scholarship.

"Are we finally ready?" he asks. "If we are, for God's sake let's go."

"You go on," Charity says. "We'll catch up. We have to give the babies a hug that will last a whole week."

"Couldn't you have been doing that while we repacked?"

She chooses not to notice his surliness. Having won whatever it was she thought she had to win, she indulges what probably strikes her as his childish resentment, she sends him off with little business-like pats. "Wait for us at the Hazen Road," she says, and then she notices the canes hanging from the limb of a maple. Sid and I hung them there an hour ago hoping to forget them. But Charity, smiling her most brilliant smile, unhooks them and hands them to me. "Don't go off without your *protection*."

The canes are bent willow things with spikes in their ends and *Lauterbrünnen* carved on their shafts. Charity must have bought a gross of them in Switzerland on their wedding trip, for the Madison house has a half dozen in its hall closet and every cottage in the compound has several. On this trip they have been declared compulsory. Pritchard, whose book on the outdoors Charity has been reading in preparation for the trip, recommends walking sticks, blackthorns, alpenstocks, or some other support for rough terrain and as a protection against hostile dogs.

Other suggestions of Pritchard's include instructions on how to make a wooden leg out of a forked branch if you sprain your ankle or break a leg in the woods. Also instructions for what to do if you must set your broken leg before hobbling out on your forked stick. The thing you do is find a tree with a crotch a few feet above the ground, wedge the heel of your broken leg in this crotch, and throw yourself backward. This is like the old method of pulling a tooth by tying one end of a string to the tooth and the other end to a doorknob, and slamming the door. Sid and I had a good deal of fun with Pritchard while we packed last night. But here we are with our canes.

We walk two or three hundred yards before either of us speaks. Finally I say, "Sorry about the tea. I just must have mislaid it. I know we had it last night."

"We had it this morning. But Charity goes by the book. And what a book!"

A western buckaroo, I share his scorn for people who go camping by the book, relying on the authority of some half-assed assistant scoutmaster whose total experience outdoors probably consists of two overnight hikes and a weekend in the Catskills. But we have just had that confrontation. The one who goes by Pritchard's book is Sid's wife, and I am wary. It is not my expedition. I am a guest here.

Still, I can't help saying, "I have to admit I was hoping she was wrong."

He gives me a strange look past Wizard's ewe neck and bobbing head. "She's never wrong," he says.

At the four corners we turn up a dusty secondary road. Dust has whitened the ferns along the roadside, gypsy moths have built their tents in the chokecherry bushes, the meadow on the left is yellow with goldenrod, ice-blue with asters, stalky with mullein, rough with young spruce. Everything taller than the grass is snagged with the white fluff of milkweed. On the other side is a level hayfield, green from a second cutting. The woods at the far edge rise in a solid wall. In the yard of an empty farmhouse we sample apples off a gnarled tree. Worms in every one. But Wizard finds them refreshing, and blubbers cider as he walks.

We come up a long hill onto high ground just as the sun edges out of the clouds and touches a green whaleback ridge ahead. Beyond that, more hills, and beyond those the main range, gray-violet with haze. Almost as if making sure he is free from supervision, Sid sneaks a look back down the road we have come. I look too. Charity and Sally have just come into view at the corners, tiny at the end of the white road.

We turn back to the view ahead. "Too bad we couldn't have waited to do this till October," Sid says. "Some year we're going to stay on through the color if I have to resign from Wisconsin to do it. In October those hills must be something."

Slouching in his faded khaki, a lunch pack on his back and a machete at his belt, one hand holding Wizard's lead rope and the other stabbing the cane's spike into the gravel, he intones to the horizon:

"There is something in the autumn that is native to my blood,
Touch of manner, hint of mood . . ."

How does it go? You don't know it?

"And my lonely spirit thrills
To see the frosty asters like smoke upon the hills?"

Kind of a nice poem, one of those *Vagabondia* ones of Bliss Carman's. Proper for the country and the occasion.

He squints, remembering lines.

"There is something in October sets the gipsy blood astir.
We must rise and follow her
Where from every hill aflame
She calls and calls each vagabond by name."

As I dream of a jail sentence, he dreams of vagabondage and irresponsibility, which would probably drive him crazy as fast as jail would drive me. But it is a fine morning for fantasy, and I say, "Why don't we just keep on going?"

"Ha, wouldn't I like to!"

"I've got forty dollars. The grub box is full. We could eat Wizard if we ran short. You could give poetry readings in the villages and I could write travel articles. We'd be like those traveling colonial painters who used to paint the children for a weekend's room and board.

And Charity's got Pritchard in her pack to tell us how to survive in the wilderness."

Mistake. He makes a sour face. Vagabondage has become bondage again.

We move to the side of the road to let an approaching pickup go by. Two heads show over the cab—a couple of kids standing up to stare, and why not? Here are two dudes with canes, leading a horse as high and humped as a camel. To them, we must look like something out of Exodus.

They rattle by, their dust swirls around us. The boys, hanging on to the cab top, are half-turned, still staring. Their teeth flash, they caper and make derisive gestures. I wave at them, but Sid stops, holding his cane as if it were a wet horse-biscuit somebody just handed him. He barks out a one-note laugh.

"Good God! To see ourselves as others see us. A couple of god-damned British gentlemen. All we need is gaiters." He lifts the cane in the air. "Oh, *bugger* Pritchard and his bloody book!" He throws the cane fifty yards into the goldenrod.

Astonished, I keep my peace. Also my cane. As a matter of fact, I rather like the feel of it. But then, nobody is making me carry it.

On a stone wall, with dense smells of growth and mold and an autumnal tartness of vegetable decay in our nostrils, we sit and let Wizard crop the roadside grass. There is a drowsy sound of bumble-bees and flies. Brown crickets hop and crawl around our feet. On our left begins a dim track, more like a bay or opening in the woods than a road, that closes in after a hundred feet or so. A stone wall runs along it, disappearing into chokecherry and popple and mountain ash. Out of the scattered stones of the wall grow trees as thick as my thigh. Down the shaded opening where it deadends against woods in a patch of sun there is a quivering that might be a will-o'-wisp but is more likely a cloud of gnats.

Sid is telling me that during the Revolution, forces under Generals Bayley and Hazen cut a road through this wilderness from Newbury, on the Connecticut, to the flank of Jay Peak, on the Canadian border. The intention was an invasion of Canada that never came off. The result was a track that, like the Wilderness Road across the Cumberland Gap, became a road of settlement once the Revolution was over.

Some parts of the old Bayley-Hazen Road have been obliterated by modern highways, some have been used for generations as farm roads, some have been lost in the woods. Sid thinks this opening here, bordered by stone walls that nineteenth-century farmers built along it to fence fields long since gone back to trees, is one of the lost stretches.

On the map he shows me where the trace was cut up through Peacham, Danville, Walden, Hardwick; how it bent around Battell Pond and over the hill to Craftsbury; how it crossed the Black River Valley and the Lowell Mountains and entered the main range by way of Hazen's Notch.

All this is news to me. For me, roads of settlement have always run east to west, and my private interest in them never took me east of Bent's Fort, Colorado. But this history, and this country romantically returning to wilderness, speaks to Sid like bugles. He could not be more eager if the woods across there hid the sources of the Nile.

While he talks, he keeps looking back down the road to where Charity and Sally are coming. As usual, they pause now and then to ponder weeds, bugs, berries, or ferns. "Come on, come on!" Sid says in a voice like a crow's; and then, looking at me sharply and laughing in an awkward insincere way, "She'd botanize on her mother's grave."

He is still sore from that scene at the loading, his nose is still bloody. But notice: When they are within a few hundred yards he stands up and goes along the wall picking late raspberries and ripe chokecherries, and when they chug up, pink with exercise, exaggeratedly puffing, he goes to them, Charity first, and holds out his handful of berries as if expiating something.

"Why, *thank* you!" she says, extravagantly pleased. "Oh, don't they taste good, and natural? I love their *pucker.*"

In a few minutes we start again, Charity now in front with Sid, Sally and I leading Wizard behind. But as we begin to move, Charity notices a lack. "Where's your cane? Have you left it somewhere? *Already?* Oh, Sid!"

Sally and I walk the trail that the two ahead have made through the wet grass. Our hips bump. I put my arm around her. "Ready to plunge into the pathless woods?"

"Oh, yes! Isn't it great?"

"Now that we're sure we've got our tea."

Her eyes flash up, her lip curls. "Wasn't she preposterous? But she knows it. She's sorry."

"She ought to be."

Sally stops, and Wizard, walking in his sleep, almost runs over us. "Larry, let's not let it spoil things. It'll blow over. It already has."

"She acts like his mother, not his wife. If she'd treat him the way she treats, for instance, you and me, everything would be dandy."

"Friends come first, family comes last. She treats him the way she'd treat herself."

"Oh no no no no no."

"She's the most generous person I ever saw!"

"That's not what I mean. I mean she wouldn't treat herself or anybody else the way she sometimes treats him. She has to be boss. Maybe she tells him when to wash his hands and brush his teeth. I don't suppose she can help it, but she's as blunt as a splitting maul."

She thinks about that, walking again. "I don't think she *can* help it. She grew up in a family where her mother was boss, and she got both the genes and the example. She told me that the only thing her father ever said about her marriage was to advise her against it. 'He's not strong enough for you,' he told her. Poor man, I guess he knew all about it."

"Off to your think house," I say. "Out of my parlor."

We laugh, kicking the wet grass. "Did he tell you about his poems, and the fuss they had yesterday?" Sally says.

"No. What poems?"

"I guess there were several. You know how she's been riding him to finish those Browning articles. Well, he's been writing poetry instead. He sent some to some little review and they took a couple. He was so pleased he couldn't keep it secret, and she blew up. He didn't tell you about that?"

"Not a word."

"She told me just now, while we were walking. I guess she was ashamed about this morning, and wanted to explain. She says she absolutely *knows* Wisconsin won't promote him on the basis of poems, and he absolutely *must* write something scholarly. She says the department only values what it can do itself. But then he sneaks off and wastes his summer, as she thinks, and she got mad. They had a real quarrel, I guess, and she was still mad this morning. That's why she had to prove him wrong about that tea."

I stop in the trail and wrap my arms around Sally and give her a big smack. She laughs. "What's that for?"

"That's for being a sensible woman. That's for not getting sore if I sell something to a magazine. That's for valuing what I do. My God, why shouldn't he take an hour off now and then to do what he most loves to do? You'd think she'd caught him in the pantry with the maid."

"She says after he gets tenure, then he can do what he wants."

"Then she ought to write his Browning articles for him."

"Why? Have you seen them? Has he finished any?"

"He's finished two, and already got one back from *PMLA*. Did she mention that? I suppose he hasn't dared tell her. Right away it came back, right back in his face."

"Oh," Sally says, "that's bad! You mean they aren't any good?"

"Not very. Informed. Uninspired. A-minus term papers."

"Did he ask you to read them? What did you tell him?"

"What *could* I tell him?"

Just talking about it makes me angry at myself, because the fact is, I didn't have the nerve to tell him what I thought. I wish he had told me about the poems. I would have made him feel good about those, instead of guilty.

"What's the matter with them?" Sally asks.

"Nothing in particular. Everything in general. His heart isn't in them. Only her heart is."

"But what will happen to him, then?"

"Yeah," I say. "What will? I suppose they'll either promote him because he's so good with students and such a good guy, or they'll ding him because he hasn't published enough. Or they could promote him to assistant professor, and then bust him when he comes up for tenure. That'd be worse. He won't decide his own fate, anyway, and neither will Charity. Departmental politics and the departmental budget will. My guess is they'll agonize and string it out. They won't find it easy to let him go, because he's rich, and popular, and Rousselot likes him, and Charity is such a force in Madison. But they could."

Walking along with her lower lip thrust out, Sally raises her eyes to watch Sid slashing away with the machete up ahead, where the bushes have almost closed our dubious road. Charity is behind him, out of the way of his swings. "She'd just die," Sally says. "Could you be wrong about his articles? You're not very sympathetic to scholarly writing. Maybe the department will like them better than you do."

"I hope they do. *PMLA* didn't, though. Hell, what do I know? They fired me after one year. But you should see what he's been doing. Browning's use of music. Browning's debt to Vasari. Those aren't what a scholarly journal wants. Those are Charity's notion of what makes an article. Maybe she wrote term papers on those topics at Smith. Why is she so hot for promotion and permanence anyway? Sid might be a lot better off in some small college where publications don't matter and teaching does, some place where he could be Mr. Chips. For that matter, if they want to stay in Madison, they could stay whether he gets promoted or not."

"She'd be ashamed."

"*She'd* be. I doubt that he would, or only if she was. What he'd probably like best of all would be to move up here the year around and write poems and dig in the local history and folklore and jot down in his journal when the Jack-in-the-pulpit and Calypso orchids come out, and how the crows get through the winter."

"His New England conscience would bother him if he'd failed."

"His conscience or her pride?"

We swish through the long wet grass. Sally says, "If it were Charity bucking for promotion, she'd make it."

"You bet she would. But she's crazy if she thinks she can make him make it against his will. When you're nailing a custard pie to the wall, and it starts to wilt, it doesn't do any good to hammer in more nails."

Now I have made her angry. "You can't possibly think he's a custard pie!"

"She'll make him one if she doesn't let up."

When Sally is annoyed, she seldom flares up; she smolders. Well, let her smolder. I have said nothing but the truth, which I would be as happy to see changed as she would. We walk in silence. Up ahead, Sid is slashing again. Charity follows behind like a dutiful subservient wife. Is she doing penance?

I swing my cane. Sally says, with a look out of the corners of her eyes, "You seem to like that walking stick."

"A touch of class."

"So Charity is right sometimes."

"Charity is always right."

Walking with her body twisted sideways, she studies my face. Finally she says, "Neither of you would win any prizes for self-doubt."

I am surprised. How did I get into this discussion? We were talking about the Langs.

"You can't stand to see anybody else with that sublime self-confidence," Sally says. "I suppose it's what makes you both what you are. But it shouldn't make you self-righteous about people who don't have it. Poor Sid doesn't have any at all. He ought to, but he doesn't. Maybe that old Presbyterian banker of a father. Maybe marrying a woman as strong-minded as Charity. Anyway, can't you see how much worse it must be for him. knowing she'll be devastated if he doesn't make it in her terms?"

"I thought that's what I was saying."

"No, you were being superior, you were being scornful of both of them. It's sad, that's what it is. She wants to be proud of him in the sort of disparaging way she's proud of her father or Uncle Richard. But she's getting afraid, and the more afraid she gets, the more she tries to put her will into him."

Wizard stumbles over a root, and a surprised *whoof* comes out of him. The woods whisper and hum, my face prickles with spider webs, light winks off globules of water in a patch of ferns. "Well," I say, "let's not spoil the trip arguing about something we can't do anything about."

"No." Then, after a pause, "Promise me something."

"Maybe. What?"

"Don't challenge her on this trip. On *anything*. I know you both sort of like those arguments, but this isn't a good time. She's afraid the summer's been wasted. So don't get your back up, even if she's outrageous. Just be nice."

"Have I sassed her? I never said a word, even during that scene this morning. I'm as nice as old Sid himself. Yes, ma'am. No, ma'am. Very good, ma'am."

"You watch it," Sally says. "Honestly."

I watched it, naturally. But the day that had started crooked insisted on going crooked, like a cross-threaded screw.

The Hazen Road turned out to be something less than a turnpike. The guiding stone wall vanished in the woods within a half mile. Then we got into a swamp where beavers had dammed a brook and flooded several acres. Drowned trees stood up bleached and bare out of brown water and hummocky grass. The ground we tried to make our way across was more liquid than solid. When we finally decided to make a wide circle around all that, we found ourselves in a blowdown where a wind from Hudson Bay or somewhere had laid down trees the way a scythe lays grass.

Hot, tired, mud-footed, and mosquito-bitten, we fought our way through and around that, and discovered when we came to clear solid ground that we were lost.

Or not really lost. We just weren't quite sure where we were. Our USGS quadrangle map told us that we wanted to come out just where the brook that we had left backed up behind the beaver dam met a country road leading to Irasburg. The brook was north of us, the road west of us. We could either bear right and hit the brook below the beaver dam, and follow it down to the road, or we could take a compass course due west (Pritchard had told Charity to bring a compass) till we struck the road. Sid and I were for working back to the brook, along which fishermen would probably have beaten a path. Charity was for the compass course. Guess which we did.

And guess what it got us into. After floundering a half mile through heavy woods, we came to a blowdown worse than the one we had had to circle earlier. Trees lay crisscrossed, down and half down, their trunks leaning, their root tables on edge above torn pits masked by raspberry vines. It was impossible for poor Wizard. He got into a hole where he might have broken a leg (and how would we have got him to wedge his heel in a forked tree and throw himself backward?), and after we had hauled and pried him out we decided once again to go around. It took us three hours to make what looked on the map like a mile and a half, and it was only by the grace of God that we didn't all come out on wooden legs.

The road, when we finally hit it, was a welcome pair of little-used ruts. Turning right, we came in a short while to a plank bridge across the brook. Sid got the canvas bucket off the load and dipped up a drink for Wizard, who couldn't get down to the water. Charity sat on the bridge and took off boots and socks and stuck her feet down into the brown stream. I raised Don Quixote's battlecry, *Dulcinea del Toboso!*, and Sally, who read my mind, gave me a warning look. So I made no remarks to the brookside about doing things the hard way. It was never Charity's habit to do them the easy way. Most of the time she preferred to set a compass course (adopted sometimes from eccentric authorities) and follow it, whatever it led her into. Once or twice that day I wondered if she hadn't secretly, under an assumed name, *written* Pritchard's book.

Leg-weary, we pursued the remnants of a sultry afternoon down the easy going of the road. We bought a couple of chickens from a farm wife who talked a blue streak while she swiftly beheaded, plucked, and gutted them. From that same woman we bought ten ears of sweet corn. About five o'clock, two more miles down the road, we fell into camp on the little lake that I will always remember as Ticklenaked Pond, though that wasn't its name, that's another pond altogether.

It was sunk in woods, the late sun glared off the water, there was a clearing with decent grass for Wizard and with room for spacing our pup tents. We unloaded Wizard and picketed him out and poured him some oats and fell into the lake, which was shallow and warm. Three of us just floated around on our backs and looked at the blue overhead and sighed with beatitude. Sid, charmed by the camp and as vigorous as a spaniel, swam all the way around a little island that sat offshore in the oval pond like the pupil in a cocked eye.

Revived, we came ashore. I dragged in wood and Sid built a fire and we put water on for the corn. Charity and Sally took a while, sitting on a log and combing their hair like mermaids, leaving Sid and me to unload the hampers and set out plates, knives and forks, bread and butter. While we were still unpacking, the girls went off together into the woods.

Among the things I took out of my hamper was the package of tea Sally had gone to get that morning. Halfway down the hamper I found another of the same.

Sid was feeding the fire. "Look," I said.

Squatting in the smoke, he looked. Then he stood up quickly and came over and took a package in each hand as if comparing their weights. Almost furtively he looked from them to me. "Well," he said, "since we aren't a York boat that will be out for months, we shouldn't need more than one, do you think?" He set one package on the log we were using for a table, and threw the other in the fire. There was a strong herbal smell, but by the time Charity and Sally returned, it was gone.

The fire was ebbing to good hardwood coals, the water was boiling, I had the corn stripped and lying on a bed of husks, Sid had split the chickens down the middle with the axe. "How long on these?" he said. "I understand steaks, I never barbecued chickens."

Before anyone else could venture a guess, Charity jumped up, intensely smiling. "Let me look," she said. "Pritchard has a chapter on outdoor cooking."

That name was a spell that immobilized us. Sid squatted by the fire and waited. Sally and I carefully avoided letting our eyes get entangled. Charity sat down on a rock, her combed wet hair hanging down on both sides of her face, and consulted her bible. She turned pages, stopped, read, flipped another page, read again.

"Ah, here! 'First rule for camp cooking: better underdone than overdone. Three minutes to a side, over good hot coals, is about right for any camp-cooked meat.'"

I took that in, but I couldn't keep it in. "He's talking about hamburgers."

"No, he says *any* camp-cooked meat."

"They'll be raw."

Charity raised her head and looked at me. The morning was still with us. It was her against the world, or at least against me, since I was male, and Sid's coadjutor. She had learned nothing by following her compass course. "Well, I'm going to have mine three minutes to a side. The rest of you can have yours any way that suits you." She said this smiling.

What Sid slid onto our plates a little later had been cooked exactly six minutes by the watch. It was barely seared, still bleeding internally, tough as life in a Vermont barnyard.

I tried, though I am a rotten-roasted westerner and hate raw meat. I suppose the others tried too. We sat there on our rocks and logs in the late thin sun, with the heat of the fire in our faces and the growing coolness at our backs, and did our best. When I couldn't cut my chicken with the table knife, I used my Swiss army knife. That cut all right, but what it cut could hardly be chewed. After a couple of mouthfuls I fell back on the corn, which was marvelous.

I was already on my second cob when I heard a clank down the log. Charity had set her plate down hard. "Oh, *phooey!*" she said. "It *is* raw. You were right, three minutes aren't *nearly* enough. Now why should a man who writes books on camping be as wrong as that?"

"Never trust people who write books," I said. "We're all a bunch of liars."

"Well, anyway, I *apologize,*" she said. "It was going to be such a nice dinner, and I spoiled it. Here, give me your chickens and I'll do them right."

Sid stood up without a word and started raking the coals together, but she chased him away. "No, *I'm* going to do it. I deserve some penance for being bullheaded and not listening to Larry."

Listening to Larry. I approved of that, but I thought it might have been a good time to bring up that second package of tea, so that Sid could get some vindication too. He was at least as well worth listening to as Larry was. While we were at it, we might have discussed the dangers inherent in conducting your life according to rules whimsically adopted from some book, and ignoring the testimony and experience of the people around you.

I'll tell you who she reminded me of—a desert tortoise I once had, an armored hero named Achilles that my father had picked up in the Mojave. There was quite a fad of keeping them in the twenties. People painted their shells blue and red and gold, even painted their toenails. We used to call them Hollywood Bedbugs. This Achilles friend of mine was an amiable fellow—slept all winter in a closet among the shoes and gave no trouble. But when he came out in the spring he had one thing on his mind, and he went looking for it. Food. He loved lettuce, string beans, broccoli, cabbage. He went sedately nuts over strawberries. It got so we teased him, setting out something he liked and watching him make a beeline across the lawn to it. He would get stuck in the bushes and flowerbeds, sometimes for ten or fifteen minutes, but eventually he would break through and make his ponderous, slow-motion rush to the table. Put a book in his way, he would never go around. He went over. Put two books, he would still go over. Put three, he would push them out of his way. Put something immovable like an automobile tire in his predestined track and he would butt up against it and stay there, pushing and spinning his wheels. Come back an hour later and he'd be half dug in, still trying.

Now here we had evidence that Charity was not quite as Achilles-like as I had thought. She could change her mind, given incontrovertible evidence. She could be sorry for being bullheaded.

Everybody felt better for her conversion. We gave her our raw chickens and she finally got them broiled, about fifteen minutes more per side, and cheerfully served them up. We gnawed the last cobs of corn and had an orange apiece and some chocolate for dessert. I dug a hole and buried the garbage while Sid washed the dishes and the girls dried them and put them away. The sun over the pond was red, the water was red, the little island was black. Black woods surrounded us. Off at the edge of the clearing Wizard clinked his halter rings and cropped the grass. The sound of his hoofs as he moved was more a vibration through the ground than a noise. It gave him a heavy solidity out there, though as the light faded he became only a shadow.

We were tired, not talkative. Charity in particular seemed subdued. She sat on the ground, leaning back against Sid's shins, and he ran her hair through his hands, spreading and shaking it to dry it. I saw the fire glint in her eyeballs as she bent her head back against him. I saw him kiss the top of her head. Sally and I sat opposite them, hugging our knees, soaking up warmth.

Then I stood up to throw more wood on the fire, and a beaver's tail slapped the water at our very doorstep, loud as a shotgun in the stillness. We laughed, full of pleasure. "Hey, we've got company!" We held still and listened. Silence, a ripple, a clink of halter rings. Stars were entangled in the tops of the trees.

"Anybody feel like joining him?" Sid asked. "How about a swim before bed?"

None of us felt that energetic. For a little while we sat on, just enjoying the fire and the surrounding darkness and the feel of listening trees. Then we got up all at once as if on cue, checked to see that no food was left out where squirrels or raccoons could get into it, moved Wizard's picket pin to give him fresh grass for the night, made our pilgrimage with flashlights, ladies left, gents right, said our goodnights, admitted we were tired and lame, agreed that the red sunset should mean good weather tomorrow, and went to our separate tents, pitched on opposite sides of the clearing. We undressed outside, vaguely visible to each other in the starlight and the last glow of the fire. The shapes of the Langs disappeared; Sally and I slid feet-first into our sleeping bags in the sausage-tight space.

"How do you feel?" I asked.

"Good. Tired."

"Too tired?"

"Shhh. They'll hear you."

"Can you hear them?"

We listened. Nothing, not even the earth-transmitted thud of Wizard's slow feet.

"Well, *are* you too tired?"

"Yes, of course I am," she said. "So are you. We'll both be stiff as planks tomorrow. *Ugh!*"

"What's the matter?"

"Rock. I thought I'd. . . . Uh. Oh. There. Now goodnight. I'm dead."

Her face came poking out of the sleeping bag, her thrust-out lips found mine. She was warm, and smelled of cold cream and woodsmoke and toothpaste. "Goodnight," she said again. "Ugh, I wonder if I really *can* sleep on this. Maybe if there'd been any hemlocks around we could have made beds as soft as mattresses, the way Pritchard promised. I wish there'd been room on Wizard for air mattresses."

"Take-um deep breath," I advised her. "Blow-um self up like water wings."

I remember—my bones remember—how it felt to wake up, aching from the hard ground, one arm asleep, my pillow of shoes-rolled-up-in-pants-and-shirt gone somewhere and my face on a groundcloth sweating cold dew. Stre-e-e-etch, extend the legs, tighten the knees, push against the bottom of the bag as a diver pushes up from the bottom of a pool. Khaki light overhead. I determine where I am. What woke me? Birds? Wizard whiffling a hayseed out of his nostrils or stretching his picket rope toward better grass? Beside me Sally is still asleep, only a mass of dark hair showing.

Carefully I reach the flap and pull it aside. Through the opening I can see trampled grass, the log, the corner of the grate over the dead fire. The dew has been heavy—while I am holding it, the flap drips on my wrist, and the grass outside is blue. Birds I don't recognize are skirring and chirping. Was it they who brought me out of my aching sleep?

No. There. Splashings. Our friend the beaver?

I slide out of the bag like a snake out of his skin, and stand up in my underpants. The ground is wet, cold, and rough with twigs, and I grope inside for my shoes with my clothes wrapped around them. Sally does not stir. The tent across the clearing is closed and quiet.

Then voices, male and female, just a word or two. I turn. The lake, obviously warmer than the air, steams. The island lies green in the lead-colored water. Out of its brush, splendidly naked, come Sidney and Charity Lang, picking berries into a metal saucepan.

They are in sight only a moment, and they are intent upon what they are doing, and do not look my way. Standing in my startled goose-pimples, I watch them pick along the fringe of brush and out of sight again, glimpsed and gone, woods creatures.

But one impression is inescapable. If there was ever a dominant male, Sid is it. He is muscled like Michelangelo's Adam anyway, but this morning he looks proud, sure of his power, even arrogant. And Charity? Docile female, following obediently, turning to pick from a bush he designates as hers, needing no Pritchard to give her crosswise advice. It is not Pritchard who calls the shots this morning, nor was it Pritchard, I am sure, who called the shots last night.

I have ducked half down, for I have the instant perception that if Sid looks over and sees me he will bellow for me to come over and join them, for both of us to join them. And I don't want to, for complicated reasons. Perhaps I am uneasy with broad daylight skinny-dips. I am pretty sure Charity would be, too. Perhaps I feel that this is their moment, they should have it alone.

But also, Sid's physical presence is overwhelming. He stalks like a god over on that island. It may be that I remember a day on the dock when, as we all lay sunning, he reared up on an elbow and laid his hand on Sally's instep and said, as if unaware of my presence, "What a dainty, feminine little foot!" More than once, since we have known them, I have had the impression that Charity does not always match his physical vigor, and that when she resists or repulses him he can lean toward anything that is feminine, comforting, and at hand.

Do I shrink from comparisons and competitions on his terms, preferring my own that I am confident in? Maybe. In any case, I get into my clothes and go over and start a fire, being careful to make some noise about it so they will know I am up. Pretty soon I am aware that the two of them are in the water, swimming back to camp, Sid pushing ahead of him the floating pan of berries. When they stand up, they are wearing suits. Rowdily they come ashore, shaming us as slugabeds, and towel themselves before my fire. Beautiful people, blazing with life.

Being who she was, and as honest as she was, Charity had obviously made up her mind to admit her mistake, and not make that particular one again. And when she made up her mind to something, it stayed made up. All the rest of that trip she was gay, amusing, malleable, endlessly enthusiastic and interested, thoughtful, generous. We loved her all over again, as fresh as new, from the moment when she came like laughing Venus out of the water of what I remember as Ticklenaked Pond.

Later, of course, the roof fell in—but let that rest a while, let me try to remember this in sequence. There is still something of that walking trip left.

We were camped, on the next to last day, beside a brook that came down through marble basins, overflowed down marble cascades, filled other basins, and overflowed again. The banks, like the basins and chutes, were clean stone. The sun was out after two days of rain. We spread out and spent the morning drying tents, clothes, and sleeping bags.

The days before had been without flaw or jar, even through the rain. We had outdone ourselves in cheerfulness, helpfulness, and good nature. We had sung one night in a dry hayloft. We had made sport of yesterday's soaking morning when everything except our mason jar of matches was wet. Now we sprawled in swimming suits on the clean marble while green and white water, veined like marble itself, went past us and Wizard rolled in deep grass at the foot of the cascades, kicking his feet in the air and rolling clear over. Worth a hundred dollars, we said. Good for you, Wizard.

Our gear was spread out along the bank like a *National Geographic* photograph of washed carpets drying along the river in Isfahan. We were utterly at peace, comfortable, indolent, basking. Charity and Sally, who had telephoned home at every chance—well, twice, once from a village store and once from a farmhouse—seemed to have forgotten their abandoned babies. There we lay, young, healthy, relaxed, without a care, forgetful of everything except comfort and sun.

"Larry," Charity said without preamble, into the noise of the brook. "Sally. What are you going to do?"

"Do about what?" I said. "Do when?"

"About how you'll live, and where."

The sun lay on my back like a poultice. Warm, safe, and untroubled, I raised my face off my wrist and looked toward Sally, who did not move, and then toward Charity, who was on her stomach with her chin propped in her hands. Beyond her lay Sid, a sea-lion bull whose work is done and who doesn't give another damn.

"What brought up that repulsive subject, in this moment of euphoria?"

"I've been thinking. Sid and I have been talking. *Are* you going down to Boston to try to make it free-lancing?"

"I guess so, unless Uncle Richard rescues us with a job."

"Do you think you *can*?"

"Fate will let us know."

"You're a brute," Charity said. "You've got a *wife and child.*"

"I give thanks for them. Don't you think they'll like Boston?"

"Not if they don't have enough to eat. I worry about them. I even worry about you. You're so short of resources."

"The Lord will send His ravens," I said, not especially believing it, saying it only because we lay under that beneficent sun and I didn't want to look past the day. "Events will transpire. I will win the Pulitzer Prize. We will sell a lot of copies. Magazines will come hat in hand to our door. Uncle Richard will find that he can't get along without my editorial talents. The Fairy Godmother will appear."

As, of course, she already had. That was she speaking.

"Do you think you could survive a Vermont winter, with the baby?"

Sid had rolled over onto his back and was squinting up at the strato-cumulus clouds that coasted over in armadas. Sally had not moved, but her bare brown back was listening.

"We won't *be* in Vermont," I said.

"What if you were? That's what we've been talking about. What if you just stayed on after we leave? The Big House has a wood-burning furnace, and is winterized. It's hard to heat, with that cathedral ceiling, but you could shut off everything but the downstairs and one bedroom. The cellar is full of wood, and there's plenty more if you want to cut it. You might want to put in a telephone, so you could call out if anybody got sick. That would be up to you. But there the place *sits*. Why shouldn't you use it? Finish your book and make yourself famous and come out in the spring like the groundhog."

Sally now had turned her head and was looking at me, startled, past her shoulder. Down the rock Sid sat up, indolent and sleepy-eyed, as if God's finger had just touched him. "Please," he said. "Sally, Larry, please. It would give us both so much pleasure."

They worried more about us than we had the sense to worry about ourselves. What they had, and they had so much, was ours before we could envy it or ask for it. One sort of morality, a somewhat stiff-legged kind that I used to think I subscribed to, would have told us to refuse, to stand on our own feet, to be poor but proud, lest we become the hungry poor relations of the rich. But if we had said no, we would have been depriving them as much as ourselves.

The ethical niceties are academic anyway. Like much else that Charity planned during her bouts of constructive daydreaming, our winter in the Big House never happened. Thomas Hardy, whom I had recently been teaching to Wisconsin high school teachers, might have guessed that the President of the Immortals had other sport in mind for us. My own view is less theatrical. Order is indeed the dream of man, but chaos, which is only another word for dumb, blind, witless chance, is still the law of nature.

You can plan all you want to. You can lie in your morning bed and fill whole notebooks with schemes and intentions. But within a single afternoon, within hours or minutes, everything you plan and every-thing you have fought to make yourself can be undone as a slug is undone when salt is poured on him. And right up to the moment when you find yourself dissolving into foam you can still believe you are doing fine.

Exhilarated by the sudden solution to the Morgan problem, we decided not to move on that afternoon, but to stay in our pleasant brookside camp and walk the whole distance to Battell Pond, a little over twenty miles, the next day. By then we were trail-hardened. We had demonstrated to ourselves that we could keep up a good three-mile-an-hour pace for hours on end. If we got any kind of start, we would be in by early afternoon.

Sally, though she didn't press for that decision, admitted that she welcomed it. She didn't feel especially well today—headachy and dull, perhaps some allergy. After lunch she took a couple of aspirin and lay down in the shade to sleep it off. She has that gift: Illness makes her sleepy.

The rest of us took a swim in the marble pool, and came out and lay like drying salmon on the stone bank, and plotted another walking trip for the next year, and spoke of the possibility that Sid and Charity might leave the children with their nanny between Christmas and New Year's, and spend a few days with us, cross-country skiing. We discussed some repairs and improvements that I might make, if I chose, around the compound; and what I should do about the spring that kept breaking out in the Big House basement during wet spells. Charity revealed that she and Sid had talked about the possibility that, once he was promoted to tenure, they might start a movement to bring us back to Madison. She admonished me to be *immensely* productive so that the mossbacks could see what a mistake they had made.

From that we got to talking about the ideal department in the ideal university. It contained us, of course, plus certain friends like the Abbots and the Stones. I wanted to establish this university in the West somewhere, maybe at Chaco Canyon, but they both thought it should be planted in some little New England town under the elms. We com-promised on Battell Pond. We lay there cutting the future into happy stars and circles like girls making Christmas cookies.

Finally Charity got up and went tender-barefooted across the hot rock and close to where Sally lay. She craned and peered and came back saying that Sally was asleep, just as she ought to be. She thought she might take a nap herself. That released Sid and me for an expedition up the creek.

The marble basins lasted only a few hundred yards. Then the mountain steepened, the woods thickened, the gulch deepened and became impassable, so that we were forced up and around, following a trail worn by animals or fishermen, up through dense brush, across a swale waist-high in ferns (ostrich ferns, Sid said, remembering past instruction), and finally out onto a stony level. We were sweating; the air was still. We started together across the open.

And suddenly a misty coolness breathed in our faces, we heard the sounds of water, stereophonic, many-toned, reverberant. The earth gaped before us, and we looked down into a fantastic gulch, shadowed and light-shot, where the stream appeared and vanished and appeared again through grottoes and potholes as slick and twisty as the waterslide at an amusement park. Below us on the right the water burst from the rock and fell ten or fifteen feet into a green pool. Opalescent bubbles streamed along the wall, currents stirred the pool into whorls and upwellings. At its lower end, the water swelled out over a lip and into a second fall, which we could not see but could tell by its rainbow. Down below the second pool, the stream twisted in and out of sight.

"My God," Sid said. "Can there *be* such a place?"

I expected poetry. Sometimes I have joined Charity in mocking Sid's habit of bursting into quotations whenever he meets something sublime. He drips poetry as Pavlov's dog salivated, on cue. No Folsom Hill sunset or druidical old maple or green pocket of woods is safe from him. Here, at the very least, I should hear about Alph, the sacred river, running through caverns measureless to man down to a sunless sea.

But within two seconds I realized that it was my mind, not his, that Coleridge invaded. After all, we had been programmed in the same system, stuffed like Strasbourg geese with the best that has been known and said in the world during man's long struggle upward from spontaneity to cliché. That was one of the things we had most in common, and I learned something about us both during the minute or two we stood looking. We were two of a kind, the only difference being that he was reverential before all the traditional word magic, and I would steal it if I could. He came to the tradition as a pilgrim, I as a pickpocket.

In this case it was the pilgrim who was more spontaneous in his response. He wagged his head, smiling delightedly, his eyes shining. Then he took off his glasses and laid them carefully on the ground. He unbuttoned and tore off his shirt. "This calls for a baptism," he said.

For the best part of an hour we played in that rock-and-water funhouse, diving off the brink of the falls, swimming the pool, diving off the second fall, climbing up out of the second pool, sliding down the twisting chute below it, and scrambling back up the cliff to dive and slide again. We stood up to our necks in the seethe and bubble of water, assuring each other that we had to bring the girls up here, tonight or the first thing in the morning, to give them a chance at it before we started our walk home. We revised next year's itinerary so that we would end up in this same magical place. And if next year, why not every year? Why not make this our place of refreshment and renewal, a retreat that we revealed to no one, keeping it a secret between ourselves and the few locals who might know it?

It felt like a purification before the next fateful, hopeful chapter of our lives. Up to our chins in the water that foamed through its marble bowl, tiptoeing the smooth bottom to keep our noses above the surface, the light wavering and winking down on us and flickering off the curved walls, trees overhanging us and the sky beyond those, and all around and through us, a soul-massage, the rush and patter and tinkle of water and the brush and break of bubbles. It was a present that made the future tingle.

What I didn't know as I stood blissful in the foam was that I had begun to foam too, though I hadn't yet felt the salt.

I felt it soon enough. We came down after five, and were met by Charity at the edge of the camp. She was distracted, close to infuriated by our long absence. She would have come hunting us, but hadn't dared leave Sally, who was burning up with fever, her head splitting so that the lightest jar or footfall made her moan, her neck and back aching. "She's really *sick,*" Charity said. "It's not just a headache. We've got to get her to a doctor."

I confess that I hoped her irritation at us made her exaggerate. But when I went over to where Sally lay on her sleeping bag I found her on her back, her parted lips enameled with fever, her breath coming hoarsely through her mouth. She heard me, and her eyes opened, but after the first wincing look they closed. I was not sure she recognized me; and when I put my hand on her forehead to feel how hot she was, she rolled her head away and cried out with pain. She said something and I could not understand her wandering voice. I tiptoed back to where Sid and Charity stood, and we had an anxious huddle.

Within a half hour Sid had improvised a hackamore out of a halter and two lead ropes, and was riding Wizard bareback down the brook, headed for the nearest village, seven or eight miles away. Charity was sitting by Sally's sleeping bag, every now and then wringing out a towel in a bucket of water and laying it across Sally's eyes. And I was assembling the gear, grimly packing hampers, rolling up bags and tarps and getting it all in a pile to be carried out somehow, sometime, to the road where the car that Sid would summon would meet us.

Good fortune, contentment, peace, happiness have never been able to deceive me for long. I expected the worst, and I was right. So much for the dream of man.

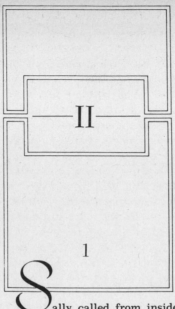

II

1

$\mathcal{S}$ally called from inside. I went in and helped her dress and held the door open for her and brought her folding high chair out onto the porch. Sitting down in that is not the collapse that sitting down on an ordinary chair is, and its arms give her something to push against when she wants to stand again. She sat there breathing deeply, or as deeply as she *can* breathe.

"Doesn't it smell fresh and wonderful! Have you just been sitting here?"

"That's all."

"Still feeling sad?"

"You invented that."

"You were feeling something. Maybe you were just pensive."

"That's it. I'll settle for pensive."

"I guess there's reason. Have you seen anybody?"

"Not a soul."

She started to say, "Doesn't it seem a little odd . . ." and then I saw her eyes focus on something beyond and below. I turned, and there were Hallie and Moe, standing in the path in shorts, beaming at us.

They made a striking pair, Baltic married to Mediterranean. She is tall, fair, and blue-eyed like her father; he is pear-shaped, Jewish, swarthy as Sennacherib. For the week before they were married, he lived with us in this guest cottage, and we kept him out of the way of the bride and the family and the preparations, and learned to know and like him well. At first we wondered how a Jew, ten years older than this adored daughter, would blend into the New England matriarchy, but we needn't have. The matriarchy simply unhinged its jaw and swallowed him as it swallows all sons-in-law.

Sally from her high chair was sending them back their smiles. It was plain in her face, the slight trembling, the eagerness below the surface of her serenity, how glad she was to be with them again. They are like our own; in every way but birth they *are* our own.

One after the other they came bounding up the steps to lean and kiss her. I saw them hold back from embracing her too hard and perhaps hurting her. I saw her hand, the half-clenched one, fold over each bent back in turn, pressing, and it struck me in a way it had never struck me before (why not? why ever not?) how touching and attractive the gestures of human affection are. Moe pumped my hand. Hallie kissed me. We could not keep from smiling and smiling.

"Are you rested?" Hallie said. "We didn't want to come too early."

"You're just right," Sally said. "I had two lovely sleeps, one last night and one after *hazari,* and Larry's already taken a walk."

"Has he cut any wood? That used to be the pattern. You'd hardly arrive before I'd hear you and Dad sawing and splitting like a couple of poor woodcutters in a fairy tale." She did not wait for a response. "How about brunch? Could you eat something?"

"Don't go to any trouble," I said. "Any little snack will do. Maybe half a papaya? Orange juice? Cereal with some Vermont raspberries? Eggs Benedict and a little ham? Muffins of some kind, or a waffle? Coffee?"

Hallie laughed like her mother. "Dream on. The girls ate early so they could go with Lyle to Montpelier. They might have left some Rye Krisp and cottage cheese."

"Some welcome," I said. "How *are* those twin monsters we've never seen?"

"Overfed," Moe said. "Inexhaustible. Exhausting. P-p-p-praise God Lyle's got them till the picnic."

"It all sounds so natural," Sally said happily. "So as usual. I want to hear all about you. Is the whole family here?"

"If we were, it wouldn't be as usual. Nick *was* here, but he had to go back to Ecuador. Barney and Peter will be up today, Lyle's picking them both up at the airport. David's been living here since last fall. He built himself a sort of *yurt* up on the hill and lives like a Mongol. Mom must have written you."

"Nearly everybody," Sally said. "It is critical, then. How long does she have?"

It is hard for Hallie to look grave even in grave situations. Like her mother, she was made for smiling, and she smiled now, a rueful, puckered flash. "Two weeks? A week? She holds herself together by willpower, but she's terribly weak and thin, and eats hardly anything, and has to rest a lot. You know her, though. *She'll* decide when it's time. For one thing, today's her birthday . . ."

"Oh, Lord! It is! It never crossed my. . . . That's why the picnic. Oh, I should have remembered!"

"Don't worry about presents," Hallie said. "You're her present. Don't think she didn't have that in mind, too. She lies up there in her lounge with her notebook, and plots like a Mafia godfather. She isn't going until everything is in order. She's been through all her papers and burned most of them. She gave each of us the book she kept on us from the time we were born. That really made me weep. You have this idea of her as the boss woman with all the reins in her hands, telling everybody what's best for them, and then you look in this baby book and see her watching every move you make, loving you and studying you and hoping for you and predicting what you might turn into."

"I know," Sally said. "I've seen those books."

"And she's been having the grandchildren in, one per afternoon. Last visits. That'll tell you everything. Monday it was the twins, they went together. Yesterday it was Margie. You remember Margie. Barney's oldest."

"Of course. She must be all grown up."

"Half," Hallie said. "And miserable. Barney and Ethel are splitting up, did you know? It's bitter—shouting, quarrels—awful. They can't live in the cottage together, so whenever he comes up from Hartford she moves with the children over to Aunt Comfort's."

"You'd think they'd call a truce."

"Till Mom goes. Yes. Ethel might, but not Barney. He thinks Mom takes Ethel's side against him. Which, of course, she does. Anyway, Margie came back crying, and cried the rest of the afternoon."

"Poor child."

"It's a mess. Not just that Mom's going to die. She makes no bones about that—cracks *jokes,* if you can believe it. I don't suppose it's the split that bothers Margie so much, either. She has to be used to that by now. But she saw this stream of grandchildren going up to the Ridge, pretty solemn, really, and then it came her turn. She said she came out feeling she'd been checked off one of Mom's to-do lists. She felt completely finished, as if the world had ended. And she loves her mother and her granny but she sort of sides with Barney and Dad."

"Sid?" I said. "Does he take sides in this? And how is he holding up?"

Hallie answered only the second question. "About as you'd expect."

We waited, but she didn't offer any more. An indefinite awkwardness settled like pollen on the porch. Moe finally scattered it. "How about that food? I don't know about y-y-you, but I'm starved."

"Me too," Sally said. She unhooked her canes from the arm of her chair.

Moe rushed to help. His sensitivity is more acute than his muscular coordination. Several times Sally and I have seen him on *Today* or some other broadcast as he explains or predicts the economy, and remarked on how much faster his head works than his tongue can. His wisdom comes off the air as a slurred stammer. If he wasn't such a tangle-tongue he would be the chief economic adviser to every Democratic administration during his lifetime. You have to read his books and articles to know how bright he is, and you have to know him personally to comprehend how much gentleness and consideration his clumsiness obscures.

To keep him from getting in the road, I said, "Take care of the chair, will you, Moe?"

With my hands in Sally's armpits I lifted her to her feet. Moe pulled the chair out of the way. Hallie was watching with a wincing, unwilling expression on her face. Though Sally has been in irons since before Hallie was born—we have always assumed, from the evidence, that Hallie was conceived that night on Ticklenaked Pond—it has been eight years since we have seen each other, and I suppose it is a shock to her to see afresh how helpless leglessness can be.

When Sally had planted her canes and was turning, Moe again jumped to help. She gave him her serene smile. "Thanks. I can manage."

"The steps?"

"I can manage."

"You've heard of a hog on ice," I said. "She makes the independence of a hog on ice look timid and tentative."

Reluctantly he fell back. Sally swung to the top of the steps, leaned and planted her canes on the step below, swung her iron-bound dangling legs, just scraping the porch boards, and made it down the first step. Then the second. Then the ground. Moe, entangling the chair in the raspberry bushes, hovered close behind her as she lurched into the path. He was in my road, for I wanted to be close. If she caught a cane or hit a soft spot it could be bad. She has had a broken hip and a broken wrist to demonstrate that she isn't as invulnerable as she acts.

I couldn't get around him, but after a few lurching steps Sally took care of herself. She stopped, turned, thrust out her lips humorously, and opened her eyes wide. "Moe, I love you, but if you keep offering me a gentlemanly arm I'm going to fall on my face."

She made it a laughing matter, and we laughed. Moe, as I edged past him and got behind Sally, shook his head at me in admiration. Sally has always been a legend among the Langs and Ellises for her gameness. And why not?

The path was narrower and more overgrown than it would have been if Sid had still been living in the compound. Then it widened, and we were at his old think house/shop—weathered shingles, sagging porch, cobwebs in the window corners.

Sally stopped to take it in. "It looks absolutely the same as it used to."

"It ought to," Hallie said. "We haven't touched it."

"Since they moved up to the Ridge?" I said. "That was the summer you got married. Eight years ago. How come you haven't taken this over, Moe?"

"What do I need of a shop? I can't fix a leaky t-t-tap. For a study I use the downstairs bedroom."

"It's still Dad's hidey-hole," Hallie said. "The Ridge was Mom's project. Remember how she had the Bruce boys cutting with chainsaws all one summer and fall to clear the road? The Turnpike, we used to call it. It's grown in some, but it's still wider than a lot of town roads. Dad never had much to do with any of that. His heart's down here. He likes to keep this place for mending furniture, and stenciling names on mailboxes, and watching warblers, and keeping his journal, and writing poems."

"He's still writing poems."

Sideward flash of eyes, downward curve of mouth. "Wouldn't he?"

"Your mother used to think his poetry was a waste of time."

Hallie laughed. "She still does. Especially since last spring when she found out he'd written one to a girl student."

"My goodness," Sally said, astonished. "Don't tell me. He was always so much in her apron pocket."

"He still is. This wasn't any Abelard and Heloise, just sort of soft-headed. He was her adored professor, she was his adoring disciple. I guess he liked being adored. But it sure irritated Mom."

So nothing much had changed. Sid was still trying to go up a road that was blocked by her thought police, she was still trying to keep him from doing something that she thought embarrassingly amateur. To change the subject, I said, "Could I take a look inside? I used to envy him this place."

"Of course. Sally, can you make it up there?"

"I'll wait here. You go ahead. You too, Moe, if you want."

"I'll wait with you," Moe said, and offered to unfold her chair.

She cried out, "Moe, you're too gallant! I can stand here perfectly safely. Really."

Hallie and I went up on the porch and I slid open the barn door. There lay the sun in its shortened late-morning rectangle, just as it used to lie when I came past before swim time and ventured to intrude (he welcomed intrusions) summer after summer.

Every tool was in its place. The foot-powered grindstone, which he liked to call a grinstun in the Vermont fashion, stood like a paleolithic bicycle in the middle of the floor, with its stone wheel and its iron seat and its funnel-shaped water can. The anvil was where it had always been. There was the bench with its several vises. There was the paint locker, such a paint locker as I had copied when we moved to Pojoaque, but when I opened the door I saw how this one differed from mine. These cans were arranged by size. They had no slops of paint down their sides. Their lids were firmly on. Each can wore a circlet of masking tape marked with a felt pen: *Big House Kitchen. Children's House Trim. Guest House Bath.*

On the pegboard wall were the carpenter's tools, not a power tool among them, all of them designed for doing things the hard hand way. Each hung within its drawn outline: hammers, everything from a magnetized tack hammer to six- and eight-pound sledges; wooden and rubber mauls; hatchets and axes, single- and double-bitted; a hand brace and a staggered array of bits; screwdrivers and chisels in ascending sizes; hacksaws, keyhole saws, pulp saws, rip and crosscut saws wearing a bluish film of oil. On the opposite wall, also hung within their drawn outlines, the rakes, hoes, shovels, scythes, sickles, pruning hooks, machetes, splitting hammers, and the seven-foot lumbering saw with three-inch teeth, a relic now retired by the chainsaw.

And along the top of the bench the shelf containing capped and labeled mason jars: nails graded by size and type, wood screws likewise, stove bolts, rivets, brads, tacks, staples. Below the bench, on the plank that was its central brace, a row of two-pound coffee cans, also labeled: *Switches. Plugs. Outlets. Electrical Cord.*

"See?" Hallie said, as if she had brought me there to prove something. "Everything but 'string too short to save.' Was he this way when you first knew him? Did he save things in the refrigerator—saucers of leftover rice, and half a baked potato, and a little rhubarb sauce, and two or three asparagus spears? It drives Mom wild."

The light in the shop was dusty and cool, the sort of light the past always affects. "Why should he get miserly?" I asked. "Does he think he has to be penurious because she's extravagant? Is he scared of being part of a three-generation pilgrimage from shirtsleeves to shirtsleeves?"

"It isn't money," Hallie said. "He never tries to make her economize. She thinks she's contemptuous of luxuries and comforts, and she is, sort of, but when she wants anything she'll throw money around in a way to scare you. He never complains. He's always been generous."

"Nobody knows that better than we do."

Her eyes on my face, she hesitated. "If either of them is contemptuous of money, he is. It's just . . . I don't know whose side you see it from."

"Are there sides? Is there an it?"

"I only meant . . . I don't know. Neither one of them could get along without the other. He needs her to manage him and she needs him to manage. I just wish it was more equal. She's always been too strong for him. She does everything she wants to do, she's got the family and a hundred different causes. She flits from socialism to Quakerism, and Quakerism to psychology, and psychology to women's lib, and meanwhile he gets to do what she lets him do. And they both seem to be disappointed. Also, now that she's dying, she almost seems to find him in the road. She's got these notions of how he should take it stoically, and he's so torn up he can't, and that upsets *her.*"

"It's not easy for either of them."

"No," Hallie said discontentedly. "But I wish he'd get up some gumption and make her behave. She's the sick one. She does herself harm. I wish he'd assert himself more."

That sounded like an attitude I had heard expressed before, years before.

"This shop is his security blanket," Hallie said. Something like resentment had heightened her color, as the heat of argument used to heighten her mother's. "Look at it. Did you ever see it messed up—shavings lying around, brushes in the paint pail, tools scattered, the way it would be if something important were going on in it? I never did. He keeps it like a hospital lab. He's always either cleaning something up or sharpening something—pencils, tools, whatever he can find that needs it. Last week I came in—you won't believe this—I came in and found him straightening used nails on the anvil and sorting them into jars. If there's ever an iron shortage, we're ready."

"That's sad," I said.

"Of course it's sad." Her laugh was a pained, incredulous bark. She troubled me. Obviously she troubled herself.

I said, "Puttering can be a comfort. It goes with rumination, and he's a ruminator. He should have been a literate gentleman farmer with a telescope in his backyard, and a big library, and all kinds of time to think."

"A rustic Newton?" she flashed. "Where's his *Principia*?"

There was something so close to contempt in her voice that she made me mad. "Is it compulsory to be one of the immortals?" I said. "We're all decent godless people, Hallie. Let's not be too hard on each other if we don't set the world afire. There's already been enough of that."

I was too sharp. She was upset enough without my scolding her. The color got deeper in her cheeks, and she made an unhappy, apologetic mouth. "I know. I sound like Mom. But it does bother me that he never gets past preparing. Preparing has been his life work. He prepares, and then he cleans up."

Trapped flies buzzed at the windows. Over Hallie's shoulder I could see, through the door that led to the lean-to study, the desk with the short shelf of books above it.

"Hey!" Moe was calling from outside. "Have you gone to sleep in there?"

Hallie turned her head as if to call back, but instead said to me, "Do you think he could have been a poet if she'd let him?"

I spread my hands. "A poet is somebody who has written a poem. He's written quite a few. Some of them aren't much good, your mother's right. He's too respectful of past poets, his head is full of echoes, the longer he teaches, the more his poems sound like Matthew Arnold. But yes, he's a poet. I remember one he published in *Poetry,* years ago. He showed me half a dozen letters he'd got about it. People said they'd been delighted and enriched by this simple little poem about how certain jeweled beetles live and make unnoticed love down among the club moss."

"The kind of letters *you* get all the time."

Again she made me mad. The women in that family are too judgmental. Even with his life getting on into late afternoon, they always have something other, or better, or more distinguished, that they want him to be, when all he wants to do is live quietly down in the club moss. The point, I felt like saying, was not a comparison between my relative success and his relative failure. The point was the unsatisfied hunger in him. No wonder he wrote a poem to a student who admired him.

Hallie made again her shrugging, apologetic gesture. "You knew Dartmouth gave him its Distinguished Teacher award last year, and finally made him a full professor."

"No. Why wouldn't they write us about that? That's wonderful. I hope he was pleased. I hope she was."

Her look was curiously evasive. "I guess he was. Sure he was. Mom . . . well, you know her. Maybe it was too late. She liked the award, and was glad for him, but she said being promoted just before retirement was a little like charity, a sort of booby prize."

"Good God!"

"I don't think she meant to be deflating. Just realistic. Aunt Comfort says she's never got over Wisconsin. She was just desolated, she broke down and had to go to a sanatorium for two months."

"I remember."

"Do you remember that great house? Did you ever see it?"

"Once, when I was bringing Sally home from Warm Springs. It wasn't quite finished yet, but it *was* a great house."

"Mom won't talk about it. I think I remember it a little—the stairway. But probably I don't, we left when I was three. Once when I looked for pictures of it in the album I found that Mom had torn them all out. 'It's dead,' she told me. 'It's gone. Forget it.' What was it, Larry? Just not enough publications? He's a better teacher than almost anybody I had in college. He can make books very important and exciting. I've sat in his classes."

"He was unlucky," I said. "He came up for tenure just when the war was emptying all the men out of the colleges, and the colleges were cutting back."

"I suppose," she said vaguely and discontentedly, as if the subject both bored and irritated her. "All I know I got from Aunt Comfort. She says Dad would have gone into the army himself, or into the OWI the way you did, though with four kids he wouldn't have had to. But Mom was in her Quaker-Pacifist phase, and all broken up besides, and she wouldn't even let him take a war job. So they came up here and just vegetated for three years. It was great for us kids, but it must have been like Siberian exile for both of them."

"Once it would have been just what he wanted."

"What he did mainly was work for farmers who couldn't get help."

"A war job."

"She thought of it as a community job. She's always been great for community."

Her eyes were very clear in the whites, the irises bachelor-button blue—beautiful eyes. I realized that they were Sid's, without glasses and in a woman's face.

"Did you see them at all, those years?" she said.

"Only a couple of times. Sally wasn't very mobile, and the war made getting around tough enough, even if you didn't have her problems."

"But you wrote to each other."

"Oh, yes."

"Were they miserable? Did they complain?"

"Not a bit. They made a game out of wartime shortages and hardships. They got into the village in ways they never had. If they could have forgotten Wisconsin they'd have had the time of their lives."

"But then you saved them by getting him on at Dartmouth."

"I did that with fear and trembling. I wasn't sure he should even apply for that job. It put him right back where we'd both been in Madison."

"Mom thinks you did him the greatest favor. They both do."

"I hope I did."

Steps thumped on the porch, and Moe appeared in the doorway. "I hate to hustle anybody, but if one of us doesn't drop a word on Clara, we'll eat about three. Shall I go get her started?"

"I'll come right now," she said, and to me, "Have you seen it?"

I hadn't quite. "Could I look in the study for a minute? You go ahead, I'll be right along."

She left. Moe worked his eyebrows at me and followed her.

The study was as neat as the shop. On the desk were the portable typewriter with its lid on, a squared stack of yellow pads, a Japanese jar full of sharpened pencils. Above the desk were the books. I read their titles in the gray light: *The Oxford Universal Dictionary,* Roget's *Thesaurus,* Webster's *Dictionary of Synonyms, The Oxford Companion to English Literature,* the ditto to American literature, Bartlett's *Quotations, The Golden Bough,* a foot or so of bird, flower, tree, and fern books. One book was backwards in the shelf, its spine turned inward. When I put it straight I saw that it was a rhyming dictionary. Imagining him jamming it hurriedly out of sight when he heard footsteps, I was ashamed for him. After a minute I turned it back the way he had left it.

2

To travel from Warm Springs to Cambridge by way of Madison was about like going to Dallas by way of Seattle and Green Bay, but that's what we did—because they would have it that way, because Charity wanted to give Sally a spell of care and affection after the long ordeal of therapy, because she wanted to check out Mrs. Fellowes and see if I had picked somebody suitable to look after Sally. She did not trust my judgment in a lot of things. And anyway, we had to pick up Lang, whom we had not seen since September, a millennium ago.

The new house, in March, still smelled of paint and plaster. The yard under its thawing snowbanks was littered with scraps of lumber and Sheetrock and tin and black flaps of building paper. The *allée* that Charity planned, a long vista through woods to a far glimpse of lake, had been cleared, and rows of bare sapling poplars planted along its edges. We could sit in the overwarm living room, behind a wall of double-paned windows, and look at the view with the eye of imagination. In a playpen in a corner of the living room a golden retriever with eight puppies dozed while we looked. Charity was noticeably pregnant. Barney and Nicky had discovered the sliding properties of the curving banister, and chased each other up and down.

It was an anniversary, or nearly one. Lang and David had a joint first-birthday party, skewed a few days to take advantage of the reunion. Lots of photographs with flash. Lots of awed talk about how much had happened since that night on Morrison Street when the letter came from Harcourt and our whole ball of string had begun to unravel. In the rush of events I had hardly noticed my book. It was out. It had had some pleasant reviews. It had sold about what Uncle Richard had guessed it would. It had solved none of our problems.

But at least one thing was settled: I was now an editor at Phoenix Books, at a salary nearly twice what Wisconsin had paid me, and we had an apartment waiting for us on Trowbridge Street in Cambridge. We decided that Charity was right, it was better to look forward, not back. I suppose her pregnancy did that to her—you *have* to look ahead if you're pregnant, I would guess. But also she had not relinquished one detail of her vision of Sid's future in the department. She had been assured by Mrs. Rousselot that Professor Rousselot thought the world of Sid, thought him the most dependable of the younger men. Reports on his teaching were full of praise. He served on a lot of committees. Charity looked down that road and it was as clear to her as the unfinished view outside her window. Soon spring would thaw the drifts and reveal the disorder and scarred earth, and she would set to work to transform it into a landscape.

Happy house, happy visit, though when we left after three days both Sally and Charity were in tears.

Then a gap that, as I count back, turns out to have been more than two years long. Once we were settled in Cambridge we hardly budged. I was as usual moonlighting and using the weeks to the last quarter-hour. Sally worked patiently and uncomplainingly on her therapy. We devised little strategies and gadgets that made life easier for her, but even with Mrs. Fellowes, who turned out to be sympathetic, motherly, and immune to illness or fatigue, we found merely living all we could manage.

No Battell Pond visit at all in the summer of 1939. None in 1940 either. Charity came down once, but stayed only a day. Other people's houses, and routines that she could not control, made her uneasy, and she was as unwilling to be a burden as Sally was.

But by 1941 Sally had rolled her stone a few feet uphill. She could get around better on her canes. She thought she could manage the woody paths and slate steps of the compound. She did not fear that the very sight of the place would break her down. And Lang, at three, was big enough to enjoy the lake and the company of the Lang children. When Charity wrote inviting us, with a scrawled postscript from Sid demanding us, we accepted.

Our other problems had eased, too. I liked my job, and Uncle Richard evidently liked the way I did it. My second novel was out, generally overlooked as Uncle Richard foretold, but again with several respectful reviews. I was selling an occasional story and reviewing books for three or four journals. We had paid off the first two thousand dollars of our debt to the Langs.

In Battell Pond everything—well, nearly everything—was as be-

fore. Order, affection, thoughtfulness, consideration, social excitement, strenuous work and strenuous play, sent us to bed blessing the
place and the people. We had half forgotten, during our long spell of
endurance, what companionship meant. Though Sally's condition
prohibited the shared walks, swims, and canoe rides that had once
filled our best hours, we had survived as a foursome. We could still
listen peacefully to music after dinner, or sit talking late on the porch,
watching the stars pass under the brow of the eaves. We read a good
deal aloud, and one story of Faulkner's gave us a watchword. "They
mought of kilt us," we declared with Faulkner's unreconstructed red-
neck. "They mought of kilt us, but they ain't whupped us."

Sally was so joyfully there that for hours at a time we accepted her
as whole. As for the rest of the world, and its grievous woes, we put
aside what we could not prevent or cure. What if Hitler had broken his
pact with Stalin, and German panzers were expanding the war into
Poland and Russia? What if the Vichy government of fallen France
had just turned over military control of Indo-China to the Japanese?
What if, at home, people came to blows over Lend Lease, America
First, Father Coughlin? What if all the front organizations met and
wrangled, what if individuals abdicated the Communist Party in despair over the indigestibility of the party line, while the diehards met
to protest the continued imprisonment of Earl Browder? What if. Forget it. Shoulder the sky, my lad, and drink your ale.

We went through those three weeks in the summer of 1941 like
people driving an open road while storms gathered ahead and to both
sides. On them, the sun still shines. Who knows, the clouds might part,
blow over, clear away; the rain might turn out to be no more than a
hard shower. Meantime, the light is lurid and lovely, the mesas reach
out of black distance and warm their cliff-ends in the sun, unexpected
rainbows arch the valleys.

What had happened to Sally and me was that the future had been
restored to us as a possibility. Despite Sally's crippling, we thought we
could make it. The Langs too. They had built themselves into Madison
like stones into a wall. Their house was the center of the department's
social life, they had friends all through the university, their guest-
rooms knew no empty weekends. And even Charity was willing to
admit that scholarly articles didn't seem as necessary as she had once
thought them. The hasty textbook that we had thrown together in the
spring of 1938 was being used in enough places to give Sid satisfaction,

and even a few royalties. He was assembling an anthology of Victorian poetry and prose that Dodd Mead had agreed to publish.

There never were hosts to match them. At first we were even a little hurt to find that during our stay we would not have them to ourselves, that a Wisconsin graduate student and his wife were coming for several days, that Charity was having a widowed college friend up from New Haven, that two of Sid's Yale classmates would be through for a weekend. People had been coming through that way since early June. They welcomed and absorbed them all. Lang was one of the children, Lang-Lang, from the hour we arrived. Mrs. Fellowes was a benevolent aunty.

Three full weeks without a hint of cross purposes. What he wanted, she wanted; what she wanted, he wanted; what they had, they both wanted. The snake that had once inhabited Innisfree never showed itself.

On the morning we left, the whole family gathered—Sid and Charity, the four children, the nurse girl. Charity's clothes had got more bizarre during the break in our acquaintance—she looked like a fortune teller. Sid was fitter than I had ever seen him—confident, superb, the demigod who had stalked the island in Ticklenaked Pond. Very shortly we would have concrete evidence that the happy resolution of the problems at Wisconsin had produced a predictable result: In October, Charity would write that child number five, already named Elsie to force it into being a girl, was on the way.

They stood with their arms around one another in the scatter of shade and early sun. "Well, Kernel," Sid said, "remember the password. They kilt us but they ain't whupped us yit."

Our hands were out the windows, our necks craned for a last look at the people who above any other two on earth made us feel good, wanted, loved, important, and happy.

"Good-bye," we cried. "It was wonderful. Thanks for everything."

"Oh, thank *you*!" they cried to our departing dust. "Thank you for *coming*! We're counting on you again next year. *Every* year!"

Re-enter the law of nature. On December 7, a Sunday, the radio announced the bombing of Pearl Harbor, and the war that had been everybody else's was abruptly ours too. By May I had taken leave from Phoenix Books and we had moved to Washington for the duration, bent upon helping Elmer Davis prove that the way to have an informed public opinion was to inform the public. At about the same time, Professor Rousselot, almost in tears, told Sid that the department could not promote him after all, and since it could not promote him, it could not retain him either.

It was not from the Langs that we heard the news. We heard it from the Stones, already at the Great Lakes Naval Training Station learning to be a warrior and a warrior's wife. Sid and Charity simply dropped out of sight like weighted bodies in a pond. No letters came back in answer to ours; we were unable to reach them by telephone. When we finally did hear, Charity had recovered from her breakdown and left the sanatorium, and the family was together in Battell Pond.

That was August, 1942. We did not see them until June, 1945, and when we did at last get together, the snake was back in Eden. At least once during our ten-day stay it stood on its tail like a spitting cobra and menaced our eyes.

About nothing. About who should do the dishes. Standing in the quiet lean-to that for years had been Sid's prison and hideout, I could hardly credit what I remembered, it was so bizarre and unnecessary.

We got a hint of trouble when we came in from the porch with our sherry glasses in hand and found Barney, ten or eleven years old by then, sitting at the table. Charity left us in the doorway and crossed quickly to where he sat. "Have you finished?"

"I can't eat it."

"Yes, you *can* eat it. You'll sit here till. . . . No, you can go now. Go on up to your room. I'll save it for you. You can eat it for breakfast."

She picked up the dish from in front of him. With her other hand she hoisted him to his feet and pushed him off toward the kitchen. I had a glimpse of his sidelong, sullen eyes, his wedge-thin face, before the door closed on them both. Sid was making quite a production of building a fire in the fireplace. Sally and I said nothing.

After a minute Charity came back out, shooting one of her exasperated smiles across the big living room as she bent to brush Barney's crumbs away and begin setting the table for the five of us. "Vegetables!" she said. "You'd think they were being poisoned."

"Poor Barney," Sally said. "I never much liked vegetables either. Where are the other kids?"

"Up in the nursery playing canasta."

"And Barney can't?" Mrs. Fellowes said. "Why don't I just. . . . Maybe I can. . . ."

"No," Charity said. "He knows what he has to do. He can solve his problem in three minutes whenever he wants to."

We had a splendid dinner that Charity had cooked herself—four courses, with a Bordeaux that must have been gathering dust in their cellar since before the fall of France. We warmed up, there was a lot of laughter. I had managed to avoid all talk of the war or of Washington, either of which might stir up Charity's irritable, and, as I felt it, irrational pacifism. Well fed and comfortable, we sat over coffee for a good while.

Then Charity stood up and announced that we would now go in and sit by the fire and listen to some music. They had a new Toscanini recording of Beethoven's Ninth that they had been saving just for tonight. Something joyful, to celebrate. She meant celebrate our reunion, and we were all for that. But victory in Europe was only a few weeks old; the war in the Pacific could end any time. There was more to celebrate than Charity wanted to talk about.

Fine, wonderful, we said. Wasn't the Ninth pretty long, though? Shouldn't we do up the dishes first?

Mrs. Fellowes stood up promptly, saying why didn't she do them? She hadn't been allowed to do a thing all day. We should go on in and have our music, she'd have them done in a jiffy.

"No," Sid said, and Charity said, intensely smiling, "Mrs. Fellowes, you're a *guest,* and in this house we don't let guests do dishes."

"But you don't have any help!"

"Sid will do them."

"Sid will?" I said. "Sid and *I* will. Pride will not suffer a Morgan to sit at his ease while his host is up to his elbows in dishwater made necessary by the Morgan presence. You ladies have three choices. Wait a few minutes for the music, or let me help with the dishes after the music, or have the music without the comforting presence of the gentlemen."

"You're a windbag," Charity told me. "And you are not doing any dishes. You can be the *opérateur* of the music machine. Sid does the dishes."

"Why should he get to do dishes when I can't?"

"Because that's our agreement. That's the way it's been ever since our last help went down country. I cook, he cleans up."

"Say it isn't so," I said to Sid.

He said it *was* so. No amateurs allowed in the kitchen.

Sally and Mrs. Fellowes were looking from face to face, smiling, trying to find an agreeable way out of the impasse. "Why don't we leave them till afterward, then?" Sally said.

Sid looked as if that might suit him, but then he looked at Charity and saw by her clouded face that it wouldn't suit him after all. "I'll just get them done before they all dry out and harden."

"Then you'll miss the music," I said. "You'll be cut off from our intemperate joy. Really, I want to help. I insist."

"Insist all you want, you aren't allowed to," Charity said. "You'll find the Ninth Symphony on top of the pile over there."

Sid had quietly got up and begun to stack dishes on a tray. Charity snuffed the candles. Sally, who had stayed out of the argument because however much she would have liked to, she would have been no help doing dishes, was telling me with her eyes to knock it off and submit. So I went and helped her stand up; and because it was now pretty dim in the dining room, I held her while she bent to lock her knee braces. People who can't feel their feet must be able to see them, or they lose their balance when they bend down.

I took her chair over by the fire, and she caned over and sat down in it. Charity curled up in a big chair. Mrs. Fellowes said uncomfortably that she would just pop upstairs and take a look at the children, then, and despite Charity's objections went on up. Sid was backing through the swinging kitchen door, carrying his loaded tray.

"Now let's just be joyful," Charity said. "This horrible war is almost over, and we've got you back."

With the records stacked on the changer, I still hesitated. "It would only take the two of us ten minutes to do up those dishes. Then we could all sit and be joyful."

"Sid is not unhappy," Charity said. "He's not out there crying into the dishpan. He'll come in when he's through. This is the way we *do* it. This is our *agreement.*"

Mine not to make reply. I pushed the automatic switch. The arm lifted, swung, hovered, and came carefully down. Scratching began, then a quaver of violins against sober strings and horns that quickly rose to a musical shout. Charity stretched up and snapped off the floor lamp. We sat in firelight, watched by the eyes of the owl andirons. The kitchen door, over at the dim dining-room end, was outlined with the light beyond it.

Ordinarily I am an admirer of the Ninth Symphony, but that night it struck me as pompous and overstated. I couldn't listen because I kept thinking of Sid out there, inferior and unneeded, dismissed to the scullery. And why? Because Charity had set up a schedule and was too inflexible to change it. Either that or she was whipping him for something.

The longer I sat in the firelit dusk, the more annoyed I got. When the first record ended and the changer clashed and the second one dropped, I stood up. It was too dark to see expressions, but I saw that both Charity and Sally had turned their heads and were watching me. I held up one finger and tiptoed out.

The downstairs bathroom was off the hall that ran from the front entrance past the stairs to the kitchen. The whole passage was out of sight from the living room. Bypassing the bathroom, I went down the hall and pushed open the kitchen door.

Sid, at the sink in the middle of chaos, looked around. Every counter and table was loaded with dishes, bowls, pots, pans, milk bottles, strainers, and garbage. Good cooks dirty a lot of dishes, especially when they themselves don't have to wash them. Out beyond the doors, the music was working back up from pianissimo to fortissimo. "What is it?" Sid said, frowning.

"I thought I'd come out and lend a hand."

The very thought agitated him. "Come on! You're supposed to be out there. I'll take care of this. Get out of here."

I opened the refrigerator door and put away a butter dish, a bottle of milk, and half a head of lettuce. I scraped some peelings and rinds off a counter into a paper bag and looked around for the garbage pail. Sid had hold of my arm.

"It's my job. Go on back and listen."

"They don't need me to listen."

"Charity will eat your gizzard out."

"That's a giblet that will poison her." I found an overflowing wastebasket and crammed the sack of peelings into it. There were dishtowels hanging on the oven door handle. I pulled one out and began drying the plates that Sid had set on edge in the drain rack. He tried to take the towel out of my hands.

"Look," he said, "I'd really appreciate it if you'd go back. I'll join you in a few minutes."

"If we go together we can go in half the time."

He let go of the towel. For a moment he stood frowning. Then he shrugged and went back to his sink full of suds.

"Have you been a bad boy?" I asked. "What have you done to deserve three years of K.P.?"

"It hasn't been that long. And it's a fair arrangement."

"How do you tell it from punishment?"

Looking sideward, sharp and at first offended, he raised his eyebrows and shoulders and gave a little laugh. "I guess it *is* punishment."

"What for?"

Shrug. Another sideward glance. "General incompetence."

I was wiping and stacking the clean plates on a corner of the counter. "Explain, Professor."

Sid laughed again, looking at the black window above the sink as if something outside had caught his eye. His tongue came out to touch his upper lip. "I proved I couldn't hit big-league pitching."

"Horsefeathers. They called the game on account of wet grounds."

"Whatever." His hands paused in the dishwater. "The taste of failure is like the taste of cabbage soup, you know that? It rises sourly in the gorge. Just an echo, hoo hoo. Now you go on back and let me finish my work."

"With permission," I said, "the hell with you."

Once he submitted, we made progress. The stacks of clean dishes grew, the counters and tables got mopped clean, we reached the pots and pans.

"One reason I'm here wiping is that I want to talk to you," I said. "People are going to be coming back to college. Johnny'll come marching home. The colleges are going to start hiring again."

He glanced up, but said nothing. I saw scorn in his face.

"The head of the Dartmouth English Department has been in my section of the OWI," I said. "He's just gone back. He's already looking for people."

No comment.

"If you think you'd like to go back to teaching, and lay this ridiculous rumor that you're not competent, I can put your name in."

Now he did look fully up, and his hands were quiet in the greasy water. The scorn had been wiped from his face; he looked close to terrified. For a long second he stared at me, and then went irritably back to work.

"Slave labor," I said. "Off the promotion ladder, at least for now. They'll protect their regular faculty and bring in irregulars for the rush."

"What as?" Sid said. "Instructors?"

"Mostly. Not you. With your experience you shouldn't take less than assistant professor. You ought to get associate, but that's out."

For a while he scoured the bottom of a saucepan with a Brillo pad. He held the pan under the hot tap and the black scourings rinsed away and left clean red copper. He put the pan upside down on the drain.

"After the Wisconsin debacle I wouldn't have the chance to take anything. Not at a place as good as Dartmouth."

"Yes, you would, if you want it."

"I just reminded you, I proved I can't hit big-league pitching."

"And I just told you horsefeathers. You can hit anything they can throw."

"What makes you think I'd have a chance?"

"Because I've talked to Bramwell about you."

"You have?"

"A couple of times. He's been beating the bushes. There weren't many Ph.D.'s produced in the last three years. All of a sudden it's a seller's market. *If* you want to go back to teaching."

He worked away at a colander. In the living room I heard the music swelling up to a passion. "Did you tell Bramwell all about me?"

"Every shameful detail."

"And he still thought I'd have a chance?"

"You'd have to apply," I said, irritated. "Remember what old McChesney told Sally when she asked him when the wild strawberries would be ripe? 'Wal, you have to let 'em blossom first.' You'd have to act as if you *wanted* a job. You'd have to send him a letter and a *vita.*"

"And if I should, do you think there's a chance?"

"If you do, you're in," I said. "He's crazy enough to think you'd be a catch. For the kind of job he's got, you would be."

He stood motionless, staring at me across the steam of the sink. His eyes began to open, his lips drew back, the vertical creases in his cheeks deepened, his smile broadened. "You sly bugger," he said. "Morgan . . ."

The door to the dining room was pushed open. Music shouldered into the kitchen. Charity stood in the door. She took in the stacks of wiped dishes, the cleaned counters, the clean pans, Sid with his hands in the water, me with my guilty dishtowel in my hands. Red flooded into her face.

"Really!" she said.

"We're just finishing," Sid started to say. He said it to the closing door.

In silence we finished up. He dried his hands, I hung the wet dishtowel with the others on the oven door. Out in the living room a *Heldentenor* was shouting into the fog and the eclipse: *"Freunde . . . Freunde . . ."*

I said, "I guess it's time we tiptoed contritely to the doghouse."

He was not amused. His face was stiff and his eyes veiled. Quietly we went out the hall door and up the hall and stood at the top of the steps leading down into the living room. The tenor was through shouting. Now everyone was shouting. Choral exultancy filled the house and rattled the windows.

For a second or two we stood letting our eyes adjust to the darkroom gloom. The chorus rose and fell in waves, the music skittered from sopranos to tenors to basses and back again, really joyful, so joyful that the blood took off, trying to catch the beat. More than once we had sung that Ode to Joy in the Langs' Wisconsin living room with Dave Stone at the piano and nobody but friends in sight and the future a challenge that we would meet when it came. Uplifted, I joined in the chorus now, and came down the steps roaring.

No one else joined in. We found chairs. I stopped my clamor. Sally's face, rosy in the firelight, looked rueful. Charity was only an outline folded into the big chair. In silence we let joy sing itself out.

Long time ago. Better times grew over and healed those bad war years as grass and bushes heal scarred earth. Why did I think of that bad evening when there were so many good ones to remember? It was over next day—would have been over even if the Dartmouth opportunity hadn't altogether changed the atmosphere.

I am sure now, and was pretty sure then, that she didn't even know she was punishing Sid for disappointing all her hopes. Probably she had evolved the rationalizing theory that he needed a function, something useful to do—like dishes!—that would persuade him that he mattered in the scheme of things. Something his alone, humble perhaps, but his, a responsibility that he could accept and discharge. It sounds unlikely, but some of her ideas were. That didn't keep them from being, to her mind, totally logical.

He didn't need me to get him a teaching job after the war. Almost any of his dozens of friends could and would have done it, or he could have done it himself. All he had to do was write around and indicate that he was available. So even if I hadn't known Steve Bramwell's needs, Charity would have had to renounce her dramatizing of failure, and consent to resume life among the living. Still, they chose to think I had done him—done both of them—the greatest favor. If I did, it was not in finding him a job. It was in inducing Charity to end their self-imposed withdrawal and her pose of proud humiliation.

In the little spartan study, that furtive sanctuary, I felt airless and oppressed. I went through the dust-moted streak of sun to the shop door, and out onto the porch. The door slid heavily shut behind me, shutting in the tools waiting to be put to use, the pencils sharp for expression, the pads awaiting words, the dictionary of rhymes with its face turned to the wall in the hope of going undiscovered. With a feeling that I was escaping something, I went on over to the Big House.

3

The porch of the Big House overlooks a lot of family history. The cove itself, which Aunt Emily used to swim across every day before lunch, is private water, a family sea. We sit above it, at a table set with bright, flowered pottery, and look across at the Ellis dock and boathouse, and beyond those, backed by woods, the weathered cottage that is now inhabited by Comfort and Lyle Lister.

Our talk goes as inevitably backward as our eyes. Hallie steers it, obviously trying to get away from the discomfort of our talk in the study, and give us back the Battell Pond we used to know. Sally and I corroborate or amplify as we are called on. Moe listens with his Levantine smile, his watchful, comprehending eyes moving from his wife to us and back to his wife. He listens as an anthropologist might listen to the stories and gossip of primitive villagers in an effort to hear the heartbeat of a culture. He and Sally have something in common, something ancient, knowing, sympathetic, unfretful, and ultimately sad.

It is less a conversation than a series of recollections, reminders, and questions. We are affectionately scolded.

—Doesn't your conscience bother you? All the time I was growing up, the Morgans and Langs were part of the same family, back and forth between Hanover and Cambridge, and up here together every summer. Then you go and move to New Mexico. Even Lang quit coming.

—It's my fault. I wanted to get away from Cambridge winters, and once we were out there it was hard to get back. And Lang was on the West Coast, and her job and Jim's job were obviously going to keep them there.

—Doesn't she get vacations? Doesn't she ever want to see her old friends? She's only brought Jim here once, to our wedding. I always thought of her as my big sister, and wanted our kids to grow up together like cousins, and they've never even *met*. How *is* the selfish wretch? Does she like being a banker?

—Securities analyst. She's fine. Yes, she likes working. I guess she's good at it. She makes more than Jim does.

—She sold us out for dirty dollars.

—Come on, Hallie. Is it a one-way street? It's no farther from here to the West Coast than it is from the West Coast here. You could go visit her. She'd love it.

—But this is where we all *belong*! Don't tell me you've become a chauvinistic westerner.

—I was always a westerner. New England was a rainy interlude.

She is so outraged that I have to back off.

—I take it back. It was no interlude. It was the best time of our lives.

—You'd better not be one of those boosters selling sunshine. What's the matter with this sunshine? Oh, you know, you really do belong here! You and Mom and Dad were always so in *tune*. I remember you going off to those Sunday evening concerts that Mom started. This was long before you ever saw Battell Pond, Moe. They used to play phonograph records through a loudspeaker from the town dock and everybody'd gather in canoes and rowboats. We could hear it clear over here when we quieted down enough. We'd all get left with Flo or whoever it was that summer, and we'd watch the four of you row away and as soon as you were around the point we'd tear the place apart.

—Charity knew that. She thought it was good for you, once a week. I always felt guilty about making us go in the dumpy old rowboat, but I'd have swamped us if I'd tried to get into a canoe. I loved those concerts. Mozart and Schubert across the water, people drifting around stirring a paddle now and then, and the sunset gathering behind us. Your father loved them too. He couldn't get his lungs full enough. He *breathed* sunset. By the time the music was over it would be dark and chilly. Charity and I were always wrapped up in those Algerian burnooses.

—Which would have drowned you if we'd capsized.

—I wouldn't have been any safer in a bathing suit. What nicer way to go, anyway? And Charity had always thought ahead and brought flashlights so we could see to get home. Larry and Sid had to carry me up the path on their hands while Charity and I held the lights. This was the blackest place, at night, I ever saw. I suppose it still is. You couldn't see the dock till the boat bumped it. You couldn't see your hand if you had hold of your nose.

—What she is struggling to express is expressed by an old New Mexico saying: It was so dark you couldn't find your ass with both hands.

—Why, thank you, darling. You took the words right out of my mouth.

Laughter. It is fine to be on that porch, in that company. The sun is full on us, warm but not too warm. It will be a while before the shadow of the nearest tree moves across.

—You were so much a part of us, like aunt and uncle. Meals and swims and hikes and picnics and expeditions. Larry and Dad always had some project—fencing the tennis court, or building a new dock, or putting a cattle guard in the gate up to Folsom Hill. Do you suppose other men get fun out of coming to the country on vacation and working like day laborers? And you and Mom were so close. You really deprived her when you moved west. She's never found anybody else it's so much fun to do things with. Actually it isn't as nice here as it used to be, I think. It's got dressier, the country-club crowd sets the tone. The way I remember you two, neither of you ever gave a hoot how you dressed. Strangers could never figure you out, you on your canes with your cocky little Bavarian hat with a feather in it, and Mom in one of her bedspread skirts, clear to the ground, and huaraches, and ankle socks, and a *mouchoir* around her head. I'm ashamed to tell you this, Sally, but that winter we were together in Italy I used to walk forty feet behind you two so that nobody would know I belonged with Mom. What was I? Fourteen or so. I just died at some of the things she'd do, and the way she looked. Did I ever tell you about the time you got out of the Marmon in front of McChesney's, and these two summer people, Upper Montclair types, were standing there? They were fascinated. They couldn't make out whether you were a rich invalid and Mom was your nurse, or whether you were gypsies, or servants driving the master's car, or hippies from Stannard Mountain, or what. I heard one of them say, 'That car's an absolute heirloom, Ed would be mad for it,' and the other said, 'That's a Liberty's scarf on the big one, and the one on crutches is wearing a hand-loomed skirt.' You made this a happy place for all the Langs.

—What are you saying? You made it happy for us. We were privileged visitors.

Hallie is nearly as striking as her mother used to be, and softer, more feminine. For an instant, on the sunny porch, brushing a wind-stirred strand of pale hair away from her face, she looks like Charity in a contentious mood.

—No no no. I won't have it. Not visitors. Family.

Moe, who has been working on a cork, stands up and goes around pouring.

—Speaking of family. Larry, do you talk a lot about your p-p-p-parents?

—My parents died more than forty years ago.

—Did you talk about them before they died?

—It wouldn't have occurred to me.

—Wh-*when* they died?

—I shut the door.

—Sally?

—I never had a father. My mother died when I was twelve.

—Then it must seem as strange to you as it does to m-m-me. I sit in, I hear all this family recollection, dissection, analysis, speculation, puzzlement, outrage, rebellion, pity, whatever, and I'm astonished. My father m-m-meant a lot to me, he taught me a lot and I respected him. My m-m-mother was a Jewish Mama, smothering, but you had to love her, right? Well, I never discussed them when they were alive, even with old f-f-f-friends, even with my b-b-brother. I don't think I've talked about them with a dozen p-p-people since they died. This family, though, you can't b-b-believe them. The minute any two of them get together they're off on M-M-Mom and Dad.

—You do it yourself! You're as much into those bull sessions as any of us.

—I didn't mean to irritate you, sweetheart. I didn't m-m-m-mean to exempt myself. I just meant, how those two people do occupy the m-m-minds of the family.

—Not Dad. Mom, yes. But that's because . . .

—Long before she got s-s-sick. Both of them. The other day I was r-r-reading that Katherine Anne Porter novel, whatsitsname, *Ship of Fools*. There's a scene where she's passing in a b-b-bus and catches a glimpse of these two, a man and a woman, she's stabbing him with a knife, he's hitting her with a r-r-rock. Stab, clonk, stab, clonk. Mortally locked together. It's like that.

—Good heavens, Moe, you've been reading too much! It isn't like that at all. It's never violent. It's never even competitive. He always loses.

—Maybe so. Just the same, it's mutual crucifixion. They aren't individuals, they're a c-c-c-c-confrontation. They're an insoluble dilemma. Your father is a captive husband, like m-m-me . . .

—Oh, like you!

—Exactly. And like your Grandfather Ellis. Aunt Emily k-k-kept him in his th-th-th-think house, and looked after him kindly, like the family dog. She admired the way he could read G-G-Greek and Latin and H-H-H-Hebrew. I'm sure she loved him, but she wore the pants. This isn't a f-f-f-family, it's a pride. Females run it. Us males lie around yawning and showing our two-inch t-t-teeth, and get swatted when we get out of l-l-line. We have only one function.

—Oh, Moe, I feel sorry for you!

—Sorry for me why? I love to yawn and show my t-t-teeth, and have my d-d-dinner brought to me, and service all the l-l-l-ladies. I just wish the family would acknowledge its p-p-p-p . . . its p-p-p-p . . . admit what it's doing. You've written a lot of books, Larry, but you've n-n-n-neglected one that's screaming to be written.

—You can't write about your friends.

—Why not? None of us wants it to happen, but this confrontation, if that's what it is, is almost over.

—People leave unfinished business. They leave unanswered questions. They leave children, sometimes quite a few.

—Some of us children might like to see them written up. It might help answer some of the unanswered questions. Such as, why have they stuck together all these years. It's been a kind of agony for both of them.

—Oh, not all the time! Not even very much of the time. I don't think there's ever been a question of their splitting up. Neither one would think of it. It would destroy them both.

—I suppose. Just the same . . .

Moe passes the bottle across, and I pour. He looks in the window, frowning. "Is the fool girl *laying* the eggs?" But Hallie pays no attention. She is watching me. She is serious about this. She'd like a book about her parents.

—Hallie, you've got the wrong idea of what writers do. They don't understand any more than other people. They invent only plots they can resolve. They ask the questions they can answer. Those aren't people that you see in books, those are constructs. Novels or biographies, it makes no difference. I couldn't reproduce the real Sid and

Charity Lang, much less explain them; and if I invented them I'd be falsifying something I don't want to falsify.

—I thought fiction was the art of making truth out of faked materials.

—Sure. This would be making falsehood out of true materials.

—If you can't do it, who can?

—Maybe nobody can.

—Doesn't it bother you the way it does us? It must. They hang in the air like an unresolved chord. Some Mozart has to go downstairs and bang the right notes and let them rest.

—Some other Mozart than this one.

There are further considerations I might raise. How do you make a book that anyone will read out of lives as quiet as these? Where are the things that novelists seize upon and readers expect? Where is the high life, the conspicuous waste, the violence, the kinky sex, the death wish? Where are the suburban infidelities, the promiscuities, the convulsive divorces, the alcohol, the drugs, the lost weekends? Where are the hatreds, the political ambitions, the lust for power? Where are speed, noise, ugliness, everything that makes us who we are and makes us recognize ourselves in fiction?

The people we are talking about are hangovers from a quieter time. They have been able to buy quiet, and distance themselves from industrial ugliness. They live behind university walls part of the year, and in a green garden the rest of it. Their intelligence and their civilized tradition protect them from most of the temptations, indiscretions, vulgarities, and passionate errors that pester and perturb most of us. They fascinate their children because they are so decent, so gracious, so compassionate and understanding and cultivated and well-meaning. They baffle their children because in spite of all they have and are, in spite of being to most eyes an ideal couple, they are remote, unreliable, even harsh. And they have missed something, and show it.

Why? Because they are who they are. Why are they so helplessly who they are? Unanswered question, perhaps unanswerable. In nearly forty years, neither has been able to change the other by so much as a punctuation mark.

Another consideration, a personal and troubling one. I am their friend. I respect and love them both. What is more, our lives have been so twisted together that I couldn't write them without writing Sally and me as well. I wonder if I could recreate any of us without my portraits being tainted by pity or self-pity. *Amicitia* is a pure stream. Too many ppm's of pity might make it undrinkable.

The girl interrupts our somewhat awkward silence. She is perhaps the twentieth local girl to work summers in this house. The tray she carries is loaded with a coffeepot, a pitcher of orange juice, and a bowl of raspberries. She plugs the coffeepot into an outlet and hustles back inside, returning almost at once with a platter of ham, hot plates, biscuits, and a big omelet. Moe grunts and shakes out his napkin. Hallie begins to serve. We eat, and the pressure is off me.

—Is everything all right? Is what's supposed to be hot, hot, and what's supposed to be cold, cold? Clara doesn't always get it all together.

—Marvelous. Heavenly.

—Is the sun in your eyes, Sally? Want to be moved around a little?

—I'm fine right here. Always was.

—But you still went and moved to New Mexico.

—It wasn't this I moved from.

—I was just talking. Even if you did move from this, who could blame you? This was where you had your terrible bad luck.

—Bad luck?

—The polio.

—I could have caught that anywhere.

—Just the same, Mom blames herself. She says they took you out on a pack trip when you were still anemic and run-down from having Lang. She thinks you might have thrown it off, the way some people do, if they hadn't overworked you.

—That's ridiculous. I was feeling as good as I ever felt in my life. They'd been fattening me up and looking after me all summer. And after it happened, they were both simply wonderful.

—They say you were the wonderful one. How you stood being brought out on the horse, and afterward. But then, we know you, we've seen you all these years.

I can see those years stretched out in Hallie's mind, more years than her own total experience of living. All the time of her infancy, childhood, girlhood, adolescence, college, marriage, poor Sally Morgan has been pegging around on crutches, needing help to go to the toilet or get out of bed or even out of a chair, and yet refusing to be either helpless or hopeless. Drives her own specially equipped car.

Travels, or used to, all over the world. Cooks, scooting around her kitchen in her high chair on wheels. Does all but the heavy housework. And smiles, is cheerful, and amused, and amusing. Doesn't complain, thinks of others. Hallie's eyes are moist as she looks at her. Love is there, and admiration.

Properly. I have wet an eye myself in contemplation of that woman.

—Did they ever tell you what *they* did?

—What they did? When?

—While I was sick. If I'd been picking the very worst time to get sick I couldn't have done better. They were just about to go back to Madison, the dream house was already started, Charity was on fire to get back and oversee it. And she had three children under five, and you in the oven, though she couldn't have known that yet. We were out of a job, and they'd offered us this house for the winter. They never missed a chance to be generous. So I go and get sick.

She sits very erectly, forgetting to eat. Her eyes are wide and glowing. The mere thought of what they did melts her with affectionate gratitude.

—They just abandoned everything because of me. Charity went with us in the ambulance to Burlington, and when I was in the iron lung, and so to speak safe, she and Larry took turns talking me back to life. Poor Larry, he had to support us, and all he had was book reviews at fifteen or twenty dollars apiece. He'd try to read while he sat watching the air being pumped into me and out again, and when Charity came and took over he'd go back to his room and try to write. Without her there, he'd never have been able to do a thing, and I'd have worried myself to death. In the meantime, Sid had loaded up all the kids, Lang with them, and driven them back to Madison, and Aunt Emily had abandoned your grandfather and gone out on the train to hold the family together. Talk about solidarity!

The girl reappears on the porch, looking questioning, and Hallie motions her back in. She and Moe are both intent on Sally, stiff in her stiff chair. Her voice comes out of her in a tranced stream, interrupted by pauses while she catches her breath. If I were filming the Delphic Oracle, I would get Sally in that mood to play the Pythoness.

—You get a new perspective in an iron lung. I was nothing but a suffering vegetable. I couldn't move anything but my head, but I could certainly worry. I worried about my baby, I worried about poor Larry, dying on his feet. I worried about Charity's house, going up without her after all her preparations, just because of me. I worried about Sid with that house full of children, and poor helpless Mr. Ellis, left to look after himself in Cambridge. I worried about the enormous bills we were piling up, and about whether I'd ever get well enough to justify all that was being spent on me. When the 1938 hurricane hit us, I worried about the power going off and cutting off my air, and some-times I almost wished it would. But then I'd look up into my mirror, and there would be Larry half asleep over his book, or your mother with that smile. You've inherited it, Hallie. It's a wonderful gift. It has life in it. I couldn't think of dying with that shining on me.

Pause while she draws a ragged breath. None of us speaks. Moe, with his eyes on Sally's face, gropes his coffee cup down blindly, feel-ing for the saucer.

—She paid the bills, too—just went to the office and settled the whole thing and asked them to send any further bills to her. Larry was upset, but my goodness, how much she took off our minds! He got her to take his note for it, and later for a lot more she advanced us. We were years paying it back, and every time we'd send a few hundred dollars they'd act as if we were some kind of paragons of honesty, as if nobody ever heard of people who tried to pay back a precious debt.

—I never heard any of that. It sounds like Mom.

—Like both of them. He'd write me these letters full of news and funny little poems, and snapshots of Lang, and sound as if it was a privilege to take care of all those children while he was starting a new term. Nearly every day, something to cheer me up. Then when the doctors said my best chance of getting back some muscular control was Warm Springs, that really sunk us, it was so utterly impossible. This was the Depression, remember, there wasn't any unemployment insurance, or health care, or anything. Larry didn't even have a job. But Charity and Sid just jumped at it. Yes! they said. Do it, whatever it costs. Don't *worry* about costs. So Larry took me to Georgia, and at first I was terribly depressed. My legs were gone, and one hand not much use, and I was surrounded by people as bad off or worse, people who gave me an idea of what I could expect my life to be like. Some parts of the therapy were all right, but some were so rough and callous they almost killed me. They'd put you on a treadmill, for instance, with rails to hold on to, and you were supposed to try to walk. There was a nurse behind you with a hand in your belt, but she never kept you from falling. They were careless, they didn't hang on tight. We all fell. I found out later they did that on purpose, to harden your will. Unless you'd grit your teeth and take any amount of punishment and failure and still go on trying, they knew you'd never improve. I was so discouraged I cried all the time, and when Charity heard that, she abandoned the family again, and came down. When they put me on the treadmill she was right there to help me and encourage me. She made me try, and try, and try. I never did get so I could walk, but I got more control in other ways. There was a boy there, about seventeen, a high school athlete from Chicago, a very nice boy. They put him on the treadmill and he fell like everyone else. I'll never forget the desperate look on his face. They hoisted him up and tried to make him start again, and he wouldn't. He just hung there with his teeth in his lip and tears running down his face. He never did get on again, and after a while they sent him home. He's written me for years. He's lived ever since in a wheelchair.

The tranced voice pauses, the tranced eyes become aware of what they see. Sally blinks, and sends a startled, apologetic-defiant look around the table. She laughs, a strangled little hiccup. We are all silent. Surely Hallie and Moe never heard anything like this passionate rush of feeling from Sally. I never did either, not in public, nowhere except once in a while in bed when she has awakened from a dream to find herself still imprisoned in her helpless flesh.

—So who was wonderful? I was just a crippled thing that had to be made to want to live. They made me—Charity especially, but both of them. I had to live, out of pure gratitude.

The girl looks out again, gets a nod from Hallie, and begins loading dishes on a tray. Sally, her thin shoulders pulled together, sits stiffly, her eyes downcast and her breath uneven. Her hands, the half-clenched one on top, are folded in her lap, in the sun. Her feet are quiet on the metal step of the chair, also in the sun. But her face is in the shade that moves and changes with the movement of leaves up above.

—I'm ashamed. For years now we haven't been as close as we used to be. I let myself get irritated at her way of taking charge of everything. I thought she was a tyrant to all of you in the family. I still do. But I shouldn't have ever let myself forget what a wonderfully unselfish friend she has been. I should have had the grace to forgive what I knew she couldn't help. We parted almost as if we *weren't* friends, and it's been eight years.

She sits. Her eyes go quickly around from one to another of us. She forces the tension out of her lips and cheeks; the *kore* smile tries to return. But something will not quite loosen. Under the returning placidity some tight muscle gives her expression a shadow of sternness. Her eyes lift, and fix themselves on Hallie.

"Tell me exactly how she is. Is she in pain? I can't tell from her letters."

"If she was, she wouldn't let on. But I don't think so. Stomach cancer is supposed to be less painful than other kinds. Of course, it's metastasized, it's all through her now. Earlier this summer, just in case, she and David did some meditation training—controlling pain by a sort of self-hypnosis. I don't know if she's had to use it. I do know she hasn't taken any pain-killers. Won't."

"No. I remember when she was having David, she didn't even want any ether. She wanted to experience everything. She isn't afraid, is she?"

"Not a bit. She's incredible. The other day we were talking, and somebody—Nick, I guess, he was still here—forgot for a minute how things were, it was such an ordinary kind of family conversation, and asked her how she was going to vote in November. You know what she said? She looked at him with her eyebrows cocked in that way she has, and her eyes just dancing, you'd have thought she was letting some happy secret out of the bag, and said 'Absentee.' We cracked up, we couldn't help it. No, you're absolutely right. She wants to experience everything, and she won't be shortchanged. You know how she likes to plan. Well, she's planning this the same way. She's like a choreographer, every little step is plotted out. Even . . ."

Hesitation. "What?" Sally says.

"Better not," Moe says.

"Oh, they have to know! I hate it, I can't bear to think about it. But she's already signed the papers. She's willed her body to the organ bank of the Hitchcock Clinic in Hanover. God, I just . . . I blew up when she told me. I said, 'Mom, who *wants* a sixty-year-old kidney or a pair of sixty-year-old corneas? You're doing this for some theoretical reason. It'll torture us. Let your poor body go in peace.' But she says she wants to be a good steward. Whatever's worn out can be cremated and go back to the earth, but whatever's still useful ought to be used by someone who needs it."

Indignant tears stand in her eyes. She bends her head and puts her fist to her lips, then looks up, laughs, shakes her head. Sally, from her edge of shade, looks out broodingly as if from a cave.

"She's really getting ready."

"Oh, yes."

"Oh, I wish she'd let me know sooner! We should have come weeks ago. It's what she would have done for me. But she sounded as if it was under control."

"She's known since May. But there was a remission, it just seemed to mark time. She didn't want to worry you."

"She knew I couldn't do anything," Sally says, with a sad mouth. "She'd have been trying to look after *me*." She broods at the crumpled napkin in her hand as if she can't make up her mind what it is or how it came there. Then she lays it on the table. "When can we see her?"

"Anytime."

"Won't they be having lunch?"

"She hardly eats anything. Dad generally has just a sandwich at noon. She said bring you when you're rested and have eaten." She looks at her watch. "We've got a couple of errands to do before the picnic. We'll leave you there and meet you later, on the hill. So anytime you're ready."

"I should make a couple of telephone calls," Moe says. "Maybe now is the time."

Sally reaches for her canes and props them against her chair. Moe leaps up, but I sit still, because I can see that she is still brooding, not ready to move. I know what she is doing. She is looking, in her steady way, at what we have until now pretty well covered over with a mulch of nostalgia.

Hallie, thinking aloud, says, "Moe, you'd *better* make those calls. I want to talk to Clara, too. Would you two mind waiting just a few minutes?"

"Of course not," I say. Sally says nothing, sitting stiffly and staring into the past or the future, whichever it is that oppresses her.

Hallie has paused in mid-departure, watching Sally's face. "Is something wrong? Can I do anything?"

Sally lifts her eyes, huge wide-spaced eyes in a face whose skin is tightly stretched on its bones. The slight pucker in her forehead smooths out, the plane of her cheek softens, the look that only seconds before glared out like the high beam of a headlight is shuttered and focused down.

"Nobody can do anything," she says. "It's the way things are."

Left without anything to do but mutter agreement, Hallie and Moe delay awkwardly for a moment and then excuse themselves. We sit on. Sally blots her eyes one after the other with a knuckle.

"I guess I was hoping I'd wake up and find it wasn't so."

"It seems to be closer than we thought."

"It's hard to take in, there are so many reminders. She *lives* so. She's everywhere you look. Did you notice the dishes?"

"Cantigalli, weren't they?"

"Yes. From Florence. Remember the day we went with her to buy them?"

"Was I along?"

"Sure. We went out to the factory. She bought sets and sets of them. Later they arrived in Hanover in three big barrels."

"I take your word for it."

"You can. I haven't forgotten one hour of that year."

"A year without housework."

"Oh, more than that! That year was all spring, even when it snowed. Every so often I wake up and that little poem of Lorenzo's is running through my head. Remember? The one they teach to every tourist?

> Quant' é bella giovinezza
> Che si fugge tuttavia"

She shakes her head. "Youth did flee, too, but that year we were young—that was the second year. The first was Madison. Before that it was all kind of gray, and since then it's been mainly hanging on. Is that the way it's been for you? But that year in Florence we were young. Youth hasn't got anything to do with chronological age. It's times of hope and happiness."

"Che si fuggono," I say, and then, because I don't want to add to her desolate mood, I say, "You weren't the first to find your youth there. Remember Goethe? *Kennst du das Land, wo die Zitronen blühen?* And Milton? When he couldn't stand any more English winters and English politics you know what he'd do? He'd eat an olive to remind him of Italy."

"I don't need any olives," Sally says.

4

Once, at a Cambridge dinner party, I had an imaginary debate with the sociologist Pitirim Sorokin, who was holding forth on upward mobility. He called it "vertical peristalsis in society." Obviously he liked the phrase; he thought he had invented something pretty good.

Since he had been born nameless in a nameless Russian village and had risen to become a member of the Council of the Russian Republic and secretary to Prime Minister Kerensky, I granted that he knew more about upward mobility than I did. I had only my own limited experience to generalize from, and three martinis to make me skeptical of other evidence. But I didn't like his metaphor, and muttered to the lady on my left that social scientists should stick to semantically aseptic language, and leave metaphor to people who understood it.

Peristalsis, I informed this lady or someone else, consists of rhythmic contractions in a tube, such as the gut, that force matter in the tube to move along. In Sorokin's trope, society was the tube and the individual the matter to be moved, and the tube did the work of moving him. I thought the individual had something to do with moving himself, not necessarily rhythmically.

And why that word "vertical"? Man being an upright animal, at least in his posture, any peristalsis he had going was bound to be vertical, unless we conceived him to be lying down, which there was no reason to do.

Finally, I had the impression that normal peristalsis worked downward, not upward. Upward peristalsis was reverse peristalsis, whose name was emesis. Did Professor Sorokin mean to suggest that he had been vomited up into revolutionary prominence, and later into an international reputation and a distinguished position on the Harvard faculty? Probably he didn't. But there was no way out of his metaphorical difficulty. He couldn't extricate himself by reversing directions and accepting the normal alimentary flow, for that not only ruined his upward metaphor but left him looking even worse than if he had been vomited up.

Professor Sorokin never figured in my life. I had never seen him before that night and I never saw him afterward; and our argument never took place except in my head and out of the corner of my mouth. But we had just returned from a Guggenheim year in Italy, and in Italy I had discovered, rather to my surprise, that I had myself been ferociously upward-mobile since my first day in school. In reducing my strenuous life to a social inevitability, and giving it that taint of routine communal digestion, Sorokin insulted me where I lived.

Until Italy, I had been too busy to notice what I was. I was learning, and interested in the learning. Or I was diving into a hole and pulling the hole in after me. Or I was simply trying to survive. But even in our most oppressed times, I was a cork held under, my impulse was always up.

According to Aunt Emily's theories, I should probably have been led to walk in my father's footsteps. I loved him, we got along, I worked off and on in the shop. There was no reason why I should not succeed him as proprietor and make a life out of transmissions, brake bands, ring jobs, lube jobs, yard chores, neighborhood barbecues, baseball, and beer. But I had no intention, ever, of doing that. It wasn't snobbishness. I was never ashamed of him. Nothing in dusty Albuquerque led me to envious comparisons. I just expected more than Albuquerque offered. I took it for granted. And everybody important to me—my parents, my teachers, my professors in college, Sally when we met in Berkeley, and for that matter the Langs when we met in Madison—made the same assumption. I was headed somewhere.

Without knowing what I was after, I pursued it with the blind singlemindedness of a sperm hunting its target egg—now there is a metaphor I will accept. For a long time it was dark, and all I could do was swim for my life. Union and consummation finally took place in the fourth-floor front room of the Pensione Vespucci, an old palazzo on the Lungarno a little below the American consulate in Florence. There, one September morning, it hit me that things were altogether other than what they had been for a long time. Wherever it was that we were going, we had arrived, or at least come into the clear road.

·   ·   ·

Usually the bells from churches over on Bellosguardo awoke us at six, but this morning I awoke earlier, before dawn. For a while I lay on my back and sent my ears abroad in search of what had brought me awake. But I heard nothing, not the slightest whisper of *rumore* from the street that was practically never silent, no switching of trains in the stony distance, no bells or whistles, no snarl of a Vespa starting off up some alley, no footsteps on bare stone, no stir of our awakening house communicating itself through marble and plaster, no voices of early fishermen down in the trough of the river.

Nothing but Sally's soft purr beside me and the ticking of the clock, sounds so near and comfortable and reassuring that they accentuated the hush into which they fell. In the bed that was still strange to me I lay listening for outside sounds that I was not sure I could interpret, and I had a thrilling sense of the safety of *hereness* and the close dark. It didn't really matter what noise out there had caught my sleeping ear. Sally breathed quietly beside me. The clock ticked us toward morning.

Then I woke up another notch. Clock? We had no clock. Then what was I hearing? Holding my breath, I listened. *Tick-tick-ticket-tick-tickety-tick-tick,* not one clock but many, unsynchronized. I brought my watch to my ear: inaudible an inch away. But the faint, hurrying, ratchety, dry ticking went on.

Folding back the covers, I went to the French doors, opened one, and stepped out onto the roof terrace. The night was lighter than the room, and the ticking was much louder, hastier, its rhythms more broken—such a sound as several children might make running sticks at different speeds along a picket fence a block away. I went to the balustrade and looked down into the street, and *ecco,* there it came, a bobbing line of lanterns that curved off the Vittoria Bridge and came on up the Lungarno toward the city. Every lantern swung from a two-wheeled cart, and beside every cart walked a man, and drawing every cart was a donkey whose hasty feet ticked on the pavement.

The swinging lanterns threw exaggerated shadows of spoked wheels, scissoring legs, and long donkey ears onto the stone parapet of the river. Below the pattering and ticking of hoofs, now that sounds were not partly cut off by the jut of the roof, I heard the grit and grate of iron tires on pavement, the squeak of axles, scattered talk, a laugh. When someone stopped to light a cigarette, his face bloomed red for a moment in the flare of the match.

I sprang back inside, stopping long enough to unlatch the other half of the doors and leave both sides standing open. When I snapped on the bed light, Sally lifted her head. "What is it?"

"I'm going to pick you up," I said. "The quilt too. Up we go."

I scooped her out of the bed, gathered the quilt over her legs, and started for the doors. "But what is it?" she cried, alarmed. "Is there a fire? What's the matter?"

"No fire," I said. "No time either. It might be gone. You've got to see it."

On the balustrade I set her down, wrapped the quilt around her, and got my arm around her to hold her. Her arm came around my neck before she dared look down.

I needn't have worried that the procession would be over. It was still ticking and grating past, a half mile of moving lights and half-seen shapes of men and donkeys and loaded carts that constantly renewed itself off the bridge.

"Oh, look at them!" Sally breathed. Inside my arm she was warm with sleep. "What are they, do you know?"

"Market carts, I guess. Bringing in the zucchini and *carciofi.*"

"They're beautiful! How did you know about them?"

"I didn't. I heard their hoofs going tickety-tickety."

"Isn't it a nice sound. Like Ferde Grofé."

"Better than the farm trucks banging in toward Faneuil Hall."

We watched for quite a while, and still the stream turned in off the bridge and the lanterns swung past. My feet were getting cold, and were punctured by the gravel embedded in the roof.

"Have you seen enough? Want to go in?"

"Oh, not yet! Let's see how long it goes on."

"Sure you're not cold?"

"Not a bit." Then her hand went up and down my back, pressing the cold cloth of my pajamas to my skin. "But *you* are! You're freezing. Come under the quilt."

My feet were killing me, but she was so enchanted by what was passing below us that I couldn't have admitted it. Anything she was enchanted by she was entitled to. I came under the quilt.

"Better?"

"Great. You're like a heating pad."

"It's my warm heart. Feel it."

I did. I stood there on my icy feet with my arm around her and her breast in my hand, and such a sudden flood of complex feeling went through me that I could have groaned or ground my teeth. Thin and eager, she crowded against me, and I was acutely aware how under the quilt her pipestem legs hung lifeless from the balustrade. A hundred what-ifs and might-have-beens swung in my skull as the lanterns swung in the street. I kissed her. "Cold nose," I said. "Healthy dog."

Eventually the procession of carts tailed off to occasional hurrying stragglers. The lanterns had lost their luminance, the street was gray with daylight, we could see the mounded vegetables, the boxes and sacks of onions, potatoes, or artichokes on the carts. The sky had paled, silhouetting the hills across the river from Bellosguardo to the Belvedere. Against the shadowed hills were the curves of streets, angles of red roofs, black spires of cypresses. Down in the river bottom two fishermen with long poles had appeared, and were throwing their lines into the meager stream that flowed below the weir.

Upstream, the river's pewtery shine was spanned by the bridges— Vespucci, Carraia, the sweet catenary curve of Santa Trinita, all of them recently rebuilt from the stones the Germans had left in the river; and beyond those, blocking any further view, the crowded ocher-and-umber buildings and the enclosed causeway of the Ponte Vecchio. It was like looking upriver into the pour of history, seeing backward toward the beginnings of modern civilization.

I would get used to ancient history in the next ten years, when we traveled a lot, and Florence, choked with crowds and automobiles, would lose some of its glamor. But right then, history-less and green, gawky newcomer and pretender to the culture of my kind, I watched the city and the river grow into daylight reality and could hardly believe that it was Sally and Larry Morgan, people I knew, who were on that balcony taking it in.

By the time I had carried Sally back to bed, got my slippers on, and put the water heater in the pitcher to make hot water for tea, the bells had begun over on Bellosguardo, a polyphony in four or five voices. They had rung out over many centuries of blood and striving, and I intended to learn from the city they rang into wakefulness. There would be whole long afternoons and evenings with no manuscripts to read and no hackwork to write. We could learn Italian, we could read about the Medici, we could walk the streets that Leonardo and Galileo had walked, we could catch up with the Renaissance and grow into our world and ourselves. At past forty, with a daughter starting college, we could begin.

Now the incomparable Florentine *rumore della strada* was growing, coming with the fresh morning air through the open doors. The voice of the Vespa was heard in the land. Bubbles were rising along the heating element submerged in the pitcher. I set out two cups and a tea bag. Propped against the carved headboard with a plaster *putto* looking down on her from the corner of the ceiling, Sally watched me.

"Can you believe we've got a whole year of this ahead of us?"

"It gives me the intellectual bends."

She studied me as if she suspected hidden meanings, and after a moment shook her head slightly and made an apologetic mouth. "I should think. You've had to work so hard, so long."

I poured hot water into the cup with the tea bag, and said nothing. Sally thinks too much. She has guilt feelings for what God has done to her.

"Well, you have," she said. "Look, you even have to make tea. I should at least be able to do that. You didn't come over here to be a kitchen maid."

I moved the tea bag into the other cup and poured the cup full. "Look yourself. Let's get something straight, once and for all. Repeat after me: 'I am not the millstone around your neck.'"

Shrugging and smiling, she finally repeated it. "I am not the millstone around your neck."

"'I am not the cross you bear.'"

"I am not the cross you bear."

"'I never *have* been the cross you bear.'"

"Oh, come on, let's not go clear overboard."

"No say, no tea. No tickee, no laundlee."

"All right. I never have been. I hope."

I handed her the cup, and she lay with it close to her lips. Her breath blew the steam across the cup toward me. "Let's pretend it was that debt that was your cross," she said. "Can you realize it's over with? It's like waking up and finding a big ugly birthmark has vanished overnight. They hated it as much as we did. Remember Charity, when you handed her the last check? 'Thank goodness, now we can just be *friends* again!' They'd have cancelled it ten years ago if we'd let them."

"If we had, would you feel this good now?"

"No, of course not. But I hated it that you were so driven. If it hadn't been for that, we might have been able to do this years ago."

"I survived. We all survived. We couldn't have come on account of Lang, anyway."

"Maybe not. I wonder how she's liking Mills by now?"

"That is not something that's going to keep me awake nights. My selfish mind is on the *vita nuova*. I give you John Simon Guggenheim."

We drank to John Simon in Bigelow's English Breakfast.

"You've got a resilient temperament, Mister Morgan," Sally said.

"I have to compensate for a woman who lives in constant anxiety, depression, and alarm."

Her eyes registered a question: Was I serious? She decided I wasn't. A warm, rich smile began to gather and take over her face. "Not any more," she said. Just at that moment the sun looked over Bellosguardo and a pinkish beam came flat through the doors. Sally, the pillows, the headboard, the wall, the *putto* in the ceiling corner, all blushed. Sally set her cup on the bed table and scowled at me. "Why are you over there? How can I kiss you if you're clear across the room?"

I came over and bent down and was kissed.

"You know what I'm going to do?" she said. "I'm going to be a really helpful wife. I'm not even going to speak to you between breakfast and lunch. I'm just going to read or study Italian and never peep a word and let you work."

"You can't get through a whole morning. Not without Mrs. Fellowes."

"I can teach Assunta. We can give her a little extra at tipping time."

"I won't be exactly unavailable, thirty feet away, or forty if I'm out on the terrace."

"No, I won't call on you. You're going to write the book that will show them all what you might have done long ago if you hadn't had a millstone around your neck. After lunch we'll take a nap—nothing's open till three anyway. After three we can soak up Florence. Charity's got a list of museums and churches and frescoes and expeditions three pages long."

"Charity has? I thought we bought the Fiat so they wouldn't feel responsible for us."

"They won't be. That doesn't mean we can't do things together."

"No. But let's not be *on* them. It feels too good to be free. Charity's agenda can get binding. Anything on for today?"

"Just our Italian lesson at five. Before that, they'll be taking Hallie out of the Poggio Imperiale."

"Taking her *out*? They just put her in."

"It isn't working. She's miserable. She'll be a lot better off in the American School."

"As anybody but Charity could have predicted. You tried to warn her. I heard you. So she does to poor Hallie exactly what her mother did to her in Paris. And what did Charity do then? She went over the wall. Somebody should tell her about people who refuse to learn from history."

Sally laughed. "She says she *did* learn. She learned her mother was right. She'd have got a lot more out of France if she'd stuck where her mother put her. She's been hoping Hallie would have better sense than she had."

"She's so incredible she's wonderful. It's good for her to have to eat crow once in a while. Is she eating it gracefully?"

"She's perfectly cheerful about it. She tried something, and it didn't work. So she's trying something else. She even thinks it's a kind of joke on herself. But she's really sorry about Hallie. It must have been grisly, not a word of Italian, not knowing a soul."

"We ought to try to get Lang over here for Christmas, you know."

"I thought you thought it would cost too much."

"Maybe we should do it no matter what it costs."

"You know," Sally said, "Italy's good for you. Let's do it. She'd love it. So would we. So would Hallie. She could use a playmate."

"She could show Lang the Poggio Imperiale." I stood up. "How about taking you to the bathroom so I can get to work?"

"Fine. But isn't it early to be typing? You might disturb the people across the hall."

"If they complain, I'll stop. But if I'm going to set the literary world on fire, the only way to do it is to rub one word against another."

So I was at the typewriter—hard at it, with my back to the morning and my face to the blank wall—when breakfast came. Maybe I had acquired the habit back in the furnace room on Morrison Street, but I found it easier to see what was in my head if I didn't have distractions in front of my eyes. I was writing up a New Mexico snowstorm, and I had it coming down thick and heavy, muffling the roads and mounding on adobe walls and windowsills and whitening the piñons and junipers when the tapping came on the door.

"Permesso?"

"Avanti."

The door opened and Silvano came in with the tray on one flat

211 || CROSSING TO SAFETY

hand, shoulder high. He wore his white gloves. He always wore them when serving food, to conceal his scarred, cracked workman's hands. He also wore his morning smile, which was gentle and tired. Distributing *buon giornos* to Sally in the bed and me in bathrobe and slippers, still with a few New Mexican snowflakes on my shoulders and hair, he lowered the tray onto the table in the early sun. His look took in, with sympathy, the typewriter and the paper and the wastebasket already half full of crumpled pages.

"*Sempre lavoro,*" he said. He affected to believe that I worked harder than he did, but his phrase contained sympathy for us both. *Sempre lavoro,* no fooling. Silvano lived out in Scandici, which he left before six every morning to stand for forty minutes on the jammed bus. For the first half hour after arriving at the Vespucci he would be mopping the marble entrance and sweeping the sidewalk and polishing the door handles. At seven-thirty he would start serving breakfast to fifteen rooms. Then there would be a time of cleanup in the kitchen and another time of raking the back courtyard where several of us kept our cars to preserve them from the *auto topi,* who would gnaw down to the chassis any vehicle left overnight in the street. For a few minutes around noon he would get to sit down to eat in the kitchen. Then he would put on his white gloves and serve lunch.

After lunch, I hope, he got a little siesta like everybody else, but I never knew for sure, and he was always subject to the ringing of a bell. In the afternoon he vacuumed the halls, ran errands, polished more brass. If anyone wanted tea or a drink, he left whatever he was doing and put on his gloves and served it, and afterward carried away the cups and glasses and went back to what he had left undone. If the *signora* or her daughter Albarosa had to leave the desk and telephone, Silvano took over. At seven he was back in his white gloves serving dinner. By nine he was ready to catch the bus back to Scandici.

Unless. The doors of the Vespucci were locked at eleven, and people who were out late had to come in through the courtyard entrance. That meant someone had to stay up to let them in, and that meant, generally, Silvano. I have never felt guiltier than one night soon after we arrived, when we went with the Langs to a concert, then to Doney's for a drink, then to the river to look at the lights, and then, on an impulse, up to the Piazzale to see the night city from above.

We got in about two, and had to bang pretty loud to be heard. Silvano finally opened the gate, so groggy he had to hang on to it to keep from falling down. His lids closed over his eyes as we made our apologies; he fell asleep on his feet while closing the gate. But his sad smile forgave us, even while we were telling each other that we must never do that to him again. On nights like that, of course, he didn't get home at all. Once, getting up early to walk in the Cascine before breakfast, I found him asleep in his clothes on the bench by the back door.

During the war Silvano had been unhappily a soldier, and toward the end a prisoner of the Americans. He hated war, trouble, and Tedeschi, who were associated in his mind, and loved the Sunday *calcio* games in the Campo di Marte. He considered himself very very lucky to have a secure job, with people who treated him well, and with every Sunday off. By not having any, or any hope of any, Silvano taught me a good deal about my own upward mobility.

"Sempre lavoro," he said to me on mornings like this, shaking his head. It astonished him that I, a rich American who could obviously afford to be idle, and to his knowledge had at least six drip-dry shirts, should be up and pounding a typewriter before seven-thirty. Now he sent Sally his sad, kind smile—*la poveretta,* he called her when he spoke of her to me, wished us both a soft *buon appetito,* and backed out of the door.

"He's such a sweetie," Sally said as I was getting her established in her high chair in the flood of sun. "He makes me feel so lucky and so guilty."

I poured some black sludge from the coffeepot into two cups, and filled the cups with hot milk already beginning to skim over. The *panini,* two apiece, were still faintly warm from the oven, and creased like a cherub's behind. I broke one and spread it with butter for Sally, and looked through the bowl of little plastic jam pots to see what we had. *"Arancia, ciliegia, e fragole. Cosa vuoi?"*

"Ciliegia," Sally said. "Hey, you're getting good."

"I still mix it up with Spanish. I'll never catch up to you. None of us will."

"I ought to be a lot better than I am. I had all that Latin, and I can study all morning while you write."

"In addition to which you have the gift for it. You'll be reading Dante before Sid does."

She looked at me sharply. "For heaven's sake, don't even suggest such a thing."

"Why not? He isn't vain about how much Italian he knows."

"Just the same. He's always comparing himself, or getting compared, to other people. Charity compares him to you, and it isn't fair. You're a producer, he's a consumer, a sort of connoisseur. But this spring, the minute he knew he'd got tenure finally, and was a real associate professor and not some ambiguous sort of lecturer, and we began to plan this trip, Charity was right back on her hobby horse. She started to wonder if maybe, in Florence, Sid could get back to those Browning studies she set him at years ago. She'd still like him to prove to the world that he's as good a scholar as anybody. I hope I talked her out of all that. I think I did. Because all in the world he wants out of this year of grace is to learn enough Italian to read Dante in the original. Reverently. That's what he should do."

"Fine. I agree. That doesn't change my opinion that you'll be reading Dante before he does."

She accepted the jam-spread *panino* I handed her. "If I do," she said, "let's just keep it a secret, shall we?"

The bells started up again on Bellosguardo, where Browning had once lived, and where, in some square or other, we had seen a monument bearing his name and other literary names. Let them rest in peace. Sally was right, the way to spoil the year for all of us would be for Charity to start imposing ambition on Sid again. The way to keep it loose would be just to let him be a receptor. He had the appetite, the curiosity, and the energy for it, so long as his feelers didn't detect a compulsory publication at the end. It struck me that he was a little like Silvano. Now that he finally had tenure, and was safe for life, and was getting his first sabbatical, let him enjoy his safety.

From their villa up behind San Miniato the Langs could make forays into the art, antiquities, color, picturesqueness, history, food, and wine of Tuscany. This week, Sally informed me, was to be Brunelleschi week, starting with the Duomo and going on to San Lorenzo, Spirito Santo, the Innocenti, the Pazzi Chapel, and God knew what else. Fine with me. I would be happy to go along and profit from her impeccable planning.

In the afternoons and evenings only. In the mornings I had other fish to fry. Mornings such as this I could hardly wait to finish the *caffe latte.* I wanted to get back with my face to the wall and my mental windows wide open. Mornings it didn't matter where we were so long as I had working space. If the day stayed as fine as it had started, and it often did, I would move out onto the terrace at nine o'clock, and leave the room to Sally and Assunta, the maid.

Assunta did not soothe the soul as Silvano did. She stirred up dust with her turkey-feather broom and stirred up the morning's placidity with her fierce denunciations of a whole anthology of wrongs and wrong-doers: her worthless husband, her shiftless son, her wicked mother-in-law, the *sindaco* of her town of Settignano, the malignant driver of the bus that had brought her in that morning, the taxes, the prices, the government, the times. She talked to Sally all the while she made the bed and dust-mopped the floor and cleaned the bathroom and changed the linen, stopping every now and then in sheer disbelief of how impossible everything was. *"Pazienza!"* she cried, throwing her eyes and the spread fingers of her right hand toward the ceiling; and again, denying the possibility, *"Pazienza!"*

Good advice. In my shirtsleeves, out on the sheltered deck, I turned my back on her life of turmoil and went on complicating the lives of some people I had once sort of known, involving them in, among other things, a monumental Christmas snowstorm that stopped them in their knee-deep tracks and forced them to some hard acceptances and decisions. Later, I supposed, I would come wallowing like a St. Bernard, with a little brandy barrel around my neck, and if not rescue, at least reprieve them. They were people whom, having invented them, I rather liked. I didn't want to do them in, only make them see a little better. One of them was a little like Charity, in that she thought she saw very clearly without any assistance.

And every morning of a whole year would be like this one.

It almost was. With my face to the wall and my back to temptation and distraction, I spent the mornings in New Mexico, a world of mixed recollection and invention where I moved with the freedom of a god. I controlled the climate. I knew every mesa, pueblo, road, street, and house because I had put it there. I knew everyone's mind, emotions, and history. I could anticipate, even plan, every event, and predict, even dictate, every consequence.

The New Mexican phase of my life was all order and good management, among people I knew, in a country, climate, and social milieu in which I was completely at home—which did not belong to me so much as I belonged to it by reason of birth and experience. I ran my New Mexico mornings about the way Charity had always tried to run the life of the Lang family—evocatively when possible, arbitrarily if necessary. That, if you can get away with it, is a very satisfactory way to live. When the writing went well, and it generally did, I was without pain during my mornings in Albuquerque-on-the-Arno.

But it was also satisfying to surface—not with the bends, never with the bends; those were only talk, part of the hyperbole of euphoria. No, I surfaced easily, sweetly, eagerly, full of expectation, into this world of origins that was all discovery, and only rarely evocation or manipulation. Sally had been studying it while I was gone, and could tell me about it at lunch.

I suppose I was peculiarly susceptible because of our recent emancipation from debt and duty, as Sally was susceptible because of her long imprisonment. But I would have been susceptible anyway. Anyone who reads, even one from the remote Southwest at the far end of an attenuated tradition, is to some extent a citizen of the world, and I had been a hungry reader all my life. I could not look up the Arno without feelings of recognition, as if, somewhere off downstream, the river drained into the Rio Grande. I knew names, books, some of the art. I was myself the product of ideas that had been formulated right here. I lived now in a pensione named for the man who had given America its name.

But I had experienced far less than I knew. Though I had worked among people who traveled constantly, dispersing America throughout the postwar world, we had not been able to travel ourselves. Europe and the European past were to me words in books and reproductions on coated paper and exhibitions at the Boston Art Museum or the Gardiner or the Fogg. It thrilled me to think how the people of this little city had lighted mankind—both kindling and matches had been here in profligate plenty. It never ceased to amaze me to look across the river and see, small and sharp as if seen through a reversed telescope, a landscape of hills and cypresses cribbed from Leonardo.

Here I was not producer and stage manager but audience, pupil, respectful country cousin. Every white American who wants to know who he is must make his peace with Europe. He is lucky if he can conduct the negotiations, as we did, in the valley of the Arno.

To cap it, we were not alone, we could share it. We were once again four in Eden. And that is not a mere verbal flourish. We felt it, talked about it, argued its meanings. It affected our perception of the things we took in. We were conscious that we had been given a second chance.

Thus, visiting the Carmine to look at Masaccio's *Expulsion from Paradise,* studying his Eve clumsy with woe, stricken with desolate realization, and Adam stumbling beside her with his hand over his eyes, one of us wondered if Masaccio or anyone else could have done anything with the reverse situation. Ours. Could a painter capture in expression and posture the delight-touched-with-humility, the almost tearful gratitude and thankfulness, that ought to mark paradise regained?

It was the sort of question made to order for Sid, an intellectual hare that he went after like a terrier. Well, Milton had tried it, both sides of it. We had all read *Paradise Lost.* Had any of us read *Paradise Regained*? (He and I had, because we had been forced to.) And Dante. What better example? The *Inferno* boiled with hot life, but the *Paradiso* was theological meringue. The wicked and the unhappy always stole the show because sin and suffering were the most universal human experiences. Technically, Christ was the hero of *Paradise Lost;* actually, Satan was. Fallen grandeur was always more instructive than pallid perfection. Or look at painting, all those Christs whose bland faces belied their bloody wounds, all those characterless angels. Saintliness had no possible expression but a simper. But Judas, now, sitting at the Last Supper trying to disguise his treachery, with that symbolic cat behind him, he was something else because of his human complexity. And if you were walking down the Tornabuoni and saw, at the same instant, Beatrice with her beneficent smile and Ugolino gnawing on Ruggieri's skull, which would catch your eye?

As usual, Charity found these classroom verities less than convincing. Of *course* you could make great art out of happiness and goodness—look at Beethoven's Ninth (we laughed); look at Fra Angelico. But most artists—writers too, you're all alike—found it easier to get attention with demonstrations of treachery, malice, death, violence. *Sure* you'd notice Ugolino gnawing on his skull, but how long could you stand to go *on* watching him? Art ought to set standards and provide models. What model could you find in Ugolino? Dante used him as a horrible example, but he cheated too, he made Ugolino so horrible he drew attention to him.

Should he have walked on by? I wondered. Ignore him? Focus on the beauty of the flames of Hell? Whistle past the Ninth Circle?

Oh, come on, Charity said. Really. Art and literature have these fashions. Why don't you just ignore all that stuff so many modern writers concentrate on, and write something about a really decent, kind, good human being living a normal life in a normal community, interested in the things most ordinary people are interested in—family, children, education—good *uplifting* entertainment?

She made her demand on me with her most vivid smile, her

friendly, interested, outgoing, life-loving smile. She made it out of affection and good will, half taking it back even while she expressed it, saying it mainly because she wished it were possible.

I said I would think about it.

Whatever we thought about art and its relation to life, we knew that the Faulkner motto we had adopted in harder times no longer served. "They kilt us but they ain't whupped us yit" was no watchword for this world so full of interest, instruction, suggestiveness, possibility, and friendship. So after a day or two of searching through Dante, Sid found us a new one, not so succinct but satisfying to Charity's didactic imperative.

> Considerate la vostra semenza:
> fatti non foste viver come bruti,
> ma per seguir virtute e canoscenza.

"Consider your birthright," we told each other when fatigue or laziness threatened to slow our hungry slurping of culture. "Think who you are. You were not made to live like brutes, but to pursue virtue and knowledge." Very high toned. We all hitched our wagons to the highest stars we could find.

For me it produced an odd dichotomy. Part of my time I lived in a managed, controlled fictional world, the rest in this world of cultural wonder and discovery to which I was as submissive as cottonwood fluff is submissive to the current of a ditch. Coming out of the morning isolation I had a sense of almost unbearable stimulation, of daily and even hourly growth. In the past I had had periods when I learned and grew very fast—when I came from dusty Albuquerque and my native cow college into graduate school in Berkeley, when we were assaulting the hopeful future in Madison, Wisconsin, when I first stepped inside the door of Phoenix Books on Beacon Street and felt all that challenge of a new profession to be learned, new people to know and work with. But I never felt any such explosion of capacity as I felt shuttling between the Albuquerque of my mornings and the Florence of our afternoons.

I balked at nothing, I was above nothing. Everything had something to teach me. I say *me;* I think I mean *us.* The Langs were as insatiable as we were, for they had been held back as long as we had—by the failure at Wisconsin, the hibernation of the war years, the demands of the new job at Dartmouth, the obligations brought on by a family of five children. Now, with one in graduate school, one in college, one at Exeter, one knocking around the world on a self-restricted shoestring, and one finally settled in the American School in Florence, they could continue what they had begun with enthusiasm in 1933. Not even all that eye-glazing marble of the Medici tombs, nor the icy stone floors of the Bargello that numbed us to the knees, could discourage us.

Sometimes we wondered what it would have been like to be part of the generation of Americans who discovered Paris in the twenties, and remade the world from the Left Bank. Had they felt as we felt? They were younger, some of them were greatly gifted, some of them were infected with fashionable literary despair, most of them were theatrically pleasure-bent. We thought them luckier. They had had only a war to damage them, and war's damage is, when it isn't fatal, likely to be stimulating rather than the reverse. Living through a war, you have lived through drama and excitement. Living through what we had been given to live through, we had only bad luck or personal inadequacy to blame for our shortcomings.

But one thing we did not feel. We did not feel any despair, literary or otherwise. We were having too good a time.

We were no lost generation, despite our losses. It was no Dada Nada that we hunted up and down the streets of Florence and through its museums and churches and out into dozens of hill towns and villages, but something humanized, something related to mind and order, and hence to hope; something that, as we kept reminding ourselves, was the dream of man.

I suppose we all wanted out of Florence corroboration of things we already believed, and Charity had her tendency to assert what she could not clearly discern. But every one of us, even she, was open to Florence simply as experience. We wanted contact in the most particular and sensuous ways, and we lived at a pitch of sensibility that was probably absurd. Given earlier chances, we would not have been such super-tourists. Being what we were, we seized whatever we could get. Every excursion was an adventure, and excursions were almost as common as sunrises.

Wasn't it a *satisfaction,* Charity asked, to be able on our *stranieri* passes to drop into the Uffizi at any time, maybe for only ten minutes, maybe just to stand a while in front of the Primavera or ponder the lugubrious Byzantine Christs out of whom, strangely, all the glories of

Florentine painting had evolved? Less lucky people might save up for years, just to be able to visit the Uffizi once, on some flying trip, between breakfast and departure for Assisi, under the rod of a brassy tour guide; and having seen it once they would hoard all their lives the postcards that were their most lasting benefit from the place. People even less lucky never *heard* of the Uffizi. And here we could go in and be enriched four or five times a week, whenever we weren't too busy being enriched by Ghiberti's doors, or Giotto's Tower, or San Marco, or the Loggia dei Lanci, or the Bargello, or I Tati.

The Bargello was difficult for Sally because of the steep stairs. She tried them once on her own; after that Sid and I carried her up. But even so, we were there so often that Donatello's David took to tipping his helmet when he saw us top the stairhead. As for San Marco, that was a favorite, especially of Charity's. She dragged us there so often to refresh ourselves with Fra Angelico's sweet innocence that the guides broke into smiles when they saw Sally coming on her crutches, and when we turned down any more of their assistance they would begin to intone, mocking their own spiels which they knew we knew by heart, "... *Delizioso!* ... *Meraviglioso* ... !"

And not only Florence itself. Through a long spell of Indian summer, using either our car or the Langs', or both if the trip was long, we grew familiar with Lucca, Pistoia, Pisa. We rehearsed the laws of the pendulum from the Leaning Tower and tried the acoustics of the baptistery with some barbershop harmony. Once, on a cool, sunny, windy day, we picnicked beside a country road on the way to Siena, taking shelter on the sunny side of the banked roadway, and a *contadino* on a bicycle, passing above us, gave us grave welcome, looking down on us with interest. Picnics generally look a little silly and uncomfortable and unnecessary to someone not participating in them. Not to this countryman. He came steadily, his feet going solemnly around, his head canted to look down at us benevolently. *"Buon appetito,"* he said gravely, and wheeled on. It was as if he had blessed us.

"I love it," Charity said when we had quit laughing at his decorum and self-possession. Her eyes were snapping with the enthusiasm that rarely died down in her. She could never have a good time without calling her own and others' attention to what a good time she was having. She wanted no experience, even the slightest, to go unmarked. "I love it that you're finally rich, too, so we can do things like this together."

I could have replied that, thanks to them, we had done quite a lot of things like this with them, long before we could have afforded them ourselves. And I could have cited her some figures—the Guggenheim stipend plus the rent on our Cambridge house plus the few royalties that dribbled our way, minus Lang's expenses at Mills—and asked her if she thought they added up to riches. But I didn't. All she meant was that she was glad we were out of the woods. We were too.

"Rich enough," I said. "I'll drink to that," and Sally said from her high chair, looking stiff and incongruous for a luncheon on the grass, but very happy, "Amen. Who needs more than this? Is there any more wine in that *fiasco*?"

I filled the glasses around, and we sat sipping the acid Chianti. Birds came hopping close, looking for crumbs. Sid said nothing. Talk about money, his or anyone else's, always bothered him. But I knew he felt our emancipation as we all did. That debt, which he had been unable to forgive because we would not let him, had been a weight on all of us.

The wind blew the roadside grass with a faint whistling sound, as if it ought to be cold, but our bank was protected and warm. Perfectly content, we lay a while with Sally sitting straight and looking down at us. We may even have slept a few minutes with our faces turned to the sun before we drove on.

Our daily schedule was like that of Battell Pond—mornings for work and study, afternoons and evenings for whatever we were attracted to and the weather permitted. We knew no one in Florence except the woman from whom we took Italian lessons twice a week; and needed to know no one. Like Frost's farm couple who went from house to wood for change of solitude, we sometimes let our afternoons be guided by whim and association, but most of the time they were guided by Charity.

One day we went to Volterra, where they mine alabaster, a town that glittered faintly with crystal dust. Another, we went to Vallombrosa, just to check up on Milton and see if autumnal leaves did strow the brooks there. No leaves, no brooks, only a plantation of Douglas firs from Oregon, the Cascades rejuvenating the Apennines, and a pen of wild boars that would soon be *cinghiale* in some game restaurant.

In Assisi we pondered the shriveled mummy of Santa Chiara in the crypt, still devoted to St. Francis after seven hundred and fifty years. We spent an afternoon at Orvieto, up on a mesa that might have been imported from New Mexico. At Gubbio, where St. Francis civilized the wolf, we slept one night in an old monastery, a San Marco with comforts, and while buying gas at the local AGIP station the next morning, heard a passionate *cri de coeur* from the girl who manned the pump. She said she was trapped in this medieval prison of a town. She turned her lips inside out when we protested that it was the most picturesque town we had ever seen, a jewel-box of a town. Oh no no no no no. There was no news, no entertainment, no action, no life. She held her nose and gagged, yearning upward toward more breathable air. She wanted to see the world—Paris, London, America. She was disappointed and scornful when she learned that we came from places named Boston and Hanover, places she had never heard of. Americans who mattered came from New York or California.

Just the same, if we had wanted a maid, a driver, a cook, a *sarta,* a concubine, a faithful follower until the first better opportunity showed, we could have had that girl for a thousand lire a day. She would have abandoned her gas pumps and climbed into the car in the clothes she wore, not asking where we were going so long as it was somewhere not Gubbio. We regretted afterward that we hadn't asked her. It would have been interesting to see her expression when she found herself expected to stand respectfully before the Della Robbia lunettes in the Pazzi Chapel, or asked to wait with the car outside Santa Maria Novella.

There was another time, after the mildest winter in memory had relaxed and the valley of the Arno was greening and the blossoms bursting out and the river running bank full, when we drove to Arezzo to see the Piero della Francesca paintings, and then came back through the hills, stopping at Sansepolcro, where we routed out a sacristan or some such and got him to open the chapel in which Piero's resurrected Christ started up behind the tomb and the sleeping drunks who had been set to watch it.

Until then there had been a good deal of frivolity in us, a springtime response to the blossoms and the mild, clear air. But Piero's Christ knocked it out of us like an elbow in the solar plexus. That gloomy, stricken face permitted no forgetful high spirits. It was not the face of a god reclaiming his suspended immortality, but the face of a man who until a moment ago had been thoroughly and horribly dead, and still had the smell of death in his clothes and the terror of death in his mind. If resurrection had taken place, it had not yet been comprehended.

Three of us were moved to respect, perhaps awe, by that painting, but Charity thought, or pretended to think, that it was another instance of an artist resorting to shock for his effects. Instead of trying to paint the joy, the beatification, the wonder that would naturally accompany the triumph over death—an uplifting idea if there ever was one—Piero had chosen to do it backwards, upside down. She thought he was anti-human in his scornful portraits of the drunken soldiers, and anti-God in his portrait of Christ. It seemed to her an arrogant painting. Instead of showing pity for human suffering it insisted on grinding down on the shocking details. Instead of trying to paint the joyfulness of Christ's sacrifice Piero almost seemed to call it hopeless. Why hadn't he, if only by a gleam in the sky or the glimpsed feather of an angel's wing, put in *anything* that suggested the immediacy of heaven and release? And what *terrible* eyes this Christ had!

We did not argue with her. She was still developing her sundial theory of art, which would count no hours but the sunny ones. But I noticed that Sally stood a long while on her crutches in front of that painting propped temporarily against a frame of raw two-by-fours. She studied it soberly, with something like recognition or acknowledgment in her eyes, as if those who have been dead understand things that will never be understood by those who have only lived.

In the sunny, unseasonably warm afternoon we came back along the spine of the mountains on a crooked, little-traveled road. The hillsides oozed, the gulches gushed water, here and there the road was invaded by slides. *Attenzione,* said a sign. *Sassi Caduti.* Then we came around a bend and were stopped by a gang of men gathered in the middle of the road, surrounding one who held his right wrist in his left hand, supporting against his bloodstained shirt a right hand that was smashed, swollen, smeared with blood and mud.

They swarmed around us, all talking at once, too fast and too loud and too many at a time for me to understand. The hurt man stood alone, holding his wrist, and dripped blood into the road.

"Piu lentamente, per favore," I said. *"Non cosi in fretta. Non capisco."*

But if I had enough Italian to ask them to slow down, and if they did slow down some—no Italian on the scene of an *incidente* can slow down *much*—I didn't have enough to understand what they were saying. It was Sally, cranking down the rear window, who finally talked to them. They wanted us to take the hurt man to his village, eight kilometers further on.

We had a hasty discussion about space, while the men outside listened to our strange tongue and interrupted us in theirs. The Fiat, barely adequate for four small people, already held three large ones and one medium-sized one. At first Sid insisted that he would get out and stay here while we took the man in, after which we could come back and get him. But I was afraid that the man might pass out, or need to be carried, and I might not be able to handle him alone. Sally couldn't be left behind on her crutches. Charity couldn't either, though she was willing and though she probably would have been safe enough. But when she got out and stood by the car, tall and striking and dressed like the queen of the gypsies, I saw a couple of workmen behind her wag their heads and wink, appraising her like men admiring a horse. So in the end we decided that Charity and Sid would cram into the front seat with me, and the hurt man could ride in back with Sally. For five miles it ought to be bearable.

His friends pushed and lifted the man in. He held his mangled hand carefully and did not raise his eyes except for one brief flash around the interior. I saw him take in Sally's legs, in their braces, hanging lifeless from the edge of the seat. One swift glance to see the face that went with those legs, a glance quick and surprised, and then he was looking down again, and never looked back up until we stopped. His shirt and the front of his pants were bloody, and blood and mud were drying into a crust on his hand.

We tried getting Charity in beside me and Sid beside her, but there was no room. So she got out, Sid got in, and Charity crawled in on top of him, her head jammed against the ceiling, her neck cramped, her voice full of cheerful assurances that it was all right, it was fine. "Only don't dawdle around!" she said over my head.

Sid's leg was so tight against me that I had trouble reaching the gearshift lever. To a chorus of advice we pulled away, edged around the slide the men had been clearing, and went on up the road.

"How's it go?" I said, to all and sundry.

"Fine, fine," they said. The car filled with the smells of sweat and blood and garlic, and Sally opened a rear window. The hurt man said nothing, and Sally said nothing to him. Seeing his grim, unshaven, rocklike face and downcast eyes in the rear view mirror, I understood why. He invited neither conversation nor sympathy. Once or twice, when we hit rough patches of road, I heard squeaks from Charity, jammed against the ceiling on my right. I drove somewhere between fast and carefully, unable to decide which was better.

After seven kilometers I saw the village on a hilltop to the right. The road that turned off to it was a wet clay cart-track with a grassy crown. Not at all sure we could get up there—it might be like climbing a greased pole—I turned off, but the man in back squawked in a raven's voice, *"Qua! Qua!"*

I stopped. "Tell him I think we should take him up," I said to Sally. "Ask him if there's a doctor or first-aid station or *farmacia* up there."

"Qua!" the man said. He was trying to fumble open the door without letting go the wrist of his hurt hand.

"Dov' é la sua casa?" Sally said. *"Dove si trova un dottore? Un medico?* Oh, how do you say it? *Ce ne uno lassú?"*

The man continued to fumble at the door handle, which he didn't know how to work. I reached back and opened the door for him and he lurched out and stood. He was a man of perhaps fifty, gray and weathered as a boulder, thick in the shoulders. His eyes, suspicious and quick under heavy brows, darted across the car to where Sid and then Charity came untangling out of the cramped front seat. When he looked back at me I had a little tingling shock. He had the eyes of Piero's Christ—and what was that? Regional type unchanged since the sixteenth century? Community of pain? Or merely suggestion from my own hyperstimulated imagination?

The man said something—grunt or *grazie*?—and with his bad hand cradled against his stomach started off up the track that led in a long steady incline up the hill until it disappeared among walls and buildings.

"Wait!" Charity called after him. "Oh, we can't let him *walk*! *Signore!* Hey!"

The man walked on, his right shoulder low, and did not look back.

"Oh, *shoot!*" Charity said, distracted. "What are we going to do? Drive after him, Larry. We can't just let him walk away. That's a *terrible* looking hand. Drive after him. Hurry. We'll stay here."

"I don't think he wants any more help."

"But he needs it, whether he wants it or not. He could lose his hand, and what would a workman like him do with only one hand? He's got to have a *doctor.* They'll probably just soak his hand in dirty water and wrap it in a rag, or poultice it with *cow* manure!"

"What would we do?" Sid said. "Tackle him, and load him back in by force?"

"Oh," Charity said, "why did you let him *out*?"

"Because he *wanted* out," I said.

The man had reached the foot of the long slope and started up it. He walked steadily, leaning into the hill. Charity said no more, but I could hear her boiling. After a minute or two she climbed into the back seat beside Sally, Sid got in beside me, and we drove on.

In Pontassieve I looked halfheartedly for a *farmacia*, knowing that in Italy pharmacists treat minor injuries and bandage wounds. But it was getting late, the traffic was thick, we were all tired from a too-long drive in that sardine can of a car. Seeing nothing on the main street, I went on through without a further search. With only monosyllabic communication, we eased down into the traffic of suburban Florence, crossed the river and climbed the hill, turned left short of San Miniato, and stopped in front of the Langs' villa. Politely, they suggested that we stop for a drink. We pleaded fatigue. Hastily, almost curtly, we said good-bye for that day.

"Bad ending," I said to Sally as we threaded the little walled streets toward the Viale Galileo. "Good start, bad ending."

"She wanted to help."

"Of course. We all did."

"It frustrates her when she can't."

"You can say that again. Lie down. Shut up. I want to *help* you."

"You exaggerate," Sally said wearily. "Charity hates pain, and you could see in every move he made how much pain he was in. A rock must have come down on his hand—it was just mangled. And did you notice how stoical he was? Not a whimper or a blink. He just closed around his pain and set his teeth. But you could tell by the way he moved."

We circled with the traffic around the Piazzale Galileo and into the Viale Machiavelli, heading toward Porta Romana. "Well," I said, "she can blame it on the Artist Upstairs. How's she going to count only sunny hours if He keeps throwing things like that in her path?"

"You know she doesn't really believe that Pollyanna theory. She knows about the unsunny hours. She was more upset than any of us. She always is when anybody is sick or hurt or unhappy."

"I suppose," I said. "Hell, I don't have to suppose, I know. She just made me sore with her suggestion that I'd abandoned the poor guy on the roadside."

For a while the cars were thick and I couldn't talk. Sally sat in back, holding onto the strap I had rigged back there. Down the Petrarca we had fairly clear sailing. "Did you notice his eyes?" I said.

"Yes! Yes, weren't they awful? So gloomy and set inward, as if they couldn't see out at all, they could only see in, toward the pain he had bundled up inside."

A Vespa cut around me, ducked in front so that I rode the brake, and darted off between two cars ahead. "Tell me something," I said.

"What?"

"When you remember today, what will you remember best, the spring countryside, and the company of friends, or Piero's Christ and that workman with the mangled hand?"

She thought a minute. "All of it," she said. "It wouldn't be complete or real if you left out any part of it, would it?"

"Go to the head of the class," I said.

I raise my eyes. Sally's legs hang quiet in their braces, her feet are placed precisely on the metal step of her chair. The sunlight lies diagonally across her breast, the shadows of leaves or thoughts move on her face.

"Do you remember Christmas Eve?"

"All those red hats."

"More than red hats. Remember the torches along the river, and in sconces on the walls? And what an icy, glittering, transparent night it was? How the whole city bloomed with light when we went up to the Piazzale for the view? And all the churches. Even grim old San Lorenzo was festive. You must have pushed me miles in the wheelchair that night, from one church to another, and every one with what looked like two dozen bishops and archbishops and cardinals saying mass, and thousands of people coming in and out, and hoisting their children on their shoulders for a better view. Lang was enchanted. She thought we must live that way every day."

She sits looking down at her hands. Then her eyes come up and meet mine. She sighs and tightens her mouth and smiles a bleak little smile. "Wouldn't it be nice if we were all walking down the Tornabuoni right now, on our way to look at all the Ghirlandaios in the Santa Trinita, and watch the red hats and the brocade doing mumbo-jumbo around the altar?"

Her face says she is unconvinced by memory and unpersuaded by wishfulness. She throws her eyes and her fingers skyward and says, in imitation of Assunta's croak, *"Pazienza!"* Her hand reaches for the canes leaning against her chair. "Will you get me up? I'd better go, before we start."

5

oing up the hill she is attentive to the woods we climb through. When we first saw this hill in 1938, before the Langs had bought the farms that contained it, it was only in the first stage of metamorphosis from pasture back to forest. Now it is authentic woods, mostly maple, beech, and white and yellow birch. All through, among the larger trees, tall saplings as thick as a man's arm or leg have been shade-killed, and many, in falling, have got hung up in the trees around them. They give the woods the look of an Uccello or Piero battle painting with long slanted lances; and those dark angled lines, with the bursts and patches of sun that penetrate the leaves, create precisely the illusion of depth that Uccello and Piero were after. We seem to see a great distance into the trees, though it can't be more than fifty yards to where the hill rises steeply and shuts off the view.

Goldenrod and raspberry bushes crowd the shoulders of the road, which has been washed in the rains and kicked into a washboard by spinning tires. Moe grinds the gears, shifting. We climb steeply, then level off a little. Sally's warped hand clings to my sleeve. Her eyes never leave the woods. She says nothing.

Now the paddock with its stake-and-rider fence opens on the right, a green opening hewn out of the trees. This is one of Charity's works, a facility for the grandchildren as they grow. Farther up the hill, a half mile beyond the house, there is another—a meadow two or three acres in extent, bulldozed flat and planted to grass, designed to be a playing field for soccer and softball. It would not surprise me to find, when we go through this afternoon on our way to the picnic, that Charity has erected bleachers for the old folks to sit in while they watch competitions among the family young. She does not think small.

As we reach the turn by the stable I see that the gate is open. A girl in jeans sits a sorrel horse just outside it. From the front seat Hallie waves and calls. "Hello, Margie!"

The girl's arm comes up, she stares nearsightedly, her rather sullen face is broken by a flash of very white teeth.

"Oh, is that Margie?" Sally says. "Why, she's all grown up!" She waves, we all wave, but Moe does not stop. He challenges the hill somewhat grimly. Our tires chatter for a few yards, and then we level out on the grass before the front door of Ridge House.

Moe hops out and opens the door on Sally's side. She pokes her canes out and rests them against the car, and when he starts to hold them for her she shakes her head at him with a smile. Laboriously she lifts her feet with her hands, one at a time, to the edge. Bracing herself on one cane, she pushes with her good hand, stands up, bends to lock her knees, gathers in the other cane, and stands straight. I see her eyes go to the closed front door.

"Mom will be on the terrace," Hallie says.

There is no walk. We go around the house on the dense, closely mown grass. The mountain ash that Sid and I planted the year they moved up here has grown to be twenty feet high. Near it a wild apple, growing from below the wall that holds the hilltop in, leans its load of green nubbins over the lawn.

We round the corner and there is Charity's view, first imagined and then created in defiance of the genius of this country, which tries always to hide itself in trees. Broken by an occasional tall maple or birch that she had the cutters leave for visual effect, the hill drops away, furred with raspberry and dense hardwood seedlings, to the untouched woods below. The view swoops down and then levels to the lakeshore, across the lake and its far meadows, then up again to broken hills, the blue mountain ridge, the sky with traveling snow-white clouds. It is the sort of high blue day that Charity must have had in mind when she imagined and began to expose what she would see from this hill.

And there she sits who made it—there *they* sit, or half recline, she in a lounge with a steamer rug over her legs, he on the grass in his faded summer khaki. They have not heard us. Charity's face is turned toward the outline of Mount Mansfield on the horizon, and seen from the rear and half in profile she looks as stony as the mountain. Something in the set of her head and the stiffness of her neck says *no,* says refusal, says obstinate rejection. Sid, leaning on his elbow with his eyes slanted up at her averted face, slaps his flat hand against the ground as if baffled.

Then they hear us. Their faces turn. Sid leaps to his feet, nimble as a young man, and comes yelling across the lawn. I get an instant impression—not much changed, a little older, only a little gray, in good shape, still a formidable physical presence, his voice the remembered musical, slightly metallic tenor—and brace myself for the crushing of the hand and the greeting.

But I am also aware, even in the violence of his welcome, of the other part of this reunion: Sally floundering forward, all but running on her canes, her uncontrollable iron legs trying to keep up with the crutches; and on the lounge Charity half rising toward their awkward, maimed meeting, her face a thin wedge, and on it that incredible, gleaming, ardent smile, a transfiguration, a bursting to the surface of pure delight, uncomplicated love.

Now we are finally here. This, in all its painful ambiguity, is what we came for.

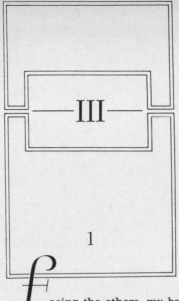

III

1

*F*acing the others, my back to the view, I
could see us reflected in the plate-glass windows, like a stage set or a
photograph of eternal summer: a lot of blue and white distance for a
backdrop, then the curve of stone wall that kept the flattened hilltop
from sliding lakeward, then the spread of grass with Sally's chair and
the two striped canvas deck chairs grouped around Charity's lounge.
We made a colorful constellation on the lawn, and at our center the
Lady in the Chair, Cassiopeia. Even in reflection she gave off light.

I had been prepared to find Charity a transparent husk all but
eaten away from within and held together only by pride and will. I
should have known better.

True, she was thin, and for sure she was held together by will. But
there was nothing feeble about her looks or her manner. Hers is a face
that does not depend on flesh; it is built from the bones outward. And
her skin was tanned, and her brown, freckled hands took hold of me
with a bird's strength when I bent to kiss her. Her voice piped and
cracked with excitement, her smile was a window onto an internal
incandescence. Her spirit gushed and overflowed and swept us up,
making us forget pity, caution, concern, everything but the pleasure
of her presence.

All her life she has been demanding people's attention to things
she admires and values. She has both prompted and shushed, and

pretty imperiously too. But she herself never needed or accepted prompting in her life, and she is not going to be shushed, not even by cancer. She will burn bright until she goes out; she will go on standing on tiptoe till she falls.

"Now!" she cried, in the same voice and with the same emphasis she used to employ when she cried us to attention for music and digestion after dinner. "Now we've *finally* got you here again we want to know all about you! Oh, it's been so *much* too long! Sally, are you well? You look it, you look wonderful. Was the trip too hard? I won't ask about Larry, he's obviously disgustingly healthy. Tell us, are you still doing therapy? Have you got more muscle activity back? You must have, you practically came *running* across the lawn just now. New Mexico must be good for you, much as I'd like to think you'd be better off here. Do you still like it? Do you move better, and breathe better, where it's high and dry? How's Lang? And your grandchildren, tell us about them. Tell us *everything*. At once!"

Time has not dimmed her, sickness has only increased her wattage. She lights things up like a photoflood. There was so much animation in her that I wondered why she had held off this meeting through the whole empty morning, when she was apparently as eager to see us as we were to see her. Letting us rest, I supposed, whether we wanted to or not. Lie down, you're tired.

She would not have let her own tiredness interfere with something she wanted to do. Theatrical, Hallie called her, the choreographer of her own *Totentanz.* I didn't mind. I had no will to resist or bait her as I often had in the past. If she wanted to heighten this fatally late reunion with a little deliberate dramatic delay, who lost by her theatrics? I didn't feel anything false, I didn't feel manipulated, and I am sure Sally didn't either. I just felt warm and friendly, and grateful that Charity made it easier to talk by making us talk about ourselves, not her.

So we sat in the sun discussing Pojoaque, and our house, and our all-gray garden, and altitude and aridity, and Indian cultures, and Sally's daily routines, and what I was working on, and Lang, and Lang's job, and Lang's two boys. Not much about Lang's husband, whose promotion to a professorship has already been held up once because he hasn't got his book finished. Perishing for lack of publication was not a subject we wanted to open up in that company.

We were voluble, we all but babbled. Charity was interested and animated, Sid attentive. Sneaking a look when I could, I saw that he had aged more than I first thought. He has the kind of rugged athlete's face that does age—the bones get heavier, the lines deeper, the skin rougher—instead of the academic face that George Barnwell, for instance, had, the kind that stays smooth and boyish into the seventies. And his eyes, when he took off his glasses to clean them, were more faded and watery than I remembered them. Circling his handkerchief with thumb and finger around a lens, he laughed at something Sally said, and laughed too loud.

Anybody listening might have thought this just any coming-to-gether of friends after a long separation. But it was an exercise in levitation, not indefinitely supportable, and it was Sid, listening but not contributing much, who by his soberness slowed us down. He sat among us, one of us, but with an unease about him, as if he might at any minute tiptoe away, like a man at a meeting that has gone on so long he is afraid of missing his plane, or someone trying to pay attention while resisting an irresistible need to go to the bathroom.

The chatter for which I had at first been grateful began to be objectionable, a sort of flippancy in the wrong place at the wrong time. There came a moment when we all felt it. The web of talk broke, and we dropped into a lull from which we blinked and smiled at each other. The only questions remaining to be asked were those whose answers we already knew and did not want to hear.

I say *we;* I mean *I.* Sally is far less cowardly in these situations than I am. Also, she had more at stake. Charity and I like each other well and somewhat warily. Half of our pleasure in each other's company comes from resisting each other. But Charity and Sally are stitched together with a thousand threads of feeling and shared experience. Each is for the other that one unfailingly understanding and sympathetic fellow-creature that everybody wishes for and many never find. Sid and I are close, but they are closer. Apart from Mrs. Fellowes and myself, Charity is the only person Sally ever willingly allowed to help her up or down or to the bathroom, the only person besides the two of us that her disability is comfortable with.

The cant word these days is "bonding." I suppose some people see in a relationship like that signs of an unacknowledged lesbianism—the same people who probably speculate about the sex life of somebody like me, a perfectly healthy man with a crippled wife. I don't care how they speculate, or what their answers are. We live as we can, we do what we must, and not everything goes by either Freudian or Victorian patterns. What I am sure of is that friendship—not love, friendship—is as possible between women as between men, and that in either case it is often stronger for not having to cross sexual picket lines. Sexuality and mistrust often go together, and both are incompatible with *amicitia*.

We ran down. We sat. Eventually Sally, on the heels of something frivolous that had left her laughing, sent across at Charity's lounge an abruptly earnest, pleading look, and said what she was thinking. "Charity, I have to know. What do they say? How *is* your health?"

"Right now, wonderful."

"Then it isn't true, what Hallie tells us?"

A long steady look held between them. Charity's mouth was a little slack, as if caught unexpectedly between expressions, but her forehead was untroubled and her eyes were candid and, I thought, pitying. "That I'm going to die soon. Yes."

"Charity . . . !" Sid said. The frail canvas chair creaked with his sudden leaning.

"Oh, Sid, don't," she said. "Of course it's certain. There's no sense in pretending otherwise."

"There's all kinds of sense in not just accepting a sentence like that! If you'd only agree to radiation or chemotherapy. Cobalt. Whatever. All of them! You've got chances if you'll take them. But no, you won't. You give up. You won't try to save yourself. You won't let me take you down to Sloan Kettering."

"The doctors say there's no point."

"You put the idea in their heads!"

"Sid, dear, hush," Charity said as if to a nagging child. "You're not helping. I don't want to go into all that again."

"But. . . ."

"*Please!* Let's not make a scene."

For a moment her look was hot and peremptory. Then, when he looked away, blindly searching the grass as if for four-leaf clovers, her face softened. She seemed about to say something consoling, but by then he had distanced himself. His face bleak and bruised-looking, his eyes hooded, he had settled back in his chair and was looking at the view.

Sally, with her eyes filling, said, "Charity, I didn't mean to distress you. Sid, I'm sorry if. . . . But it isn't like you, Charity. When I was sick and wanting to die, you sat by my bed and made me live. You wouldn't let me give up hope. Isn't there some way we . . . something we can . . . ?"

"Bless you," Charity said. Her neck looked too thin to carry even her small head, but her eyes were dry, and she had pushed her lips into a little Gioconda smile. "All I needed was to have you here, and here you are. You make it complete. It was different with you. I wanted you to hope because hope could make you well. You just had to set your will on it. But hope would be foolish for me. It wouldn't do me any *good* to set my will on living. I thought it would, before I had the operation. That's why I had it. I had so much to live for I was *determined* to live. But they just sewed me up again, and I had to learn to face the facts, and make the most of what time I had left."

"What did they tell you after the operation?"

Charity smiled and spread her hands.

"They didn't suggest radiation, or chemotherapy, or anything?"

"It had already metastasized."

"But sometimes even then . . ."

"They said I might have a little time," Charity said. "They were right. I could have had the treatments, but they didn't hold out any hope except maybe for a little delay. And there's all that appalling nastiness of losing your hair, and the people I've known who took those treatments were sick all the time. I decided I'd rather be intact for whatever time I was given."

Holding the little smile, she shut her eyes. She looked like a woman carved out of pale wood. Figure of a goddess, remote and removed, cleansed and pitying. Proserpine. That used to be Sally's role.

Her eyes opened, still crinkled with the faint, grave smile. I saw them rest a moment on Sid, heavy and somber in his striped chair. Then they came back to Sally. "Dying's an important event," she said. "You can't rehearse for it. All you can do is try to prepare yourself and others. You can try to do it *right.* In a way, cancer is a blessing, it generally does give you a little time."

Now Sid looked up. His eyes were as hot as if he hated her, and he pounded one hand against the other in a parody of applause. "Oh, wonderful!" he said. "Cancer's a blessing. It gives us that precious time. And just think, without it we wouldn't have all that useful cancer research. God Almighty, darling, you've been reading some novel that bids farewell to life in a dying fall of sweet relinquishment! I've talked to the doctors, too. They're the first to tell you that the patient's attitude makes all the difference. There are all kinds of cases of people who lived just because they refused to give up and die. Just what you've been advocating all your life. And now when it's *your* life on the line, you. . . . You do have a chance. Even if it's only ten percent, even if it's only five, why not take it? Are you so tired of living? Are you so tired of *us*?"

For a long time they looked at each other. Finally she shook her head. "You wouldn't want the five or ten percent they might save. Neither would I."

Sid jerked his glance away, and in the reflecting plate glass his eyes met mine with a jolt that was like running into a door. His twitched away a fraction of a second ahead of mine. Pitying and inexorable, Charity continued to study him, and Sally, her precise shoes propped precisely on the chair's step, kept her wide eyes on Charity's face. No one said anything. I was thinking that this was a Charity I did not know. Or was it? And she was not through talking.

"There's no decent literature on how to die. There ought to be, but there isn't. Only a lot of religious gobbledygook about being gathered in to God, and a lot of biological talk about returning your elements to the earth. The biological talk is all right, I believe it, but it doesn't say anything about what religion is talking about, the essential *you*, the *conscious* part of you, and it doesn't teach you anything about how to make the transition from being to not-being. They say there's a moment, when death is certain and close, when we lose our fear of it. I've read that every death, at the end, is peaceful. Even an antelope that's been caught by a lion or cheetah seems not to *struggle* at the end. I guess there's a big shot of some sedative chemical, the way there's a big shot of Adrenalin to help it leap away when it's scared. Well, a shot will do for quick deaths. The problem is to get that same resignation to last through the weeks or months of a slow one, when everything is just as certain but can't be taken care of with some natural hypo. I've talked to my oncologist about it a lot. He has to deal with death every day, seventy-five percent of his patients die. But he can't tell me how to do it, or give me any references in medical literature that will help. Medical literature is all statistics. So I'm having to find my own way."

Bemused and listening, we sat around her, thinking more things than we would have said. At last Sally ventured, "But you could be *wrong* about it, Charity! And if you're not absolutely sure . . ."

"I'm sure," Charity said. "Oh, I'm sure! That's one of the few things I *am* sure of. Another is pain. If there's pain, I can handle it. Most pain is mental anyway."

Sid jerked in his chair and pressed his lips together. Looking at him with an expression that I could only define as stern pity, Charity went on.

"It's the *fear* of cancer that hurts, and there's a whole library of palliative medicine that can help us over *that*. We just need to learn not to panic. Then we can meditate pain away, or just ignore it."

What should anyone say to that?

"Still another thing I'm sure of is how lucky I am," Charity said, and smiled around our attentive circle in a proud, self-congratulatory way. "I don't have to do this alone. I'm *surrounded* by the people I love, and I'm doing my best to teach them what I'm trying to learn myself: not to be afraid, not to resist, not to grieve."

Her smile, directed now at Sid alone, widened; her face took on a look at once monitory and mischievous. "It's as natural as being born," she said, "and even if we stop being the individuals we once were, there's an immortality of organic molecules that's absolutely certain. Don't you find that a wonderful comfort? I do. To think that we'll become part of the grass and trees and animals, that we'll stay right here where we loved it while we were alive. People will drink us with their morning milk and pour us as maple syrup over their breakfast pancakes. So I say we should be happy and grateful, and make the most of it. I've had a wonderful life, I've loved every *minute*."

She stopped. Her eyes touched us all, Sid last. A wistful, questioning, pleading smile hung on her lips, a smile that held and wavered as her look wavered and held on his face. Any man would be shaken to have a woman look at him like that. Sid was.

"I've had the man I loved," she said very softly. "I never lost him the way so many women do. I've had bright, beautiful children. I've had dear friends. You may not believe this, but this has been the happiest summer of my life."

Still none of us found anything to say. Air moving uphill from the woods and lake stirred the seeding flower-heads of Delphinium that rose above the wall. A Monarch butterfly caught in the draft was lifted twenty feet over our heads. I saw Sid look away from Charity's unsteadily insistent glance to follow the Monarch's movement. Perhaps he was fantasizing, as I was, that there went part of what had once been the mortal substance of Aunt Emily or George Barnwell or Uncle Dwight, absorbed by the root of a beech tree in the village cemetery, incorporated into a beechnut, eaten by a squirrel, dropped as a pellet in a meadow, converted into a milkweed stalk, nibbled and taken in by this butterfly, destined to be carried south on a long, unlikely, interrupted migration, to be picked off by a flycatcher, brought back north in the spring as other flesh, laid in an egg, eaten by a robbing jay and laid as another kind of egg, blown out of a tree in a windstorm, soaked up by the earth, extruded as grass, eaten by a freshening heifer, some of it foreordained to be drunk, as Charity said, by its own descendants with their breakfasts, some of it deposited in cowpads, to melt into the earth yet again, and thrust upward again, immortal, in another milkweed stalk preparing itself to feed more Monarch butterflies.

Fragile as tissue, the butterfly wavered off and away. From her lounge Charity urgently demanded our agreement; her strained smile pinned us to our chairs. She widened the smile by an act of will as definite as the shoving open of a jammed window. Her freckled hands fluttered over the steamer rug, straightening it across her knees. When she spoke again, her voice was screwed up close to shrillness.

"So I'm trying to do it *right*. Most of the family are helping. They find it hard, but they're trying. I hope you will too. When the time comes, nobody should be unhappy. It shouldn't be made a production of. I'll just go away."

We assented in silence. Of course. Of course, dear Charity. However you want it. Whatever will help you. Sid stared gloomily at something beyond the hilltop, off in the air.

"I knew I could count on you," Charity said. The shrillness was out of her voice; she sounded happy. "Well! I'm glad we got it out in the open right away, so there'll be no pretending and long faces, and we can make the absolute *most* of what's left." Now she managed the full, unforced smile. "That's more than enough of *that*! Now let's forget it. This afternoon we're not dying. We're *together* again. The whole family's coming for a picnic on the hill, did Hallie tell you? Oh, you don't know how grateful I am that you could come! I hated to ask you, I know how hard traveling is for you now. But I'm glad as I can be."

She did not look glad. The smile had already faded. She looked ghastly, as if the effort of talking had forced all the blood from her face, which was jaundice-yellow. She wet her lips and closed her eyes and turned her face sideward against the cushion that hung on loops from the back of the lounge. Her thin throat worked. When she opened her eyes again it was as if marble had awakened.

"Now!" she cried in a wan effort at decisiveness. "Now we're going in and rest awhile so as to be ready. Sally, you come with me. If you don't want to rest, we can talk, and if you don't want to talk we can

meditate. We won't leave for the hill till four. Larry can help Sid load the Marmon."

"My goodness, is that still running?" Sally said. "Oh, it *will* be like old times! I love that car."

She sounded tinny and false. Poor lady, she found it as difficult as I did to know how to act or what to say. Later, with practice, we might do better. The star had her part down cold, but the male lead didn't like his lines, and the walk-ons had never seen the script until forty minutes ago.

Watching Sally, I saw her eyes widen and her body start forward in the chair. Her hand reached helplessly out, two yards short of its mark, and I became aware that Charity had leaned sideward and was vomiting over the side of the lounge. Sid leaped out of his chair with an exclamation and got his hand under her forehead. He held her, looking down with a face like granite on her dry retching.

Weakly Charity leaned back and wiped her lips. "I'm sorry," she said. "You must excuse me."

"Oh, we've been too much for you!" Sally said. "We should have known."

"It's nothing," Charity said. "It happens now and then. Now let's go in and take our rest."

Silently Sid helped her to her feet. He was careful and gentle, she was grateful for his arm. The opportunity to help and be helped was good for them both.

For a moment Charity stood tottering. I saw her discipline her body and mind before she tried to take a step. With his arm around her, Sid threw an unreadable look over his shoulder and started her slowly across the grass toward the house, where a woman in white nylon, who had apparently been watching from the window, had appeared and was holding open the screen door. From the lawn I watched the two careful backs receding. In the plate glass I saw the two careful faces approach.

Without waiting for my help, Sally had pushed herself to her feet and locked her braces, and with her weight on her spread canes was also watching the receding backs.

"Will you want your chair?" I said.

Her somber eyes considered. "No, leave it here. We'll be lying down, I suppose. If I want it the nurse can get it for me."

She turned and swung after them toward the door. The Langs had disappeared, the one faltering, the other attentive. Inside, I saw Charity and the nurse go past the windows, moving slowly, and in a moment Sid was back holding the screen open for Sally. She had trouble with the two high steps, and I saw him start to help her, then hold back. She struggled up onto the landing, and with an upward flash of eyes passed him and entered. He eased the door shut behind her. In a moment they went together past the windows.

I waited—troubled, supernumerary, out of it. It was as if Charity had just, in that brief spasm of nausea, disproved her own statement that you cannot rehearse for your own death. I could not have been much shakier if I had watched her die. I was bothered by the ruthlessness with which she disciplined and drove her sick body—picnics, in that condition!—and I remembered the time the four of us were lost in the woods somewhere off the overgrown Bayley-Hazen road, and Charity disagreed with Sid and me about the best way out. She had chosen a compass course and forced it on us, and we had plowed through swamps and blowdowns, making a beeline like Achilles the tortoise over and through obstacles that we might have avoided by finding and following the brook. She had put her trust in Pritchard, the authority, and been betrayed by him, and eventually had to repudiate him. This time she was writing the guidebook herself, as she went, and its authority could not be challenged or repudiated. But the method was the same. She still preferred a compass course.

What would she do if she broke a leg in those woods she was heading into? Did she have contingency plans? Would she find a handy tree crotch into which she could wedge her heel? Would she come out on the other side on a peg leg whittled out of a forked stick?

Pitying and shaken as I was, I had to admit she was the same old Charity. She saw objectives, not obstacles, and she did not let her uncomplicated confidence get clouded by other people's doubts, or other people's facts, or even other people's feelings. Nor by weakness. Once she had nerved herself to accept the death sentence, it would not have occurred to her that others, Sid especially, might not share her determination to suck every drop of sweetness out of the experience.

It was her death. She had a right to handle it her own way. But I felt sorry for Sid, a reluctant stoic, and I dreaded the coming hour or two when I would be alone with him. I was the person he was most likely to confide in, and I feared his confidence and had on tap no word of consolation or comfort. It crossed my mind, while I sat waiting on the lawn above the green and blue view, that down under his anguish and panic he might even look forward to her death as a release. Then I decided not. Charity had mastered him, but she also supported him. She not only ran his life, she was his life.

I didn't like to think what would happen to him with her gone. His resistance and resentment were only expressions of his dependence. Sally resented her crutches, too, but without them she would have been hardly more than a broken stick with eyes.

*f*inally Sid came out. Whatever he had been doing inside, he had got himself in hand. When I asked how she was, he acted as if it took him a moment to know whom I was talking about. All right, he said. Fine now. Inside, our wives would already be deep in confidences, but Sid and I would pretend that this was an August afternoon and we were getting organized for a picnic. Nothing is so safe as habit, even when habit is faked.

He looked me up and down as if estimating my weight. "Eh-yuh," he said. "I wonder what you're good for. Ever done any work?"

"Once I was a hired man in a Vermont compound."

"Long time ago. Still, maybe there's a little left in you."

As we walked down the road toward the stable he took off his glasses, wiped his eyes, and blew his nose. When he saw me noticing, he said, "Damn the goldenrod."

"Still bothers you."

"I don't know how I ever got fond of this place. Drip, drip, drip."

Snuffling, wiping a leaking eye with a finger, his hay fever about as persuasive as his cheerfulness, he led me down to the stable. Inside, the whole right side was divided into four stalls, each one opening onto the paddock. The left side of the stable was drive-through space, with doors at each end, and in this corridor, soaking in the odors of hay and oats and horse manure, the Marmon sat with its top down, its seats and furled roof and long hood whitened with dust and straw. Inside were the relics of past picnics: a flashlight battery, an empty Coke bottle, some crumpled paper napkins, a bandanna, kernels of trampled popcorn, crumbs of crushed potato chips. A toy revolver was stuck behind one of the jump seats. The space between the back seat and the plate-glass partition that prevented fraternization between passengers and driver looked big enough for a square dance.

243 | CROSSING TO SAFETY

"She hasn't been used for a month," Sid said. "If she won't start, we could be in trouble."

But he did not look troubled. He had perked up. A certain alacrity had come into his expression and his movements. He eyed the Marmon as he might have eyed a cliff he was about to climb.

Everything about that behemoth was an anachronism—hand choke, starter button on the floor, a switch instead of a key, a hinged hood that lifted up on both sides, a chrome radiator cap in the form of a naked lady who leaned into the wind. Sid unscrewed the lady, stuck his finger down the pipe, and screwed her back on. He lifted one side of the hood and found the dipstick and pulled it out and carried it to the light and squinted at it and brought it back. With one foot he flattened the folding luggage rack on the running board, opened the door, and climbed in. Squinting down into the shadow, he pulled out the choke. I heard his foot pump the throttle three times.

"Hail Mary full of grease," he said, and stepped on the starter.

A subterranean grinding, heavy and hoarse. I could imagine pistons the size of gallon jugs trying to move in the cylinders. Sid took his foot off the starter, adjusted the choke, and stepped down again. The grinding resumed, went on patiently for a good minute, grew slower, weakened. Another tired half turn—*uh-RUH!*—and on the last juice from the battery she coughed, raced, faded, caught again, and was running.

"Ha!" Sid said. He sat nursing her, easing the choke in until she talked to us comfortably. Looking in under the propped hood I could see that the engine was not twelve in line, as I had always half believed, but a V-16. It would have pulled a fire truck. At every stroke a stream of gasoline as thick as my finger must be pulsing through the carburetor. She panted at us in the whiskey-and-emphysema whisper of an Edith Wharton dowager. *"Dollar-dollar-dollar-dollar-dollar,"* the Marmon said.

I lowered the hood and locked the catches. "How about opening the door on this end and we'll drive her out on the grass and give her the treatment," Sid said. He looked ten years younger than he had up on the terrace.

We gave her the treatment—took off shirts and shoes and socks, rolled up pants, and swept her out, washed her down, rinsed her off with the hose, went over her chrome and glass with damp chamois skins, wiped off the seats and the wheel and the dash and the gearshift knob, even wiped down the wooden spokes of her wheels and the two vast spares that rode in wells on her front fenders. Then we drove her up and parked her gleaming by the kitchen door.

The running-board rack we pried up again, and behind it we stowed Sally's chair and Charity's lounge, brought folded from the terrace. When we went inside, I saw that Sid had already been busy at preparations. On the kitchen counter were two Styrofoam coolers full of beer and soft drinks and ice cubes. On the floor were two thermos jugs of water, and next to them two stained pack hampers half loaded. I thought I recognized them.

"Those look like what we hung on old Wizard, away back before the Deluge."

A quick, curious look, as if I had recalled him from thoughts so different that he needed to reorient himself. "The hampers? I guess they're the same ones. I can't remember ever ordering new ones."

I might have asked him if he had remembered to pack the tea, but heard my own intention in time, and said instead, "They're going to last forever."

"Longer than any of *us.*"

He was a man in a briar patch. So long as he kept still he was comfortable, but every time he moved he found thorns. Or put it the other way around. Busy, he could forget where he was. The minute he paused, he was reminded.

"Have you ever been back to that Shangri-La we found?"

Again he gave me the curious, sidelong look. "No."

"Ever been tempted to? It shouldn't be hard to find."

"Charity and I have talked about it once or twice. We decided not to."

"That's probably sensible."

Dead end. I kept trying. "Looks as if you've got a standard Lang picnic on the planning board."

I didn't need to ask him, or look in the hampers, to know what was in them: two grills in stained canvas bags, a canvas sack of cutlery and toasting forks, a nest of smoked, scoured kettles, two dozen tin plates and cups, packs of plastic glasses, paper plates, napkins, and table-cloths, a roll of paper towels. And packed in and around all that, dozens of sandwich rolls, bags of sweet corn, jars of mayonnaise and mustard, boxes of crackers, chunks of aged Cabot cheddar, bottles of apple and cranberry juice. In the refrigerator, ready to go into the hampers at the last minute, would be bowls of salad ready for the dressing, carrot and celery sticks wrapped in a damp cloth, Sara Lee cakes thawing toward edibility, whatever fruits of the season McChesney's offered, and above all the centerpiece of this pagan festival, the steaks, a dozen of them, great marbled slabs two inches thick, each a surfeit for three lumberjacks. Steaks for a platoon, and scraps left over for all the platoon's dogs.

Nothing would have been forgotten, any more than the tea had been forgotten years ago, and nothing would be out of place. In his way, Sid was as rigid a planner as Charity. It was probably she who inherited or instituted the ritual family picnic, decreed its forms and abundance, and selected its vessels and instruments; but it was Sid who conducted the ceremonies, and he knew them as a priest knows the mass.

We finished packing the hampers and loaded everything onto or into the Marmon. As we reentered the kitchen we met the nurse, putting the teakettle on a burner. Sid introduced her: Mrs. Norton. She had frizzy hair and a curiously whittled nose, and she was glad to meet me, she said, though I did not think she was excessively cordial. Her eyes were suspicious and pocketed in radiating wrinkles.

"Are they awake in there?" Sid asked.

"They rested awhile. Now they're talking. Too much, to my notion. I'm taking them a cup of tea. You want some too?"

"Do you, Larry? No? I don't think so, thanks, Mrs. Norton. I feel more like a beer. How about you two?"

She declined, I accepted. We stood drinking out of the cans, watching her put a tea bag in a cup, pour boiling water over it, let it steep only a second or two, move it into another cup, pour water over it again, and rescue it again within seconds.

"Pretty weak tea," Sid observed. "I suppose that's best."

Mrs. Norton, for some reason, looked offended. "She likes it cambric. Cambric's all her stomach will *take*." Angrily she set sugar bowl and milk pitcher on her tray and dug spoons out of a drawer. Sid watched her.

"I suppose," he said vaguely. He looked at his watch. "Well, there's still plenty of time, but you can tell them anytime they're ready, we are."

The nurse did not answer at once. She shook Arrowroot biscuits out of a box, thought a moment, went to the refrigerator and spooned some custard out of a bowl into a glass dish. She folded two paper napkins into triangles and picked up the tray. With her hip against the swinging door she looked back and said, "She oughtn't be going, you know."

The look that passed between her and Sid was so long and unrelieved that I felt it like a bar in the air, something that would stop you if you tried to walk through it. Finally Sid said in the quietest voice, "Can you think of a way to *keep* her from going?"

Mrs. Norton's face was red. "I've told her. She won't pay any attention to me. She might to you."

"She might not, too," Sid said. "Today's her birthday. She's got her heart set on it."

"Yes, and she's weak's a cat. She threw up again a half hour ago. She's running on her nerve. Two, three hours up there in the wind, all the hooraw and excitement, I already told her she's not up to it. I won't be responsible."

"Nobody will hold you responsible," Sid said. "You can only do what you can do. What did she say?"

"What?"

"When you told her she shouldn't go."

Mrs. Norton breathed through her nose. "She said, 'Oh pooh!' "

Sid laughed, shaking his head. "I can hear her." He shrugged and spread his hands, asking her complicity, admitting his helplessness. "I don't think anything we say will make her stay home. We'll just have to keep an eye on her and try to keep her from overdoing."

"I most generally do keep an eye on her," Mrs. Norton said, offended all over again.

Patiently, wearily, Sid said, "I know. It's hard. I'm grateful for all you do. I just meant, up there on the hill I'll be cooking, I may not notice. You'll have to let me know if she starts having trouble."

"She'll have trouble," Mrs. Norton said. "You can count on it." She pushed the door open with her hip and backed through it with her tray. Sid stood watching the door's dying oscillations.

"She's got a case," he said. "Can you imagine a more difficult patient?"

"Sid," I said, "why do we do this at all? Why don't we take all this stuff up and leave it for the others, and then come back here? Charity and Sally can have their talk out, or if Charity's too tired we'll go back to the guest house. Then we can come again tomorrow without feeling that we've done her in."

He started shaking his head the minute I started to talk, and he shook it as long as I was talking.

"Maybe she'll stay home for Sally's sake," I said. "I can get Sally to say she's too tired."

For a moment that idea half appealed to him, then he rejected it too. "That'd make Sally into a party pooper. No, there's no way. Charity planned this, and she won't be kept home. It'd probably be worse for her to be kept home than to go."

"Mrs. Norton seems to think she can do herself real harm."

He looked at me as if he could not believe what he had heard. "For God's sake, Morgan, of course she'll do herself harm. *All* her harm is real! She's fixed her mind on dying, and when she fixes her mind on something nothing is going to stop her. Her *pride's* at stake. She's planned it all, every step." In the gray north light his face wore the challenging, sneering expression of a man talking his way into a fight. "While she was planning for herself, she didn't forget the rest of us, either. Want to know how the script goes?"

I said nothing. We stood in the kitchen as if on the brink of a quarrel.

In a mincing, schoolteacherish voice, Sid said, "This is how it'll go. Once she's carried out her part of the program, or before that if it can be managed, Barney will patch it up with Ethel, and the family will carry on without that lesion. Nick will come back from Quito and get a job at some American college, preferably Harvard or Yale, and marry some nice girl and raise another branch of the family. Only Nick didn't agree, he was insubordinate and went away without agreeing. She was very upset. Still, she holds to the plan; she thinks he'll come to it. David will quit living like the hermit of Folsom Hill, and give up looking for whatever self realization he's been looking for, and go to law school and become a civil-liberties lawyer and do good in the world, and marry some nice girl and start raising still another branch of the family. Hallie's all right the way she is, I guess, except that she should have a couple more children before it's too late. Peter's to quit playing the field, and marry *yet* another nice girl, and build a cottage on the lake, down by the boathouse, and start raising, you guessed it, *another* branch of the family. He's nearly thirty, it's time he got going. Charity's had a lake lot surveyed, and she's given it to him as a premarital bribe. Everything tight and orderly. No loose ends."

"Sid," I said, "would you rather she sat wringing her hands?"

"All kinds of real-estate plans," he said, ignoring me. "She's had all the hill land resurveyed and divided, grandchildren to take their pick of lots when they reach eighteen. The top of the hill, four hundred acres of it, is to be kept as a nature preserve, given to the town if the town'll accept it, or to Nature Conservancy, or as a last resort managed by the family trust. That's her bequest to Battell Pond, a permanent picnic ground."

He flattened his lips in a smile of derision and distaste. "Her bequest to me is more personal, naturally."

I waited. He watched me with his crooked grin.

"After a suitable interval," he said, "I am to remarry. 'Oh, no, I won't,' I tell her, and 'Yes, you will, of course you will,' she says. 'Why shouldn't you? You *need* someone, it's best for you.' She's never been in any doubt what's best for me. 'But not somebody our age,' she says. 'Not some comfortable widow. Somebody younger, quite a bit younger, somebody with lots of energy and ideas who will keep you lively and not let you sag back. Because that's what you'll do if you're not watched,' she says."

Meeting his eyes was like taking hold of a hot wire. I said, "Sag back into what?"

"Into what? Into myself. Into my dilatoriness and incompetence." A scrape on the back of his hand attracted his attention. He examined it carefully, pinching the skin around it. Then his eyes lifted to mine again. He puckered his lips as if about to whistle. The pucker widened into a smile. "Know what she's done to guide me? You'll never guess. Don't even try. She's made a list. Women here and in Hanover it would be okay for me to marry. Five names, listed in their order of suitability."

The refrigerator came on with a behind-the-scenes whir. I felt the warm gush of its exhaust against my ankles. "You're kidding," I said.

"I am not kidding. Want to see the list?"

"I guess not."

"No," he said with sudden gloom. His hand reached out and turned on the tap in the sink. For a few seconds he watched the water run as if he had never seen water run out of a tap before. Then he shut it off.

"Plans," he said. "She lies with that notebook on her stomach and lays out the future of everything. She's written and rewritten her will ten times. The lawyer is over from Montpelier every Monday, Wednesday, and Friday. She's foreseen every contingency and plotted everybody's life. All any of us will have to do in any crisis is consult the master plan."

"I still can't believe she made you out a list of prospective wives."

"She did just that."

"Out of the most loving motives, surely."

"Of course. Out of the most loving motives. And with the most scrupulous regard to common sense."

"She's been looking after people all her life. She's made a career of being thoughtful. Isn't it kind of wonderful that even now her mind is on others, not herself?"

Sid turned his seamed face and stared out the window above the sink. To the leaves and sky out there he said, "She hasn't forgotten herself. She's got plans for herself, too. Horrible plans."

"Hallie told us. That's hard to take."

"You bet it's hard to take. Did Hallie tell you the rest?" His voice rose, he pushed at the nosepiece of his glasses and looked at me furtively through his hand before he turned half away and said, "You heard her, out on the lawn. When it's time, she thinks she can just slip quietly away. Not bother anybody, just quietly withdraw, like someone having to leave a party early."

"She wants to spare you."

"Sure. What am I supposed to do, wave bye-bye and forget her, just go on fixing the vacuum cleaner or whatever I'm doing? Just erase her from mind and memory, while she goes off to the hospital and lies there refusing to eat or drink—well, she'll have to drink water, I guess, she couldn't get the doctor to agree to not even water. But she did get him to agree he wouldn't force-feed her. That way, she thinks it won't be drawn out."

It took me a while before I could think of anything to say to him. "But don't you approve of that?" I said finally. "I do. I hope they'll do as much for me when I come to that situation."

The muscles were suddenly ridged in his jaw; his eyes were blue blurs behind the glasses. "Oh, it's sensible! Everything she does is sensible. It can't be argued with. I just wonder sometimes if she knows people have feelings."

High and constricted, his voice came out almost as a squeak. "Think who it *is* we're talking about! Think who it *is* we're supposed to close the door on as if she were someone selling magazine subscriptions!"

His hands went out in a violent gesture, and the can he held in or of them shot a spurt of beer out onto the floor. At once, not looking at me, he grabbed a handful of paper towels off the roll and knelt down and began mopping. I saw that his hair had grown thin on the crown. The skimpy whorl on the top of his tanned skull reminded me of something Lyle Lister had told me once, whether in earnest or as a joke I never knew—that south of the Equator the crowns and cowlicks of the natives, like the whirlpools in bathtub drains, go counterclockwise, the opposite of the way they go up here. Sid's went clockwise.

"So, to return to your original question," he said to the floor between his knees, "what if this picnic is too much for her? From her point of view, does it make any difference whether she dies Thursday instead of Saturday? What right has anybody to tell her she can't spend her last hours roller-skating, if that's what she wants? How are you going to keep her from doing what she's going to do whether you forbid it or not?"

Standing up, he slammed the wad of towels into the wastebasket. His eyes slid around to meet mine, hot with outrage. "I could refuse to take her—she can't go without help. But you know what she'd do. She'd find the help. She'd persuade somebody. She'd go if she knew she was going to die right there on the hill. She'd go to her death fighting me. She'd sew her lips shut. She's the mistress of the implacable silence. I couldn't stand it. I never could."

The beer can went into the wastebasket after the towels. "Great way to celebrate her birthday. Deathday. Great setting for our loving farewells."

A prickly, electric energy agitated his hands and moved the muscles of his face in spasmodic grimaces. He fixed me with his eye as he might have fixed a student in a class, someone he intended to drop a hard question on. "So what's the proper procedure here?" he said, almost ruminatively. "What do decorum and common sense advise? She wants to leave her love and thoughtfulness in an irrevocable trust that will protect us all forever. Life betrayed her by not always going as she told it to. Now she hopes she can make death behave better. All my life she's stopped me and started me and run me like a lawn mower or a dishwasher. She knows I can't run myself. I'll need somebody— why not a plump young handmaiden? So she comes up with that list. It's a shrewd list, too, it says a lot about both her and me. And now she's going to have this final picnic if it kills her and everybody else."

His shoulders slumping, his hands jammed down in the pockets of his worn khakis, he brooded again out the window, and said, so low that I wondered if he was talking to himself, "She's dividing herself like some inexhaustible Eucharist. She's going around to everybody she loves, saying, 'Take, eat, this is my body.' "

"She's trying to do it right, she says."

"Sure." The quick glint of his glasses was eloquent with a kind of helpless derision. "Sure. If she can't do it right, she'll refuse to do it." His words made him laugh. "And if we won't eat, she'll cram it down our throats. God, I don't know, I don't know."

Once more he turned on the tap and watched the water run. When he turned it off he squinted at me sideways. "It's a hell of a way to treat a friend." Then he must have seen that I was confused, thinking he was still talking about Charity, and added, "Dumping all this on you."

"It's what friends are for."

"I appreciate that." He took off his glasses and polished them. Carefully he hooked them back over his ears and looked at me through them. Polishing the lenses had done nothing to change the expression of his eyes. He said, "You've always thought my marriage was a kind of slavery."

"What are you talking about?"

"No, of course you have. I'm not so stupid I can't see my own situation, or understand how it looks to others. My trouble is that it's a slavery I couldn't bear to part with. I value it above anything that might have taken its place, even a plump handmaiden."

"I don't think any of us ever doubted that."

"Never? Well, maybe. You're part of us, you know us as well as we know ourselves. We're two of a kind, in a way. I don't mean you're henpecked. I mean your marriage has been a sort of bondage, too. You fell in love with a good woman, just as I did, and are chained to her."

I stood looking at him.

"Does this bother you?" he said. "Kick me if it does. But I admit I've taken a kind of comfort from your bad luck. I've seen someone else tied and helpless, though for very different reasons. You've been con-stant, a rock, and I've admired you for that. But I've wondered what your life might have been if Sally hadn't got polio. You were upward bound when we first knew you, headed up like a rocket. Success might have taken you away from her—you wouldn't have been the first one. You've done a lot anyway, but maybe not all you might have done if you hadn't had the greater obligation of looking after her. I think your marriage did to you something like what mine did to me."

"If you're suggesting I regret it, I don't. I never wanted out."

"No," he said. "No, of course not, that's not what I meant. I never wanted out either. I just wish . . . I mean I can't help envying you because she needs you, she can't get along without you." He broke our rather frowning look with an embarrassed movement of the shoulders. "She couldn't survive you. Could you survive her?"

His question jolted me. It was not what I had been expecting. We stared at one another in the north light of the kitchen. Finally I said, "If you're wondering about yourself, don't. We're all tougher than we think we are. We're fixed so that almost anything heals."

"I wonder."

"No, you don't. You know Sally could survive me, dependent as she is, and that I could survive her. We wouldn't be the same, but we'd survive. You'll survive Charity, too. You know what would happen if you let grief and despair overcome you? She'd come back and shake you out of it. She'd have none of that."

I made him laugh. "I suppose," he said. "God, why are we on this subject? I'm sorry. I let self-pity take charge."

Straightening, he stretched his hands as high toward the ceiling as he could reach. I could almost hear his muscles creaking for some sort of saving action. He brought his arms down. "We're still up against this damned picnic. Can you imagine going up there and playing games, and stuffing ourselves, and making pretty toasts, and wishing her many happy returns, and singing 'Happy Birthday to You' through gritted teeth while *she* grits her teeth to keep from screaming? Jesus. It's fiendish to ask you and Sally to contribute your bit to another round of traditional family fun."

He wandered around the kitchen, looking at anything rather than me. To the wall of cabinets, throwing the words aside as if they were not intended for ears, he said, "No birthday cake. Hallie was going to bring one, and then we both started to imagine her blowing out the candles."

A sound at the dining room door. Sid spun around by the sink and busied himself rinsing his hands. When he turned back, drying them with a paper towel, Sally was braced in the door, trying to keep her balance while holding the door open with one hand. I went and opened it all the way so that it would stand.

"Are we ready to go?"

Her eyes were telling me something grave. Already she had her body half turned, ready to go back the way she had come. "She wants you both to come in."

Blotting his hands a last time, Sid threw the towel in the sink and came quickly across the kitchen. He fixed Sally with a hard, searching look before he went past her and through the dining room and out of sight.

"Trouble?" I said. "Is she worse?"

She only gave me a mute, clouded glance, tilting her head to indicate that I should go first. "You," I said, and when she started I followed her.

3

We went through the dining room, then the living room with its big rock fireplace, then the alcove where books, blocks, cars, dolls, dump trucks, and board games filled shelves and cabinets on both sides of a bow window, ready on an instant's notice for the visits of grandchildren. The hall into the bedroom wing was dark, the room at its far end bright. Then we were in it, a big, glassed-in promontory exposed on three sides to the view. From the first time we ever saw it, Sally and I had envied them that room. It would have been like sleeping in a treetop.

Charity was in bed, propped against the pillows and looking through slitted eyes at Sid, who had stopped with his back to the windows and his hands on the spooled footboard. Alarm and foreboding made his face look accusing. Charity's face, in the uncompromising full-front light, was yellow-gray.

"Thank you, Mrs. Norton," Charity said, and dropped her head in a slight nod. For a moment I thought the nurse was going to refuse what the look implied. Her face was rebellious, her odd little eyes screwed themselves deeper into their surrounding wrinkles. But after a moment, without a word, she picked up the tea tray and came out past us. I saw that the biscuits and custard were untouched.

"What is it?" Sid said. "Is something wrong? Have you had another spell?"

"Nothing's wrong. I feel all right." But her voice was low, without animation, missing the usual fluty emphasis. She kept her eyes almost shut against the light from the windows.

"Why did you send for us?"

"I thought we'd better talk."

"Mrs. Norton says you've been talking too much."

Impatience flashed in her face and voice. "Sid! What a wretched thing to say in front of Sally! It's been *wonderful* talking to her, it's what I've been wanting for years. I wouldn't have missed one word. Mrs. Norton thinks I should lie here like a cat on a comforter while she tiptoes around drawing curtains."

"She doesn't think you should go on the picnic."

"I know she doesn't," Charity said. Her eyes closed completely. After a few seconds they opened again. "That's what I want to talk about. I've decided she's right. I shouldn't."

He was like someone who has hurled himself at a door and found it made of paper. It took him a second or two to pick himself up. "Well, good," he said confusedly. "I'm glad you finally. . . ." Then the implications must have struck him. His eyes widened. As if apologetically, acknowledging some undue vehemence, he took his hands off the spooled footboard. "I think that's best," he said. "It's too bad about your birthday, but they'll . . . I'll call Moe or Lyle to pick up the Marmon. It's all loaded. They might as well go ahead with it."

She cut in on him. "No, I want you to go. Larry too."

Now he did stare at her—glared at her was more like it. "With you feeling this way? That's absurd."

"It isn't absurd at *all,*" she said. "I'm not feeling any particular way. I'm just tired. I don't think I could stick it out. I'd spoil it for everybody. You'll all get protective and think you should bring me home. If I'm not there you can go ahead and enjoy yourselves."

He was shaking his head.

"Sid, be sensible. It's a *family* picnic. You're *needed.* Who'd broil the steaks? I'm *sorry* I don't think I should go, but that's no reason everybody else has to be done out of it. And it's such a perfect day for it."

His head went on stubbornly shaking back and forth. "They can have their picnic. All they have to do is come by and pick up the Marmon."

"Yes, and then they'll get the idea I'm too ill to go, and they'll get upset and hover around here trying to look after me. I don't need any looking after, I'd just rather be quiet. You don't have to say anything to them except that Sally and I felt a little tired. We'll take it easy down here, and think about you up there playing Kick the Can and eating steaks and singing around the fire."

"There isn't going to be any singing around the fire. Not by me."

"Yes!" Charity said. She started to sit up straight, lost her balance, slipped sideways, pushed herself awkwardly upright again, and said intensely, leaning toward him, "Sid, I *want* you to! You *must!* David's

bringing his guitar, and the kids will want to toast marshmallows and sing. You must go, and you must stay till after dark so they can have the fun of the stars."

Mulish, his eyes full of suspended panic, he kept on shaking his head. "What's the point of a birthday picnic if you're not there? We'll have your birthday down here. The picnic's expendable. Let the kids and the others have it."

Weakly, tentatively, she let herself back against the pillows. She stared at him in impatience and frustration. "Oh, Sid, darling, why must you *argue*? If you'd like to do something for me on my birthday, just go up there and play paterfamilias. Do their steaks as only you can do them. Sing them some of your lovely sad ballads. Make Larry sing 'Blood on the Saddle,' the grandchildren have never heard that. Do that for me."

Gripping the foot of the bed, he stared back at her. Their look held and held. Beside me I heard Sally's crutch clink against the wall as she shifted her weight.

"I can't," Sid said in a tense, harsh whisper. "I won't. I know what you're planning."

"What? What am I planning?"

"You're planning to slip away while I'm gone."

I felt Sally move again. Our eyes touched. But Charity caught even that slight movement. Without taking her eyes from Sid's she said, "Stay. Stay, please." To Sid she said in a tone that was at once pleading and hopeless, "Darling, what if I was? That was our *agreement,* that when it came time. . . ."

"I never agreed to that! That's your plan, not mine. How would I know when it's *time,* as you put it? You never tell me honestly how you feel. You keep it a secret from me, how long you. . . . You think it's time now, and you want to send me out on a *picnic*?"

His feelings strangled him. Violently he turned away and stood with his back turned, his face set rigidly out the windows toward the blue line of mountains across gulfs of summer air.

"Ah, ah," Charity said. She was crying. "Ah, *don't!* Why do you . . ." Her tone softened. She said, as if the reasonableness of what she said could not be questioned, "You weren't to *know* it's time, not till I'd gone. And it isn't the end, darling. It may be days yet. You'll be visiting me, it's only eighty miles. Is it so awful that I want to go away quietly, without any fuss, and get *braced* there?"

His head did not turn, and he said nothing. His shoulders looked as if he were holding his breath. Staring from her pillows into the light, her yellow-pale cheeks wet, Charity was shaken by sudden impatience. Her face darkened and grew forbidding, her voice burst out with an edge of anger in it.

"I don't want to die where I've lived so much!" she said. "Can't you *understand*? I want to go gradually, a step at a time, in some kind of decent order. Is that too much to ask? I'm trying to do it right, and you won't help me. Oh, it was just to avoid scenes like this that I . . . I don't want to *bother* anybody, I don't want a lot of crying and breaking down! I *hate* it! All I want to do is go away quietly while the family is together and enjoying itself."

A long silence. Then, without turning, Sid asked, "Who was supposed to take you?"

"We called Hallie and Comfort. Sally says she'll come along. And of course Mrs. Norton. I'll be *well* looked after."

He continued to stare out the window. The sun pouring past him lit a halo in his thinning hair, and showed me once more the somehow pitiful clockwise whorl of his crown. Slowly he turned around. He said as if in puzzlement or wonder, "Your daughter, your sister, your friend, and your nurse all get to go with you. Your husband doesn't."

Her eyes closed for a moment, her head moved slightly, a spasm quirked her lips. She did not reply.

"Why?" Sid said. "In God's name, why am I shut out? At least let me drive the car. We can take the Marmon. It'll only take five minutes to unload it. There's room for everybody, even with you lying down."

"Comfort's bringing her station wagon."

"I'll drive that, then."

"No! That would only *complicate* things! I want you to go to the picnic and hold things together."

Sid stood very still for a moment. Then I saw him begin to shake. He shook all over, like a man with a chill. He cried out, "The hell with the picnic! The hell with holding things together! I'm going with you!"

Once again, as if he needed it for a brace, he put his shaking hands on the footboard. He leaned on it, the tears streaming behind his glasses so that he raised his hand and ripped the glasses sideward and off. They fell somewhere below and beyond. Without protection or disguise, his naked face hung contorted at the foot of her bed.

"Why?" he shouted. "Do you hate me? Am I a handicap, or an embarrassment? Am I so troublesome you have to invent errands to send me off on? I'm your husband! I have a right to be with you. It isn't as if you were going shopping, or off to a luncheon. Have you *thought* where you're going, or were you too busy planning how to get me out of the road? Have you thought what it means to exclude me?"

She lay quiet. Her braids lay across her collarbones, which rose and fell with her quick breathing. Her eyes glittered, her mouth was unyielding, her voice rose against his and cut him off.

"Because I can't stand it when you break *down!*" she said. "I haven't the strength. I'm trying to do it right. If you'd just let me do it my way it'd be best for everybody, it'd be *ever* so much better. But you won't!"

Sally and I stood in the doorway wanting desperately not to hear this, wanting to wipe out what we had heard, wanting to be gone. If sympathy means literally "suffering with," we were utterly sympathetic. Also helpless and miserable. What I heard in Charity's voice, I was sure Sid heard in it too: the exasperation of an assured, competent, organized, supremely confident woman having to deal with a fumbling man. *Must I hold you up even now?* that sub-voice said. *I've picked you up after every failure, I've kept you from falling more than once, I've tried to give you some of my strength, I've been loyal, I've been a helpmeet. You know you can trust me to do what's best. Why can't you now, when it's all I can do to keep going, just do as I ask, and spare me all this?*

There was hardly enough life left in her to let her lift a hand—both hands lay strengthless at her sides—but the old fighting pink showed in her cheeks, and as soon as she stopped speaking her mouth was a hard thin line. Mistress of the implacable silence, she stared him down.

Then, in the midst of that confrontation, I saw her face change. Some tension pulled it out of shape. A whimpering sound bubbled from her throat, her head drew backward, the cords of her neck stood out, her body arched under the blanket, her eyes closed, her lower lip was bitten between her teeth. I could feel the effort she made to lie still.

Sid sprang around the bed and bent over her.

Until then I had somehow not thought of pain as a problem, perhaps remembering Hallie's word that stomach cancer is relatively painless, perhaps taking at face value Charity's confidence that she could handle any pain that came. As of course it would come. Had come. The thing had already metastasized away back in May, when she had the operation. By now she could have it in the lungs, liver, pancreas, bones, brain, anywhere.

For what seemed an unbearably long time, maybe as long as ten seconds, she lay with her teeth in her lip and her eyes shut. Then—of itself or by an act of will?—her body relaxed in a series of little jerks. Her breath drew in and was breathed out again in a long sigh. Her eyes opened blindly. Fumbling a Kleenex out of a box on the bed table, she wiped her wet face.

"Better?" Sid said. "Okay now?"

No answer.

"Shall I call Mrs. Norton?"

It was as if she neither heard nor saw him.

He offered her the water glass with its bent sipping straw.

Her hand came up and brushed it away from her mouth.

For a few seconds he stood looking down at her. His hand set the rejected glass back on the bed table. Then, with a sound like someone trying to breathe with his throat cut, he dropped on his knees. His arms spread across her, his face was buried in her shoulder. Sobs shook him. They shook her too, her face broke up in suffering and pity, and she bent her neck as if to kiss the top of his head.

But the will took over, the emotional impulse was put down. Her right arm, which had moved as if to go across his back in an embrace, drew back and stretched itself along the pillow, as far from him as it could get. Her face, still twisted with the feelings at war in her, turned away from the head that burrowed in her shoulder. She lay rigid, every muscle in her body repudiating him. Though with his face buried that way he couldn't see her, he had to feel how completely she rejected him.

Almost at once, without raising his face, he surrendered. "All right! All right, whatever you want. Any way you must. I'll stay out of it, I'll try to . . . I just can't. . . ."

That was all she wanted. From her deathbed, practically, she had mastered him once more. Her will would be done. But the moment she had beaten him he was her hurt child. The arm came off the pillow and clenched around him, the lips touched the whorl of his crown.

"It's best," she whispered. "You'll see it is. You can come over and see me when I'm . . . settled. Come and see me tomorrow."

Sally touched my arm, set her canes, and turned into the hall. I started after her, but as I went through the door I could not keep my eyes from going back to the bed. Charity, holding Sid's head against her shoulder, looked straight at me. Her mouth made an indescribable, wistful, begging, please-understand, pained and painful smile.

Her eyes, to my fascinated imagination, were like the eyes of Piero's gloomy Christ—a painting that she had once, wanting to count no hours but the sunny ones, affected to repudiate.

Sally and I had barely stopped in the alcove where the grandchildren's toys were stacked when Mrs. Norton put her head out the kitchen door. Sally had been standing with one hand to her mouth. She took it away and said steadily, across living room and dining room, "Give them a few minutes." Mrs. Norton's head withdrew. We stood flooded with light from the bow window.

I said, "Has she been having these pains often?"

"One other time while I was with her."

"Shouldn't someone call the doctor?"

"I did."

"What did he say?"

"He thought it was time she came to the hospital. He said Mrs. Norton should give her a hypo."

"It doesn't seem to have had much effect."

"She didn't give it. Charity wouldn't take it. That's why Mrs. Norton was upset."

"Doing it what she calls 'right,' she makes it awful hard on everybody else."

Thoughtful, sober, her thin shoulders pushed upward by the weight she put on the canes, her collarbones starved and vulnerable, her face puckered in the ancient, sorrowful acceptance that is increasingly its basic expression, Sally said, "She says what she's trying to do is *save* everybody else. Especially Sid. She says if she lets him take her to the hospital he'll have to acknowledge it's all ending, and he'll go all to pieces. You've been talking to him. Do you think he would?"

"I don't know. Maybe. At least he wouldn't feel shut out."

"She wanted him to be kept busy with something physical. She thinks he can reconcile himself better if he finds out afterward, when it's at a distance. She says he's so dependent and emotional that even looking at her breaks him down. He weeps. She was going to have this picnic for a last farewell, she'd be as they all remember her. Then in a day or so, maybe right the next morning, she'd send Sid on some errand and she'd slip away."

"Forethoughted," I said. "Not necessarily sound."

"Oh, it's all spoiled now. She realized she didn't have strength for the picnic, so she was going to get away this afternoon. But he guessed, and now it's all happened just the way she didn't want it to."

"But she's still going to shut him out."

"I guess," Sally acknowledged. "I wish . . ."

"What?"

But she was not ready to tell me what she wished. She said instead, "I found out she hasn't eaten anything for two days. She hides the things Mrs. Norton brings, and manages to flush them down the toilet."

I thought about that. "You mean she'd already started two days before you got here? That seems strange."

"She expects it to take a while, maybe as long as a week."

"But she was really going to the picnic? Fasting? You'd think she'd have tried to keep up her strength that long."

She gestured with her hands—a kind of shrug without letting loose of the handles of the canes.

"How about you?" I said. "Aren't you about done in? You've had a trip through the wringer."

"I'm all right."

She did seem so—all right, but sad.

"What do you suppose they're doing in there now?"

"I hope," Sally said, "I hope they're doing what they were when we got out. *Hugging* each other." Her eyes flashed up, swimming with sudden tears.

"Wouldn't you think she could just let him drive her to the hospital? If she's trying to save him she's doing it in the cruelest possible way."

She didn't bother to wipe away the tears that ran down her cheeks. She only looked at me, shrugged hopelessly, and shook her head.

"She's the most bullheaded woman alive."

"Larry, she's *dying*!"

"By compass."

Sally did not answer. She brooded out the bow windows into the glorious afternoon.

"Would you do it this way?" I said. "If you die before I do, am I to have access to your last hours?"

Before she could reply, fast hard steps came down the hall. Sid went past, never seeing us. His heels left hardwood, pocked across the slate pavement in front of the fireplace, and went silent in the dining room rug. The kitchen door burst open, light from the other side outlined him, the door swung shut. Sally moved one of her canes and shifted her weight so that she could lay her fingers on my arm. We stood that way while Mrs. Norton came out of the kitchen and hurried off to the bedroom.

"I keep trying to remember she has to be forgiven what she can't help," Sally said. "We're different people. You're not dependent the way he is. I'm not strong the way she is. I don't have to protect you." Her voice ran almost out. "Couldn't."

We stood. Finally I asked, "When are they coming?"

"They said they'd be here about four-fifteen, after you and Sid would have left for the hill."

My watch read ten of four. "When will you be back?"

"I don't know. We'll probably get her settled and have dinner there and go see her afterward. If it gets too late we might stay all night. I'll have to call and let you know."

"We'll be at the picnic."

"Till when? Nine or so?"

"At least."

"Keep him as late as you can. Take him for a walk afterward. He always loved late walks with you."

"If I know him he'd rather walk by himself tonight. He might not be at the picnic, either."

"Well, stay with him if you can. I'll call here, and if I can't raise anybody I'll leave word with Moe. Or I may be home before you are."

"If you are, how will you get to bed?"

"Mrs. Norton."

"Pretty grumpy help."

"She's all right. She's just frustrated that Charity won't be treated like a patient. I won't give her that kind of trouble."

We had a sort of smile between us. I said, "So everybody will have somebody to take care of."

"Yours will be the hardest."

"Yours doesn't strike me as easy."

"There'll be three of us. And she's so brave about it she makes me feel proud. It's a sort of privilege."

Her hand came up, with the crutch still sleeved on it, and she wiped a knuckle along her cheekbone before she tilted her face to be kissed.

"Stay with him," she said again. "Walk him. Make him forget

she's gone. If you have to, stay up here with him overnight, or bring him down to the guest house. The other bed's made up."

"All right." For a moment I studied her sad, resigned, trying-to-be-cheerful face. I thought of how it might be to look at the face of the woman you loved and had lived your life with, and know that this might be the last, or the next-to-last, or the next-to-next-to-last time you would see it. I said, "Are you up to all this?"

"Yes."

"I hate to think of you being at the mercy of Charity's plans."

"Oh, she wouldn't *think* of putting us out! We'll have to fight for everything we get to do for her."

"It's only Sid she's willing to put out."

Long dark look. "But that's because he's so much herself," Sally said.

She planted her canes and went off down the hall, frail, contorted, devoted. I went looking for Sid.

4

*N*ine forty-five. It seems a geological age since I awoke this morning. Since I opened my eyes and looked around the familiar shabbiness of the guest cottage, continents could have regrouped themselves, species and genera could have evolved and vanished, the ice could have come and gone more than once. At the very least, lifetimes must have passed.

I sit on the porch step, dead tired from all the walking. The sun set nearly two hours ago, the long twilight has ebbed, the sky behind the hill spiky with spruce has gone the color of buffed iron. But over the lawn before me, over Moe's gray Rambler, over Charity's lounge and Sally's chair lying folded where I dropped them, spreads a pallid, dusty, trembling wash from the moon. By craning to look up past the porch eaves, I can see it almost straight overhead, something over a half moon, enough to dim the stars.

It is the kind of evening that calls for meditation, nostalgia, vague religious thoughts, remembered lines of poetry. But I am not meditative. I am anxious. I have exhausted myself to no purpose, and my mind frets itself with worry and obligation. For I have not found Sid, and I do not know what to do next.

When I left Sally I expected to find him in the kitchen. He was not there. Neither was he on the terrace. Neither was he waiting in the Marmon. Neither was he down at the stable cleaning stalls or filling mangers, trying to make his muscles do for him what his mind would not.

He must have gone blindly walking. Should I try to follow him? If so, where? The hill was a network of trails, miles of them. I didn't relish the thought of going through the woods calling his name. I liked neither the idea of seeming to pursue him nor the idea of his perhaps hiding from me, watching from cover as I went calling past. If he wanted to be alone, he should be allowed to be.

On the other hand, the family would probably already have started for Folsom Hill by the village road, and Charity's peace of mind depended on their having a picnic, and all the wherewithal of the picnic sat here in the Marmon. What was more, the station wagon would be coming for Charity at a quarter past four, twenty minutes from now. Charity must not come out for her last ride and find the Marmon still there and Sid rebelliously off in the woods. If he did not soon appear, I should probably take the car up. I might meet him on the road. Perhaps he was walking up to the hilltop, disciplining himself to the master plan and depending on me to bring the picnic.

But I still had a few minutes to look for him. Where? The idiot boy sent to find a lost horse asked himself where he would go if he were a horse, and went there, and there the horse was. In my experience, horses never strayed downhill, always up. If I were a horse—or if I were Sid Lang—I would not stray downhill either.

So I went for a quarter of a mile or so up the hayroad that Sid and Charity used as a shortcut to the picnic site: through a gate, along a warm fragrant tunnel under the balsams, and into the empty meadow that Charity had had bulldozed for a playing field.

It seemed to me an absolutely characteristic Charity artifact. She had prepared that field in a burst of enthusiasm without considering that it was a steep mile and a half from the lake where all the children lived. The uncut grass was eighteen inches high. Obviously nobody had played anything there all summer.

But then, as I neared the far edge, I saw off to the left a trampled circle marked by horse dung. Margie, undoubtedly, the bewildered and desolated granddaughter, had been there training her sister-companion-friend to trot, canter, and change leads, in brooding repetitive circles. Not so different from what Sid was doing out here somewhere, and without even a horse for company.

It didn't seem right to call out in that quiet place. Quiet—only when I stopped at the edge of the spruce woods did I realize how quiet. The sun beat down on me, angled but still hot. The air hummed and buzzed with insects, but their noise was a form of silence, not a sound, and over the whole hill lay a cushiony emptiness that absorbed and blotted up every vibration of air. I listened until the stillness rang in my ears. The meadow, unstirred by the slightest wind, darkened as I watched it, like a curing Polaroid film.

Then I heard a car. As first I thought it must be the station wagon coming up for Charity, and I started to run back, thinking I must somehow get the Marmon—no, too late. Then I realized that the sound was coming from behind me, and turning, I saw Moe's old Rambler nosing out of the woods into the open.

We had a hurried, baffled conference. He had seen nothing of Sid on his way down from the hill, though as he said, he had not been looking for Sid, he had been keeping his eye out for the Marmon. Charity's directions, relayed by Sally over the telephone, had been to get the family up to the hilltop, and if Sid and I were not already there, to come and get us—at once.

Moe was sober and upset. "It's like something out of K-k-Kafka," he said. "Where is he?"

"I don't know. Walking, I guess."

"Is the c-car still there?"

"Yes."

"Hallie and Comfort haven't shown up yet?"

"They hadn't ten minutes ago."

"We'd better h-hustle," Moe said.

I climbed in beside him and we went on down, leaving the gate open, and parked beside the Marmon on the grass. There was no sign of anyone, or any movement through the kitchen windows. Charity's bedroom, on the other side of the house and at the far end, was out of sight and out of earshot.

Moe, in a tearing hurry, motioned for me to drive, but I said I thought I'd better try to find Sid. We could walk up, or come in Moe's Rambler. Moe agreed after only a moment's hesitation. Obviously the thought of being caught there by the station wagon caused him intense anxiety. He climbed into the Marmon and looked distractedly down at its mysterious dashboard. I had to show him where the switch and the starter button were. He bucked the car a foot forward trying to start it in gear. Finally he got it going.

"If I run across him I'll take him on up," he said. "We'll h-h-honk all our h-h-horns. If you find him, b-bring him. The key's in the car."

"Fine."

At the last moment, I yanked Charity's lounge and Sally's chair from behind the running-board rack and dropped them on the lawn. Charity wouldn't need her lounge ever again, but Sally could not get along without the chair. Standing on the running board, I rode with Moe up the hill to the gate. With a relief that surprised me, I stepped off as we pulled behind the screen of birches and brush, and just before I stepped off I grabbed a flashlight out of the top of one of the hampers in the back. So powerfully did Charity's instructions and training direct our every move.

At the gate Moe gave me a sober look, grimaced, and drove away, looking small and childlike behind the wheel of that leviathan. He rocked ahead and disappeared down the balsam tunnel, leaving me standing in the spritzy smells of raspberry and hazelbrush, my ears alert for the sound of the station wagon coming up the hill.

I heard it almost at once. While I waited for it to come in sight below me, I was wondering what effect the sound of cars might have on Sid. First the Rambler, then the Marmon, now the station wagon— any one of them might be the sound of the end of his life. Would it drive him deeper into the woods, or would it draw him to lurk by the side of the road and watch?

The station wagon topped the steep pitch and drew up beside the Rambler. Hallie and Comfort got out and hurried inside. I waited. The door, left open behind them, stared back at me, as pregnant with unfulfilled possibility as an open door on an empty stage.

Then in a very few minutes it filled. The white outline of Mrs. Norton appeared in it, carrying a suitcase. She backed through, set the suitcase down, and leaned in to help Hallie and Comfort get Charity through.

Intent on the step down, Charity did not look up. I saw her cameo profile and the graceful, weak, flowerlike droop of her neck and head. Her helpers moved with her in synchronized steppings and bendings. They were like the chorus of women in some Greek drama, or Morgain le Fay and her maidens bringing wounded Arthur on board the barge for Avalon. *Totentanz.* Grave and solicitous, intensely concentrated, they crossed the porch and descended the other step to the lawn.

From behind the screen of brush I watched them, hoping that Sid was not hidden anywhere, watching as I was. In his shoes, I could not have borne this.

Then the doorway filled again, and there, hobbling and lurching, helpless to help or even keep up, shrunken and warped out of shape, came Sally—no part of the dance, but harder to watch than any of it.

The vision of her floundering in the wake of the concentrated helpers and their feeble charge turned my distress into outrage. Not at any of the helpers, not at Charity's willfulness, not at the solidarity of women collaborating in what only they could do as well, while excluding male intrusions. No, at *it,* at fate, at the miserable failure of the law of nature to conform to the dream of man: at what living had done to the woman my life was fused with, what her life had been and was. What she had missed, how much had been kept from her, how little her potential had been realized, how hampered were her affection and willingness and warmth. The sight of her burned my eyes.

The other three helped Charity into the middle seat and propped her with cushions. Mrs. Norton got the suitcase and herself into the back. Outside, Hallie and Comfort stood a moment looking, it seemed to me with satisfaction, at the Rambler. They said something, but I could not distinguish words. They looked up my way, so that I shrank behind my screen of brush like a discovered peeping tom.

Then Hallie got into the back beside Mrs. Norton. Comfort slid into the driver's seat. Sally braced her canes and boosted herself awkwardly in beside her, pulled in her canes, and shut the door. The engine started, the station wagon backed and headed down the road. I watched it until it dipped down behind a clump of birches. For a little while I heard the engine, then only the humming quiet of the hill.

Down at the house I found the door unlocked. For some reason, the fact that I could get in, and Sid too if he should return, reassured me. On an impulse, perhaps to see what he would find if he did return, I went through the house to the bedroom. It showed no signs of precipitate flight. The bed was made, books and magazines were stacked neatly on the bed table, the curtains were drawn against the dropping sun, the implements of sickness—sipping glass, bottles, Kleenex, mohair comforters, heating pad—were out of sight, put away, disposed of. An empty bedroom, no more.

Outside again, I scribbled a note on the pad that hung beside the door. I said that Moe had taken the Marmon, and that I was walking. If Sid came back here, he should take Moe's car and go on up. I would see him there.

This note I stuck on the Rambler's aerial, and with the flashlight in my hip pocket went up the rise to the pasture gate, through the balsam tunnel, and across the playing field's tangled grass to the edge where woods met meadow in a line as abrupt as a cliff. Tentatively, not as loud as I intended, I called. Listening brought me no answer. I found the masked entrance of the path and stepped inside.

In one step I was in brown twilight. Nothing grew in that dense shade. The lower branches of even healthy trees were shade-killed, spiky, scaly with gray lichen, and many trees had been broken or tilted by wind or snow, and lay crosswise, hung up, down and half down. The path that I remembered wound through this tangle, soft underfoot with duff and moss, and where trees had gone down across it someone with an axe or machete had cut through the trunks or trimmed the branches. I knew who. In a summer like this, Sid would have spent a lot of time clearing paths like this. He might be doing it right now.

I listened, but I heard nothing. Nor did I call in there. The shrouded quiet forbade noise. Anyway, there was no use to call, or search the skeleton woods for a sign of him. If he was in there, he would be on the path, and that went secretly ahead of me. I followed it.

And found nothing. I walked every trail on the hill, some of which I knew from past summers and some of which I found with my feet. I went to the hidden spring deep in the woods that he had shown me once, a place like a boys' hideout. Nothing. I walked the long trail clear around the hill, a tiring hour and a half of up and down, because it occurred to me that what he wanted was the most strenuous walk he could find. Nothing.

There were scuffs in the trail, and chunks of moss had been kicked off an outcrop in one place, but I was not tracker enough to know whether those marks had been made that afternoon or last month. The woods were silent, except once when I came into the open and heard the yelling of kids, a good way off on the hilltop. It offended me, and I drew a gloomy parallel between Charity and the bare, gnarled, immoderately branched, very dead seed trees that I had come across here and there in the spruce woods—trees that had obviously grown up in an open meadow and seeded the area around themselves, and then been choked out by their profuse offspring. It was unfair to blame those children for having the fun that Charity had arranged for them, but that's the way I felt.

Later, at nearly seven o'clock, I came close enough to see them. They were all spread out on the knoll above the cooking fire, eating, while Lyle and David squatted in the smoke, carving up steaks, and Barney circulated with a wine jug on his finger. They irritated me too. Why were they so carefree, when they must know why neither Charity nor Sid, nor Sally nor I, nor Comfort nor Hallie, was there? But a moment's thought convinced me that they didn't know. At most, Moe and maybe Lyle knew; and they would not have told, because Charity's orders were very clear. If they were worried about Sid, they must have persuaded themselves that I had him somewhere, or was walking his legs off for therapy.

That I didn't, that it was only my own legs I had been walking off, was all the more reason for not going over to join them and partake of the feast whose smells across the hill watered my mouth. If I went over there I would get sidetracked into a lot of greetings and questions and sociability, or else I would have to tell them why I couldn't get sidetracked, and that would break up the picnic.

But where, then? Back to the Ridge? I could think of nothing better, and having started, I grew more convinced with every step that I would find him there. I went fast down the old hay road, past the cellar hole full of fireweed where a farmhouse had burned, through the sugarbush where spruce trees were growing up and choking everything, across the playing-field meadow and along the balsam tunnel and through the gate. From above, I looked down on the house and its quiet lawn.

The Rambler sat just where Moe had left it. The note was still on the aerial. The folded lounge and the folded chair lay on the grass.

Since then, wild goose chases have followed one another. It occurred to me, the idea going on in my head like a light bulb in a comic strip, that he might have found his way, perhaps without intending it, down to his study/shop in the compound. He might be down there now, straightening used nails on the anvil.

Of course, of course. The idiot boy would have thought of that long ago.

I climbed into the Rambler and drove on down, parked in the grove of the parking lot, walked down past the woodshed to the shop, opened the sliding door on the quiet room smelling of linseed oil.

"Sid?" I said.

Nothing.

Later, back at the Ridge, sitting on the porch step eating crackers and cheese and trying to think what to do next, I saw that the sun was over the hill, and that all along the west a bed of cloud with fiery edges was turning orange. The sunset was going to be fine, just what Charity would have ordered. Another light bulb went on in my head. Over on the western slope of the hill was a place where the ice had gouged a long trough through an outcropping of schist. What was left when the ice withdrew was a bench a hundred feet long, with a sloping back and moss cushions, where at least a dozen times we have gone to be quiet and watch the fire die out of the sky. Whatever he had been doing for the last four hours, wouldn't Sid be drawn there now? I thought he would. I could imagine him sitting there in the flat red light, brooding on his loss and on the fact that he was excluded from it, like a child, for his own good; and I could imagine him savaging himself with the unconsoling lines that education and habit would have brought to the surface of his mind:

> It is a beauteous evening, calm and free.
> The holy time is quiet as a nun
> Breathless with adoration. The broad sun
> Is sinking down in his tranquility . . .

If I wanted to drive down the hill and a mile around, I could get there by car. But I did not want to risk having Sid return to find the house empty, the car with its note gone, nobody around. Tired as I was, I would walk—it was no more than a half mile through the woods.

Before I left I turned on the porch light and pulled the note a little higher on the aerial. Then I walked, so tired my hip joints ached in their sockets, through the darkening hardwoods till I came to the western edge, and the sky opened, with the whole main range cut out in black against it. The long bed of cloud that had been fiery at the heart and silver at the edges had cooled to purple, dying like a coal. The ice-cut trough, nearly clear of trees, angled along the hill. My eyes hunted along it for a reddened khaki figure.

"Sid?" I said again.

Nothing.

Coming back, I found the woods so dark I had to use the flashlight. See? My mind said to me as I played it on stumps and ferns ahead. You can understand his dependence. She told you that sooner or later you'd need a flashlight, and she was right. As usual.

By then I was really alarmed, not merely concerned. I had let more than four hours go by when I should have been organizing a search party and letting the picnic fall apart as it might. The porch light, when I came up the hill from the stable, did not cheer me, for I saw at once that the Rambler was still there, and the note a tip of flame above it, catching light either from the porch or from the moon.

I was headed for it, intending to go straight to the hilltop and enlist the family in the search, when I heard the telephone in the kitchen. I burst in the door and answered it. "Hello?"

"Ah, darling," Sally said. "You're back. How did it go?"

"What?"

"The picnic. How was it? We saw you'd gone when we came out— the Marmon was gone."

"Oh," I said. "Yes, it was all right."

"They didn't miss her, then. They went ahead."

"They went ahead. But of course they missed her. They went ahead because most of them didn't know."

"You sound out of breath."

"I just ran in from the yard."

"How's Sid?"

"Okay. Playing his role. He'll be all right."

"Oh, I'm so glad," Sally said. "I was afraid . . . How are *you?* Did you have any trouble with him? He didn't break down?"

"Not that I noticed."

"Good. Because, you know, *she* did. She sat and looked out the window and cried all the way over. Having done that to him, she found she'd done it to herself."

"It's a mess," I said. "Have you got her settled? Are you coming back tonight?"

"No, that's why I called as soon as I thought you might be back. We'll be home before noon tomorrow. We didn't stay with Charity long because she was so tired and weak. We saw her again just now, after dinner, and we'll see her tomorrow before we start back." There was a pause. "Larry?"

"Yes?"

"I love you."

"I love you too."

"Are you going to spend the night at Ridge House?"

"We haven't discussed it. I suppose I might."

"Do. I don't want to think of either of you alone. Did you have a walk?"

"My legs are worn down to stumps."

"Poor fellow, I *bet* you're tired."

"How about you? You must be worn out after a day like this one."

"Oh, I don't know. A little, maybe. Not too. Just . . ."

"What?"

"Sad. You know?"

"I guess I do know. Get to bed. Get a good sleep."

"I will. You too."

"All right. Goodnight, sweet."

"Goodnight."

Sound of her kiss in the receiver, then *click.* I went back outside.

The moonlight has gathered and concentrated itself, the lawn lies out there pallid and even, the Rambler squats upon its shadow, the note is now a petal of pale flame. The folded chairs lie on the grass, faintly gleaming, like a pile of bones. From far off, drifting down from the hilltop, comes the sound of singing.

I have made up my mind that I will not drive up there after all. If they are singing, they are close to finished with their family duty. Moe and Lyle, and perhaps others, will surely be stopping by here to check with Sid and me. I would gain only a few minutes, and risk breaking up what they have loyally held together, if I went up now.

And anyway, Sally's voice is still in my ears, wearier than I have ever heard it. Even in her worst spells she doesn't sound like this, and she takes care to see that there are very few bad spells, and that when she has them they do not show. On the screen of my mind appears her struggling image, floundering across the grass toward the station wagon, left behind by the others, even by the friend to whom she gives her whole store of love and gratitude. She is like some unbearable, sticky-sweet Disney character, some hurt and wistful little creature scorned by her kind. In a Disney fable, there would be a transformation—Dumbo would find that his big ears let him fly, the Ugly Duckling would sprout the white plumage and grow the imperial neck of a swan. But in this script there will be no such ending.

"Could you survive her?" Sid asked me this afternoon. I read his question as being aimed really at himself, and answered it accordingly. Now that I ask it seriously of myself I don't know how to reply.

One of the peculiarities of polio is that its victims, once they have recovered from the virus and settled down to whatever muscular control it has left them, live a sort of charmed life. Crippled as they are, they are rarely ill, they are surprisingly tough and durable, they astonish their sound companions with their capacity to endure.

But that is not forever. There comes a time in the life of every such patient when the whole system—muscles, organs, bones, joints—begins to fall apart all at once, like the wonderful one-hoss shay. Every polio patient is warned to expect that time, every polio family lives with that foretold doom waiting for it at some unknown but expected time in the future. One learns to live with it by turning away from it, by not looking. And yet on occasion one is aware of an intense, furtive watchfulness, and the victim, the doomed one, must surely have just as often the vulnerable sense of being watched.

Could I survive her? More accurately, *can* I? Suppose the tired conversation we just had on the telephone were the last, what would I do? Run mad through the woods like Sid, to be found later in some pond, or hanging from a tree?

The image is too clear to me, and I rise, intending to head for the Rambler, to drive up and start what I should have started hours ago. But then I see on the sky, above the wall of trees, a long dim movement of light. Someone up on the hilltop is turning or backing around, his headlights pouring off into the sky. Better to wait. And brace up— answer the question.

I am so tired that I melt back onto the step. Too old for this physical and spiritual exertion. I will be worthless now for any further searching. I should have gone straight on up with Moe, we should have roused the whole summer colony, the farmers around, the police. Guilt comes to join anxiety in my mind, I am near to tears for my own incompetence.

The lawn spreads out before me under the moon, light gleams off curving metal surfaces, I see the moon's reflection in glass, reflected as if from water, and looking out with unfocused eyes I see it as another scene. My tired mind, dreaming or inventing or remembering, moves reality ahead as a carousel moves a color slide, and another slide takes its place.

I am in our walled yard at Pojoaque, standing beside the swimming pool that we installed for Sally's therapy. The moon shines down on me from a polished black sky, and shines up at me from black water. I have been hearing the screech of a hunting owl, and now I see him on the telephone wire, a Halloween silhouette, cat-size and cat-eared. A moment only, and then he is not there, gone as soundlessly as a falling feather. The moon stares back at me from the pool.

Then it cracks, crazes, shivers, spreads on tiny, almost imperceptible ripples. Some moth or night-flying beetle has blundered into it, I think. But when I put my flashlight on the spot from which the ripples seem to emanate (and who is ever without a flashlight?) I see that a mouse is drowning there. He is a very small mouse, hardly bigger or heavier than a grasshopper, and he apparently cannot sink. But he must have been in the water for some time, for his struggles are feeble, and as I watch, they stop completely. He lies on the surface, his ripples spread and dissipate and smooth out.

I am not unused to things drowning in our pool. Rabbits and ground squirrels come in from the dry country around in search of a drink, and sometimes, like this mouse, fall in and find themselves trapped by walls of shiny, unclimbable tiles. Once in, they have no way to get out, though twice I have found bedraggled mice crouching in the opening where the Jacuzzi drains into the main pool. That is no escape, only a respite, for as soon as the filter pump starts they will be washed into the pool again.

And once, on a morning after a big thunderstorm, I came out and found a neighbor's bulldog dead on the bottom. He had wandered in the open gate, probably blinded and scared by the cloudburst, and fallen in. Heavy bodied, heavy headed, and short-legged, he had swum, I suppose, a round or two of the slick walls before he went down. That was not a good morning.

Now this mouse, intruding on my prebedtime breath of air with his trouble. Generally when I find mice in the pool they are dead, and I can scoop them out with the net and throw in an extra gallon of chlorine to disinfect their intrusion. I will do the same with this one, I think, and get the net.

Even while I am dipping him up, I wonder why I do it. Perhaps the owl scared him into the pool. If he is alive when he comes out, the owl may get him. Or I may have to thump him on his paper-thin skull, for fear his mouselike reproductive capacities will people the patio with skittering offspring, to endanger Sally on her canes.

I lay the net on the pavement and turn the light on it close. A wet wisp, thoroughly dead, the mouse lies in the nylon web. I pick up the net and carry it to the low back wall and turn it upside down on the other side. In the flashlight beam the mouse is so tiny I can hardly see him, there at the edge of a grass clump—a tuft of fur, a recently sentient little chunk of complicated proteins now ready for recycling.

Then miracle. The fur stirs, finds itself on dry ground. In a scurry of legs it disappears among the grass and weeds.

Survival, it is called. Often it is accidental, sometimes it is engineered by creatures or forces that we have no conception of, always it is temporary.

I squeeze my eyes hard shut, and when I open them again, New Mexico is gone from my sight. But what put it in my mind is not. I remember Sally's face, contracted with pain, when we brought her out of that last camp to the road where the car waited—I riding behind her to hold her on, Sid leading old Wizard, Charity walking alongside to steady and hold as she could. It was not a rescue according to any Pritchard formula, but a desperate improvisation like much that has followed. And every detail of that long improvisation has tightened the bonds that hold us together.

Suppose she had died in childbirth under the care of that doctor whom I can't think of even yet without anger—whose name I have carefully forgotten. I would have left that delivery room a nothing, made nothing by the nothing that remained on the bloody table, but I would have survived her. I would probably even have gone on writing, for writing was the only thing besides Sally that gave meaning and order to my life. A nothing, writing nothings, I might have gone on a long time, out of habit or brute health.

It would have been an appalling fate. I am flooded with gratitude that I wasn't asked, quite yet, to survive her, that down under her cone of pain and ether she heard the anesthetist's exclamation, "She's going, Doctor!" and brought herself back, thinking, "I *can't!*"

But of course she is going, as surely as Charity is though not quite so soon. The sentence is handed down and recorded and understood; some shadow of it was in Sally's voice just now on the telephone. You can't be close to the mortality of friends without being brought to think of your own.

Of all the people I know, Sid Lang best understands that my marriage is as surely built on addiction and dependence as his is. He tells me what under other circumstances would infuriate me—that he takes some satisfaction in my ill luck, that it gives him comfort to see someone else in chains. He says too that he would not be unchained if he could, and he knows I wouldn't either. But what he doesn't understand is that my chains are not chains, that over the years Sally's crippling has been a rueful blessing. It has made her more than she was; it has let her give me more than she would ever have been able to give me healthy; it has taught me at least the alphabet of gratitude. Sid can take his guilty satisfaction in my bad luck if he pleases. I will go on pitying him for what his addiction has failed to give him.

But where *is* he? Out in the woods somewhere debating between what he has lost and what he can't give up, wandering without her guidance in a freedom he has never learned to use.

Perhaps, in some obscure desk drawer in his mind, is that list she left him. Assuming he is all right, and will come back, will he ever take it out and ponder it, and act on it? It could be the saving of him—as she undoubtedly knew when she lay in bed with her notebook making it out. She is often right.

She is also capable of a noble generosity, and of cramming it down on the head of the recipient like a crown of thorns. She wept, Sally said, going in the station wagon to the hospital. Was she already thinking ahead for him, breaking him away from her by an act of cruelty and preparing him for healing and the list?

If we could have foreseen the future during those good days in Madison where all this began, we might not have had the nerve to venture into it. I find myself wondering whatever happened to the people, friends and otherwise, with whom we started out. Whatever happened to poor Mr. Hagler, who had only his salary? Whatever happened to Marvin and Wanda Ehrlich, and the Abbots, and the Stones? How much would they understand, from their own experience, of what has happened to *us*?

I hope they have done more than survive. I hope they have found ways to impose some sort of order on their chaos. I hope they have found enough pleasure along the way so that they don't want it ended, as Sid may right now be trying to persuade himself he does.

There is a car, or more than one, coming down the hay road. In the stillness I can hear the growl of low gear, the creaking and bouncing in rough ruts. Lights grope through the highest treetops, turn, are lost, reappear. I stand up readying my tongue for what it must tell them, my mind for more uncertainty, and my legs for more walking.

And now I see the figure, dusty-gold in the moonlight, coming steadily up the road from the stable. It is blurred, its shadow encumbers its feet, but it comes without pause, as if timing itself to meet the family coming down from the hill.

"Sid?" I say.

"Yes," he says.